Romantic Suspense

Danger. Passion. Drama.

Crime Scene Secrets

Maggie K. Black

Wilderness Witness Survival

Connie Queen

MILLS & BOON

Maggie K. Black is acknowledged as the author of this work
CRIME SCENE SECRETS

First Published 2024
First Australian Paperback Edition 2024
ISBN 978 1 038 91074 5

WILDERNESS WITNESS SURVIVAL

First Published 2024
First Australian Paperback Edition 2024
ISBN 978 1 038 91074 5

Published by
Harlequin Mills & Boon
An imprint of Harlequin Enterprises (Australia) Pty Limited
(ABN 47 001 180 918), a subsidiary of HarperCollins
Publishers Australia Pty Limited
(ABN 36 009 913 517)
Level 19, 201 Elizabeth Street
SYDNEY NSW 2000 AUSTRALIA

Printed and bound in Australia by McPherson's Printing Group

Crime Scene Secrets

Maggie K. Black

MILLS & BOON

Maggie K. Black is an award-winning journalist and romantic suspense author with an insatiable love of traveling the world. She has lived in the American South, Europe and the Middle East. She now makes her home in Canada with her history-teacher husband, their two beautiful girls and a small but mighty dog. Maggie enjoys connecting with her readers at maggiekblack.com.

Visit the Author Profile page
at millsandboon.com.au for more titles.

Let the words of my mouth, and the meditation of my heart, be acceptable in thy sight, O Lord, my strength, and my redeemer.

—*Psalm* 19:14

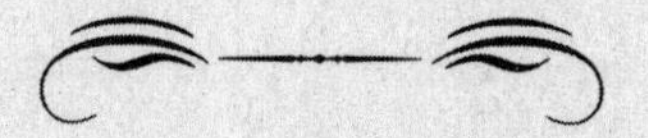

DEDICATION

With thanks to our new fearless series editor, Katie,
for taking all of us on and piloting us through
her first LIS K-9 series

Chapter One

The sweet scent of yucca flowers filled the warm June air as Ophelia Clarke pulled her car up the narrow Sangre de Cristo Mountains road on the outskirts of Santa Fe, New Mexico. An early sunset spread across the endless sky above her, in a breathtaking array of orange, pink and purple brushstrokes. To her left, a playful goat-shaped sign beckoned her to visit the Cherish Ranch Petting Zoo. Tempting. Instead, she turned right through a large archway that welcomed her to the ranch's wedding venue and the marriage of her second cousin Jared Clarke to his new bride, Gabrielle Martinez.

Rustically elegant adobe buildings seemed to cascade across the mountains ahead of her, their soft, clay-colored walls punctuated by dark wooden beams called vigas. A handful of people mingled, chatted and nibbled on appetizers in a huge courtyard underneath strings of patio lights. A large barn lay beyond it. She parked her small car at the main building, in between two far more lavish vehicles, each of which Ophelia guessed cost more than she made in a year in her job as a crime scene investigator for the Santa Fe PD's Crime Scene Unit. Then she took a deep breath. As much as she loved her cousin Jared, their personalities had never really meshed. She'd always felt far more comfortable stepping under yellow police tape in a full-body white protective jumpsuit than she did standing around hobnobbing with his wealthy friends in a sundress and sandals. Not to mention her beloved great-aunt Evelyn, who was like the grandmother she'd never had, also had an incredible and accidental knack for making her feel inadequate.

Lord, please protect my heart and my mind from getting all hung up on what other people think of me. Even the opinions of well-meaning people I love.

She tossed her long blond hair out around her shoulders, stepped out into the hot, dry air—and heard a voice screaming her name.

"Ophelia!" The woman's panicked voice seemed to be coming from all directions at once. "I'm so glad you're here! There's been a terrible crisis and I need your help!"

Ophelia yanked her phone from her pocket and was about to dial 911 when she saw Gabrielle running down a narrow flight of steps toward her.

"What happened?" Ophelia hastened to her. "Everything okay?"

"No!" Gabrielle shook her head and bell-shaped, yellow yucca flowers tumbled from her intricately braided black hair. "Chloe didn't show up!"

"Who's Chloe?" Ophelia asked. "Is she okay?"

"She's my roommate from Albuquerque!" Gabrielle's well-manicured hand grabbed her by the arm and started dragging her up the steps toward one of the buildings. Words poured from the bride-to-be's lips so quickly Ophelia could barely catch them, let alone make sense of what she was safying. "The rehearsal starts in thirty minutes, but when Nolan went back to the hotel to pick her up Chloe still hadn't checked in yet—"

"Who's Nolan? I don't understand."

"And then I got a text from Chloe saying she wasn't coming to the wedding at all!"

"So she's not here?" Then where was Gabrielle dragging her so quickly? What was she so panicked about? "Where is she? What happened to her?"

"I have no idea!" Gabrielle said. She stopped before a door that seemed to be made of four horizontal planks of wood with huge metal hinges. The sign on it read Wedding Party Only. Gabrielle pushed it open. "Thankfully Jared's grandmother said you'd be happy to rescue me."

"From what?" But the words had barely left Ophelia's lips when she stepped through the doorway and saw the ruffled monstrosity of lavender chiffon that hung alone on a clothes rack in the middle of the room.

Oh, no...

"I told Gabrielle that you'd be happy to help her out of her little crisis." Evelyn's voice rose from the corner of the room. "Aren't you, my dear?"

Ophelia had been so distracted by the purple dress she hadn't even realized her great-aunt was sitting in the corner of the suite. The seventy-four-year-old stood and crossed the floor in a haze of beautifully coiffed gray curls, flowing golden fabric and rose perfume. Now a widow, Evelyn had been a beauty pageant contestant when she was younger, and always dressed impeccably.

"Hello, Auntie, I didn't see you there." Ophelia hugged her gently, her own heart still racing from the fear there'd been an actual emergency. But as they pulled apart she saw a flicker of what seemed to be genuine worry cross her great-aunt's face, and Ophelia felt another twinge of concern.

Hang on, was her great-aunt actually worried about this? Or was there something else going on?

"You sure everything's okay?" Ophelia asked Gabrielle. "When you said there was a crisis, I thought something was actually wrong."

"Of course, something's really wrong." Gabrielle's brown eyes widened and Ophelia couldn't help but notice she was only wearing one contact. "I'm getting married on a cliffside at sunset tomorrow and one of my bridesmaids didn't show. I can't just have three bridesmaids standing on one side and four groomsmen on the other. It will completely throw off the symmetry."

Symmetry? Ophelia bit the insides of her cheeks and managed to stop herself from snorting.

"I got all the bridesmaids matching heart-shaped lockets to wear," Gabrielle went on. "Sadly, I've already given Chloe hers, but it's too late to do anything about that now. I guess this means none of the other bridesmaids will get to wear theirs, either, so your outfits match." She sighed. "Of course, you're welcome to stay in Chloe's hotel room. It's a five-star hotel and I'd love to have the whole wedding party staying together. Now, there isn't any way you can rustle up a date for yourself, can you? Jared told me you're hopelessly single, but it'll also throw off the seating plan if you don't have a date."

Hopelessly single? She was a thirty-one-year-old career woman, not some teenager in a 1950s movie who'd just been dumped on prom night. Ophelia felt her jaw clench. She hadn't wanted to be a bridesmaid in the first place and now this whole thing was snowballing. It was just one weekend, she reminded herself. And this was family. She'd just grin and bear it. By tomorrow night it would all be over. "No, I won't be bringing a date," Ophelia said.

Gabrielle's lips turned down in a pretty pout.

"I'm sorry, but did you know you're missing a contact?" Ophelia added. "Do you need help finding it?"

"Wow, you're right!" Gabrielle blinked twice

and then laughed. "What an odd thing to even notice about someone! I guess I've been so distracted with wedding plans I didn't realize."

"Sorry," Ophelia said automatically, then wasn't exactly sure why she was apologizing for trying to be helpful. "It's a hazard of my job. I'm used to noticing the little things. You never know when one victim's missing contact is the key to catching a serial killer."

She meant it as a joke, but Gabrielle didn't laugh. Out of the corner of her eye, Ophelia could see her great-aunt frantically signaling her to drop the topic. She definitely seemed a bit more on edge than usual.

"But Jared said you were some kind of science nerd who worked with animals?" Gabrielle asked.

"Well, I'm working on a PhD in using DNA markers to help track the endangered Rocky Mountain wolf population," Ophelia said, "and also working full-time for Santa Fe PD's Crime Scene Unit."

In fact, she'd received a wonderful financial grant that covered most of her studies, so most of her salary could go to covering her day-to-day living expenses. She'd always felt passionate about conservation but had also realized pretty quickly during her undergraduate science degree that her greatest strengths lay in the lab. Now all she had to do was successfully juggle her work with her research, and she'd be able to fulfill both her dreams of being a CSI and doing life-changing research. It just meant hitting some pretty tight PhD deadlines that often had her researching and writing late into the night. She barely had time to eat and sleep, let alone think about finding a date for her second cousin's wedding.

"Ophelia has always loved animals," Evelyn said, "and I'm sure she won't mind stepping in as an emergency bridesmaid." She turned to her great-niece. "Do you, Ophelia?" Evelyn asked, firmly.

"No, of course not, Auntie." Although Jared had promised he wouldn't try to rope her into the wedding party. Ophelia and Jared were both only children and, despite their differences, were the closest thing each had to a sibling. With the same blond hair and blue eyes, they even looked like brother and sister. Ophelia's parents had traveled a lot for work and her own grandmother had died before she was born. Evelyn had stepped in, inviting her to spend every holiday and vacation with her and Jared. Ophelia could do this much for them.

"See, I knew this would be sorted out," Evelyn said, turning to smile at Gabrielle. "Ophelia's been a bridesmaid more times than I can count."

"Four, actually," Ophelia said softly. "This will be number five."

She was practically an expert at smiling uncomfortably in a dress she'd have never chosen for herself, while standing next to a beamingly happy couple.

"Five times," Evelyn said brightly. "You know what they say—"

Please, don't say it.

"Always a bridesmaid, never a bride!" Evelyn said. "You know, I worry sometimes that nobody's going to marry this one. Which would be a shame, because Ophelia is so wonderful and I love her like my own grandchild. I thank God every day for bringing her and Jared into my life."

That was her great-aunt in a nutshell—accidental insults and a genuine compliment in the same breath.

Evelyn waved her hand toward Gabrielle.

"Now go visit with your guests. Ophelia and I will see how the dress fits."

"Thank you so much for this. I owe you one." Gabrielle disappeared out the door and closed it behind her.

Evelyn sighed. "I wish you wouldn't do that."

"Do what?" Ophelia pulled the dress off the hanger and disappeared with it into the adjoining room. The sooner she got trying the dress on over with, the sooner she could go join the party.

"Talk about things like murders and crime scenes," Evelyn said. "It's impolite. Besides, you never know who you're going to meet at an event like this, and no man wants to marry a woman who pokes around in blood and guts for a living."

"Which is why I expect I'll never get married," Ophelia called, lightly. A few minutes later she emerged again in layers of flowing purple fabric and did a little spin. "Thankfully, the dress isn't terrible."

Her great-aunt looked her up and down, critically.

"No, it's not," she conceded and dropped into a chair. "Which is a relief, considering."

"Considering what?" What exactly was Evelyn concerned about? Ophelia knelt down beside her. "Auntie, what's wrong? You can tell me."

"Absolutely nothing you need to worry about," she said firmly. "Gabrielle's parents are just running late because their flight from Europe was delayed due to a storm. So Jared just needed some help sorting some money things with the venue. You know they're buying Jared and Gabrielle a piece of land near the Pecos Wilderness as a wedding present?"

"Yes," Ophelia said, "he took me up there a few weeks ago to show me, before he put the offer in. Got my help to tie balloons to the trees for when he took her up to surprise her with it. Said they were going to build a house there 'where the mountains meet the sky.' It was all terribly theatrical." The land had been beautiful but completely undeveloped, except for a small shack the previous owners had left behind, but the views had been extraordinary. "Is there some problem with the land?"

"Oh, I'm sure it's nothing." Evelyn waved her hands airily as if batting away invisible cobwebs. "There was just a minor hiccup with the initial down payment, due to restrictions on foreign buyers, so he had to step in and cover it.

They'll pay him back. Plus, this whole wedding has just been so lavish."

Evelyn pressed her lips together as if she'd been about to say more and caught herself.

"Are Jared and Gabrielle struggling for money?" Ophelia asked. "I thought he had an excellent job."

"He does and everything's fine," Evelyn said, with a tone that Ophelia knew meant that even if it wasn't, she was changing the topic. "You should really consider staying with us in the hotel. The rooms they've booked are just gorgeous. Now, I have a plan to get you a date for this wedding. One of my friends told me about this wonderful telephone thing she used to help her grandson find a wife."

"That's kind, but I'm not looking to date anyone right now. Between my full-time job and a PhD, I don't really have time."

But Evelyn had already gone to get her large cell phone from her purse. She opened it to a bubble gum pink dating app. Ophelia gaped as her grandmother started to swipe through the smiling faces.

"It's called Loving Meddlers," Evelyn said. Her blue eyes twinkled. "Isn't that perfect? You can put your grown children and grandchildren on it, and it shows you lovely young people nearby who you can introduce them to, through whoever put them on the thing. Like, see, this man's mother just logged in that they're visiting a petting zoo less than a quarter of a mile away. He's a cop and has a little boy."

Ophelia glanced down at the screen and felt a rush of heat rising to her cheeks, to see the dark hair and intense brown eyes of FBI Agent Kyle West of the Mountain Country K-9 Task Force looking back up at her. Ophelia bit her lower lip as if the incredibly handsome detective could see her through the screen.

"I actually know that one," she admitted, "or at least I know of him. We've worked several of the same crime scenes. He's an FBI agent who specializes in serial killers."

"Oh." Evelyn grimaced. "Maybe not him, then."

A loud bang sounded from somewhere on the other side of the door. Instinctively, Ophelia froze. A second bang sounded. A distant voice screamed.

"Is somebody setting off fireworks?" Evelyn asked.

"No." Ophelia could feel a danger warning tingling at the back of her skull. "Those were gunshots." The property didn't have a range and handguns were prohibited for hunting in Santa Fe. She snatched up her bag, opened the door a crack and listened. Voices were shouting in what sounded like panic and confusion. "Stay here and don't open the door to anyone but me or Jared."

"Don't be ridiculous, sweetie," her great-aunt called. "If there's something wrong it'll be handled by law enforcement."

"I'm a part of law enforcement."

One without a gun, but still she wasn't about to just hunker down and hide when someone might be in danger.

She locked the door handle behind her and slipped back out into the heat. The courtyard was empty, leaving nothing but fallen chairs and plates of food. The gunshot and scream seemed to have been coming from the direction of the barn where the wedding reception would be. She made her way toward it, gleaning what bits of information she could from the shaken guests she passed.

Then she saw Jared running toward her in an expensive tan suit, his eyes wide with panic. He grabbed her arm. "Ophelia!"

"Are you okay?" she asked.

"Have you seen Gabrielle?"

"No," she said. "But your grandmother is safe and inside one of the suites."

His blue eyes scanned past her. He still hadn't answered her question and she wondered if he'd even heard her.

"What happened?" she asked.

"I don't know." His skin was paler than she'd ever seen it before and so clammy she wondered if he was about to be sick. "I heard this popping sound. People dropped their food and ran into the building. Somebody said someone was shot."

"Who?"

"I don't know," he said. "But I heard someone scream."

"I did, too," she said. "Has anyone called 911?"

"I… I don't know…" His head shook. She wondered if he was in shock. "I have to find Gabrielle."

"When you find her, get inside!"

In the meantime, she was going to call 911. She dialed the number and ran for the barn, down stone paths hemmed in by tall, flowering bushes. A dispatcher answered immediately.

"This is CSI Ophelia Clarke of the Santa Fe

PD," Ophelia told her. "I'm at Cherish Ranch's wedding venue in the Sangre de Cristo Mountains. I heard gunfire and there's a report of someone being shot. I'm trying to find that person and see if I can help them."

And if not, she was going to secure the scene and keep people from trampling on whatever evidence there was. Her sandals slipped on the terra-cotta tile, threatening to trip her up. She kicked them off and ran for the barn barefoot.

"We've got law enforcement heading your way," the dispatcher told her. "But they're twenty-two minutes out."

Which might be too late if the victim was bleeding out. And an eternity if the shooter was still on-site.

"Call FBI Agent Kyle West of the Mountain Country K-9 Task Force," Ophelia said. "He's apparently less than a quarter mile away."

"We'll try to reach him."

She silently thanked God for her great-aunt's ridiculous app for alerting her to that. Ophelia reached the barn. A handful of guests were standing around the front, taking pictures on their phones, while a couple of men in suits, who she guessed were ranch security, tried to stop them from getting too close.

She wedged her phone into the crook of her neck, yanked her identification badge from her bag and flashed it at them. "CSI Clarke, Santa Fe PD," she said. "I'm on the phone with dispatch now."

They waved her through. The huge sliding door was open a couple of feet. She came to a stop.

"Hello?" she called. No answer.

She took a deep breath to steal her nerves and stepped inside. The barn was deep and cool. Chandeliers constructed from hundreds of vintage lightbulbs hung down from the ceiling above. Tables were stacked along one side, covered with mason jar oil lamps. Chairs decked in flowing fabric sat in clumps waiting to be set up for the reception, along with pedestals of flowers and buckets of soapy water and cleaning supplies. Silently, she tiptoed through them.

Then she saw him.

The man lay on the floor behind an empty cake stand. He was tall, blond, casually dressed in a T-shirt and jeans, and dead from a gunshot wound to the chest.

"Down!" Brody said. The toddler wriggled in Kyle's arms and waved his hands toward the scampering baby goats as Kyle stepped through the gate to the Cherish Ranch Petting Zoo's goat pen and closed the gate behind them. "Want pat!"

Kyle chuckled.

"Me, too, buddy." He knelt down, set the little boy on the ground and held him steady with one arm strong around his waist, knowing that otherwise he'd run off and try to climb on the very same wooden climbing frame the tiny hooves now balanced on. "But I'm not sure any of them are going to stay still long enough for that."

It had been a long afternoon at the petting zoo. They'd finished their picnic dinner and the sun had begun to set. But still, Brody's energy level hadn't even begun to flag. Keeping up with his nephew had been an adjustment since he'd been unexpectedly thrust into single fatherhood after his brother and sister-in-law had passed. With green eyes and a mop of curly dark hair, Brody was the spitting image of his father, Kevin. Kyle's heart ached with the thought of how Brody's parents would miss seeing the little boy grow up. Thankfully, he had the help of his widowed mother, Alice West, who had moved in to help raise Brody. Together, the three remaining Wests had formed a small, fractured family.

Kyle's phone buzzed in his pocket. Jostling around the squirming toddler, Kyle reached in, fished it out and glanced at the screen. It was his Mountain Country K-9 Team Leader, Chase Rawlston. Kyle sent it through to voice mail and made a mental note to check it later. Chase had promised Kyle a week off to spend with his family, and Kyle had been determined not to let anything get in the way of spending time with Brody.

It had barely been two weeks since Kyle had gotten back from assisting Selena Smith, a sheriff's deputy in Sagebrush, Idaho, and a member of the Mountain Country K-9 Task Force, in protecting a targeted convict. And while, thankfully, the case had been closed and the convict found to be innocent, the entire MCK9 Task Force was still working flat out to catch a pernicious serial killer—dubbed the Rocky Mountain Killer—who'd murdered six people so far across Wyoming, Montana and Colorado. The RMK had also managed to evade them.

"I can pat!" Brody declared confidently. He stretched his tiny fingers out toward a small kid with black-and-white fur and tiny curling gray horns. "Come here, pat!"

"He definitely doesn't lack confidence, does he, Kyle?" Alice West chuckled.

Kyle turned and looked through the fence, to where Brody's grandmother stood, holding the dogs' leashes. With her long gray hair in twin braids and clad in blue jeans and cowboy boots, his sixty-two-year-old mother had a deep faith and perpetual joy that belied the tragedy of having been married to an abusive man and then losing her eldest son. To Alice's right sat Kyle's K-9 partner, Rocky, a magnificent black-and-tan hunting hound who specialized in cadaver detection, especially in the rough and hilly terrain of the Rocky Mountains. Rocky watched the goats, with his head cocked and his long, velvety ears attuned to any sign of trouble. Rocky's half sister, Taffy—a three-month-old puppy who was the spitting image of her big brother—was tangled up in the leash as she tried to run in multiple directions at once. Kyle had adopted her as a family dog when the puppy's sweet but goofy temperament had been deemed to be unsuitable for the rigors of K-9 training. Truth was that most days he felt more like Taffy than Rocky.

It had been over a year since Brody's parents—Kyle's brother Kevin and wife, Caitlyn—had died when their small helicopter had suddenly gotten caught in a treacherous thunderstorm in the Rocky Mountains. To Kyle's surprise, Brody's parents had specifically mentioned in their will that their hope was Kyle would adopt Brody and become his father if anything ever happened to them.

"He reminds me of Kevin," Alice added. His mother's smile faded as the words froze on her lips. An old familiar ache turned in Kyle's chest.

"Me, too," Kyle said wistfully. His fraternal twin might've only been six minutes older, but he'd been Kyle's hero and filled with a strength and confidence Kyle could only hope to find.

Lord, I feel like I'm never going to be able to fill the hole left in this little boy's life. Please guide me in Your path.

His phone buzzed again. Kyle frowned. Chase was calling back.

"Do you need to get that?" his mother asked.

"Yeah, I probably should." He scooped Brody up into his arms and stood, despite the boy's wails of protest, and carried him back out of the goat pen. "He knows it's my week off, so hopefully nothing's wrong."

Deftly Alice handed him Rocky's leash with one hand, while taking her still-protesting grandson into her arms. "We're going to go get ice cream. Come find us when you're done or give me a shout if you've got to run."

"Will do. Thanks, Mom."

She waved a hand for him to go, and he silently thanked God for her.

Kyle glanced down at his partner. Rocky's serious dark eyes looked up at him, silently asking him what was going on. Yeah, he wondered that, too.

He started toward the privacy of the parking lot, with his partner at his side, and answered the phone.

"Kyle here," he said. "Hey, Chase, what's up?"

"Hey," Chase said. His boss sounded a bit tired, but with every ounce of the same determined grit Kyle had come to appreciate from the task force leader. A supervisory special agent with the FBI, Chase had lost his wife and child in a revenge bombing in DC five years ago. A lesser man might've packed up his badge and given up his faith along with it. Chase had moved back to Elk Valley to work in the Wyoming bureau, before heading up the task force Kyle was so proud to be a part of. "Sorry to bother you on your week off, but there's been a report from Santa Fe PD about an incident at the Cherish Ranch wedding venue in Sangre de Cristo Mountains. Guests reported hearing gunshots. Victim was found in the barn, male in his twenties, with a single gunshot to the chest."

That was the Rocky Mountain Killer's MO.

"But the crime scene investigator, who was first on-site, told dispatch that you were in the area and requested you by name," Chase added.

"I'm at the petting zoo next door." But he had no idea how anyone would know that. He and Rocky jogged toward his truck. The cell signal crackled and he hoped it wouldn't cut out. Phone reception wasn't the best here in the mountains and made worse by the fact that he was on the move. "I'm on my way and two minutes out. Who requested me?"

"A CSI Clarke."

An unexpected wave of relief washed over him. "Oh, she's excellent."

In the year or so since he'd come into contact with Ophelia Clarke, Kyle had quickly pegged her as the very best investigator he'd ever worked with. Her work was both thorough and meticulous. Not that Kyle thought they'd ever exchanged two words. Or, come to think of it, even knew what Ophelia looked like under her full-body protective gear, booties and mask. But between the old-fashioned name and her excellent work, he'd always envisioned her as being around the same age as his mom, with curly gray hair, a sharp gaze and well-disciplined grandchildren.

Kyle knew nothing would be missed whenever he saw Ophelia Clarke's name on a case.

"Got it." Kyle opened the back door of his SUV for Rocky. The dog leaped into the back seat and lay down. Kyle hopped in the front and plugged his phone into the vehicle's hands-free system.

"Do we know if it's connected to the RMK?" he asked.

"That's what I'm hoping you'll be able to find out," Chase said.

It had been a decade since three young men had been found shot dead in Elk Valley, Wyoming, on Valentine's Day night. The three friends had all been members of the Young Rancher's Club, known to local police as troublemakers and lured to a barn by a flirtatious text from a burner phone. They'd been shot—each with a gunshot wound to the chest. The murder weapon had never been found, but ballistics had matched the 9mm slugs. The case had gone cold for ten years until, four months ago, two more men were found shot the same way, one in Colorado and another in Montana. Then recently a sixth victim was found in Idaho. Every weapon left its own unique pattern of ridges and marks on each bullet it fired. CSI had determined the three bullets found at the new crime scenes, and those from the original murders, had not only been fired from the same type of gun, but the exact same gun.

Could this new shooting be connected?

"Santa Fe PD and paramedics are fourteen minutes out," Chase added. "You and CSI Clarke are the first on the scene."

"Understood."

Thank You, Lord, that CSI Clarke was there. Please help us get the evidence we need to stop the RMK and crack his case.

"Let's meet up via video call tomorrow morning at eight," Chase went on. "I'm going to ask Isla to join us, too, and maybe others. If this does turn out to be related to the RMK, I want to make sure you have the backup you need."

"Sounds good." The MCK9 Task Force's technical analyst, Isla Jimenez, was second to none and someone Kyle was thankful to call a friend.

"I'll also coordinate with the Santa Fe PD," Chase went on, "as I'm sure it'll end up being a joint investigation if there is a RMK connection. But at the moment it's too soon to know anything really."

"Understood. Talk soon."

They ended the call. Kyle sent his mom a quick text letting her know that he had to work a scene nearby and would be in touch later. Then he peeled out of the crowded petting zoo parking lot as quickly as he safely could and followed a small sign directing him to the wedding venue. In a matter of moments, he pulled through an arch welcoming him to the wedding of Jared Clarke and Gabrielle Martinez. The top of the rustic barn appeared ahead through pine trees. He drove through the parking lot and down a small access road. He stopped the vehicle as close as he could to the barn, got his badge and gun from his glove compartment, then hopped out and ran down the winding path, with Rocky by his side.

There wasn't another emergency vehicle in sight. But a couple of men in crisp black suits and sunglasses, who he guessed were ranch security, were standing by the entrance, holding back a small gaggle of well-dressed gawkers in pastel dresses and paisley ties, who seemed to be trying to film whatever they could with their phones.

He held up his badge and identified himself to the security officer closest to the door.

"FBI Agent Kyle West, Mountain Country K-9 Task Force," he said. "Has anyone been inside?"

"No, sir." The guard shook his head. "Just the chick."

Chick?

He couldn't imagine anyone referring to Ophelia Clarke like that. Had one of the party guests breached the perimeter? Whoever he was talking about, she shouldn't be in there.

"We need a twenty-five-foot perimeter around this barn," Kyle said. "Get everyone out of here and keep them back. They'll all need to be questioned. The priority is figuring out where everyone was at the time the gunshots were fired and not giving anyone the opportunity to coordinate their stories." Not to mention, the last thing he needed were people trampling all over the evidence or crime scene pictures ending up on social media. "Make sure the entrance is clear for emergency services when they get here."

The guards nodded and started yelling for people to get back. Kyle signaled Rocky to stay close to his side and started for the door. The double barn door seemed designed to open all the way on both sides, but for now it was only open a couple of feet. For someone to slip in and out without being seen? A soft growl rumbled in the back of Rocky's throat, letting him know that death lay on the other side. Kyle pulled his weapon.

"Agent Kyle West, Mountain Country K-9 Task Force," he called. "Drop your weapons and get down on the ground with your hands up."

"It's clear," a female voice called. "He's already dead."

"I'm sorry, ma'am," he said. "You really can't be in here. I'm going to have to ask you to leave."

He stepped through the door and froze. The most beautiful woman he'd ever seen knelt on the floor in a flowing purple dress beside the bloodied body of a man in jeans and a T-shirt. She seemed to be checking the corpse's pockets.

"No wallet, no phone and no identification,"

she said, as if he hadn't just politely told her to leave. "We seem to have a John Doe."

She tossed her long blond hair around her shoulders and stood. Dazzling blue eyes fixed on his face. He felt his mouth open and close again, like a goldfish.

"Single gunshot wound to the torso," she went on. "Pretty much dead center and still imbedded in his chest. I checked his vitals and attempted CPR. But I'm afraid he's gone."

She ran her hands down her skirt, leaving bloody streaks on the delicate fabric. Only then did he notice she was wearing plastic gloves. She looked down at them as if debating extending a hand to shake his, before deciding against it. "I'm glad you got my message."

He holstered his weapon. "I'm sorry, who are you?"

"Ophelia Clarke." Something hardened in the blue of her eyes. Her chin rose. "Crime Scene Investigator for the Santa Fe PD's Crime Scene Unit. It's good to see you again, Agent West."

He just stood there and blinked, while his brain struggled to compute the fact that the most impressive crime scene tech he'd ever worked with also just happened to be the most beautiful woman he'd ever seen. *Come on, man*, he chided himself. He'd worked with a lot of strong and talented female officers, detectives, agents and CSIs for his entire career. So, what was it about this particular one that had suddenly robbed his tongue of its ability to form words?

"The groom is my second cousin," Ophelia added. She pulled her gloves off. "I came for the rehearsal party and they were trying to rope me in as a bridesmaid, when I heard the gunshots. Thankfully I always keep a few gloves and evidence bags in my purse." Ophelia glanced at his partner and a warm smile crossed her face. "Hello, Rocky."

She ran her hand down his side. His partner's tail thumped against the floor. Seemed Rocky had no problem recognizing her.

"I'm so sorry," he said. "I didn't recognize you without the protective gear. I assumed you were a guest who'd just wandered in and started playing detective."

He'd meant it as a joke, but she didn't smile.

"I'm glad you're here, too," he plowed on, hoping to find the right thing to say to put the investigation back on track. "You're a really good CSI."

"Uh, thank you?" Now it was her turn to blink.

Had he said something else wrong? Or was she just not used to being complimented? Either way, it seemed he'd managed to put his foot in it again.

Then she glanced past him and her face paled.

"There's a man in a mask in the trees," she said. "He's got a gun pointed right at the barn."

Before he could turn, a gunshot sounded and the barn door behind him exploded into splinters.

Chapter Two

"Take cover!" Kyle shouted. "Rocky, stay low!"

But Ophelia froze, her body suddenly too paralyzed by fear to move. She felt Kyle throw his strong and protective arms around her. He cradled her to his chest as they fell together to the ground. In one strong kick, Kyle brought a flower pedestal crashing down in front of them, creating a limited barrier between them and the man outside, just as the gunman let off a second shot. This one ricocheted across the floor.

For a second she lay there on the ground, with one of Kyle's arms around her shoulder and her heart beating painfully in her chest. Kyle pulled away, unholstered his weapon and rolled up to a crouching position.

Then it hit her. "Kyle, there are people out there!"

"Not anymore," he said. "I asked security to

create a wide perimeter. Everybody should be out of harm's way, except us."

Thank You, God.

She glanced around. Rocky was crawling toward the cover of a stack of tables to their right. The gunman was a tall and indistinct form, with a black baseball cap on over his ski mask. Some kind of dark mesh covered the eyeholes, so she couldn't even clock the color of his eyes. He raised his handgun and fired. A third and fourth shot sounded in quick succession. A chandelier crashed down from somewhere above, sending broken glass cascading across the floor.

What did the assailant think he was doing? He wasn't firing at them. She wasn't sure he even knew they were there. It was more like he was treating the barn as his personal shooting gallery.

"We've got to move," Kyle said. "Can you crawl?"

"I think so." She gritted her teeth and grabbed her bag. "If not, just drag me until my limbs decide to cooperate."

He snorted. "Will do. We're heading for the tables by the wall. Just follow Rocky."

She rolled over onto her hands and knees and

started for the spot where Rocky was now sheltered under the tables, thankful that her body seemed to have finally agreed to become unstuck. Kyle positioned himself between her and the gunman and matched her pace. When they reached the tables, once again she felt Kyle's protective hand brush her shoulder. His dark eyes scanned her as silently he checked her face.

"I'm okay," she said. "Thank you."

"Thank You, God," he murmured.

Amen. Thank You that Kyle was here. Thank You for my safety. Please keep anyone else from being harmed.

Then Kyle moved away from her, pulled out his phone and started talking. She assumed he was contacting emergency services. Rocky crawled over beside her and gave her fingers a reassuring lick. She ran her hand over his head. The hound was almost entirely black except for his tan snout and paws. She always had a soft spot for the beautiful canine with his long, silky ears and serious eyes.

"Backup is six minutes out," Kyle called.

In the meantime, it was almost as if the gunman was intentionally trashing the scene. A bucket full of soapy water went flying, sending suds cascading across the floor.

"He's destroying evidence!" Ophelia shouted.

Kyle pulled the phone from his ear. "You mean on purpose?"

"Maybe. I don't know."

But she hadn't thought to start snapping pictures when she'd arrived, or even take notes. She'd been too focused on seeing if she could save the victim's life. And now the only record of what she'd observed when she first arrived on the scene existed solely in her mind.

She could now hear the faint sound of sirens in the distance. Kyle's attention had turned back to the phone again. Impulsively, she grabbed Kyle's free hand and squeezed it. His eyes snapped back to her face.

"Listen to me," she said urgently. "He's destroying evidence and I didn't take pictures, so I need you to remember everything I'm about to tell you."

"Will do," he replied, without question.

She closed her eyes and prayed.

Lord, help me remember what I need to.

"The barn door was open only a couple of feet when I got here," she said, keeping her eyes closed in concentration. "I don't think the lights were on, but there was enough daylight to see. I didn't notice any obvious signs of a struggle. No broken glass, no overturned furniture, nothing spilled, nothing in disarray."

"Got it," he said. She felt him squeeze her hand. "Go on."

"I didn't see the body until I stepped in a few feet. He was partially blocked by planters. He was dressed casually in jeans and a green T-shirt. One bullet wound, fatal and close range." She opened her eyes. His dark gaze was locked on her face and she realized his hand was still enveloping hers. She pulled away. "My job is to focus on gathering evidence. Your job is to interpret it. But if I had to guess, he knew his killer."

"I'd go a step further and say the victim was probably looking him dead in the eye when he was shot," Kyle added, dryly. "Have you heard of the Rocky Mountain Killer?"

"Vaguely."

"He lured all his victims into barns and shot them at point-blank range. Six so far. Maybe, this guy is number seven."

"Well, I didn't see any evidence that our John Doe wasn't lured here," she said.

"Yeah," Kyle said. "Only question is why didn't the killer choose a more isolated location."

Ophelia scanned the room, silently praying

that she'd remember anything important that she hadn't focused on.

A glimmer of something gold caught her eye. The item was slightly smaller than a bullet. Just a few feet away from the next table over and seemed to shine in the refracted light of the glass on the floor surrounding it. The gunman fired ahead. A table full of kerosene mason jar lamps shattered, sending the pungent fuel pouring down inches away from the object.

Ophelia didn't even hesitate. She yanked a fresh pair of gloves from her purse, slid them on and grabbed an empty evidence bag. Then she slowly crawled under the next table over.

"What are you doing?" Kyle asked, sharply.

"I'm rescuing evidence!"

"That's not your job!"

To crawl into the line of fire to rescue a shiny object from a murder scene? Maybe not, but it was close enough.

"Stop!" Kyle called. "Get back here."

For a moment she wondered if he was actually going to grab her ankles and try pulling her back. But it was too late; she was already ducking her head out and slithering on her stomach across the floor. A second later, her fingers wrapped around the object. She ducked back under the table and dropped the item into the bag, just as another gunshot sounded.

In an instant, Kyle was at her side. They crouched side by side below the table.

"What were you thinking?" he asked. "You could've been killed."

"But I wasn't." And hopefully had rescued a clue. She held up the evidence bag. Together they peered at it. His shoulder brushed hers. It was a cuff link. So shiny it looked new and yet also marred with what appeared to be the victim's blood. "Why would a man in a T-shirt and jeans have cuff links with him?" she asked.

"I have no idea."

"There's some kind of inscription on it. But between the blood and the small, stylized letters, I'm having a hard time reading it." She squinted. "Looks like an *R*. The second letter might be an *H*, an *N* or an *M*. I'm not sure. And I can't make out the third."

The sirens roared even closer. Kyle's back stiffened. "Could the letters be *RMK*?"

"Maybe," she said. "Definitely, looks like it. Why? What does that mean?"

"It means this murder very well could be the work of that serial killer I mentioned," he said, "and the Rocky Mountain Killer might be the man shooting at us now."

★ ★ ★

A cold chill ran down Kyle's spine as he glanced to the masked figure, praying God would give him the opportunity to get a clean shot. Instead, he watched as the shooter turned tail and took off running through the trees.

But Kyle wasn't about to let him get away. The MCK9 Task Force had been tracking the killer for months.

"I'm going after him," he called. "Stay low and stay safe. Backup will be here any second."

"I'll be fine," Ophelia called. "Just go!"

He slid out from under the table, summoned Rocky to his side and took off sprinting through the barn and out into the mountain air. To his right he could see the flashing lights of police cars and ambulances lighting up the sky. The sound of voices shouting just beyond the hedges told him backup was moments away.

But he didn't let himself break stride. Instead, he and Rocky dove through the pine trees and juniper bushes, after the departing figure. The ground sloped steeply. Loose rocks tumbled beneath their feet, threatening to send them falling. He could barely see the figure through the forest. But he could hear the sound of brush branches snapping beneath his feet. The sun was setting lower in the sky now. Soon it would disappear beneath the horizon altogether, leaving an inky blue darkness behind.

Then suddenly the trees parted and Kyle could see him.

The figure was at least six feet tall, stocky and strong. A sheer cliff lay ahead of him, jutting out into the air.

"Stop!" Kyle shouted. He raised his weapon. "FBI!"

But the man vaulted over the edge and disappeared from view.

Kyle pressed faster. He and Rocky raced to the edge and looked down, just in time to see the masked man scrambling down to the bottom of a steep slope. An expensive-looking silver car stood on the road beneath it. The man dove into it and Kyle fired, catching him in the left calf. Shouting and swearing loudly in pain, the man struggled as he slammed the car door. Kyle set the vehicle in his sights and fired, just as the engine roared to life. The back window shattered.

The car sped off around a bend and out of sight.

Kyle re-holstered his weapon. Then he pulled out his phone to call dispatch and told them to be on the lookout for a man with a gunshot wound to the left calf and a silver car with a broken back window. But he couldn't get a signal. He groaned.

He lifted his gaze to where the golden sun was disappearing, leaving just a sliver of light at the edge of the horizon.

Lord, whether that man is the RMK, an accomplice of his or not connected to the other murders at all, please help me catch him and bring him to justice. And guide everyone else involved in the investigation.

He looked down at Rocky. The dog whimpered sympathetically and bumped his head against Kyle's side. Kyle chuckled and ran his hand along his partner's neck.

"You are a very good dog," he said. "It's not your fault he got away. You weren't trained for that, and you're excellent at what you are trained for." Which was finding the dead, not only giving law enforcement the evidence needed to bring the killers to justice, but also bringing peace and closure to the friends and family left behind. "Now come on, let's get back to the crime scene and see what the witnesses can tell us about the John Doe in the barn."

They turned and jogged through the trees toward the ranch. Truth was, when Kyle had joined the FBI's K-9 Unit, he'd envisioned himself partnered with the kind of imposing beast who'd help him physically chase down killers. He'd never expected to be paired with an animal who was so patient, dedicated and diligent in finding victims instead. But the moment he'd laid eyes on the two-foot-tall, black-and-tan hound, something in his heart had known that he and Rocky were meant to work together to find those whose bodies had been lost. It was a sobering job, one filled with a lot of sadness, but also a lot of hope and the certainty they were making a difference.

And Kyle thanked God for his partner every day.

It was no surprise that his son, Brody, was absolutely besotted with Rocky, too, and would charge across the room to throw his little arms around the dog whenever they came home from work, while Rocky sat patiently and accepted the small boy's enthusiastic squeezes with a gentle lick. Brody had been beside himself with joy when Taffy had joined the family as well, giving him a pint-size canine playmate who stayed home with him when Kyle and Rocky went off to work.

Kyle had felt blindsided by happiness when he'd first cradled Brody in his arms, a few hours after the little boy's birth. He never could've imagined the tragedy that would lead to him adopting Brody just six months later, when the child was too young to even understand what had happened. Kyle could also never understand why Kevin and Caitlyn had specified in their will that they wanted Kyle to adopt their son in the event of their deaths, when they had so many incredible friends, many of whom were already married with kids of their own.

How could they possibly be sure that he was the right man to be Brody's father? He was an expert in catching serial killers, who'd never had a serious girlfriend and whose K-9 partner tracked the dead.

Lord, I love Brody with all my heart and there's never been a doubt in my mind that I want to be his dad. I just worry I'm going to let him down.

After all, his own father had been a brute. He couldn't imagine the courage it had taken Kevin to get married and start a family, considering they'd hardly had a decent role model.

He could see law enforcement's flashing lights ahead and followed them back to the barn. He couldn't have been gone more than fifteen minutes, but already yellow police tape surrounded the scene and the chaos of the barn had been taken over by a small army of CSI agents in white protective gear. He scanned the scene for Ophelia but couldn't spot her.

"Agent West!" a woman's voice called to him from within the cordoned-off area.

"Over here!"

He turned toward the sound. It was Detective Patricia Gonzales, a senior investigator within the Santa Fe Police Department and one of the most dedicated officers Kyle had ever had the privilege of working with. She was in her early sixties, he guessed, not that he'd ever risk asking. Her black hair was streaked with white and tied back in a crisp bun.

"Detective Gonzales!" As he strode toward the police tape, a Santa Fe PD officer lifted it up and let him through. "It's good to see you."

"Likewise." She nodded at him and Rocky in greeting. "I heard you were the first investigator on the scene."

"I was," he said, "after CSI Clarke, who was on-site for a family event, found the body and called it in."

All of which she'd already know. He quickly filled her in on the suspect he'd been pursuing, the fact that he'd managed to clip him in the left leg, the silver car with the shattered back window and that Kyle hadn't yet been able to call it in. Then he waited while she contacted dispatch and told them to be on the lookout for the suspect and vehicle. Then she turned back to Kyle.

"And what's the Country Mountain K-9 Task Force's link to this case?" she asked.

"I was close to the scene, so they called me in. But the shooting seems to match the MO of the Rocky Mountain Killer," he said. "Male victim, in a barn, with a single gunshot to his chest."

"A lot of people get shot in barns," Patricia said. She sounded skeptical.

"True," he said. A lot of people got shot in the chest, too.

"I thought all those killings took place in Wyoming," she added, "and the victims were connected to some Young Rancher's Club."

"The first three murders were in Elk Valley, Wyoming, ten years ago," he said. "The next three were more recent, in Idaho, Montana and Colorado. All were connected by a party the Elk Valley Young Rancher's Club had a decade ago."

"And all those states are on a pretty straight line down the I-25 Highway to Santa Fe," Patricia said. "We've got no ID on the victim yet. Do we know if anyone from this wedding was connected to this Young Rancher's Club?"

"No," Kyle said. But he was looking forward to finding out. "My mother and son are at the petting zoo. Do you know if I have any reason to be concerned for them?"

"No," Patricia said, and he appreciated her bluntness. "Not at all. We have no reason to believe anyone there is in danger or was impacted."

He breathed a sigh of relief. "Yeah, I couldn't even hear the shots from there."

"We do have an officer on-site checking vehicles on the way in and out of the petting zoo," the detective added. "I'd be happy to get someone to pick your family up and escort them home, if you'd like."

"Actually, could you get someone to drop my SUV off to them at the petting zoo?" Kyle asked. It was past Brody's bedtime; Kyle had a hunch that he was going to be here awhile and was sure he could get a ride home.

"Will do."

Kyle sent off a quick text to his mom, who wrote back right away, telling him not to worry and that she'd put Brody to bed, but that Kyle would have to sort breakfast as she had to run some early morning errands. He thanked his mom and then he silently thanked God for her.

As Chase had suggested would happen, Patricia said that for now they'd proceed with the case as a joint investigation between the local Santa Fe Police Department and the Mountain Country K-9 Task Force. Which was good by Kyle. He was the only MCK9 team member based in Santa Fe and hardly had the manpower to search for the suspect on his own. And at this point, aside from the MO and a few letters on the golden cuff link, he didn't have anything solid to tie the murdered John Doe to the RMK.

"I'd like you to take lead on questioning the party guests and staff," Patricia added. "My priority right now is clearing the civilians and letting them get back to their homes and hotels. I'm hearing that they're all claiming they have an alibi for the shooting. But it's possible that somebody saw or heard something."

"I get that," Kyle said. He ran his hand over the back of his neck and felt the beginning of a sunburn. "But at the same time, something doesn't smell right about this."

The detective's dark eyes narrowed. "How so?"

"Let's say, hypothetically, our masked man lured our John Doe to the barn," Kyle said. "Maybe because this barn was close to where his victim lived or because he knew it would be hard for police to get to. Our killer stashes his car nearby to make a quick escape. Then he shoots John Doe in the chest and flees. On the surface, it looks like it matches the other RMK murders."

Patricia nodded.

"But there are discrepancies," Kyle said. "Why did he come back and keep shooting after the murder? CSI Clarke thought he was trying to destroy evidence. Did he realize he'd left something behind, see us go into the barn and try to stop us from getting our hands on it?"

"So you're saying that if it is your guy, maybe he's getting sloppy," Patricia said.

"Maybe," Kyle conceded.

And if so, what did that mean for the case? He couldn't even assume that the person who shot up the barn was also the man who killed John Doe.

Lord, guide Ophelia and the other crime scene investigators in gathering evidence. And guide me in questioning witnesses.

"I do have one thing for you," Patricia said.

"One of the CSI photographers got a good clear pic of the victim's face. I'll send it to you now."

She hit a couple of buttons on her phone and Kyle heard his own cell ping. He glanced down at the screen and got his first real, clear look at John Doe's face. The man was in his midtwenties and clean-shaven. That made him older than the RMK's first three victims, who'd been between the ages of nineteen and twenty-one, but younger than the most recent three who'd been in their late twenties and early thirties. His blond haircut looked expensive. So did his simple T-shirt. The victim definitely looked like the kind of guy who'd have been invited to the wedding.

Who are you, John Doe? And what were you doing here?

Chapter Three

Kyle's feet itched to head back into the barn to check in with Ophelia and see if she'd discovered anything. Or even if she had any new theories. But instead, armed with as much info as Kyle could be for now, he and Rocky made their way to the ranch's main building to question the wedding party and potential witnesses. When he arrived, he was greeted by the cops at the door, who quickly briefed him on the investigation so far.

There were fifteen people who'd been there for the rehearsal party, including the bride and groom, four groomsmen, three bridesmaids, the groom's grandmother, his parents and three of the couple's friends. Then of course, Ophelia made sixteen, but obviously she wasn't being questioned. To his surprise, none of the bride's family was there, but apparently her parents had been flying in from overseas and their flight had been canceled due to a storm. The ranch staff consisted of two servers, a cook, a cleaner, the manager and two security guards.

So that made over twenty potential witnesses—or suspects.

It also turned out almost all of them had somebody else willing to vouch they'd been together when gunshots were fired. Only three people had nobody to back them up—the elderly cleaner, one of the security guards and the groom, Jared Clarke.

Kyle set himself up in a small lounge with low wooden tables and pale blue couches, and questioned each person, one by one in turn. Rocky lay by his feet and watched the proceedings.

Kyle verified where each person had been when the first set of gunshots sounded, and double-checked their answers matched the info the local police had already gathered. Then he showed them the picture of the victim and clocked their expressions. Thankfully, if anyone was nervous about talking to police, Rocky was an excellent icebreaker and the hound was quick to make friends among the people Kyle questioned. But any hope Kyle had of gleaning something new from the witnesses was dashed, again and again, and nobody claimed to recognize John Doe, or had seen him before the shooting, or had any idea what he was doing at the ranch. And although most had heard of the Rocky Mountain Killer from social media or the news, all of them said they'd never been to Elk Valley, Wyoming or knew anyone who was a part of the Young Rancher's Club. Then one by one, he let them go, making sure he had their contact details on file and reminding them not to discuss the case with anyone and to keep their phones handy.

Everything was uneventful until he got to the groom, Jared. A few inches taller than Ophelia, with the same tanned skin, blond hair and blue eyes, he could be mistaken for her sibling, although he was her second cousin. Jared's tan suit and haircut were expensive. But they were coupled with the charisma of a damp sponge. He told Kyle he'd been alone at the time of the shooting. But he also claimed he didn't know or remember anything remotely helpful, and instead just waffled about how much he loved Gabrielle and needed the wedding to be perfect for her.

The whole endeavor was endlessly frustrating. His final interview was with the bride.

Gabrielle Martinez was about five-foot-two, with glossy black hair that both twisted around the crown of her head and fell in waves around her shoulders. Her dark eyes brimmed with worry. She plucked a candy from a bowl on the table and twisted the end of the wrapper back and forth, opening and closing it again.

"Are you sure that everyone is okay and that nobody else was hurt, Officer?" she asked.

"It's Agent, actually," he said, "and with the exception of our unknown victim nobody else was hurt."

She exhaled. "I'm so glad. They kind of ushered us in here and didn't tell us anything, or even let us talk to each other. Who was shot?"

"We haven't identified him yet," Kyle said. He slid his phone, with the picture open, toward her. "Do you recognize this man?"

"No." She shook her head.

"You sure you haven't seen him before?" Kyle pressed. "Take a good look."

Gabrielle stared down at the phone for a long moment. Then she shrugged.

"I'm so sorry," she said. "He might be one of Jared's colleagues from work. I know he invited a few I haven't met. But no, I've never seen him before in my life."

"Jared wasn't able to identify him, either," Kyle said.

He left his phone on the table and leaned back. How was it possible a man showed up in the barn on the evening of a wedding rehearsal party and nobody knew who he was?

"And where were you when the shots were fired?"

"With Nolan Taft," Gabrielle said. "He's one of Jared's groomsmen. I'd just left Jared's grandmother in the suite where the bridesmaids would be getting dressed. Her name is Evelyn Clarke. Jared's cousin, Ophelia, had agreed to step in as a replacement bridesmaid because my friend Chloe Madison had canceled at the last minute and I was making sure Ophelia had everything she needed. When I left them, I went looking for Jared. I thought he might be at the outdoor, cliffside chapel where we're having our ceremony. I didn't see him there but I did bump into Nolan on the way back. We were talking about something, the weather I think, and then I heard the gunshots. We rushed toward the main building, and then ran into Jared. Then we heard a bunch of more shots."

Yeah, all this matched what other people had told him, too.

"Do you have any idea where your fiancé, Jared, was when the first gunshots sounded?"

Her eyes widened.

"No," she said. "He said he was looking for me. But I can't imagine Jared hurting anyone. He's the sweetest man I've ever known."

His grandmother had said the exact same thing. But if it did turn out the groom had something to do with this, he wouldn't be the first person to fool his loved ones about his true nature. And if Jared really was as bland and irritating as he appeared, that definitely didn't mean he couldn't also be a cold-blooded killer.

"How did you meet, Jared?" he asked. "I heard it was at a party."

"Yes, downtown Albuquerque," Gabrielle said, "about nine months ago. I was getting a degree in Design from the University of New Mexico, and my roommate Chloe and I went out to a networking party at this big hotel. But it was a really lame party, so we ended up going into the room where Jared's company was having a big dinner. He invited us to sit with him and we started talking. I guess you could say it was love at first sight." She glanced wistfully to the couch cushion beside her as if expecting to see him there. Then suddenly she gasped. Her hand rose to her lips. "Oh, please tell me that we can still get married tomorrow and we're not going to have to cancel the wedding!"

"It's not my call," Kyle said. "As for the ceremony itself, it's up to you and the venue. But even if you can't hold the wedding here, I'm sure your hotel or somewhere else will be able to accommodate you. And maybe a slight delay means your parents will make it in time. As for the investigation part of it, really, all that the police care about is figuring out who this John Doe is and who killed him." And despite his mild suspicions about Jared, he definitely didn't have cause to detain him, or anyone else, right now. "So, if you and your fiancé have nothing to do with that, you're free to go get married and live your lives."

He'd hoped his tone was reassuring. But the bride's frown only deepened.

"We just really had our heart set on getting married here," she said. "The mountains are really important to both of us and that barn was so perfect and pretty."

Well, now it's a murder scene. He imagined the bride would dissolve into a puddle of tears if she saw just how badly her perfect reception venue had been destroyed.

"Considering the look in Jared's eyes when he told me about you, I'm sure he'd happily marry you in a grocery store parking lot," Kyle said in a kind tone. "I'm sure your wedding will still be beautiful and this is just a bump in the road on the way to your happily-ever-after."

Now that came out cornier than he'd hoped. But it seemed to work, because the bride was now smiling again.

"Can I go talk to Jared now?" she asked. "The cops wouldn't even let any of us sit together."

No doubt to make sure people weren't whispering back and forth coordinating their stories.

"Sure," he said. He stood. So did the bride. "I think we're done here for now. Just please don't discuss the case with anyone, including your fiancé."

Especially considering Jared was one of the few who didn't have an alibi for when John Doe was shot.

After Gabrielle left, he waited a few moments with Rocky, going over his sparse notes from the investigation so far and praying for wisdom. Then Kyle and his partner stepped out into the warm June night. To his right, he could see a trail of brake lights flickering as party guests and ranch staff made their way down the winding mountain road. There were fewer law enforcement vehicles in the parking lot now and police presence was a lot thinner on the grounds, too. He sent Chase a quick text telling him nothing concrete had been determined for now about the crime but that he looked forward to talking to him tomorrow.

He signaled Rocky to his side and walked back along the path to the barn to find a someone who could give him a ride back into Santa Fe. As they passed the courtyard, Rocky's ears perked and his tail wagged, alerting Kyle to the fact that he'd found a friend. Then Kyle spotted her. Ophelia was standing by a low stone and clay wall, looking out over the waves of stars spreading up at the dark sky. Her blond hair was tied back in a ponytail and she'd changed from her purple dress into the standard-issue gray tracksuit and flip-flops that law enforcement kept on hand for victims needing a change of clothes.

Somehow she looked even more beautiful than she had before.

As if sensing his gaze, Ophelia turned toward them. A tired but gorgeous smile spread across her face. He felt an unfamiliar grin tug at the corner of his mouth.

He raised a palm up in greeting. "Hey."

"Hey, yourself." She started toward them. They stopped a few feet away from each other and stood in the courtyard, in a bright pool of light created by the glow of two different lamplights meeting. The smell of flowers, warm earth and pine filled the air. "Good news is that CSI is done processing the scene. Bad news is there's so much to go through and analyze it might take a couple of days. Plus, the lab is pretty backed up and understaffed. But I will do my best to expedite it when I'm in the lab tomorrow."

"Thanks," he said. "I'm especially curious about the cuff link. It's hard to imagine a serial killer going out and getting cuff links made with his moniker on them, but with the RMK you never know. A few weeks ago, he managed to get his hands on the MCK9 Task Force's compassion therapy labradoodle named Cowgirl. A few weeks ago, someone we believe to be the RMK sent our team leader, Chase Rawlston, a picture of Cowgirl from a burner phone, wearing a pink rhinestone dog collar that read Killer."

Her eyes widened. "Wow."

"Yeah," Kyle said. "Our technical analyst, Isla, is trying to track down where the collar was sold. But after pulling a stunt like that I wouldn't put getting gold cuff links with his moniker on them past the RMK. Did you find anything else interesting?"

"Well, personally, I think it's interesting we only found one cuff link," she said. "Considering they come in pairs. Did he leave one behind on purpose or by accident? But if you're looking for something more concrete, I can tell you the bullets were 9mm, if that means anything to you."

"Yeah, it really does." He blew out a hard breath. "Nine mm is the RMK's weapon of choice and all of the victims were killed with the same gun. I'll get Isla to coordinate with you tomorrow about seeing if you can confirm a match. The Mountain Country K-9 Task Force will be coordinating with the Santa Fe PD on this case for the time being."

"Guess that means we'll be working together," Ophelia said.

"We work together all the time," he said. "I just never knew that you were...you know, you. Or seen you outside of your protective gear."

"Probably for the best, considering the fact that the first time you did you ordered me out of your crime scene."

Her eyes twinkled. He could tell she was teasing him, but that didn't stop heat from rising to the back of Kyle's neck. He ran his hand over it.

"Sorry about that," he said. "The whole thing was kind of confusing, especially as we'd never really met and I didn't know why you'd requested me to respond to the scene."

To his surprise, a bright pink flush now spread across her cheeks.

"Well, dispatch told me that law enforcement was over twenty minutes out," she said, "and I knew that you were less than a quarter of a mile away."

That raised more questions than it answered. He waited, letting an uncomfortable pause lie between them as she struggled to find the words to explain.

"My great-aunt Evelyn is worried about me spending all my time with blood and death," she said, with a little laugh and a shrug, "so she created a profile for me on a dating app for elderly relatives who want to play matchmakers. She was showing it to me earlier and I recognized you from past cases we'd both worked on. It indicated you were really close by."

"Oh!" Kyle's heart stuttered a step. Someone had put him on a dating app. It had to be his mother. Yet, he'd have thought that if anyone knew that between his work with the MCK9 and being a dad to Brody he didn't have time to add a relationship into the mix, it would be her. Did she doubt his ability to be a good dad or think he was lacking in some way? Or was she worried that she wouldn't be able to be there for him forever? She'd definitely seemed distracted recently and did seem to need to drop by the drug store often these days, but whenever he'd asked her about it, she'd told him she was fine. "Yeah, I was actually at the petting zoo with my mother and son."

"I didn't know you had a son." Ophelia's eyes widened with what looked like genuine interest. "How old is he?"

"Eighteen months," Kyle said. He swallowed hard, feeling a familiar lump in his throat at the thought of how Brody had come into his life. No, he wouldn't burden her with all that. "Anyway, my mom lives with us. We also have a new puppy named Taffy, who's Rocky's half sister. It's a pretty busy house. I should probably say good-night, though. I need to see about finding a way back to town and I'm guessing you're heading out soon, too."

"Ophelia!" a man's voice called from the darkness.

They turned to see Jared running toward them. He looked worried.

"Jared!" Ophelia took a few steps toward him as he rushed toward them. "Is everything okay with Evelyn?"

"Yeah," he said. "A police officer has taken her and Gabrielle back to the hotel. Oh, and Grandma told me to tell you that she really hopes you decide to take that spare room, because you deserve to sleep in a luxury bed for a night. But there's something important that Gabrielle didn't tell you."

He glanced from Ophelia to Kyle and back, and Kyle had the distinct impression that whatever it was, Gabrielle didn't want Jared telling them now.

"Hey, you can trust Kyle," Ophelia said. "I've known him for a while and he's a great guy. One of the best."

Really? She thought that about him?

"Whatever's going on," she added, "you can trust us."

Jared glanced back over his shoulder. His voice lowered to a whisper.

"Gabrielle has a stalker," he said. "One who's been threatening to kill her."

"Gabrielle has a stalker?" Ophelia repeated.

She glanced at Kyle. His eyebrows rose as he met her gaze with a look that told her that this was the first he was hearing about it, too.

"Yeah," Jared said miserably. "His name is Bobby and he's been harassing her for months, ever since he found out we were getting married."

"And neither of you ever went to the police with this?" Her voice rose. "You could've put her and everyone else at this wedding in danger."

"But we're thankful you're telling us now," Kyle told Jared, almost gently, as if he could read the frustration in her eyes. He gestured to a table with two stools that had been set up in the courtyard for the party that had never been. "Why don't we sit down and chat about it?"

Jared hesitated, then nodded. The three of them walked over to the table and Kyle pulled up a third stool. Rocky trotted over and sat down on the ground in between Kyle and Ophelia. The hound looked up at them and whimpered softly, as if sensing something was wrong and wondering if there was anything he could do to help. Ophelia leaned down and ran her hand over the back of Rocky's head as he nuzzled her fingers, comforting her even more than she was him.

Jared rested his elbows on the tiny table and dropped his head in his hands.

"This may not have anything to do with what happened," Jared said. Her cousin's gaze was locked on the table. "She told me it wasn't a big deal and I promised her I wasn't going to say anything." He looked so racked with guilt she felt her frustration with Jared begin to soften. "Is there any way we can keep this just between us?"

Not if it was related to a crime, Ophelia thought.

"I can keep this information within the immediate investigative team," Kyle said, "and only share it on a need-to-know basis. Trust me, people in my line of work get really adept at keeping other people's secrets. Nobody has to know about this conversation unless it becomes necessary for pressing charges and obtaining a conviction."

"Can we keep this out of the press?" Jared

asked. "Gabrielle is really worried about this getting online or in the media, and I just really want to protect her."

"Absolutely," Kyle agreed. "Except in the event that it's needed as evidence for a trial."

Kyle was being so much kinder to Jared than she felt capable of being. To her, most things were cut-and-dried. As someone who collected and preserved evidence for a living, she was irked to no end by the fact that her cousin and Gabrielle had withheld potentially significant evidence from police. In her line of work things were binary. Either DNA was a match or it wasn't. Fingerprints had either been found at a crime scene or they hadn't been. There was something comforting about the certainty of that. But Kyle's tone was somehow multiple things at once. Both caring and firm. Not playing a good cop or bad cop, just a compassionate cop who also wouldn't flinch from seeking justice.

Jared paused for a moment. Then he sighed and crossed both arms on the table.

"Yeah, I guess that's fair," he said. "Gabrielle just comes from a very wealthy and very private family who are worried about her reputation. So she has to be really careful about avoiding scandals or anything that will damage their image. They're really old-fashioned and she's worried about getting disowned if she's caught up in some kind of scandal."

Ophelia wondered if that had anything to do with Great-Aunt Evelyn's earlier implication that there was some kind of tension with Gabrielle's parents missing their flight and Jared needing help dealing with some problem related to the venue. Did they think Jared wasn't good enough for their daughter?

"Yeah, I hear you," Kyle said, "and I get that."

"So, you know how I told you that we met at a party in a hotel in Albuquerque last September? Well, Gabrielle and her roommate Chloe had gone to this other party first, with some students from her college, and this guy named Bobby had shown up."

"Was he also a college student?" Kyle interjected.

"No," Jared said. "He was some kind of investments guy from Nevada, who made money in online currencies. They'd only gone on a couple of dates and he'd gotten really demanding. Anyway, I was there at a table with a bunch of my colleagues when she came in and asked if she could hide out at my table and sit with me until the guy gave up and stopped looking for her. We got talking, I offered to walk her home, and next thing I knew we'd spent hours just wandering the city getting to know each other."

Despite the worry that lined his forehead, a smile filled his eyes at the memory.

"Where was Chloe at this time?" Kyle asked. "She's the bridesmaid that didn't show up, right?"

"I don't know." Jared frowned. "She made herself scarce shortly after Gabrielle and I started talking. I was honestly so caught up in Gabrielle I didn't notice. I know Gabrielle was devastated when Chloe canceled on her today." He glanced at Ophelia. "By the way, I haven't forgotten that I told you I wouldn't try to rope you in to be a bridesmaid, but it was kind of an emergency."

Ophelia bit her tongue and stopped herself from pointing out he and Gabrielle had an odd definition of what constituted an "emergency."

"Was it love at first sight?" Kyle asked.

Jared nodded. "Yeah, absolutely, I'd never met anyone like her."

"Did you see Bobby that night?" Kyle asked.

"No, I've never seen him," Jared said. "I have noticed a large guy in a hoodie who seemed to be lurking around her apartment or following us sometimes, but I never got a good look at him. And I didn't even know if it was him. At times I thought maybe I was being paranoid."

"Did she tell you about Bobby that night you met?" Kyle pressed.

"Absolutely," Jared said. "She told me right away that someone was hassling her and I didn't really ask her for the details. I was just happy to help her."

"But you didn't realize it was a problem?"

"Not for a couple of weeks," Jared said. "We'd gone out for dinner and when I dropped her off there was this big bouquet of flowers outside her apartment door. Absolutely huge. She got all flustered and upset and told me that Bobby was fixated on her and had somehow figured out where she lived. He was really relentless, refusing to take no for an answer."

"And did you suggest she go to the police?" Kyle asked.

"Of course! But she didn't want to because she has a really big heart and I think she felt sorry for the guy."

"And because of her wealthy and controlling parents, right?" Kyle suggested.

The fact that Jared had given two different explanations for the why they'd chosen not to go to the police about Gabrielle's stalker didn't mean there wasn't some truth to both of them. But it did make her wonder if Gabrielle and Jared had been lying to themselves about how potentially serious the situation was.

"Yeah," Jared said. "I feel weird talking to a cop about this, but apparently Bobby was really well connected in law enforcement and he told Gabrielle if she called the police on him they wouldn't do anything to protect her from him." He glanced at Ophelia again. "I think it would help a lot if you assured her that you and Kyle are friends, and that you can promise us that Kyle's got our back and is on our side."

She felt her lips beginning to part to tell Jared she'd do no such thing, when she saw Kyle subtly wave his hand, a couple of inches above the table, signaling to her to let the comment go.

"Does she know Bobby's last name? Where he lives and where he works?"

"No, just his first name."

"Hmm." Kyle leaned back and crossed his

arms. "Not a lot to go on, then. Were the flowers a onetime thing?"

"No, there were phone calls, too, day and night, from different blocked numbers. He also left notes on her door sometimes, which is how I know he said that he'd kill her if she married me, and if he couldn't have her nobody could."

"There are notes?" Ophelia asked. "Where are they now? We can do handwriting analysis, track where the paper came from and test them for fingerprints and DNA."

"Sadly, she burned them all," Jared said. "She just wanted to erase him from her life. It's part of why we decided to get married in Santa Fe instead of Albuquerque. She just wanted to put him behind her and move on."

Only maybe the danger had followed them here.

"And you wanted to be her knight in shining armor and protect her," Kyle said.

"Yeah."

Ophelia sat and listened for another fifteen minutes or so as Jared spoke and Kyle asked insightful questions. But it was clear they were just talking around in circles and Jared had told him everything he knew.

Finally, Kyle reached over and placed a comforting hand on Jared's forearm.

"It's clear that you love her a lot," he said. "And you're really worried for her. You should head back to the hotel and go be with her." Then Kyle stood as if to signal the conversation was over. So did Jared and Ophelia. "I suggest you tell her that you told us about this Bobby guy and encourage her to talk to us about him. You can both sleep on it, and maybe she'll be willing to talk to us tomorrow and fill in some of the gaps. Tell her that it could really go a long way in helping with our investigation. But either way, I will do everything in my power to unravel what happened here today and keep you guys safe, okay?"

"Okay," Jared said. He still seemed a bit shaky, but lighter, too, as if he'd managed to get a weight off his shoulders. He hugged Ophelia and she hugged him back. "I don't think I'm going to be able to get her to talk to police. But maybe I can get her to talk to you, Ophelia. Because you're family and she seems to really like you. I'll just explain that Kyle's an FBI agent friend of yours and on our side."

Again, she could see Kyle's warning gaze on her face telling her to let the comment slide.

So she just pressed her lips together and wished Jared a good night. She stood back with Kyle and Rocky, and watched her cousin saunter to the parking lot.

Kyle pulled his phone from his pocket, glanced at the screen and frowned.

"Everything okay?" Ophelia asked.

"Yeah," Kyle said. "Well, no, actually. I missed Brody's bedtime. My mom usually does his morning routine and I do nighttime. He's fussing that he doesn't want to go to sleep without saying good-night to Rocky and me." He glanced down at his dog. Rocky thumped his tail on the ground. "I'm sure the one he really wants to see is Rocky. He really loves my partner."

"Well, Rocky's a very lovable dog," she agreed.

The hound woofed as if thanking her for the compliment. She laughed.

"Problem is we all came to the petting zoo together in my vehicle," he said, "and I had her take it back. I told her I'd get a ride home with one of the cops on the scene, but most of them have left by now. And I don't know how long it's going to take to get a taxi up here."

"I'll give you a ride," Ophelia said quickly.

"You sure?"

"Of course, I don't mind. It'll give us time to talk." His gaze was unreadable as she added, "About the case."

He nodded. She wished she could spend the time learning more about him and the family he seemed devoted to. Despite the work on her PhD she knew she needed to get home to, somehow she wasn't quite ready for the evening to end. And maybe neither was he. Because another look she couldn't quite decipher flickered in Kyle's eyes, one that seemed to draw her closer while also sending a fresh wave of heat rising to her cheeks. She broke his gaze and looked down at Rocky.

"Although obviously the one I really want to talk to is Rocky."

Kyle snorted a laugh. "Obviously."

He fired off a couple of quick texts as they walked to the almost empty parking lot.

"Mine's the little one," she said.

She pressed a button on her remote and her small car unlocked and flashed its lights in greeting. She opened the back door for Rocky, who leaped inside and positioned himself in the middle, in between her gym bag, a box of spare plastic gloves and some of her research books. Kyle opened the passenger door and slid the seat all the way back, before folding his tall frame inside. She got in the driver's seat and was instinctively about to apologize for having such a modest car, instead of the fancier ones the other wedding guests had, before realizing that for once she was sitting beside someone who already knew what she did for a living, understood what it entailed and even relied on it.

It was a nice feeling.

She glanced to the rearview mirror and saw Rocky's cheerful face smiling back at her, as if riding in her small and crowded car was some kind of grand adventure. She smiled and pulled out.

Slowly, they drove back through the wedding arch, out of the ranch and down the steep, narrow and winding mountain road. A drive that had seemed a bit tricky during the evening felt almost treacherous now.

"I didn't know you had a family," she admitted. She had happened to notice he didn't wear a wedding ring. But that kind of routine observation was a hazard of the job.

"When my fraternal twin and his wife died in a helicopter crash in the mountains last year, their six-month-old son, Brody, was orphaned. And I adopted my nephew."

"Oh, I'm so sorry for your loss." She clenched the steering wheel to keep from squeezing his hand reassuringly. How awful for him. "I remember hearing about the accident. I didn't realize that was your family. What was your twin like?"

"Kevin was perfect. At least in my eyes. He was confident and always seemed so certain of both himself and God. He just threw himself into everything without hesitation. I admired him so much. I always wished I was more like him, and then he was gone, and it felt like I'd lost the person who inspired me most." He ran his hand through his dark hair. "I don't think I ever admitted that to anyone before."

She swerved the car around a blind corner. Suddenly a white delivery van loomed ahead, parked at the side of the road. She turned the wheel sharply and barely managed not to clip it. *Thank You, God, that I wasn't driving faster.* She guessed somebody had picked an inopportune place to stop and stargaze. The van's headlights flickered on and then off again. Kyle glanced at it over his shoulder for a long moment, then turned back.

"I need to ask you something about Jared," Kyle said. "Are you two close?"

"Yes," she said automatically. "Well, to a point. We grew up together. My grandmother passed away when I was little, and his grandmother, my great-aunt Evelyn, really stepped in to take her place. I spent every holiday with Evelyn and Jared. My parents are both university professors who traveled a lot for work. But honestly, I wouldn't say Jared and I are close, as people."

Something about how candid he was about Kevin made her want to be honest, too.

"We're both only children and I used to assume we were close," she went. "But our personalities are really different. He's not the kind of person who stops to question how he comes across to other people."

"And how does he come across?" Kyle asked.

"I don't know how to put it," she said. "Self-centered, maybe? I'd almost say he was spoiled but that sounds too childish. Or privileged, but that word is too easily misinterpreted."

"What was your first job?" Kyle asked.

She blinked. "How is that relevant?"

"Hey, you focus on gathering evidence and I do the interpreting, remember?"

There was a grin in his voice. Yeah, she remembered telling him that back at the barn.

"I was a waitress all through high school," she said.

"And Jared's first job?"

"A friend of his dad's got him a position at his firm after college."

Headlights appeared in the rearview mirror. She turned another corner and they vanished again.

"When you and Jared visited Evelyn, was he expected to clear the table and do his own dishes?"

"No," she said.

"How about picking his clothes up off the floor?"

"No, those were my jobs," Ophelia said. "Evelyn had pretty strong opinions about gender roles, and whenever I complained she'd say Jared had the responsibility of protecting the family if we ever went to war."

To her surprise, Kyle chuckled under his breath.

"Sorry, I'm just imagining ten-year-old Ophelia standing over a sink full of dirty dishes wondering when exactly the invading armies were going to arrive."

She giggled, despite herself. Her great-aunt was certainly grounded in her opinions about women's roles, but she'd always made Ophelia feel welcome in her home. She knew Evelyn loved her. Ophelia just wished her aunt had understood how some of her comments made her feel.

"That's not far off," she said. "And you can't have missed Jared assuming that because we know each other, you'd be 'his cop' and on his side."

"No, I didn't," Kyle said dryly.

"Truth is my parents were really big on personal responsibility," she said. "Jared had it a lot easier and his side of the family was a lot wealthier than mine. Although Evelyn did say something about a plot of land Gabrielle's parents are buying for them that made me wonder if there were money problems."

"What plot of land?" Kyle interjected.

"A gorgeous place near the Pecos Wilderness that they're going to build a house on," Ophelia said. "Jared was so ostentatious about it. Said they'd decided to build a house 'where the mountains meet the sky,' et cetera. It was so pompous."

"Not cheap," Kyle said.

"No," Ophelia agreed. "Plus, this whole wedding has been expensive and exorbitant. So maybe he's been overspending. But please, don't get me wrong, they're not bad people. And even if I did end up doing a lot more housework than Jared did, I know Evelyn loves me and she would've been the first person to tell Jared to go mow the lawn and chop wood, if she hadn't had a gardener and central heating."

Kyle chuckled. Then his smile dropped almost immediately, as headlights reappeared on their tail.

"Do me a favor," he said, "and turn left at this next fork."

"Will do." She focused on keeping the pace steady as the turn ahead grew closer. Then at the last possible moment she tapped her brakes just enough to safely pull off the road that would've led them back to the highway in a matter of minutes and onto one that would take them on a longer route past hiking trails. The van kept going forward.

Kyle leaned back against the seat.

"Do you think you're able to be impartial if the evidence points to your cousin?" he asked.

"I don't think he's capable of hurting anyone."

"His fiancée and grandmother agree with you on that," Kyle said. "But the fact is that

Jared had no alibi for when John Doe was killed. Now, our victim was tall and blond like your cousin. It's possible Bobby was gunning for Jared and shot John Doe by mistake. But I also have to consider that the victim *is* Bobby, that he came here to stop the wedding and Jared shot him to protect Gabrielle."

"But then who was the man who shot into the barn?" Ophelia asked. "Because that can't have been Jared."

"I don't know."

The road seemed to stretch out endlessly in front of them. The lights of Santa Fe grew closer. Eventually ranch houses began to appear, up and down the mountain on either side. She felt like she was standing on the edge of something very tall and he was asking her to be willing to jump.

Lord, help me keep an open mind about this. Don't let my feelings blind my vision.

"Okay," she said finally. "I can promise you I'll do my job, gather the evidence, process it impartially and trust you to draw your own conclusions."

Which didn't mean she'd necessarily agree with him. Only that she knew she was probably unconsciously biased toward her cousin and would try to keep an open mind.

After all, Kyle would be the one who'd make the call on whether any charges would be laid. And she wouldn't get in the way of him doing his job.

"Good." Kyle let out a long breath. "Because Jared seems willing to tell you things that he won't tell me."

Kyle's gaze darted up to the rearview mirror and her gaze followed. The headlights had returned.

"Also, I may be wrong," he said. "But I think we're being followed."

Chapter Four

The glare of the twin headlights filled Ophelia's rearview mirror. Fear trickled down her spine. Was it the same van? Was it really following them? She couldn't even imagine how hard it would've been for a van like that to have done a U-turn on the steep mountain road to turn around and get after them again.

She spotted a residential neighborhood ahead to her right. Instinctively, she turned in through the gate and weaved her way through the houses, before coming back to the same road she'd been on before, hoping the van wouldn't follow and Kyle would turn out to be mistaken. But instead, the van followed every move.

The sense of dread grew deeper. She gripped the steering wheel so tightly her hand shook.

Help me, Lord. I don't know who this guy is or what he wants, but please keep us safe.

"You're right," she said. "I'm sorry, I just wanted to double-check."

"I respect that," Kyle said.

"So, what do we do?" she asked.

He glanced back at the van over his shoulder. "I can't get a good look at the guy and his license plate is too dirty to read. And I don't want to risk getting into a high-speed chase with the guy."

Neither did she. She had to force her eyes to stay on the road ahead and not keep glancing to the headlights on her tail. Kyle turned to Rocky and ordered him to get onto the floor and lie down. The K-9 woofed in agreement and complied. Then Kyle sat back in his seat.

"I'm sorry," he said, "I just realized I didn't think to ask if you do have any training or experience in tactical driving."

A laugh slipped through her lips. Not because the situation was funny. But because she was so used to being underestimated she couldn't actually remember the last time anyone overestimated her.

"Not in the slightest," she said. "If you need someone to gather DNA samples or process crime scene evidence I'm your gal. But anything that involves high-speed chases or action scenes is out of my wheelhouse."

She watched as his jaw set in determination.

"Well, if I could find a safe way to pull over and change places with you I would," he said. "But I don't want to risk it."

He paused for a long moment and when she glanced his way she noticed his eyes were closed and he seemed to be praying. She echoed his prayers, asking God to hear his plea.

Then Kyle opened his eyes again.

"Okay," he said. "I want you to head to downtown Santa Fe. I want to get this guy into the light and get a good look at who we're dealing with."

Another fork in the road appeared ahead. This time she turned toward the city. Santa Fe, the capital of New Mexico, was nestled in the foothills of the Rocky Mountains. The road sloped steeply beneath her tires. The beautiful lights of the city dazzled below her like dozens of tiny tea light candles floating on the surface of a lake.

The vehicle behind turned and followed. It was stalking them like an animal, not driving close enough to run them off the road and yet never getting too far from sight, no matter how many twists and turns she took. The city grew closer; ranches and houses gave way to densely packed roads dotted with stop signs and traffic lights.

As the warm glow of Santa Fe surrounded them, she could see the van pull back as if shirking from the light. But finally, they were able to get a good look at the van. It was an old delivery vehicle, with no windows or obvious markings on the side. The kind someone could buy from a used car dealership or steal from a small business lot. She couldn't see much of the man who was behind the wheel. He was hunched low and wearing a baseball cap. Traffic continued to slow. Black and yellow signs advertising road closures appeared ahead. Summer weekends in Santa Fe were a rolling feast of events and festivals, celebrating New Mexico's culture, diversity, music, agriculture and cuisine. The sound of string instruments and singing filled the air.

"Keep going," Kyle said, "right up to the barriers. We're looking for a road that's been blocked off by police. I'll get them to wave us in through the barrier and then surround the van before he can turn around again."

Kyle raised his phone to his ear, called dispatch and briefed them on his location and plan.

"We need a tight perimeter," he said. "Consider the suspect armed and dangerous. He's a possible suspect in a string of murders across several states."

But the words had barely left his lips when she glanced to the rearview mirror to see the van turn sharply, mount the sidewalk and pull down a side road.

Kyle sighed and updated dispatch of the van's new route.

"Do you want me to turn around and go after him?" Ophelia asked.

"Nah." Kyle sounded frustrated. "Last thing I want to do is get in a chase with a suspect who might be armed in a public place." After he ended his call with dispatch, he placed a very quick call to Chase, the leader of the MCK9 Task Force, and quickly briefed him on the night so far.

"We have a video chat first thing tomorrow morning," he told Ophelia when he finished the call. "We'll go over things more thoroughly then. One piece of very good news is that he's going to ask Meadow Ames to join us on the call and potentially fly out to back me up on this case, depending on how things go. She's a US marshal and an incredible member of our team. Her K-9 partner, Grace, is a vizsla who specializes in search and rescue." The relief in his voice was palpable. "Are you good?"

"Yep," she said. "I'm just driving in circles right now, waiting for direction."

He chuckled. There was something warm about it, like he appreciated her company. He rattled off his home address and she laughed. Turned out they lived in the same neighborhood on the north side of the city.

"My house is a fifteen-minute walk from yours," she said. "I'm just on Chestnut Street."

"Awesome." He turned and told Rocky he could get back up on the seat. Rocky woofed joyfully and hopped onto the back seat. A moment later the dog's cheerful face appeared in the rearview mirror again.

She waved a hand. "Hi, Rocky!"

He woofed again in greeting and she laughed.

"I've met a lot of K-9 dogs in my line of work," she said, "but Rocky is one of a kind. There's a real gentleness to him. I don't know if it's those long floppy ears or if the beige muzzle and paws make it look like he's been playing in chocolate milk, but there's a sweetness to him."

"Yeah," Kyle said. "I didn't know what to think when I was paired with a cadaver dog.

It felt like such a sad specialty. But as I started working with him, I really came to appreciate his dedication and focus, along with how our work brings peace and justice to families who've lost their loved ones."

"That's really beautiful," she said, "and kind of poetic."

"Nobody's ever called me a poet before."

Something sizzled inside her chest, like a dozen party sparklers springing to life.

"Well, nobody's ever asked me if I'm a stunt driver before," she said.

He laughed again, this time a full-throated chuckle that seemed to come from somewhere deep inside his chest.

"I like hanging with you, CSI Clarke," he said. He punched her shoulder gently, as if they were siblings. "You're a pal. This is a really hard job sometimes and people like you make it easier."

"Thanks, Agent West." Not that she was sure what to make of the fact that he'd just fist-bumped her shoulder and called her "pal."

She liked hanging with him, too. Even though her body ached for sleep, something inside her wasn't ready for the car ride to end. But all too soon, GPS alerted her that her destination was ahead on the right, and she looked up to see a large, ranch-style house with Kyle's vehicle and a smaller red car parked out front. She pulled in.

Through a window, she could see the silhouette of a woman with long hair swaying with a toddler in her arms, as if trying to get him to settle.

"Well, I should get going," he said. "Looks like my mom hasn't managed to get Brody down yet. He's a really good kid, most of the time. But he gets stubborn when he doesn't want to sleep. Thanks again for the ride."

"No problem," she said. "Have a good night."

"You, too," he said.

Yet he didn't reach for the door handle. She didn't move, either. Instead, they both sat there, smiling at each other.

"Again, I'm sorry that in all the cases we've both worked I never took the time to come over to introduce myself," he said. "I've always really admired your work. Your job is a rough one and you do it well."

"You have no idea what that means to me," she said. "I admire your work, too. My great-aunt Evelyn actually told me not to talk about my job at the wedding. 'Nobody wants to hear about murder and crime scenes. It's impolite.'" She wagged her finger in an impression of Evelyn. He laughed. "And apparently Gabrielle thought I was some kind of veterinarian, because on top of my job with the crime lab, I'm also pursuing a PhD in using DNA to track the endangered Rocky Mountain wolf population."

"That's absolutely incredible," he said. "Considering the hours we work I can't imagine juggling the job and a PhD."

"It's a lot," she admitted. "I feel like I'm never getting enough sleep and sometimes I forget to eat. But I can't imagine juggling the job and single parenthood. At least I only have to worry about me. You have Brody to worry about."

"Yeah, being his dad on top of work doesn't leave much time for anything else," he said. "Which reminds me, I have to ask my mom about that dating profile you saw and get her to take it down. The last thing I want is to fool some poor woman into thinking I'm free for a relationship right now."

And just like that, the sparklers she'd felt inside her chest went out as suddenly as if he'd dumped a bucket of cold water on them. He wasn't directing that comment at her. Of course. Kyle thought of her as a work pal and was only speaking his truth. He had no idea that she was attracted to him. And besides, it wasn't like she was looking for a relationship, either. They both had busy and demanding full-time jobs, on top of her PhD and the fact that he was raising a toddler.

Neither of them had time for anything more.

No matter how many fireworks his smile set off inside her chest.

"You should probably delete your dating profile, too," Kyle said. His dark eyes searched her face and a question hung in their gaze. "Unless you want to be on a website like that."

"Yeah, no," Ophelia said. "You're right. I should totally delete that profile."

Kyle nodded. "We should exchange numbers, to follow up with each other about the case. If that's all right with you."

"Absolutely." For professional reasons and nothing else. No other reason.

They exchanged numbers. Then she leaned in between the seats, ran her hand over Rocky's head and wished him a good night. Rocky woofed softly and licked her hand. Kyle got out of the car and called for his partner, and she watched them both walk toward the house.

There was something so sweet about them.

They were solid and comforting. She felt safe around them, like she knew they'd do what it took to bring criminals to justice.

She closed her eyes and prayed.

Lord, please help us find the identity of the John Doe who died in the barn and catch his killer. Help me focus on the evidence in front of me. Help me do my job without getting distracted by my emotions. Remind me that You called me to this work for a reason and help me trust in You.

Then she prayed that God would bless Kyle and his family, along with Jared, his fiancée, Gabrielle, her great-aunt Evelyn, the other venue staff, law enforcement and all those impacted by the murder in the barn, and those who loved the victim.

She hadn't meant to sit in Kyle's driveway praying that long, but when she opened her eyes, she looked to see Kyle silhouetted in the same window where she'd seen his mother earlier, gently dancing around the room with the small boy in his arms. The FBI agent bent low over the boy, like he was brushing a kiss on the toddler's head or whispering in his ear.

Her breath caught in her throat; it was like she was looking at a picture of something she'd never let herself acknowledge she wanted for herself one day, because she knew she'd never find it.

Slowly she pulled out of the driveway and drove home. Ophelia lived in a small stucco bungalow that sat by itself at the end of a dead-end road, with an empty lot on one side and building under construction on the other. It had a perfectly square living room, a surprisingly large kitchen, a single bedroom in the back and a small, unfinished basement. She dropped her bag on the table beside her front door and then walked through the living room and into the bedroom, tossing the remains of the purple bridesmaid dress into her closet hamper.

Her phone battery was almost dead, so she plugged her phone into a charger by the front door and placed a quick call to Evelyn. Her great-aunt assured her that she was fine and that "a lovely hotel manager" had promised her personally that his security would keep a close eye on the hotel. Ophelia told Evelyn that she loved her, wished her a good night and ended the call quickly before she could get trapped in a longer conversation.

Ophelia knew she should probably eat, considering she'd never ended up having dinner, and should also get some sleep. But something inside her just couldn't settle. Did her cousin have something to do with John Doe's murder? Had the man who'd shot at her been the Rocky Mountain Killer? What would she find when she processed the evidence?

Either way, she had to read at least twenty-five pages before bed if she had any hope of meeting her next deadline with her PhD advisor. Ophelia sat on the bed, tucked her feet beneath her quilt, pulled out one of her heavy research books and tried to get through the reading. She spun a pencil between her fingers, underlining anything she thought might be useful to follow up on her thesis and jotted notes in the margins, until finally she fell asleep with her book on her chest.

Ophelia woke up to a dark house and a gnawing in her stomach that told her she'd forgotten to eat. She reached for her lamp and toggled the switch back and forth, but the room stayed dark. She walked into the main room to find the light switch there didn't work, either, and the cell phone she'd left plugged in was completely dead.

Okay, looked like the power was out. One of the downsides of living in a hot state during the summer months was that sometimes everyone turned their air-conditioning on at once, causing brownouts.

All the more reason to get something to eat from the fridge before the food spoiled. She headed through the quiet, dark house to the kitchen, still in the same tracksuit she'd been wearing since the crime scene. A faint and foul smell hung in the air and she wondered if her food had already begun to spoil. The fridge was off, but when she pulled a carton of chocolate ice cream from the freezer she was thankful to find it wasn't too melted. She leaned over the counter and ate it straight from a carton with a spoon.

Her gaze flickered to where she'd left her laptop on the kitchen table. She still hadn't looked at the dating profile her aunt had set up for her on Loving Meddlers. And even though she knew that reading whatever Great-Aunt Evelyn had posted in her profile wasn't going to help her get back to sleep, she was curious. She opened her laptop and searched for the website. The gentle glow of the screen filled the kitchen.

The site opened quickly. It had a bubblegum pink background and photos of happy couples. Much smaller text warned users not to create profiles for their single loved ones without their permission and had a button to click for people to remove a profile that somebody had made about them. A pop-up window on the side told her that Kyle's profile had recently checked out hers and gave her the opportunity to contact him now by video chat.

A couple of clicks later, the profile her great-aunt had created for her showed up.

Ophelia sighed, feeling the ice cream turn to ash in her mouth. There was nothing actually wrong with the profile. It was sweet, actually, with a picture of her smiling in a sundress at her aunt's seventieth birthday garden party. It described her as charming, pretty, generous and kind. But there was nothing listed about her education, work or goals. Nothing about the accomplishments she was proud of or what she liked about herself.

No man wants to marry a woman who pokes around blood and guts for a living.

A thud sounded from somewhere beneath her feet. She froze. Was there something in the basement? Then she heard the telltale sound of footsteps creaking on the basement stairs. Someone was climbing up the stairs, one by one, toward her. Her heart pounded hard in her chest, blocking her ability to breathe. Her phone was dead. Should she run? Or hide? If she tried to dash for the front door, she'd have to first pass the basement to get there. Would she make it in time?

No. The footsteps had almost reached the top of the stairs. She snatched up the laptop and dove beneath the table. She needed to call for help. But how? She had no way to call 911. And while she could contact Santa Fe PD via the internet, she'd have to hurry to get to the site and there was no time. The basement door handle was already beginning to turn. The dating website's ridiculous message box flashed.

She held her breath, prayed and hit the button. The heart-shaped icon spun. The call went unanswered. She heard the creek of hinges as the basement door swung open. Footsteps sounded on her living room floor. Ophelia typed her address rapid fire into the chat box and told Kyle she needed help, that there was someone in her home.

"Hello?" A woman's face appeared on the screen. She had long gray hair and worried eyes. "Ophelia? I'm Alice, Kyle's mom. Are you okay?"

Footsteps pounded toward her.

"I need help!" Ophelia yelled. "There's someone in my home—"

But it was too late. The table that she'd been hiding under suddenly flipped over, clattering on the floor beside her. Large, gloved hands grabbed her by the hair and yanked her whimpering to her feet.

"Now, what are you doing here?" The man's voice was harsh and angry. His face was hidden in the same mask she'd seen before, with a dark mesh that even hid his eyes. For a split second she could see Alice's panicked face looking up at her. Then he kicked the laptop hard, shattering the screen and sending it flying.

Leaving Ophelia alone with her attacker.

"Kyle!" his mother's voice shouted. "Someone named Ophelia is in trouble!"

Kyle jerked awake as Brody's bedroom door swung open. He'd fallen asleep on a mattress on the floor of Brody's room, holding the little boy's hand through the crib, with both Rocky and Taffy curled up beside him. He fell asleep there most nights, gazing into Brody's face and listening to the child's tiny breath rise and fall.

Kyle leaped to his feet and rushed out to the hallway with both dogs on his heels before his brain had even fully computed what his mother was saying. Questions cascaded through his mind, like how she would even know that, but only one truly mattered.

"Is Ophelia okay?"

"No." Alice closed Brody's door. Her voice was an urgent whisper. "A man broke into her home and grabbed her."

"When?"

"Thirty seconds ago, maybe."

That was all he needed to know.

He ran for the front door, summoning Rocky to his side. "She lives on Chestnut. Do you know where?"

"Number 32," Alice said. "She messaged me on this dating app I set up for you. Should I call 911?"

"Yes," Kyle said. "But I'm not going to wait for them."

He just prayed to the Lord that he'd make it in time. Kyle grabbed his badge and gun, shoved his feet into his shoes and dashed out the front door with Rocky at his heels. His mother barely managed to grab Taffy and scoop her up into her arms before the puppy could run out after them.

He glanced at his truck, mapped the route

out in his mind and made the split-second decision he could get there faster on foot.

"Come on, Rocky!" he yelled. "We're going to make a run for it!"

His feet raced down the sidewalk with his partner keeping pace. Desperate prayers poured through his heart, begging God to keep her alive and safe until he could get there.

A swing set loomed ahead in the distance. He turned toward it and cut through the park, racing past the jungle gym and slide. A six-foot wooden fence appeared ahead.

"Rocky!" he called to his partner. "Jump!"

Kyle leaped up the fence. His toes catching the wood part way up, he braced his hands against the top of the fence and vaulted over. Then he glanced back and watched as Rocky cleared it in a single bound. He crossed another street, then ran up a driveway and cut through a stranger's backyard, praying for the peaceful sleep of those inside. They scaled another fence and came out on Chestnut Street. He gasped for breath and scanned house numbers.

Rocky growled and signaled to his right to where a house sat all alone at the end of the street. The lights were off. A white van was parked on the side of the road in front of number 32. As Kyle ran for it, his partner barked, and Kyle felt his heart lurch in response. The warning sound was unmistakable.

Rocky sensed death.

No! The single word detonated like a bomb in Kyle's heart. Rocky had to be wrong for once. Kyle couldn't have lost her. Something deep inside his core needed her to be alive. They reached the house and ran up the driveway. Rocky's nose sniffed the air and growled.

But Kyle could now hear the sounds of a struggle coming from inside the house. A second later he was at the door. It was locked. Kyle reared back and leveled a swift kick just below the doorknob, and it flew open.

"Agent Kyle West!" He burst through into the living room. "FBI!"

His eyes adjusted to the darkness. The same masked man whom Kyle had chased through the mountains had Ophelia around the throat, even as she tried to thrash and fight against him. A thick cloth he'd tied around his left calf over his pant leg was caked in dried blood. The man dragged her backward toward an open doorway, limping heavily. His left arm tightened cruelly around her neck as he pulled her in front of him like a human shield. Metal glinted in his right hand. A gun? A knife?

Rocky barked wildly, held back only by the fact that Kyle hadn't given him the order to leap.

"Let her go!" Kyle raised his weapon and set the masked man in his sights. But he couldn't get a clean shot.

Help me, Lord. I can't risk firing and hurting Ophelia!

Chapter Five

"Turn around and leave!" The masked man's shout was followed by a string of vile swear words and threats of what he'd do to Ophelia if Kyle didn't retreat.

There was no way he was going to let that happen.

Rocky snarled. The man yanked Ophelia back harder toward the door, and his arm slipped up in front of Ophelia's face. She grabbed it and bit down hard. Her attacker shouted in pain and instinctively shoved her away hard.

Ophelia flew at Kyle, barely giving him seconds to sheath his weapon before she crashed into him. He caught her and held her tightly to his side. Her weight fell into his arms as her legs collapsed out from under her.

The assailant pushed past them, bodychecking Kyle so violently he almost knocked him off his feet, and ran out the front door. Rocky barked sharply.

"I'm fine." Ophelia's voice shook even as he could tell she was trying to regain control of it. "Go after him!"

Even in the darkness he could see the tears filling the blue of her eyes.

The memory of the second set of gunshots back at the barn rattled in his mind. How could he leave her now? The criminal knew where she lived and had invaded her home. What if he had an accomplice hiding nearby waiting for Kyle to leave so he could make another attempt to kidnap Ophelia when she was alone and helpless?

Kyle couldn't have hesitated more than a few seconds, before relinquishing his grip on Ophelia's quivering frame. Then he made sure her feet were stable on the floor and pulled his weapon.

"Stay behind me and keep low," he told Ophelia. She nodded.

He signaled Rocky to his side and then he cautiously stepped out into the warm June night, just in time to hear the van door slam. The white van peeled away down the street.

Kyle pivoted quickly and ran for Ophelia's

car, with Rocky just two steps behind. Instinctively, he glanced to Ophelia's car as he debated going after him. Both of her back tires were slashed. The white van's taillights disappeared around a corner.

Kyle groaned.

"Bad news," he called. "You've got two flats."

Ophelia sighed loudly and Rocky whimpered softly as if asking Kyle how he could help. Kyle ran his hand over the back of his partner's neck.

"I'm sorry," Ophelia said. She clenched her fingers around her keys. "I wish I'd found a way to contact you sooner, or somehow found a way to stop him, or get the better of him, or..."

"Stop it." Kyle stepped toward her and her words trailed off. "*None* of this is your fault in the slightest. You did nothing wrong."

He ran his hand over his head and realized that as much as he wanted to kick himself, it wouldn't do either of them much good.

"You got help, you stayed alive and survived." Kyle's voice dropped, remembering how she'd been trembling in his arms. "Sometimes that's all you can do and it's more than enough."

She nodded and he watched as her chin rose.

"What happened to your phone?" he asked.

"The battery was dead when I woke up," she said. "The power is out."

Yeah, the lights had been off when he'd run up and he hadn't tried to turn them on.

"Okay," he said. "So you've got no power and two flat tires. I'm guessing whoever our attacker is, he didn't want you getting away."

Her hands rose to her face as if trying to blot out the fears filling her mind.

Lord, I can only imagine how scared she is. How do I help her? How do I stop the person after her and keep this from happening again?

"Flat tires are easy to fix and I'm sure getting the power back won't be that hard," he added, quickly. "I can call a mechanic and electrician for you."

"But they probably won't get here until morning." She paused a long moment, then laughed as if trying to cheer herself up. She looked at him. "Well, I told my great-aunt I didn't need a hotel room for tonight, but I guess now I do. Would you be able to give me a ride?"

"You can stay at our house with us," Kyle said. "Mom wouldn't hear of you going to a hotel."

"Thank you," Ophelia said.

Then suddenly, there was a faraway glimmer in her eyes as if she'd just noticed something. He'd seen the same look on her face when she'd spotted the cuff link, back in the barn. But before he could ask her what she was thinking, she popped the trunk of her car and pulled out a gym bag. Then she went back to the house, grabbed her phone and purse off a table just inside the door, and joined him again.

They started walking, down the sidewalk and away from her house. Rocky walked a few steps ahead of them, glancing back every now and then as if double-checking he was on the right path. They took the long way back, along the twisting sidewalks instead of cutting through the backyards and parks that Kyle had taken to get there.

"There was an odd look on your face when I told you that my mom wouldn't hear of you going to a hotel," he said. "Like it had just sparked something in your mind. What was that about?"

"You noticed that?" she asked.

"Yeah, I did."

"I don't know if it's relevant," Ophelia said, after a long moment. "But what I suddenly remembered in the moment is that the masked man seemed almost surprised to see me there, as if he hadn't expected me to be home. Which I might not have been, because Gabrielle offered me Chloe's hotel room."

"The bridesmaid who didn't show," Kyle said.

"Yeah, and Aunt Evelyn really wanted me to stay with them all in the hotel. I called her before I went to bed. She was safe and told me that the hotel manager had reassured her they had security."

"So, you think she sent a masked man over to scare you into going there." The flippant words slipped his lips before he could catch himself. "Oh, I'm so sorry! That was a horrible joke!"

Ophelia laughed and punched him in the arm. "No, it's fine. I have to laugh or I'll cry."

He tapped her shoulder back, gently and softly, though, almost as if his knuckles were kissing her skin. "Well, if you need to cry, that's good with me, too. Everybody cries sometimes and I'm always down for a hug if you need it."

"Thank you," she said again. But this time, her voice barely rose above a whisper. She swallowed hard. They walked on. "Anyway, maybe our masked attacker thought I'd be at the hotel and that my house would be empty. Which could mean he's somehow connected to the wedding party, well enough to know who I am and where I live. He might even know I'm a backup bridesmaid."

"Now, that's a scary thought," he said. "What do you think he could have possibly wanted at your house?"

"I don't know," she admitted.

"Well, you can stay with us as long as you need," Kyle said. "We've got plenty of room. It used to be Kevin's house and they were planning for a large family. Most nights, the master bedroom is completely empty. I tend to sleep in Brody's room to help settle him if he wakes up in the night. Besides, my mother would never forgive me if I didn't insist."

She smiled. "Well, your mother did save my life, as did you."

He placed a quick call to his mom, who as expected was more than happy to have Ophelia stay with them. She'd said she'd make sure there were fresh towels, toiletries for her in the master bedroom's en suite, as well as getting one of the women from the church to drop off a bag of clothes from the donation room, even though he reassured her that Ophelia was bringing a bag. He thanked her and ended the call.

He filled Ophelia in on the conversation.

Then they lapsed back into silence. Their footsteps were slow and easy, but still his mind raced with questions about the murder. If the case was connected to the Rocky Mountain Killer, then why had the white van followed them? Why had the masked man broken into Ophelia's house? Had there been something in her house he'd wanted to destroy? Surely he had to know that a crime scene investigator wouldn't take evidence home with her? And none of that matched any of the RMK's previous murders. And yet, why were there elements so similar to the RMK murders? Were they dealing with a copycat killer?

"Don't worry, we'll get answers tomorrow," Ophelia said softly, as if she'd been able to hear his thoughts.

"How did you know I was worrying about the case?" he asked.

"Your forehead was all scrunchy," she admitted. "But honestly, I was partly talking to myself."

He chuckled and they kept walking.

"Our main problem is that John Doe was killed after five and the lab doesn't run twenty-four hours a day," Ophelia said. "But it will open at nine tomorrow and we'll start processing samples then. Just know that it takes time.

As I'm sure you've noticed, things in real-life labs go a lot slower than the ones on TV. But I promise I will do everything in my power to process the evidence quickly as possible. For now, all we can really do is guess what we'll find and talk ourselves around in circles."

Now, wasn't that true?

"You said you were getting a PhD?" he asked.

"Yes, in biology," she said. "My thesis has to do with using advances in DNA analysis to improve our understanding of the migratory practices of endangered species. As you know there's a lot of concern about the endangered wolf population in the Rocky Mountains, and my hope is to use recent advances in our understanding of mitochondrial DNA to find less intrusive ways of tracking their migratory routes. My hope is that scientists in other areas can then apply that research in their own work with endangered animals, to better understand their family lineage, migration habits and how to protect them."

"That's fascinating," he said.

As they passed under a golden lamplight, he watched as a smile lit up her face. It was stunning.

"I think so, too." She seemed genuinely delighted he'd asked.

"How are you getting a PhD while working full-time for the crime lab?" he asked. "Why not finish your PhD first?"

"Because I couldn't afford to," she said. Although they'd moved back into darkness, he could still hear the smile in her voice. "PhDs are expensive and I always wanted to work with the crime lab. I did get an amazing scholarship that covers some of the cost, but it doesn't cover basic living expenses and it requires me to hit some pretty rigorous deadlines. As hard as it is to do both at the same time, it would be even harder to give up on one of my dreams. Even if it doesn't leave any time for anything else."

"Yeah, I get that," he said. "I'm juggling my work with the MCK9 Task Force, the FBI and taking care of Brody." He felt a rueful smile cross his lips. "I love that little guy with my entire heart and would do anything for him. I just hope when he looks back on his life, he'll always know I loved him and not feel like he missed out on anything because his father was off chasing serial killers."

Rocky stopped walking suddenly and sat. Kyle looked around to realize their long, meandering walk had finally led back to his front door. He couldn't remember the last time he'd gone for a quiet nighttime stroll with anyone, let alone anyone whose company he enjoyed quite that much. And there was a good reason for that.

"If I'm honest," he said, "I know I keep saying I don't have time for a life outside of work and Brody, but it's deeper than that. I don't want drama that's going to impact my life and his. I don't want to go through all the ups and downs of even trying to date anyone. Remember how I told you a few hours ago that my brother was the brave one and I always admired that about him?"

"I do." Ophelia nodded.

"Well, I think the bravest thing he ever did was choosing to get married and have a family. My dad was really terrible. He drank and yelled and treated my mother like trash. Finally, she left him when Kevin and I were still in elementary school. But he'd still show up drunk and try to start fights, or he'd call from jail when he needed someone to bail him out, until finally he ended his own life when I was twenty-two."

He hadn't even realized that he'd crossed his arms tightly across his chest, until he felt Ophelia reach for his hand. Gently she brushed her fingers along his and there was something about the simple gesture that said more than a thousand words ever could.

"I'm not afraid I'll ever turn into a man like my father." Slowly he unfolded his arms, took her hand and squeezed it for a long moment, before letting it go. "What scares me is knowing an incredible woman like my mother somehow fell in love with someone who made us so miserable. I never want to put Brody through anything like that. Not even the whole uncertainty of dating and breakups. He deserves certainty and stability, and I need to give him that."

"Yeah, I get that," Ophelia said.

"Well, thanks for listening," he said. "I don't tend to open up to people but you're really easy to talk to."

"You are, too."

They walked up the driveway and into the house, where Rocky promptly wandered off down the hall in the direction of Brody's room, probably to look for Taffy. Kyle had expected his mom to be waiting up for them in the open-concept living room/dining room. But it was empty except for a handwritten note from Alice to Ophelia welcoming her to their home and telling her where to find anything she might need. She'd also left a tray of hot lavender tea and homemade pound cake for Ophelia in her room.

She thanked him again, and he knew he should say good-night, but instead he stood there, with her blue-eyed gaze looking up into his face as he awkwardly went over all the same things, from mugs to towels, that he was sure his mom had mentioned in her note.

"The master bedroom is on the opposite side of the house than the other two bedrooms," he said and pointed, "and has its own bathroom. There should be a charger by the bed you can use for your phone. Mom's room and Brody's room are down that way. We tend to get up really early and I have a team meeting via video chat at eight. I'd really like you to be there and a part of it. Not just because you have a connection to Jared and there's a good possibility you'll be able to get vital information about this murder we won't be able to get any other way, but also because I really appreciate your professional insight."

"You don't know how much it's meant to me to spend some time talking with someone who really understands my work," she said. "Evelyn and Jared don't get it. They think it's weird at best and gross at worst, and I feel sometimes like they're embarrassed of me."

"Are you kidding?" Kyle said. "Ophelia, in case I haven't made myself clear by now, I think you are an absolutely incredible crime scene investigator. I'm overjoyed every time I know you're processing one of my crime scenes because it means that nothing is going to get missed and everything is going to go smoothly. Because you're good. You're like really, really good at your job. You should feel proud. Don't ever let anyone take that from you."

Her lips parted as if his rambling words had suddenly robbed her of her breath. For a long moment she didn't say anything. Then she dropped her bag, threw her arms around his neck and hugged him tightly.

"Thanks," she said. "I really needed that."

"Well, it's true."

He wrapped his arms around her and held her to his chest, blindsided by just how perfect and wonderful it felt to have her in his arms. Then slowly they both pulled away, their fingertips brushing as they stepped apart.

"Good night, Agent West," she said. "I think you're pretty incredible at your job, too."

"Thank you." He smiled. "Good night, CSI Clarke."

Then she picked up her bag, turned and

walked down the hallway, leaving him standing there wondering why his heart was racing.

She expected to toss and turn the way she normally did, as her busy mind struggled to slow down and rest. After all, a criminal had broken into her home. But maybe Alice's kind snack of pound cake and tea had settled her stomach. Or there was just something safe and comforting about being in Kyle's home. So as she lay there in the darkness and prayed, still in the same gray tracksuit, she found a peace that surpassed her own understanding sweeping through her heart, and Ophelia fell into a deep and peaceful sleep.

She woke hours later to the sound of tiny feet pattering up and down the hallway outside her door, along with a chorus of jingling dog tags and a child's laughter. Ophelia sat up slowly and stretched, thanking God for her good night's sleep and the safe haven she'd found. Sun streamed through a large window that looked out on a toy-strewn backyard. The bed itself had simple wooden frame and a beautiful handmade quilt that had somehow been cozy without being too hot for a June Santa Fe night. The sounds of footsteps and giggling stopped suddenly with a muffled thud that seemed to hit the door.

She swung her legs over the edge of the bed and stood.

"Is everyone, okay?" she called.

"We okay!" a small voice chirped from the other side of the door.

She smiled. "You sure?"

"Yeah!" More giggles.

She crossed the floor and opened the door to see a small barefoot boy in firefighter pajamas and the puppy who looked like a miniature of Rocky sprawled on the floor.

"Why, hello," she said.

The boy and dog untangled themselves. Taffy licked her fingers. The small dog's tail wagged rapid-fire from one side to the other. Brody looked at Ophelia skeptically.

She crouched down until she was eye level with the toddler.

"You must be Brody," she said softly. "I'm your daddy's work friend. My name is Ophelia."

"O'Felly," Brody repeated, confidently. He frowned. "You not sleeping."

She assumed someone had told him that she was and so had instructed him to be quiet.

"No, I'm not sleeping now," she agreed. "But

I was sleeping before. So thank you for being so good and quiet."

"Yes!" He nodded as if agreeing with her assessment. A huge smile spread across the small boy's face.

Seemed she'd hit upon the right answer. "It's nice to meet you."

She stretched out her hand to shake his. He slapped it hard in an enthusiastic and cheerful high five, and then took off running back down the hall again with Taffy at his heels.

She stood up slowly and watched them scamper, feeling something warm and soft glow inside her chest. So, that was Brody. He was absolutely adorable. Just as the little boy reached the living room, turned around and was about to run back toward her, Kyle appeared from somewhere out of view, scooped Brody into his arms and lifted up him.

"I good!" Brody told him, loudly.

"You often are," Kyle said, with a chuckle.

Then he glanced from the squirming toddler in his arms, down the hall to where Ophelia still stood in the doorway.

"Good morning," he called. "How did you sleep?"

"A lot better than I was expecting." She ran her fingers through her long and tangled hair.

"I hope we didn't wake you," Kyle said.

"No, not at all," she said.

"I'm glad." He shifted Kyle around onto his hip. "I'm about to feed the kid and dogs, then make some scrambled eggs and toast for myself, if that's okay by you. I've already put the coffee on. It should be ready in a moment."

"Sounds wonderful," she said.

Brody wriggled in Kyle's grasp.

"Daddy! Down!" he ordered. Kyle broke her gaze and set Brody on the floor. "Want outside!"

"Later," he said. "You can play outside after breakfast and Daddy's video call."

She closed the door, leaned against it and pressed her hand to her chest. She could feel her heartbeat racing against her palm as if she'd just run a marathon. Whatever this was that she was feeling right now, she had to nip it in the bud and fast. It was one thing to fall into a strong man's supportive arms in a moment of crisis. It was another thing to let herself stay there—especially when the last thing he wanted was a relationship and the last thing she needed was to let herself be distracted from her work. The opportunity she'd been given through getting a funding grant for her PhD was a once-in-a-lifetime thing. She'd never have been able to afford it without help, and if she lost this grant she couldn't imagine ever landing another one.

She might not have wanted to be a bridesmaid but had even less desire to be seen as a damsel in distress who relied on someone like Kyle to save her and risked blowing her PhD grant and life goals over some foolish romantic attraction. She shuddered to think how Kyle—a man who'd told her repeatedly that he wasn't looking for a relationship—would react if he knew she had a bit of a crush on him. He'd be uncomfortable. Maybe even horrified. Especially if he thought she was at risk of putting her crush on him above her career and studies. Either way, it wouldn't exactly help her career if one of the top FBI agents in New Mexico decided he didn't want her working on his cases.

She could still hear Kyle's cheerful voice coming from the large living room and kitchen area as he called to the dogs that breakfast was ready, and the clatter of paws and dog tags as Rocky and Taffy ran to their bowls. Brody's voice babbled in a cheerful mixture of real words and nonsense.

Her phone was fully charged from having been plugged in the night before. She already had a message from her boss at the crime lab, telling her that he'd heard about the shooting at the ranch and not to worry about coming in for work if she needed to take the day off. Not that she was planning on taking him up on that. Then there was the fact that Jared and Gabrielle were still supposed to get married that night.

Lord, please help me just focus on the tasks at hand and get through them.

Framed pictures hung on the wall across from the bed of a happy couple on their wedding day, who she assumed were Brody's parents, both by themselves and with a beaming Kyle and Alice. Another showed Kevin and Kyle with their arms around each other as teenagers and still another showed Kyle's sister-in-law with baby Brody in her arms.

A sudden wash of pain swept over Ophelia's heart as she remembered the stories Kyle had told her the night before. Alice had been hurt by her husband. Kyle and Kevin had lost their father. Then Brody had lost his parents.

Lord, they've seen so much loss and yet they've never let their hearts grow angry and bitter. Bless them, dear God. Help me to be a blessing to them. Please help us all solve these terrible murders before somebody else gets hurts. Help me to honor You and do my utmost whatever this case throws at me next. And please, keep my heart and mind from all distractions.

Including a handsome face with dark and fathomless eyes.

It was almost fifteen minutes later when she'd finished getting changed into the slacks and top she kept in her gym bag, packed up her stuff and walked back out into the living room and kitchen area. Her lab didn't open until nine, and even then, she wasn't expected in. She placed a quick call to her boss, got his voice mail, and left a message saying there'd been a break-in at her house the night before and she didn't have access to her laptop but that all of her research was saved on a secure cloud server. She then called the electric company who said they'd have someone out right away to check on the power at her house, and her regular mechanic who said he'd get one of his guys to pop over and replace her tires. Both assured her she didn't have to be there and they'd take care of it. She felt relieved.

Then, finally she walked into the main room to find Kyle sitting at the head of the kitchen table facing the back deck, with his laptop open in front of him and Rocky sitting by his feet. To his left, Brody sat in his high chair pushing around serial squares and banana pieces on the tray, occasionally dropping one over the edge for roly-poly Taffy to scramble after. The chair to his right was empty but set with a beautiful yellow place mat, cutlery and a glass of orange juice.

He stood as she walked into the room. So did Rocky.

"There you are," Kyle said with a grin and for a long moment his eyes seemed to linger on her face. "There are eggs in the griddle and coffee in the pot. There's bread in the toaster, too, but I didn't pop it down so that it wouldn't be cold by the time you were ready for it." He ran both hands along the side of his jeans. "I'm sorry it's not much, but we weren't expecting company."

"Don't worry, it's absolutely wonderful," Ophelia said. "I can't remember the last time I had a home-cooked meal. Most nights I just put something from the grocery-store freezer section into the microwave. Then I fall asleep reading and end up grabbing a yogurt and cup of coffee on the way out the door."

Another reason why dating was out of the question. What man wanted to come over on a Friday night to pull back the plastic wrap on a frozen entrée?

"Well, I never mind cooking," Kyle said. "It's the one thing that relaxes me. Mom and I have worked out a pretty good pattern here of divvying up the chores inside the house. It's the yard work that gets to me, because Mom can't do it while watching Brody and by the time I get home it's dark."

"That's the one thing I am good at," Ophelia said. "Because I listen to research and audio books for my PhD for hours on the weekend while I weed and mow."

"Maybe we should start trading yard work for leftovers," Kyle said, with a chuckle. He ran his hand over the back of his neck. "Anyway, I set a place for you to come join us at the table when you're ready."

She walked into the kitchen area, poured herself a cup of coffee, added a dash of cream and inhaled the aroma deeply.

"I've already got through to the power company and my mechanic," she said. "They both assure me they'll be out soon."

"Good," Kyle said. "I was going to call them myself and then figured it was better I check with you first. My mom's running errands now.

Knowing her, she'll come back with enough food to feed an army."

Then he frowned slightly.

"Everything okay?" she asked.

"Yeah, I hope so," he said. "My mom's been going to the pharmacy a lot recently. Specifically, one on the other side of town. She assures me there's nothing to worry about and the pharmacist there is just really good at recommending vitamins and supplements for her joint stiffness, but I worry."

"I get that," Ophelia said. "Truth is, I'm really worried about my great-aunt Evelyn. Before everything kicked off yesterday with the murder of John Doe, I had the odd sense that something was wrong and she was worried. But she wouldn't talk about it."

She scooped some scrambled eggs onto a plate she found waiting for her on the counter, then popped a bite into her mouth. Sprinkled with some kind of spice and cheese, the eggs were delicious. She topped up her coffee and then carried her plate around to the empty place waiting for her at the table. She sat.

"Evelyn was a model when she was younger," she said, "and did a lot of regional pageants and briefly ran charm classes for young women. She really values putting on a good face and isn't the kind of person who complains or would open up about something that's bothering her. But if she did know something—anything at all—that she thought could be related to the murder in the barn, I know she wouldn't hesitate to tell the police." She sighed. "As you know, I called her last night before the intruder broke in. And I don't want to tell her about that, because she will be beside herself with worry. I don't want to upset her that badly. Or steal the thunder from Jared's wedding day, if he's still getting married today."

"I hope for their sake the death of John Doe had nothing to do with their wedding," he said. "Although sadly we can't rule that out. But I did have a quick chat with Patricia this morning and she told me everyone was fine overnight at the hotel and that she'd email me an update on their end of the case soon. I've got to jump in a video call meeting with my team in a few minutes. I've already briefed Chase quickly over the phone, so they should be up to speed more or less, on what happened that night. After we wrap up, we'll see about heading back to your house. I don't think you should go back there alone."

"Thank you." The desire to be independent and sort her own problems didn't change the fact that she also didn't want to just blindly walk into danger. Thankfully, Kyle didn't seem like the kind of guy who'd judge her over something like that.

The adults finished their breakfast, then Ophelia cleared the dishes while Kyle pulled Brody from his high chair, helped him wash his hands and then set him up with a box full of toys on the living room carpet.

"Want outside!" Brody said.

Ophelia glanced out the glass doors. The modest backyard was completely fenced in and included a sandbox, swing set and a myriad of toddler toys.

"I know, buddy," Kyle said. "But I just need to talk to work on my computer first. I'll take you outside when I'm done. But now I need you to be quiet." Kyle ran his finger across his lips in an invisible zipper. "Why don't you make Taffy an imaginary cake?"

Brody's lower lip stuck out, but he sat politely on the carpet and began pulling plastic pots and pans out of a bin. Taffy scampered over and flopped on the floor against him.

Kyle pulled the chair that Ophelia had been

sitting on next to his and started the call. "Sorry we're going to have to share the screen."

"No problem." She held up the coffeepot. "Do you want a refill?"

"Yes, please," he said. "Just black."

She carried the pot over, topped up his mug and then sat down beside him. They were sitting so close she could feel his knee brush against hers.

She watched as three video call boxes opened one by one on the screen.

A man she assumed was Chase Rawlston was first. The task force leader had a strong jaw, broad shoulders and a cheerful-looking golden retriever poking his head into the frame. Chase welcomed them to the call and introduced his dog as Dash, before instructing him to go lie down. Next came US Marshal Meadow Ames, an athletic woman with long brown hair and bright green eyes. Her beautiful tan vizsla, Grace, lay on a bed behind her. The final face to pop up was Isla. The technical analyst had one of the most beautiful smiles Ophelia had ever seen, despite the sadness that lurked in her dark-eyed gaze.

Lord, whatever the struggles are that Isla's going through, please be with her and help her.

"It's nice to meet you, Ophelia," Chase said. "Thank you for joining us. How are you feeling this morning? I was so sorry to hear about what happened last night."

"I'm good," Ophelia said. "Thankfully, Kyle and Rocky were there when I needed them."

"Chase briefed us on what happened," Meadow said. "The whole situation sounds genuinely terrifying. And I'm really glad you're okay and I'm impressed at how you handled the whole thing."

"And I'm impressed by the fact that he said you bit the guy!" Isla said. "It's just too bad you didn't get any DNA or we could've tested it."

She laughed. Ophelia did, too. She could see why Kyle liked his team.

"Ophelia was brilliant," Kyle said and she felt her cheeks glow under his praise. "I've also been working closely with Detective Patricia Gonzales of the Santa Fe PD and she'll be emailing me any moment with an update on what they've found from their end."

"I'm going to be sending Meadow and her partner, Grace, out your way as well when we wrap up the call," Chase said. "It's clear that whoever you're after won't hesitate to strike where you live, and, Kyle, I think it's important that Alice and Brody have some protection."

Ophelia watched as Kyle swallowed hard.

"Thank you," he said.

"I think we need to discuss moving your mom and Brody into a safe house," Meadow said. "But we can talk about that when I get there."

Kyle glanced to where Brody and the puppy now sat playing happily on the carpet, and she could almost see him weighing being away from the little boy against the desire not to put him in danger. "Okay."

"Do you have any new evidence for us in terms of identifying who this John Doe was?" Chase asked. "Or linking it to the Rocky Mountain Killer?"

"Not yet," Ophelia said. "The lab was already closed for the day when the scene was processed, and I'm afraid we don't have a night crew. But they open at nine, and will be working on it this morning."

"I'm looking forward to finding out John Doe's identity," Kyle said, "and if he has any connection to the Young Rancher's Club."

"We all re," Chase said. "His photo didn't match anything in our system or anyone we know who was related to Elk Valley."

"The bride from the wedding, Gabrielle, also

had a stalker who we only know as Bobby," Ophelia said. "It's possible that either he's John Doe, or that he's our shooter."

"Well, hopefully, a DNA match will tell us who this guy is," Chase said. "Isla, if you could coordinate with Ophelia directly on any evidence as it comes in that would be great."

"Absolutely," Isla said. "I'm especially interested in that cuff link and also seeing if the bullets found at this crime scene were all fired from the same 9mm gun as the other six murders. It'll give me a break from trying to track down rhinestone dog collars."

Ophelia remembered what Kyle had told her the night before about how the serial killer had kidnapped Cowgirl, a compassion therapy labradoodle that belonged to the task force. Then recently the killer had sent Chase a picture of Cowgirl from a burner phone that showed the dog wearing a pink collar that read Killer.

"Any success on that?" Kyle asked.

"Not yet," Isla said. "It's a popular collar, sold in at least fifty shops across the Rocky Mountain region."

"I did get another taunting text about Cowgirl from the RMK," Chase said, grimly, "telling me he thinks the dog could be pregnant."

"Whoa." Kyle sucked in a breath and Ophelia's heart ached. The pain in his face was echoed in those of his team. She knew how much Kyle loved Rocky. She couldn't imagine how the unit felt in losing one of their K-9 dogs, only to have her kidnapped and now potentially be pregnant.

Kyle's phone pinged and Ophelia watched as he reached for it.

"I've got an update from Patricia," he said, his eyes scanning the screen. "The white van was stolen from a Santa Fe laundry delivery service yesterday and found on the outskirts of town in the early hours of the morning. Apparently, he torched it before abandoning it."

"To destroy evidence," Ophelia and Isla said in unison. Then they both laughed.

"Nobody's found the silver car the killer used to drive away from the murder scene," Kyle went on. "But judging by the state the van was found in, they're guessing that wherever it is, he trashed it, too. Also, according to Patricia, a gas station attendant recognized our John Doe, and while the guy didn't get a license plate, he did say that John Doe was driving a silver car that matches the description of the one our masked man drove off in. Police are guessing John Doe parked his car out of sight and walked the rest of the way to Cherish Ranch, and then the killer stole his car for an easy getaway. Apparently our victim had stopped at the gas station to ask for directions to Cherish Ranch—specifically the barn. The gas station attendant said he had plans to meet someone special there."

"So he was lured to his death," Chase said. "Just like the RMK's other victims. The question is, was John Doe killed by the RMK? Or are we dealing with a copycat?"

Chapter Six

"Let's hash this out," Chase said, "go over the evidence and see where we end up. Kyle, you argue for this being the RMK and I'll present the evidence against."

"Well, the victim is a young man," Kyle said, "who was shot once in the chest at close range, after being lured to a barn, in Rocky Mountain country. That all lines up."

"But we have no known link to the Young Rancher's Club or Elk Valley," Chase countered. "Also, he doesn't match the age profile of the other victims. The first three victims were in their late teens and early twenties. The other three were killed ten years later, but would've been the same age as the first three at the time of the first three murders. John Doe would've been nine or ten at that time. Way too young to be a member of YRC or friends with any of the members."

"Also, I'm guessing the other murders happened at isolated locations," Ophelia said, "not one in the middle of a wedding weekend."

"Hey, whose side are you on?" Kyle joked. "But you're right, this took place at a very public wedding event. There must be dozens, if not hundreds, of other barns in the area the RMK could've chosen."

"Which might be an escalation," Meadow said, "or a coincidence."

"Or it means it's not linked at all," Chase said.

"Outside now!" Brody called. The little boy climbed to his feet and toddled toward the door.

"I'm happy to take him outside," Ophelia told Kyle, "if that's okay with you." She had a feeling that her part of the call was wrapping up anyway, and it would also give Kyle the freedom to talk more freely if he wanted to discuss any of the more gruesome details of the crime without risking Brody's little ears overhearing anything.

Kyle searched her face. "You sure?"

"Absolutely," she said. "Would it be okay with you if I checked my phone and made a couple of quick calls while I'm out?"

"Yeah," he said. "The backyard is completely

fenced in and I can also keep an eye on him through the window. I just don't want him out there alone. Thanks."

She said a quick goodbye to the team, telling Meadow that she'd see her in person soon and Isla that she'd see her online. Then she thanked them all again, went to put her shoes on and headed to where Brody now stood looking out the back door.

"You outside?" Brody asked, hopefully.

"Yes," she said. "Let's go outside while your daddy finishes his call. Can you show me your backyard?"

"Yes!" His little hand reached up, grabbed her fingers and squeezed them. Something fluttered in her chest.

She opened the door. Brody dropped her hand and ran out into the yard at full speed with Taffy at his heels. Boy and dog tumbled into the grass together. She glanced back at Kyle. Something unspoken moved through his gaze.

"All good, Kyle?" she asked.

"Yeah." His Adam's apple bobbed. "See you in a bit."

She closed the sliding door and turned back to the yard, where Brody and Taffy were now playing tug-of-war with a soft plastic disk. Then she sat down on a bench and checked her messages. Her boss had texted to thank her for the call and to say that he'd have a backup laptop available at her workstation when she got in.

That made two things she could thank God for.

But worryingly, she'd missed three calls from Evelyn.

Fear rattled her heart. Quickly, she dialed her back. Her great-aunt answered on the fourth ring. "Aunt Evelyn! Hi! Is everything all right! Is everyone okay?"

"Of course, dear," Evelyn said. "Don't be all dramatic. I just wanted to let you know to be at the hotel at four thirty for hair and makeup. The photographer's booked for six."

"Right, for the wedding." Her mind flashed to where she'd left the bridesmaid's dress crumpled in her clothes hamper. Between John Doe's blood and the smoke from the fire, she couldn't imagine how bad it must look, and smell. "That's still happening today?"

"Please don't start on with me about that," Evelyn said. "We have enough chaos going on over here with Jared and Gabrielle trying to find an alternative spot at the ranch to hold their wedding reception tonight, and her parents' flight being delayed again. Poor Gabrielle has been in floods of tears all morning. She and Jared are on their way to Cherish Ranch right now to see what can be salvaged of their original plans. I know the bride and groom aren't traditionally supposed to see each other before the wedding, but Jared didn't want Gabrielle having to deal with everything on her own. My Jared is a very good boy—"

Ophelia bit her lip and stopped from pointing out he was thirty-one, the same as she was.

"And he's been really good to Gabrielle," her great-aunt went on. "You know I'm pretty choosy about who I think is good enough for you two. But she's perfect. Beautiful, wealthy, well connected. I couldn't have found a better match for him myself. But Jared is so frustrated with the ranch for trying to cancel or scale back the wedding. The police won't let them use the barn and the ranch is suggesting a quiet ceremony at the outdoor, cliffside chapel, with a downsized reception. But Gabrielle and Jared have already paid for the dinner and still want the day to feel special. Really, all he and Gabrielle want to do is put the whole unfortunate situation behind them."

Ophelia felt her fingers clench. Didn't Jared realize how self-centered he was being?

"It's not like they had a kitchen flood or something," Ophelia said. "It was a murder, Auntie. A man was shot yesterday."

And the killer was still on the loose.

"I know what happened and how terrible it was," Evelyn chided. "But this is your cousin's special day, it's his decision and we need to focus on being happy for him and Gabrielle. I'm sure Gabrielle and Jared would appreciate if you dropped by the ranch to help them, before you came to the hotel. Also, she said to remind you to check out the social media page they made about the wedding. They'll be posting all their updates there."

Ophelia had vaguely known there was one, but hadn't even looked at it yet.

"Whee!" Brody shouted cheerfully as he dashed across the yard, holding the plastic disk out in front of him like a steering wheel. "I go! Fast!"

Taffy barked cheerfully, chasing after Brody, and pretended to nip at his heels.

"What's that?" Evelyn said. "Where are you?"

"That's Brody," Ophelia said. "He's the son of my agent friend Kyle West, who questioned everyone yesterday. There was a trespasser at my house last night, but he ran off and I'm fine," she added quickly as she heard Evelyn gasp. "You don't need to worry. But Kyle and his mother said I could stay with them."

"And you're dating the handsome policeman from my phone app?"

Well, she didn't have to sound so shocked.

"We're friends," Ophelia said. "And he's an FBI agent. As I told you, I knew him from work."

"Well, you tell your friend Kyle that he's very welcome to come to the wedding as your date," Evelyn said. "I'll fire off a quick message to Jared and Gabrielle letting them know."

"You really don't need to do that..."

"Pfft, Gabrielle was already worried you didn't have a plus-one and I'm sure she'll be happy to know you that you're bringing your gentleman friend."

Gentleman friend.

She glanced over her shoulder to where Kyle sat at the table talking to his team on video chat. His dark eyes flickered to her face and then looked back down at the screen.

Well, Kyle was definitely a gentleman in all the best meanings of the word.

And yes, she would feel really blessed to have him as a friend.

"I'm sure everyone would be happy to see him," Evelyn added.

Ophelia wasn't as sure about that as her aunt was, especially if anyone there had something to hide. But she also knew that Kyle might appreciate the opportunity to attend the wedding, talk to people and see if he could discover anything new about the case.

She ended the call with her aunt, telling her that she loved her and reminding her to stay safe. Then she prayed.

Lord, this wedding is the last thing on my mind right now. I'm frustrated by the fact that part of me suspects that my cousin is a self-centered man who doesn't even realize how hard it would be for ranch staff to work today or that some guests might not want to go back on that property after what happened. People need time to heal. Please, help me let go of my judgment and anger. Help me be there for my family and do my job.

After all, she loved her cousin, and if she missed his wedding she'd regret it for the rest of her life.

"Look!" Brody ran toward her and held

out his hand. She looked into his grubby little hands. It was a rock. "See!"

"Oh, nice!" His enthusiasm and joy tugged at her heartstrings.

"Yes!" Brody turned and ran to the sandbox, where he started noisily pushing the rock around with a plastic truck.

Ophelia opened the wedding's page on the social media site. She'd avoided it for months, but it probably was good she'd checked it before the wedding. The top post was a new picture of Gabrielle and Jared holding hands, along with an emotional message about how deeply they loved each other, how sad they were for the tragedy that happened and how determined they were not to let it get in the way of starting their life together.

A flashing blue circle at the bottom of the screen told Ophelia that someone had tried to send her a message via the social media site, which was odd, as everyone she knew who'd be at the wedding had her cell phone number.

She clicked on the message. Text on the screen told her that she'd received a video message from Chloe Madison.

Gabrielle's roommate? The bridesmaid who hadn't shown up, whom Ophelia had been asked to replace? The time stamp showed the message had been sent at two thirty in the afternoon, yesterday. Hours before Gabrielle had asked Ophelia to be in the wedding party. She clicked on the message. Up came the face of a young woman, who looked to be in her early twenties, with long red hair and a gold, heart-shaped locket around her neck.

"Hi." Chloe's face filled the screen. She had the look of someone who was upset but trying very hard to be calm in order to be taken seriously. "We've never met. But I know you're Jared's cousin and I'm Gabrielle's roommate. Umm. We need to talk before the wedding. It's really important. I'm coming to Santa Fe early and maybe we can meet up. Message me here and don't tell anybody I contacted you. But I think something bad is going to go down with Gabrielle's ex-boyfriend Bobby."

After the team call officially ended, Chase and Meadow logged off, and Kyle stayed on for a few moments to talk to Isla. He'd felt a special kind of compassion for Isla, ever since discovering the single technical analyst had given up on love and decided to adopt, knowing that she'd chosen the same challenging and rewarding path that he was on. They'd bonded over his journey of becoming a sudden parent to Brody, and Kyle had thanked God when Isla was certified as a foster mother and had received her first photos of a newborn baby girl named Charisse.

But then, Isla's dreams had been dashed when the private Christian Foster-Adoption Agency had denied her application after someone had called anonymously and reported her as unfit. The injustice of the accusation and the fact that it could be made about someone as wonderful as Isla still burned in the back of Kyle's throat.

"A few weeks ago," Kyle said, "I asked you to make a list of anyone you could think of who might have ever felt slighted by you and decided to sabotage your attempt to become a mother." He'd asked her while they'd both been investigating with the task force in Sagebrush, Idaho, and staying at Deputy Selena Smith's place. Isla had left Wyoming for a few days to help the task force but also to get some R and R after her application had been denied. "Have you given any more thought to that?"

"Yes." Isla frowned. "But it's a pretty short list and nothing has really clicked yet. There are three different men who I dated briefly but decided not to see again. None of those relationships raised any red flags, but some people are able to hide their true nature. Also, I had a falling-out with a cousin last Thanksgiving, over her plan to bring her boyfriend to family dinner. He was a petty criminal and I thought she was in denial over just how scummy this guy was. They're still dating. He's in jail now, so he's not the one who placed the call. I don't want to think that my cousin could've done that to me." Isla's shoulders rose and fell. "But I'll go see if I can visit her and talk to her. I'll look into those three former dates, too."

Kyle told her that he'd pray for her and to contact him at any time if there was anything he could do to help. As Kyle ended the call, he sat for a long moment, and looked out the back window, to where Ophelia was crouched down beside Brody in the sandbox, playing trucks with him, much to the toddler's delight. It seemed Ophelia and Brody were deep in conversation. He couldn't hear what they were saying, but whatever it was had Ophelia tossing her head back in fits of laughter while Brody giggled. Something warmed in his chest, as if the simple interaction had lit the tiny pilot light of a fire that had gone out long ago. If it had ever burned at all.

How ironic that his mom had resorted to creating an online dating profile for him to try to find him a wife, when this incredibly beautiful and kindhearted woman had been under his nose all along, working alongside him, excelling at a job that meant everything to people like him and helping him do the work that mattered most.

Only, she wasn't exactly applying for the job of wife to an FBI agent, K-9 task force member and mother to his toddler.

Nor was he ever going to ask her to.

Lord, I keep telling You that I'm not looking to start a romance with anyone. And I'm really not. I don't have the time to give a woman the attention and care she deserves from a man courting her. I feel like I'm barely giving Brody the attention he deserves, and the last thing I want to do is bring uncertainty, conflict or tension into Brody's life. Please help clear my heart and my mind from whatever nonsense that's clouding it now, so I can focus on solving this case, before anybody else gets hurt.

He stood up and walked over to the sliding glass door that led to the outside. Rocky rose from his usual post on the floor by his feet and followed. But as he reached the door, Ophelia looked up, as if sensing his gaze. Their eyes met across his son's head, through the yard and the glass of the sliding back door, and for a long moment neither of them looked away.

The door opened and closed behind him. He turned to see Alice walking in.

"Hey, Mom." He smiled. "Ophelia's outside with Brody. I'll introduce you in a moment."

"Sounds wonderful." Alice smiled back and set a bright green bag down on the counter.

"You've been to the pharmacy again," he said, frowning. "Is everything okay, Mom? That's the second trip to the pharmacy this week."

"I'm fine," Alice said. There was a smile on her face, but he noticed his mother wasn't meeting his eye. "I just picked up some sunscreen."

"Are you sure?" he said. "You set up a dating profile for me without telling me."

"I'm really sorry for that," she said. "I wasn't thinking. Please forgive me."

"Of course, Mom."

"Gramma!" Brody yipped, suddenly spotting her. He leaped to his feet and charged toward the door. Ophelia stood slowly and ran her hands down her pants. Sand and grass streaked her previously pristine clothes, but she didn't seem to mind. Kyle slid the door open and stepped back as Brody raced through, past him and into his grandmother's arms, as Alice crouched down and reached for him.

"Hey, Bo!" Alice scooped him into his arms. "Were you having fun in the sandbox?"

"Yes! Snack?" he asked, hopefully.

"You need to wash your hands first," Alice told her grandson as he pressed his hands against her cheeks leaving sand in their wake. She shifted Brody onto her hip, wiped her cheeks and then walked Brody over to the kitchen sink.

Rocky slipped out the door past Kyle, brushing against Kyle's legs in hello as he passed. Rocky and Taffy ran toward each other in a flurry of wagging tails and playful growls as they launched themselves into a pretend fight.

Ophelia dodged her way around the obstacle course of darting hounds and made her way to the door, which Kyle was still holding open for her. She slid in past him and their arms bumped. "Judging by all the comings and goings through that door, if you don't close it soon you'll be stuck holding it open all day."

"Yeah." He chuckled. "It feels like some days all I do is open and close the door so that two dogs and a kid can run in and out."

But he had to admit that although life had

thrown him a pretty big curve ball, he really did enjoy sharing it with Rocky, Taffy and Brody.

"I saw you on the phone," Kyle said, keeping his voice low enough that Alice and Brody wouldn't catch it as they noisily washed their hands. "Is everything okay?"

"I don't know," she said. Her smile faded. "No specific emergencies and everyone seems to be safe. Jared and Gabrielle are at the ranch now trying to make new arrangements for their wedding and you've been invited to come now, as my plus-one. But I got a really worrying video message from Chloe, the missing bridesmaid, wanting to talk to me about Bobby. She seemed a bit scattered and I messaged her back, but she didn't reply."

"Got it," he said. "I'll just say a quick hi to Mom and then we'll head out in a second."

"I should really get changed first," she said. "Thankfully your mom laid out some clothes for me to borrow."

He turned to where Alice was standing at the kitchen sink with Brody, helping him wash his hands under the running water.

"Mom, this is Ophelia Clarke," he said. "Ophelia, this is my incredible mother, Alice West."

"It's so nice to meet you properly." Ophelia

walked toward her. "I can't thank you enough for your help and for your hospitality last night. I don't know where I'd be if you hadn't answered that video call."

"Don't mention it," Alice said. "I'm just thankful for those moments when the Lord puts the right person in our life at the right time."

Kyle and his mom had never really talked about that turbulent time she'd gone through leaving her chaotic husband, taking her two young sons with her. It wasn't something she liked talking about. And most of the time he was just amazed that she still held out hope in the power of love. But she had told him that it had taken a lot of help and support, from friends, strangers at charities and the police. He knew that she was endlessly thankful to everyone who'd been there for her.

Both she and Kevin had found a way to make peace with their past. But still, when he looked at the precious child in Alice's arms, he couldn't imagine himself ever risking bringing a new prospective mother into Brody's life. What if Kyle failed to make the relationship work? And Brody ended up getting hurt by the fallout?

"Just promise me when the moment comes

you'll pay the kindness forward to somebody else who needs it," Alice added.

"I will," Ophelia said.

Alice turned off the water, set Brody down on the floor and grabbed a hand towel. Brody scampered away before his grandmother could try to dry his hands. She laughed, wiped her own hands across the towel and then reached for Ophelia.

The two woman clasped hands in greeting.

"It's just so nice to finally meet you," Alice said, as the two women pulled away again. "Kyle has been talking about you for months. It's been CSI Clarke this and CSI Clarke that. I lost count of the number of times my son told me that he was thankful to get to a crime scene and know that you were part of the team processing it, because he knew nothing would be missed."

"Really?" Ophelia asked. Her eyes widened and she turned to Kyle. He felt heat rise to the back of his neck.

"Professionally," Kyle said. "About your work, I had no idea who you were as a person." Or that she was beautiful, sweet and kind, with a smile that made his heart flutter. She'd been nothing to him but a figure in scrubs and a name on an evidence bag. "I just told her how much I appreciated your work as a CSI. Which, as you know, I do."

Her lips parted and then closed again. But not like she was embarrassed, more like she was too pleased by the compliment to figure out that to say.

"Speaking of which, Ophelia and I need to get to work," Kyle added. He kept his voice light, knowing Brody was still in earshot. "My colleague Meadow Ames and her K-9, Grace, are on their way here to provide us some additional backup, specifically to make sure you and Brody are safe. They might stay here with us or take you, Brody and Taffy on a fun overnight vacation with them to a safe house."

Alice nodded and it was clear in her eyes that she took his meaning.

"Well, I'll make up a bed in the study for now if Meadow does stay," she said, "and start packing a bag if we do decide to take a trip."

He slipped one arm around her slender shoulders in a hug. "Thanks, Mom."

"Just give me a second," Ophelia said. "I've got to go wash this sand off me."

She slipped down the hall back into the master bedroom, and returned a few moments later in clean tan slacks, a tank top and a loose-fitting, short-sleeved, button-up white shirt that was tied at the waist.

Hang on, that was *his* shirt.

"Everything okay?" she asked, self-consciously. She slung her bag over one shoulder. "You're staring like I've got mud on my face."

"No," he said. "You look fine. That's just my dress shirt you're wearing."

"Oh." Her cheeks went pink. "I'm so sorry, I just found it in the room with the other clothes and assumed it was something Alice found. I can go find something else to wear if you want."

"No, it's okay. It actually looks really good on you."

Better than he liked to admit.

A few minutes later, Ophelia, Kyle and Rocky were climbing back in his SUV, ready to head to Ophelia's house.

"So, let's see that video message from Chloe," he said. She handed him the phone and he watched the video twice. When he was done, he whistled and leaned back against the seat. "So the bridesmaid who canceled on the bride at the last minute tried to message you yesterday about Bobby, the man Jared said was stalking Gabrielle?"

"Looks like it," Ophelia said.

Rocky woofed from the back seat, reminding him that they were just sitting in the vehicle and not going anywhere. Kyle started the engine. They pulled out of the driveway and started toward her home. "I'd honestly forgotten about Chloe. Gabrielle told me she was there the night she met Jared and that she knew Bobby was hassling her. But the fact that she didn't show up, because of some argument with Gabrielle, didn't seem suspicious to me and I didn't think it was a thread I needed to pull on."

"I honestly just assumed she'd had some spat with Gabrielle," Ophelia said. "I didn't imagine it had anything to do with Bobby."

This whole case was getting so wide and unwieldy, and he couldn't figure out what was actually connected to the death of John Doe and/or the RMK, and what wasn't. He'd started with one murdered body and since then questions had just continued to mount with no answers.

Who was John Doe and who'd killed him? The task force knew that the Rocky Mountain Killer was targeting men who'd been part of a nasty prank at a Young Rancher's Club dance ten years ago. But was John Doe connected to the YRC? Who was the masked man? Why did he shoot into the barn? Why did he break into Ophelia's home? How did Gabrielle's roommate Chloe and apparent stalker Bobby fit into all this?

He prayed to God for wisdom and thanked God for the incredible CSI sitting beside him.

"And everything was okay with your great-aunt?" he asked.

Ophelia groaned.

"I think something's bothering her," she said. "But when I tried to talk to her she just reminded me that it was important to be there for Jared on his big day. I don't know how I'm going to tell her I'm probably not going to be able to wear that purple dress."

"Did you tell her about the intruder?" Kyle asked. He turned onto her street.

"Yes, but I played it down," Ophelia said. "I never want to disappoint her. She was so good to me growing up, despite our differences. And like I told you, she asked me to invite you to the wedding tonight, as my date." She hesitated over the last word. "Look, to be incredibly honest, I told her we were just friends, but she jumped to the conclusion that either we were a romantic couple or she could somehow shoehorn us into being one by sheer will. It's like the only thing she thinks matters in my life is whether or not I've got a wedding date."

Which could be actually helpful, Kyle thought, if it allowed him to move freely through the wedding guests, gathering data while also essentially being undercover.

Her house came into view and Kyle silently thanked God to see the front light was shining. Both of her flat tires had been fixed, too. He pulled to a stop a few feet from the house and heard Ophelia shudder a breath. Instinctively, he reached for her hand and enveloped it in his.

"I'm fine," she said, like she was trying to reassure herself. "I was just suddenly hit by a visceral memory of what happened here last night."

"Hey." Kyle squeezed her hand and she squeezed it back. "You're strong and you're going to get through this. But it's also okay to feel fear, anger or whatever else is washing over you right now. Trust me, I've felt every bad feeling in the book and it didn't make me any less of an FBI agent. Sometimes life's just lousy."

"Thank you," she whispered.

She leaned against his shoulder. He pulled his hand from hers and wrapped one arm around her, pulling her close into his side.

Suddenly, Rocky let out a sharp and urgent bark from the back seat. Kyle and Ophelia jumped apart. Kyle turned back. His partner was sitting up alert. The hackles rose at the back of Rocky's neck.

"Everything okay?" Ophelia asked.

"No," Kyle said. Chills ran down his spine. "I think he detects something."

Kyle cut the engine, they got out and then he opened the door for Rocky. The dog leaped out. Rocky sniffed the air toward the house. His growling grew louder.

"What does this mean?" Ophelia asked.

"Nothing good," Kyle said. His dog was only trained to detect one thing—death. Yet, in all the confusion and urgency of everything that had happened the night before, Kyle had dismissed how much Rocky had been barking and snarling, and how determined his partner had been to let Kyle know that something was wrong.

"Does he detect something in my house?" Ophelia asked.

"I think so," Kyle said. "Stay behind me, okay?" Then without waiting for Ophelia to answer, he looked down at his partner. "Show me."

The dog woofed and ran toward Ophelia's

house, while Kyle and Ophelia ran after him. Rocky reached the front door, paused and looked back, waiting for his partner to catch up. Together they stepped into the house.

"Kyle West, FBI!" he called. "If there's anyone in here, identify yourself now."

No answer.

Okay, time to see what his partner was trying to tell him.

"Go on," Kyle told him.

Immediately, Rocky dashed across the living room, to where the basement door stood ajar. He nudged it open with his nose and ran down the stairs.

"Stay at the top of the stairs," Kyle told Ophelia. "I'm going down."

She nodded. Her eyes closed and her mouth moved, in what he somehow knew was silent prayer.

He switched on the light, pulled his weapon and started down the stairs. Rocky's growls grew until the whole house seemed to reverberate with the sound.

The basement was small and unfinished. With a plain concrete floor and sheets of plastic covering the pink insulation walls.

Rocky whimpered and pawed a spot on the

far side of the wall. Kyle ran his hand over the dog's head.

"Good dog," he said softly. He ran his hand down the dog's side.

Kyle peeled the insulation back. A moment later he saw what the masked man had tried to stash behind it. It was a large, purple suitcase. He unzipped it and the smell of death filled his lungs.

The victim was female, with long red hair and her body curled peacefully into a ball, almost as if she'd fallen asleep, except for the single gunshot to the chest. The remnants of a broken golden locket hung around her neck, as if her killer had snapped the front half of it off.

His heart lurched as he silently prayed for justice.

"It's Chloe, isn't it?" Ophelia's voice came from behind him. Kyle turned and saw her standing in the basement, and while sorrow filled Ophelia's gaze, a fierce determination burned there, too. "She's the one who tried to warn me."

Chapter Seven

Law enforcement arrived mercifully quickly. Ophelia stood on her own lawn and watched as her home was declared a crime scene.

Detective Patricia Gonzales, one of the most senior investigators within the Santa Fe PD, oversaw the scene personally. She was an excellent officer, strong and reassuring, and someone who Ophelia had always felt proud working with. Patricia calmly reassured Ophelia that the Santa Fe PD would do everything in their power to make sure those behind the murder would be brought to justice. Ophelia felt her jaw clench so tightly it ached and watched as law enforcement and paramedics went in and out of her house. Despite the warm June air, her arms felt so cold they were almost numb. She wrapped them around herself like a shield and tried to pray but didn't even know how to put words to what she was feeling.

She heard the jingle of dog tags and looked up to see Kyle and Rocky coming toward her.

"You okay?" Kyle asked. "I know it can't be easy to see something like that."

His hand reached out and touched the small of her back. It was warm, strong and comforting, and part of her wanted very much to just relax into his touch. But instead she pulled away, feeling the need to stand on her own.

"I'm used to seeing dead bodies and crime scenes," she said. "I'm a professional. This is what I do. What I'm not used to is standing outside a crime scene feeling absolutely powerless, because, for reasons I have absolutely no control over, the crime scene is my house and the crime somehow has something to do with me."

Rocky butted his head up against her leg, as if to reassure her. She ran her hand over his silky ears and the K-9 licked her fingers.

"I'm sorry," she went on. "I don't how to explain it. I just feel so frustrated I can't tell if I want to shout or cry."

"I felt something like that when my brother and sister-in-law died," Kyle said, "and when I got the news my father had passed away. I wanted to be in the thick of it, doing something, even if there was nothing I could do."

He closed his eyes for a moment, and she suspected he was praying. Then he opened his eyes again and looked around. She followed his gaze. A news van was pulling up the street.

"Patricia!" Kyle called as he jogged over to the detective. Rocky and Ophelia followed. "How long can you keep the victim's name out of the press?"

"We don't have a firm identification yet," Patricia said, "but a wallet and phone were found on the body, so we're pretty certain this is Chloe Madison. But I need to contact the family before news gets out, so they don't find out online before they hear it from us."

"Can you give us an hour?" Kyle asked.

"I'll do my best," the detective said. "And just to clarify, neither of you are authorized to tell anyone that we believe Chloe is deceased or even mention that we found a body until we've notified her family. After that, I need you to limit the details to what's officially reported to the press, so that we limit false tips in the investigation. We really take doing things the right way and notifying next of kin seriously."

"Sounds good." Kyle turned to Ophelia and gestured to his vehicle. She nodded. He signaled Rocky to his side and the three of them started toward it. She didn't know what Kyle's plan was, but she trusted him and it wasn't like standing there watching law enforcement go in and out of her house was going to accomplish anything.

"What are you thinking?" Ophelia asked.

"That we have a very small window of time before everyone in the wedding party finds out Chloe was murdered," he said. His pace quickened. "And in my experience, as an investigator, a lot of people change their tune about a person once they discover they're gone."

"Because they don't want to speak ill of the dead," Ophelia said. "Or they don't want to look like a suspect."

"Exactly," Kyle said. "I want to go try interviewing your cousin and his fiancée again and see if we can get to the bottom of what was really going on with Chloe and Gabrielle's stalker, Bobby. My fear is that they're still going to refuse to talk to police and give us a straight answer."

"Yeah, I agree with you on that," Ophelia said. Rightly or wrongly, Jared wanted to protect his soon-to-be bride, and Gabrielle didn't trust the police. Ophelia worried both of them were too focused on the wrong priorities. Besides, Patricia had specifically told them they didn't have authorization to tell them anything about Chloe until a final determination was made and next of kin was notified. "I do think that once they know Chloe's dead, they're not going to give you a straight answer." When they reached his SUV, he opened the passenger door for her and she got inside. Rocky leaped in the back. "So, what's the plan?"

"You said Gabrielle and Jared are at the ranch trying to sort their wedding plans," he said. "I suggest we swing by and see if we can get them to talk to us." He swallowed hard. "They think I'm your wedding date, right?"

"Evelyn said she was going to tell them that," Ophelia confirmed.

"Well, if you're okay with letting them think we're there as a bridesmaid and her date, instead of investigators, I think that would be helpful." He glanced at her sideways. "If that's okay with you. I don't want to ask you to do anything you're not comfortable with."

"It's cool," Ophelia said. After all, it was not like she was going to be able to stop her family from jumping to conclusions anyway. Kyle could've shown up wearing a flashing neon sign proclaiming he and Ophelia were only friends, and they'd still insist on matchmaking them. "Let's go talk to them and see what they say."

At the end of the day, all she was doing was gathering evidence with an open mind, which was what she'd promised to do. If Jared was innocent of all this, as she was certain he was, she had every confidence Kyle would uncover that.

A few minutes later the beautiful adobe buildings of Santa Fe were in the rearview mirror, as they drove up the winding mountain roads back to Cherish Ranch. Kyle had slid on a pair of mirrored sunglasses to protect against the New Mexico sun as it rose higher in the sky and she could see the beautiful orange rock of the Sangre de Cristo Mountains reflected in their gaze. He rolled the windows down and let the warm and sweet June air move through the truck. She glanced in the side mirror and watched as Rocky stuck his head out the window. The K-9's long, silky ears flapped in the wind. Ophelia leaned back against the seat and prayed, feeling that same unusual peace that had filled her heart back in Kyle's home move through her again.

How could such incredible peace, faith and even joy coexist in a place of pain, worry and fear?

"Do you know what Evelyn told Jared and

Gabrielle about us?" Kyle asked. The truck slowed as he neared the ranch. "Obviously, they all know I'm an FBI agent and you're a CSI, but I mean our relationship beyond that."

"You mean about being my wedding date?" Ophelia said. "I'm not sure exactly. But my great-aunt referred to you as my 'gentleman friend.'"

Kyle snorted, then wiped his eyes. "I've never even heard that expression before!"

"I'm glad one of us finds it funny," she said. "But then I'd hate being reduced to being seen as someone's date, and not a person in my own right. I work with an amazing group of people. But I can't tell you how many times I walked into a lab or crime scene during my training and some stranger assumed I wasn't a real tech and just somebody's girlfriend."

"True," Kyle said. Not that everyone wouldn't know he was law enforcement. "This is a first for me. I've never been anyone's wedding date. But I'll take whatever advantage I can get to solve these crimes."

The signs for Cherish Ranch and the petting zoo loomed ahead. He turned toward the ranch.

"Don't get me wrong," Ophelia said. "I know my family loves me. I just wish the things they liked about me were the same things that I like about me."

"I get that," Kyle said. "You know I told you that my brother was my hero? I also wish he'd understood how hard it was for me sometimes to live in his shadow. He used to tease me, a lot. Especially when he got better grades than me. We were both on the football team and he used to call me 'butterfingers' every time I dropped a pass. When I was a senior, Caitlyn asked me to be her lab partner, and I quickly found out the real reason was just because she had a crush on my brother and wanted me to introduce them. They told their story at the wedding and people laughed, in a good-natured way. But it still kind of stung. He never knew how to tell me he loved me without razzing me. Maybe that was a holdover from how our dad impacted me, but he's tease me and make these jokes at my expense that weren't really funny. It wasn't until I read what they'd written about me in their will, and the fact that they wanted me to adopt Brody, that I had any idea of the good things they thought about me."

He pulled into the parking lot and stopped.

"Again," he said, "our dad was a really nasty

jerk and we both dealt with it in our own very different ways."

"Families can be complicated," Ophelia said.

He sighed. "Yeah."

They got out of his vehicle and started toward the main building. Any worries she had that it might take a moment to locate Gabrielle and Jared vanished as they started up the steps and heard a babble of voices rising from the courtyard. Kyle clipped Rocky's leash on, and the three of them followed the sound.

They found Gabrielle and two members of the wedding party, whom she vaguely recognized as Nolan and Lexi, standing in the courtyard, discussing the logistics of tables and food stations with two harried looking staff, while a middle-aged photographer set up a station for photographs.

"Ophelia! Kyle!" Gabrielle called. "I'm glad you made it!" Gabrielle smiled widely and ran across the courtyard toward them. She threw her arms around Ophelia and hugged her tightly, then quickly hugged Kyle as well. "I am so happy to see a friendly face. I'm sure Jared will be thrilled to see you, too. He's just in the office trying to talk some sense into the manager. A bunch of the wedding guests have canceled and the ranch won't let us use the barn because they say it's still an active crime scene, which I'm sure it's not, is it?"

"Well, you'd have to talk to the Santa Fe PD about that," Kyle said.

"But you can ask them about that, right?" Gabrielle asked. "Or at least get the police to tell people there's no reason to think that murder had anything to do with my wedding?"

"I'd be happy to personally talk to anybody who had concerns," Kyle said. He pushed his sunglasses up onto the top of his head, and Ophelia noticed he manage to sound reassuring while completely sidestepping what she was asking. "If any of your guests or wedding party have any thoughts about what happened yesterday you can send them to me."

Gabrielle stepped back. "It's wonderful to see you two together. And, Ophelia, I just wish you'd told me yesterday that you and this hunky cop were an item!"

"I'm actually an FBI Agent. And," Kyle added with a wide grin, "in Ophelia's defense, we really haven't put a label on anything. And the last thing Ophelia wanted was to draw any attention away from you two on your big day."

Wow, he was good at this. As opposed to

her, yesterday, when she'd been asked to fill in for Chloe as a bridesmaid, and Ophelia had felt like every word out of her mouth was awkward and wrong. Then her heart sank as she remembered what had happened to Chloe. Gabrielle and Jared were like a pair of stubborn deer in headlights refusing to admit the fact that the next car on the road could be headed their way.

Lord, please help us protect Gabrielle and everyone else who might be in this killer's sights.

"You two are such sweeties," Gabrielle said. Then she crouched down and looked at Rocky. "Not to mention you are so adorable you can take the attention away from anyone! Do you think you'd be willing to carry a little basket of flowers down the aisle for me?"

Gabrielle glanced at Kyle hopefully. Ophelia watched as Kyle pressed his lips tightly together and looked like he was fighting the urge to laugh.

"I'm so sorry," he said. "He doesn't really do tricks."

"Such a shame," Gabrielle said. She turned and waved at the gray-haired man with the camera. "Hey, photographer! Get over here and get a picture of these two to update our wedding's social media page."

"Absolutely," Kyle said gamely. "Sounds like a plan."

Anything, Ophelia imagined, to increase the likelihood people would have candid conversations with him later. The photographer waved them in front of a row of flowering rosebushes and instructed them to put their arms together and turn to face the camera. She slid her arms around Kyle's neck as directed and felt his strong hands tighten around her waist. Rocky sat tall on the ground in front of them. The photographer started clicking. Ophelia tried to smile naturally and face the lens, hoping she didn't look anywhere near as awkward as she felt.

"Now if you could give her a quick kiss on the cheek for this next one," the photographer said.

Kyle's lips brushed lightly against her cheekbones just below her temple, sending an unexpected tingle of electricity through her skin.

Instinctively she turned toward him, and for one fleeting moment their lips met in a kiss.

Chapter Eight

Kyle stepped back and his eyes widened. She stepped back, too, heat rising to her face. She wanted to apologize, tell him that it was an accident and that she hadn't meant to kiss him. But the truth was she wasn't even sure which one had kissed the other first.

Kyle ran his hand over the back of his neck.

"Good, good," the photographer said and looked down at the screen as if confirming he had gotten the shots. "Now, can somebody show me where the actual ceremony will be tonight?"

"Nolan can." Gabrielle gestured to the black-haired groomsman, who was still standing at the other side of the courtyard with the bridesmaid and ranch staff. "And actually, Lexi, can you go find Jared and let him know Ophelia and her boyfriend the cop are here?"

He's an agent, not a cop, and he's not my boyfriend.

Lexi disappeared into the main ranch and within moments Jared came out, alone. He looked stressed, harried and not at all like a man who was about to marry the love of his life. But while he said hello to Ophelia and Kyle, he made a beeline straight for Gabrielle and wrapped his arm around her shoulder.

"They said we could still have the wedding in the outdoor chapel as planned," he said. "But they're insisting we hold the reception in the courtyard. Apparently they hold beautiful receptions out there all the time. It's just that after the problem with our payment going through yesterday, thanks to Gabrielle's parents being delayed, they're not being as sympathetic as they could to the fact that all we want is to get married."

"Have you considered relocating the wedding somewhere more private and quieter?" Kyle asked. "Or even eloping?"

The federal agent was still smiling, with that easygoing grin. But there was a firmer edge to his voice now. Was it because the four of them were alone? She couldn't imagine that the kiss had rattled him, too.

"We'll be fine," Jared said firmly. He stepped up and put his arm around Gabrielle's shoulder.

"We actually talked in great length last night about the Bobby situation. While she eventually agreed it was right that I told you, we also decided that as long as we stayed together, we'll be fine. He's not about to make an attempt to hurt to Gabrielle while I'm around."

But what about everyone else who wasn't them?

"Whatever's going on, I think it's bigger than just one body in the barn," Ophelia said. She felt like she was walking a tightrope between what she was allowed to tell them and the fact that she didn't want her cousin to do anything that put himself, his fiancée, her great-aunt, and a bunch of friends and family in danger. "Look, somebody broke into my house last night."

Gabrielle gasped. Her hands rose to her lips.

"Are you serious?" Jared stepped toward her. "Are you okay?"

"I'm fine," she said quickly. "Kyle invited me to stay with him and his mother."

"Well, you do live in a lower income neighborhood," Jared said and Ophelia's fingers clenched. "I'm so sorry that happened. But I'm sure it's just a badly timed coincidence."

"There's more," Ophelia went on. "I also got

a video message from Chloe saying she needed to talk to me about the whole Bobby situation."

She wasn't sure what kind of reaction she was getting to that. But suddenly Gabrielle's face paled and something like fear flickered through her gaze. Then the bride smiled firmly, reached out and looped her arm through Ophelia's.

"Okay, I think it's time you and I had some girl talk," Gabrielle said firmly. "No guys. Just us. It's clear that my fiancé got you worried. And so I guess it's time I tell you what's really going on."

Ophelia glanced at Kyle. She couldn't just go off and talk to Gabrielle about Bobby without him. He was the FBI agent and the expert in questioning suspects. Her home was in the lab. But to her surprise, Kyle waved his hand as if encouraging them to go.

"That sounds fantastic," Kyle said. "I'll appreciate the opportunity to get to know Jared better."

You've got this, his eyes added. But did she, though?

Either way, she let her cousin's fiancée walk her away down the beautifully overgrown garden path to a rustic wooden bench Ophelia imagined had appeared in a lot of people's pictures. They sat and only then did Gabrielle pull her arm out of Ophelia's. She turned to face her.

"First of all—" Gabrielle's eyes widened with sincerity "—I need you to know that I really love your cousin and would do anything to make him happy. He's everything to me and I'm really sorry for all of this." Her manicured hands swung wide as if encompassing an invisible ball of chaos. "Chloe is my former roommate and I love her. But she is also a total drama queen and busybody who spends all of her time stirring up trouble for other people. This whole situation with Bobby would never have gotten out of hand if it hadn't been for her.

"Okay," Gabrielle went on. "So, Chloe and I met Bobby in a hotel bar. She liked him, but he was only interested in me. As Jared told you, Bobby and I went on a couple of dates that didn't go anywhere. I tried to end it, he got really clingy and he didn't want to take no for an answer. He called and sent flowers. It was really annoying."

She blew out a long breath and rolled her eyes, as if she saw Bobby more like a persistent fly at a picnic than a potential serial killer.

"Chloe made it worse by trying to meddle in my business," Gabrielle added. "She would talk to him when he called and wanted to hear his side of the story. Maybe she was hoping that if she let him cry on her shoulder, he'd fall in love with her. Then she canceled on coming to my wedding. Maybe because of him, I don't know. I'm just really sorry that she tried to involve you in this nonsense."

Was that really what happened? Gabrielle sounded like she actually believed what she was saying, yet Ophelia wasn't sure if it was true.

But before she could even ask a question, she heard the sound of Jared, Kyle and Rocky running down the path toward them. Ophelia leaped to her feet. Gabrielle did, too.

"Gabrielle, baby!" Jared stretched out both hands toward his fiancée, as if she was about to fall from a great height and he was preparing to catch her. "Chloe's dead!"

"What?" Gabrielle's voice broke.

"It was leaked to the news," Kyle said softly, as he stepped to Ophelia's side.

Ophelia reached out a hand toward Gabrielle to comfort her. But instead, she watched as Gabrielle tumbled into Jared's arms, in a flurry of sobs and questions. He ran his hand over her back, soothing and comforting her. Then her cousin fixed his eyes on Ophelia. And a colder look than she'd ever seen before filled his steely blue gaze.

"I think you should leave," Jared said. He glanced coolly from her to Kyle. "Both of you. I know you must've known something about this before you showed up here today, and yet neither of you told us anything."

Gabrielle still sobbed into his shoulder.

"I'm sorry." Ophelia's heart lurched. She took a step toward them. "All I knew was that a woman's body had been found. We didn't have a positive ID and we weren't authorized to tell you anything about it."

"Can't you talk like a normal person for once?" Jared's voice rose. She stepped back as if his words had literally slapped her. "I get that your sad little life is all about work, and you don't really click with people like Gabrielle and me, and our friends. And I've never given you a hard time for that. But I don't care that you didn't have a positive ID, or you weren't authorized or whatever. You still should've told me about Chloe and everything you know about this case. I'm your cousin!"

The words "I'm sorry" still floated on her tongue. But what was she apologizing for? For being driven? For doing her job? For putting her career above the fact that her cousin wanted an inside track on the investigation?

"Look, I tried to tell Grandma Evelyn that it was a mistake to have you in the wedding party." Jared blew out a hard breath. "It would break her heart if you didn't come to the wedding. Just please, leave and stay out of our way tonight. I'll tell Grandma you didn't feel up to being in the wedding."

He turned his back on her and started down the path, with his arm still around Gabrielle.

Ophelia wanted to run after him, apologize again, do or say something to make it right.

But instead, she felt Kyle's hand brush against her elbow on one side and Rocky's head press against the back of her leg on the other, as if they were working together to lead her back to the truck.

The three of them walked to the truck in silence and got inside. They'd already pulled out, left the ranch and driven a few miles down the highway before Kyle spoke. "You okay? That was pretty harsh."

"I don't know," Ophelia admitted. "He's never raised his voice at me like that before."

"He's scared, frustrated and angry," Kyle said. "He's probably used to being in control of things and is lashing out because things aren't going his way."

"Gabrielle spun this whole story that matches all the facts we've heard before," Ophelia said. "Only she said that Chloe kept trying to get in the middle of her and Bobby. Gabrielle said she blamed the whole Bobby mess on the fact that Chloe kept stirring up drama. I definitely can't imagine her saying any of that now that she knows Chloe's dead."

"When you two stepped away to talk, Jared asked if I could give him the inside track on the RMK case," Kyle said, "and tell him some of the details that investigators haven't told the public," Kyle said. "He also asked if there was anything I could do to speed up the Cherish Ranch investigation. It became clear to me pretty quickly that he expected some kind of preferential treatment from the police that he was frustrated he wasn't getting."

He rested his left arm on the window and his right hand on the steering wheel.

"I'm not justifying what he said, but I do understand how powerless and frustrated he must feel. I know how hard it felt for me when my colleagues knew that my father had passed away due a self-inflicted gunshot wound before I was told. Or that my brother and Caitlyn didn't survive the crash. In both cases, all they would tell me was that something bad had happened and someone would brief me at the hospital. Again, I'm not saying this reaction was either right or fair. Just that I hope you can find a way to forgive him."

She tried to respond, but realized she couldn't find the right words to say. So she just closed her eyes instead and prayed the same words she felt like she'd been praying over and over again for almost twenty-four hours. She asked God for mercy, justice, guidance, compassion, wisdom and help.

When she opened her eyes and turned to Kyle again, he was watching the rearview mirror.

She followed his gaze. For a long moment she saw nothing but the empty mountain road behind them. Then a blue truck appeared over the horizon, its bright chrome almost glimmering in the hot New Mexico sun. A man in a cowboy hat sat at the wheel.

"Everything okay?" she asked.

"No," Kyle said. "This blue truck and I have been playing peekaboo for the last five minutes, no matter how many turns I take. Looks like we're being followed again. But I'm not going to run. It's time we make a stand and fight."

Kyle had always found something both majestic and intimidating about how the Rocky Mountains towered over the outskirts of Santa Fe, where tall trees, scorching deserts, red buttes and sandstone structures all coexisted in an unbelievably beautiful harmony.

It was the last he was scanning for now.

Twisted and intricate, the pale beige structures rose from the earth like giant versions of a child's sandcastles, arches and towers now frozen in time.

Well, a fortress was what he needed now.

He urged the SUV faster until the truck disappeared from view again, while his eyes continued to survey the row ahead.

"I'm looking for a place to pull over," he said. But even as the words left his mouth, he saw the trio of naturally formed sculptures, each taller than a house, standing tall like a queen with her two ladies in waiting, light brown against the darker red and orange rock surrounding them.

He took one more glance to the rearview mirror. The truck had vanished from view temporarily. He prayed he'd have enough time to do what he needed before the truck caught up with him again. Then he looked at Ophelia. Her eyes were closed and it looked like she was praying.

"Okay, so here's the plan," he said. "See those three tall rock sculptures ahead?" She opened her eyes and nodded. "In a minute I'm going to quickly stop the vehicle and hop out. I'll pop the hood to make it look like I'm having engine trouble." He glanced at her face. "I want you to stay in the vehicle."

"Alone?"

"You'll be much safer there than you will be outside," he said. "The windows are bulletproof and the walls are reinforced. Just stay low and if anything goes wrong dial 911."

"And where will you be?"

"Out there," he said. "Taking him down before he can get to you."

He watched as fear and courage battled in the depths of her beautiful blue eyes. Immediately he switched the hand that was holding the steering wheel, so he could take her hand and hold it.

"I trust you," she said.

And despite the hundreds, maybe thousands, of times he'd heard those words in his life, somehow as they flew out of Ophelia's mouth, they hit him deep inside his core in a way they never had before.

Help me, Lord. I don't want to let her down.

He pulled his hands from hers and steered rapidly off the road, in between the first handmaiden rock and the queen. He popped the hood, leaped out and was about to open the door for Rocky to join him, when the dog's large eyes met his through the window. Instead, Kyle swallowed hard and closed the driver's-side door.

"Rocky, stay with Ophelia," he said. "Guard her and keep her safe."

The dog woofed softly.

Kyle had barely managed to duck behind the sculpture he thought of as the queen when he saw the truck appear on the horizon. He pressed his back into the sandstone crevasses and hoped that the man in the cowboy hat would take the bait.

The truck drew closer and closer. Kyle held his breath and prayed. He watched as the brake lights flashed. The cowboy pulled to a stop a few yards away from Kyle's SUV. From what Kyle could see, there was just the driver in the car, no other passengers. The cowboy was tall and thin, with an expensive-looking hat pulled down over his eyes. The truck looked expensive, too, unlike the battered van and rusty car he'd seen the masked man use before.

The cowboy got out slowly and began to walk toward Kyle's SUV.

He wasn't limping. This wasn't the same man Kyle had clipped in the calf. Kyle tracked his steps as he grew closer. Thirty paces, twenty paces, ten…

"FBI! Get down on the ground with your hands up!"

Kyle leaped from behind his hiding spot. The man turned to run. Kyle was faster. He tackled him, bringing him down to the ground and deftly cuffing his hands behind his back.

"Don't shoot!" the young man yelped. The hat fell from his head showing short black hair beneath. "I'm not the killer. I promise!"

The voice was familiar. But Kyle couldn't place it straight away. He stepped back enough to let the man turn over.

It was Nolan.

The groomsman he'd seen back at the ranch, showing the photographer where the outdoor wedding chapel was. And also, the man who'd been with Gabrielle when John Doe was killed.

Unless she'd lied to give him an alibi.

Kyle stepped back to let the man breathe, but kept his eyes locked on his face and his hand at the ready should he need to pull out his weapon.

"Why were you following me?"

"I… I was trying to catch up with you to help you," Nolan spluttered.

Kyle looked the young man over. Every single item of clothing he was wearing cost more than Kyle made in a month and his eyes were darting every possible direction without meeting Kyle's eyes.

"I don't believe you," Kyle said, "because if you had been, you wouldn't have kept pulling back and slowing down like that every time I slowed down. You were following me and I'm not interested in playing guessing games about why. Two people associated with a wedding you're a groomsman in have been killed in the past twenty-four hours. And it's possible those murders are linked to the Rocky Mountain Killer who's murdered another six people across mountain country. So I suggest you spend the ride to the police station thinking hard about telling me the truth." He hauled Nolan up to his feet and prepared to steer him toward his SUV. "Don't worry, we'll get someone to come and pick up your truck."

He turned toward Ophelia. Rocky had climbed into the driver's seat to join her. They were both watching him.

"Call 911 and tell them I need backup," he called. "I've got a GPS tracker in my SUV. They can lock on the location."

"On it!" Ophelia said. He watched as she placed the call.

He had a cage divider he could raise in the back of the SUV, between the front and back seats, but he'd rather not drive a potential serial killer back to town with Ophelia and Rocky in the SUV.

"No, wait!" Nolan yelled. "All right, I was following you. But only because I saw a man put something in your SUV!"

Kyle stopped. Instinctively, his eyes locked where he'd left Rocky and Ophelia. The dog had climbed into the driver's seat. Ophelia had the phone to her ear and was saying something to someone, likely dispatch, but her eyes were tracking him through the rearview mirror. "You saw someone put something in my vehicle?"

"Maybe, I don't know." Nolan said. He was

probably only six or seven years younger than Kyle, but it felt more like fifteen or twenty. "When I came back from showing the photographer the outdoor chapel, I saw this big guy crouched down beside your SUV."

"Where exactly? Which side of the vehicle?"

"Back door, passenger side, I think," Nolan said. He didn't sound certain. "I didn't think anything at first. But then I remembered that I heard the RMK liked to taunt police with clues and messages. And I thought if I could get what was left in your vehicle, I could figure out who the killer was and maybe get some reward money or something."

"Did he have a limp?" Kyle asked.

"I think so, maybe."

Kyle blew out a frustrated breath. He believed him. The story was too ridiculous to be invented.

"Good news," Ophelia called. She got out of the vehicle and Rocky bounded out after her. "Backup is eight minutes out. Some campers got into a fight and started a fire west of here, so emergency vehicles were already in the area."

Kyle thanked God for that.

"He says he was only following us because he

thought someone might've tried to plant something in my vehicle," he called back.

"What kind of something?" Ophelia asked.

"I don't know, but he says it might be in the back seat."

She opened the back door, bent down and looked for a long moment. Then she checked the front seats.

"I don't see anything," she said.

"I'm not lying," Nolan stammered.

Ophelia looked around the outside of the vehicle. Her phone was still in her hand. Rocky sat on the ground and looked at her thoughtfully.

"Wait," she said. "There's something sticking out of the gas tank. Like a piece of string. Maybe it's a fuse, but if so it's a clumsy design because the gas tank didn't detonate."

"Don't touch it!" Kyle called.

"I won't," she said. "Thankfully law enforcement are already on their way." She closed the passenger-side door. Kyle heard a loud and metallic click. She looked up and her face paled. "It slipped inside the tank."

"Run!"

Oh, Lord...please help us.

Ophelia and Rocky both turned and ran toward him. Behind him he could hear Nolan making tracks and hoped the young man would make it out of the blast zone. But Kyle ran toward Ophelia.

He had to get to her. He had to make sure she was okay.

In an instant, Rocky had reached his side. Silently, Kyle signaled him to keep running.

"Kyle!" Ophelia shouted. "Run!"

Not yet. Not without her.

But she was only steps away from him now. He reached out his hand to grab hers. She reached out for him.

And then his truck exploded.

Chapter Nine

In an instant he watched, helpless, as a wall of orange flame rushed toward Ophelia's body. Then the force of the blast lifted her off the ground and hurled her through the air toward him. Kyle caught her with both arms and held on tight, as he felt himself tossed backward through the air. For a moment he felt powerless to do anything but grasp Ophelia to him with all his might, willing himself not to let her go. Then he hit the ground, shoulder first, and rolled over and over again on the rough ground, absorbing the impact of the blast in his body and sheltering her with his arms.

Finally, his body shuddered to a stop and he felt Ophelia slip from his arms. For a moment he lay there on the ground as soot and ash rained down around him. He looked up to see a ball of orange flame where his SUV has been. Then he felt Ophelia's hand grab his and pull him up, and he climbed to his feet.

"You saved me." She threw her arms around his neck, with such force that for a moment he thought he was going to lose his balance and fall back down again.

Of course, I saved you. I couldn't just leave you.

He wanted to tell her how relieved he was that she was okay and promise he'd never let anything hurt her. But the words died on his tongue as hot, smoky air seared his lungs.

Instead, he wrapped his arms around her waist and kissed her—or maybe she kissed him first, he didn't know. All he knew was that as their lips met he felt like it was the first real kiss he'd ever had in his life. The first one that ever had a hope of meaning all the things a kiss was supposed to mean.

Then she pulled out of his arms and it was like all of his other senses suddenly came alive and rushed back in to fill the space she'd left. He could hear the sound of Rocky barking and sirens blaring in the distance. He could feel the heat on his skin and smell the acrid scent of burning rubber. Ophelia ran toward Nolan and Rocky. Kyle followed, and as he reached his partner, he felt Rocky nuzzle his hand in greeting.

He uncuffed Nolan. The man seemed too shaken and thankful to be alive to run, and truth was Kyle knew that regardless of why Nolan had tried to follow him, he was also the reason they were all alive now. Kyle then watched as a cavalcade of police, firefighters and ambulances crossed the horizon toward them. Within moments, the sound of sirens, shouting and emergency personnel pouring from their vehicles had completely overtaken the air.

"I need to take Nolan in for questioning," he told Ophelia. "I want you to come with me and observe via the two-way mirror. There might be things you pick up because of your connection to Jared and Gabrielle."

But instead, Ophelia shook her head.

"I'm going to get someone to take me to the lab," she said. "I need to check in on how far the team has gotten in processing everything that we collected yesterday. Obviously, I won't be able to process anything found in my own house. But I can at least give Isla an update on everything we found in relation to the death of John Doe. I still haven't forgotten about that cuff link."

He opened his mouth to try to convince her that they should head back to Santa Fe together and wasn't even sure what he was going to say, when she raised her hand to stop him.

"Kyle, I need to go do my job."

He nodded. "Okay, I get it."

She bent down and hugged Rocky, nuzzling her face against the dog's snout. Then she turned and ran toward a Santa Fe PD officer. Still, part of him was expecting he'd talk to her again before she left the scene. But instead, when the flames were extinguished and the swell of response vehicles began to recede, Kyle looked around to realize that Ophelia had left without him realizing it. Rocky whimpered and sniffed the air as if he too realized that something was missing and was offering to help Kyle search for it.

"It's okay, buddy," Kyle said. "Ophelia just had to go back to work."

After all, he wasn't actually her wedding date or her partner; they were just two professionals who happened to get thrown together over one particular crime scene and might never be again.

Thankfully, Nolan quickly agreed to come in for questioning, which spared Kyle having to jump through the hoops of an arrest. Despite the fact that the incident started with Nolan following an FBI agent's SUV—and that SUV then exploding—it wasn't entirely clear what crime Nolan had actually committed.

The local FBI field office was small and not set up for questioning suspects, but Patricia had gotten an officer to drive Kyle, Rocky and Nolan to the central police station, and gave Kyle use of an interrogation room. There, Kyle and Nolan sat across from each other in the plain rectangular space with gray walls, while Rocky lay by Kyle's feet, and Nolan worried the plastic cup of water he'd been given and repeated multiple versions of the exact same story he'd told Kyle back when he'd first had handcuffs on.

"Where did you even get the idea that the Rocky Mountain Killer would plant evidence in my vehicle?" he asked.

"Because that's all everyone is talking about!" Nolan said. "If anyone tells you they're not talking about the RMK they're lying. It's all over social media." And Kyle expected that a lot of what people were talking about was either untrue or wild speculation. "But I've never been to Elk Lake or whatever it's called, or been part of anything called the Young Rancher's Club, and I don't know anyone who has."

"Are you aware that Gabrielle gave you an alibi for the time when John Doe was killed in the barn yesterday?" Kyle asked.

"Yeah." He nodded. "We ran into each other in the outdoor chapel area and talked about the weather."

His gaze darted toward the ceiling. He still wasn't being completely honest about something, but Kyle wasn't sure what.

"Nolan." Kyle leaned forward. "Is there something going on between you and Gabrielle? Some reason why she'd lie for you?"

"No!" The plastic cup crunched in Nolan's hands. "I'm not like that. I'd never mess with my friend's fiancée. She really, really loves Jared. Like a lot. And wants to marry him."

A swift knock sounded on the door. Kyle stood, and so did Rocky, and they walked to the door. It was detective Patricia Gonzales.

He and Rocky stepped outside to join her in the hallway and closed the door behind them.

"What are we looking at in terms of charges?" she asked.

He pressed his tongue against his gums. Local Santa Fe PD had a completely different jurisdictional authority than he did. For example, while he could charge people with felonies, he couldn't give anyone a traffic ticket or ding them for running a stop sign. That was the role of the local police he was cooperating with on this case.

However, when it came to Nolan, there wasn't really anything there that was chargeable.

"He's got no record," Kyle said, "and I didn't witness him commit a crime. I could charge him with resisting arrest or attempting to tamper with evidence, but it's a stretch."

"So we let him go?" Patricia asked. "Or do we hold him and hope we get something more?"

"I think we let him go," Kyle said. "As much as I'd like to hold him, I've also got to think about the fact that if I do that nobody in that wedding party is going to speak to me about anything, and I don't even know if this guy is guilty of anything except being foolish. I think our best move is to thank him, treat him like a helpful witness, and apologize for any inconvenience and give him a ride wherever he wants. Make him think we like him."

"But we keep an eye on him?" Patricia asked.

"We keep an eye on the whole wedding party."

A uniformed cop came down the hallway.

"Agent West?" he said. "There's someone at the front desk wanting to speak to you, Should I show her to a room?"

Hope floated in his chest. Was it Ophelia?

"You go," Patricia said dryly. "I'll go thank our witness for his cooperation and tell him how much we appreciate his help."

Kyle walked down the maze of hallways back to the front desk. As he turned a corner he saw MCK9 Task Force member Meadow Ames striding toward him, with Grace by her side. Incredibly athletic, with long dark hair and bright green eyes, Meadow exuded a special combination of determination and sense of adventure that seemed to match perfectly with her K-9 partner, who specialized in both tracking and search and rescue. Kyle privately thought he'd never seen a human and K-9 partner match so perfectly.

"You made it!" He clasped her on her shoulder as the dogs wagged tails at each other in greeting. "It's good to see you."

"It's good to see you, too." Meadow smiled, but genuine concern moved through the depths of her eyes. Together they walked out of the Santa Fe PD office, along with their K-9 partners. "I heard you got into some vehicle trouble today. Everything okay?"

"Everyone's okay, thankfully," he said. "Although my SUV has seen better days. Also, I know it probably seems minor in the whole scheme of things, but if you are going to be spending time with my mom on protective detail, can you try to find out why she's making so many trips to the pharmacy? I keep asking, but she won't tell me."

"Will do." Meadow nodded. "You know that Chase wants me to take your mom and Brody to a safe house. I get that you want to keep them close. But with the attack on Ophelia's home and now your vehicle, I think Chase is right that even if Grace and I are protecting them, as long as they're in your home they're in danger. At least until we figure out what's going on."

"I know." Kyle's eyes searched the bright blue sky above.

His brain knew that his boss was right and Meadow would keep his family safe. But still something in him ached. His job took him away from Brody too much as it was, and now his colleague was going to take Brody and Mom to a safe house.

Lord, I don't know to be both the family man and

lawman you've called me to be. I feel like I'm failing at both. And now this case is taking my kid away from me. Please, open my eyes to the clues I need to see and help me solve this before anyone else gets hurt.

Including his own heart.

Ophelia felt a special type of joy fill her heart as she stepped through the familiar doors of the Santa Fe PD Crime Scene Unit's forensic lab. Thankfully, her car and home had finally both been cleared, so she was back in her own clothes and able to be at the wheel of her own vehicle. But even though she knew her boss would've let her take more time off despite the fact that the forensic lab was short-staffed, right now there was nowhere else she wanted to be.

She grabbed her white lab coat from her locker and slid it on, feeling the familiar crisp and clean fabric. Then she clipped on her identification pass and started for the lab. The memory of her two fleeting kisses with Kyle still buzzed on her lips and rattled in the back of her mind. The first had been an accident. But the second? That had been full of emotions she didn't even want to begin to analyze.

After all, it didn't matter what she felt about Kyle, or his son, and that wonderful little family who'd opened their home and lives to her when she'd needed someone. Kyle had made it clear that he wasn't interested in a relationship. And even if she did have time for one—which she didn't—it wasn't good for her to go chasing after a man who'd preemptively rejected the thought of starting a life with her. She needed to focus on the life she had, and the work she did, instead of worrying about a future that would never be hers.

The forensic lab was abuzz with colleagues in matching lab coats, each hard at work and focused on their own station as their eyes peered through goggles, glasses and microscopes at the evidence in front of them. When Ophelia crossed through the room to her desk, colleagues looked up and smiled. All of them had heard about the shooting at the ranch and the body found in her house. But while person after person asked how she was doing and offered to be there for her if she needed support, once she thanked them and reassured them that she was fine, each was quick to turn back to their tasks at hand. She appreciated that.

Lord, when I'm here I feel like myself. Like I'm doing what I'm meant to be doing. That I am doing the work You've called me to do. Thank You so much for that and that I get to be a part of this work.

Nobody here thought of her as a victim, although she knew for a fact most had processed the crime scenes in the barn and her house. And definitely nobody thought she was weird or unusual for spending her life working with what her great-aunt Evelyn would call "blood and guts."

But now, she had to buckle down and get to work.

Various white boards around the room listed the evidence and process of different open cases. As she'd told Kyle, there was a backlog. There was only so much hard work and overtime she could do to make up for the lab being short-staffed and overloaded. As much as she'd have hoped that everything that had been collected less than twenty-four hours ago at Cherish Ranch had been sorted, there were still a lot of white spaces on the board.

Based on what she could see, her dedicated colleagues had processed a whole lot of different DNA and blood samples, but only one DNA profile was found in the blood in the barn—the victim's. There hadn't been any unexpected DNA samples where Chloe's body had been found in Ophelia's basement, either. Seems whoever the masked man behind the crimes was, he'd been smart enough not to leave any DNA behind. Nothing unfamiliar or unexpected had been found in the remnants of the cleaning solution in the barn, either. Or in the white van.

So many tests had been run already with so few answers. However, in her line of work, often the sooner one eliminated the wrong things the faster they were able to determine the right ones.

Sure enough, a new lab laptop was waiting on her desk, to replace the one she'd lost the night before. Ophelia found the gold cuff link in the evidence locker and double-checked with the acting head of the lab that the blood sample on it had been tested and come back to the unknown victim. Okay, now to finally get a good look at the inscription on it.

She took it back to her workstation, slid on a fresh pair of rubber gloves, carefully retrieved the cuff link from the evidence bag with a pair of tweezers and dropped it in a beaker of cleaning solution. Tiny bubbles rose from the cuff link as the solution did its work.

Then she opened the new laptop and called

Isla, the MCK9 technical analyst. Within moments Isla's face appeared on the screen.

"Hey!" Isla said. "It's really good to see you. I heard you survived some pretty scary stuff this morning and I've been praying nonstop."

Genuine care and concern filled the tech's brown eyes, but there was a brightness to her smile, too. Ophelia instinctively liked her. The whole MCK9 Task Force seemed great, but something about Isla especially made Ophelia feel like they were on the same wavelength.

"I appreciate it," Ophelia said. "The discovery that the killer took a second life is really shocking and sad. I'm just glad everyone survived the SUV vehicle explosion."

Isla nodded. "Yeah, we've all been thanking God for that, and looking forward to getting to the bottom of this."

Ophelia quickly ran her through all the results the team had uncovered so far.

"The bullets found in our Joe Doe still haven't been tested against the other bullets in previous cases involving the RMK to see if they were fired from the same gun," Ophelia said. "Can you send me through a picture so I can try to match ballistics?"

"Absolutely," Isla said. "I'm on it."

The individual lines, ridges and groves that each gun left on the bullets it fired were as unique as fingerprints, allowing investigators to not just match them to the type of gun they were fired from, but the specific weapon itself. The bullets that killed all six of the RMK victims had been fired through the barrel of the exact same gun, though that gun had never been found. Had the bullets that killed John Doe come from that weapon, too?

Ophelia left the video call open. She got one of the bullets found in the barn from evidence, plucked it out of the small clear evidence box with a fresh pair of tweezers and then created a three-dimensional rendered model of it using the lab's high-tech camera. Slowly a detailed image of the bullet appeared on the screen in front of her as the camera did its work, like it was slowly being drawn by an invisible hand. The computer chimed, letting her know the render was complete. She sent it to Isla and a moment later Isla's own image of one of the RMK's bullets loaded onto the screen beside it.

Ophelia used the computer's track pad to rotate the images this way and that on the screen, trying to line up the striation lines on the two bullets to see if they'd been made by the same gun barrel. But no matter how patiently she maneuvered the two pictures, the rifling marks didn't line up.

"They're not a match," Isla said finally.

"No, they're not." Ophelia blew out a hard breath and leaned back in her chair. "These bullets were not fired from the same gun."

"Wow." Isla looked as shocked and disappointed by the news as Ophelia felt. "So the bullets that killed John Doe in the barn were not fired from the same gun that killed the RMK's six victims. Do you think we're looking at a copycat?"

"Maybe," Ophelia said. Did that mean that the murders of John Doe and Chloe Madison had nothing at all to do with the Rocky Mountain Killer? She glanced over at the beaker, where she'd placed the cuff link. It had stopped bubbling and the liquid was slightly cloudy. "One second. I'm about to have something else for you."

She pulled the cuff link from the cleaning solution. It glistened. Gold, she was sure, not some cheap knockoff. It was worth a good amount of money. The engraving was so stylized she couldn't make it out at first. So she set it directly in front of the 3D camera and started scanning it with the high-definition lens, allowing Isla to see it in real time along with her.

Slowly, the engraving came into view in large and magnified letters on the screen.

First an *R*, then a *W* and finally an *N*.

"So, *RWN*," Isla said. "Not *RMK*. I have no idea what that stands for."

"Neither do I." So first the bullets weren't a match and now the engraving on the cuff link turned out to be *RWN* and not *RMK*.

"It's looking less and less like the murders of John Doe and Chloe Madison have anything to do with the Rocky Mountain Killer case," Isla said.

"I'm sorry," Ophelia said. "I know you guys were hoping this could be a big break in catching the guy."

Kyle had definitely hoped it would be. Ophelia's cell phone rang. She glanced down at the screen. It was Jared. She wondered if he was calling to yell at her some more, apologize or pretend their entire conflict had never happened. Knowing Jared, it could be any of the above. And any which way, it could wait until she was finished with Isla. She sent the call through to voice mail.

"Hey," Isla said. "Look on the bright side. At

least I now have a solid lead in finding out John Doe's identity. I'm going to go cross-check the picture of the cuff link with the work of jewelers in New Mexico, Wyoming and beyond. Hopefully I'll be able to track down the person who did this work and see if they have a record of who they sold it to."

"Try Nevada," Ophelia said. "That's where Bobby was apparently from. And thanks so much. I appreciate your help."

"That's what we're here for," Isla said. "I'm going to fill the rest of the team in. Talk to you soon."

The call ended and Ophelia silently thanked God for her. The phone rang. Jared was calling again. Time she answered it.

"Hey," she said. "I'm at work."

"Gabrielle's gone!" His words came out in a panicked rush. "I think Bobby kidnapped her!"

Chapter Ten

"I'm on my way." Ophelia leaped to her feet. She closed her laptop, grabbed her bag and moved swiftly through the lab, without even stopping to take off her lab coat. "What happened?"

"When we got back to the hotel, we heard that Kyle's truck had caught fire and Nolan had been arrested," Jared said. He sounded so panicked it was like he was struggling to even breathe. "Gabrielle got all upset. She blamed me and said it was my fault for telling you about Bobby because you got the cops involved and made the drama even worse."

Ophelia didn't exactly see it that way. She reached the main hallway and started down the stairs to the parking lot, not bothering to wait for the elevator.

"She went into her hotel room," he continued. "After it was over an hour I got worried and went to check on her. But she was gone."

So much for hotel security.

"How long has it been since you called the police?"

"I didn't call the police. I haven't told anyone. Just you."

"What?" Ophelia's feet nearly stumbled as she ran across the parking lot to her car. Gabrielle had been kidnapped and Jared hadn't even called police? "You have to call 911. Right away. Report it as a kidnapping and tell them you think he might hurt her. I'll be there soon and I'm going to call Kyle, too."

"No!" Jared's voice rose through the phone. "Wait! No police! If we call the cops or involve law enforcement in any way, he'll kill her."

"It's normal to think that way." Ophelia reached her car and yanked her keys from her bag. "But that doesn't mean it's true."

"He left a note!"

Ophelia paused. Her car keys shook in her hand.

"Bobby left a note?" she repeated. Hope rose in her chest. "Jared, that means there is physical evidence we can track. Handwriting, fingerprints, maybe even DNA."

"It won't help!" Jared sounded desperate. "He made her write it!"

"Bobby made Gabrielle write the note herself?"

"Yeah," Jared said.

The fleeting hope she'd just begun to feel popped like a balloon.

"Okay," she said, "that's not ideal. But maybe we can still use it. Who knows what evidence we might find."

"I Said You Can't Involve the Police!" Jared shouted. "If you've ever cared about me, please just trust me on this!"

No. Ophelia rocked back on her heels. As much as she loved her cousin, she wasn't about to let him make the call on whether or not police should be involved. But she knew someone whom she did trust.

"I'm getting into my car now and switching my phone to hands-free," she said. "I need to put you on hold and there might be some weird clicks, but I promise I'm not going anywhere and I'll be back in a second."

She put him on hold, leaped into her car and dialed Kyle.

"Hello?" Kyle's warm and reassuring voice filled the line. "Isla was just filling me in on what you guys did and didn't find. Sounds like we might be dealing with a copycat, and Nolan said everyone's been gossiping about the RMK."

"Jared says that Bobby kidnapped Gabrielle and we can't go to the police or he'll kill her," she said quickly. "I'm on the phone with him now. I need your help and for you to hear what's going on. So I'm going to mute you and then put you on the call with him via three-way." Which was risky, but she hoped Jared was too distracted to see the new name popping up on the screen. "You'll be able to hear us, but we won't be able to hear you. Okay?"

She'd just thrown a lot of information at Kyle quickly and hoped he'd been able to process it all.

"Okay," he said, and it was amazing just how much strength and security moved through her at hearing him speak just that one word. "Where are you now?"

"In my car." She peeled out of the parking lot and onto the road.

"Where are you headed?"

"To come get you." She hadn't even realized that was what she was planning on doing until the words left her lips. "So that we can go to the hotel and see Jared. I know he doesn't want police involved, but I can't do this without you."

"And you don't have to."

She glanced at the clock. Jared had been on hold for less than thirty seconds, but she imagined to him it felt like an eternity. She muted Kyle and then added Jared to the call.

"Hey, Jared," she said. "I'm back. I'm in my car and heading to the hotel."

"You can't come here," he said. His breathing was coming even faster and shallower now, like he was gasping for air. "Or he'll kill her!"

"Take a deep breath," she said, trying to think of the information Kyle would need to put the right wheels in motion to find Gabrielle. "We're going to find Gabrielle and we're going to help her. But to do that I need you to focus. How long has it been since you've seen her?"

There was a pause on the line for moment, and she worried he'd either hung up or passed out.

"An hour," he said finally. "Maybe an hour and a half."

"And you said the last place you saw her was her hotel room?"

"Yeah," Jared said. "She was really upset and said I never should've involved you in our business. She wanted to be alone. When I went to check on her she was gone. But her stuff was all still here and she'd left a note saying she was with Bobby."

"You said it was in Gabrielle's handwriting. Can you read it to me?"

There was another pause and then the rustle of papers.

"'Dear Jared,'" he began to read. "'I am so very sorry to do this to you on our wedding day. But I've realized that Bobby is the love of my life. He and I are meant to be together forever where the mountains meet the sky.

"'If you love me please forget about me. Bobby has promised to give me a good life. But if you call the police, bring law enforcement in or try to find me, then he will kill both me and himself, so that we can be together forever.

"'If you love me, don't tell anyone I've gone to be with Bobby, because you'll be putting my life in danger. I will love you forever but I have to go be with Bobby now.

"'Gabrielle.'"

Ophelia sucked in a breath, hoping that Kyle had caught every word and also wondering if that was what people sounded like when they were writing a goodbye letter to their fiancé with a gun to their head.

"That expression 'where the mountains meet the sky' means something right?" she said. "Isn't that what you called the land her parents bought for you guys to build your house?"

Jared didn't answer. It sounded like he was talking to someone else in the room.

"Jared?" Ophelia asked. "You there?"

"Sorry, I'm talking to Grandma Evelyn about the flowers. I've got to call you back."

The call went dead. She called back and Jared didn't answer. But she could see Kyle's house ahead now. His strong form was standing by the end of his driveway, with Rocky alert at his side. There were no vehicles in the driveway. Looked like Alice was out and he hadn't managed to replace his truck yet.

Kyle pocketed his phone as she drove up.

"I've alerted both Patricia at the Santa Fe PD and Chase at MCK9 of the situation," he said as he and Rocky jogged over, "including the facts that the kidnapper threatened to kill Gabrielle if police are involved, her fiancé is currently refusing to cooperate with law enforcement and that we need to search for her under the radar. But law enforcement will be on the lookout for anyone trying to take her out of the country either through the airports and over the border. Good news is that Meadow has arrived and is going to be taking Alice and Brody to a safe house."

"Got it," she said. "Get in. I think I might know where Gabrielle is. But I don't know for sure."

He opened the back door for Rocky. The K-9 leaped in. Then Kyle got in the passenger side.

"Where the mountains meet the sky," he said. "You know where that is?"

"I think so." Ophelia's hands clenched the steering wheel tightly. "That's the exact phrase they used to describe this plot of land near Pecos Wilderness that her parents bought for them to build a house. I went up there a few weeks ago to help Jared tie balloons to the trees for him to surprise her with, when he took her up there to show her. So, that has to be a clue? The solution to finding her couldn't be that simple, could it?"

Kyle's eyes flickered to the bright blue sky above, and he seemed to be praying. Then he asked, "How about you start driving that direction and we'll sort it out as we go."

"Okay." She pulled out of the driveway and

started toward the highway that led to the Pecos Wilderness.

"So you think Gabrielle left Jared a clue to where Bobby was taking her?" Kyle asked.

"I think so," she said. "But I can't be sure." For all she knew they were driving in the completely wrong direction. "If it is a clue, then Gabrielle clearly planted it for Jared and he missed it."

"Well, he seemed incredibly distraught," Kyle said. "Maybe he's so upset he can't see the obvious. People miss all kinds of things when they're upset. But something about this theory doesn't sit right with you?"

"It's too simple," Ophelia admitted. "And in my experience most things are more complicated than that."

"It would also mean that Bobby missed the fact that she put it in there," Kyle said. "Or maybe Bobby got her to use that phrase to lure Jared there, either to kill Jared or to kill Gabrielle somewhere her fiancé is certain to find her."

"So we could be driving into a trap," Ophelia said. "Or it could be nothing. I could be completely wrong. What if we get there and she's not there? What if it turns out I just wasted your time on a hunch and it's nothing but a wild-goose chase that keeps us from finding her?"

Kyle reached out his hand into the empty space between them. She took it and let the comforting warmth and strength of his fingers envelop hers.

"I don't know if Bobby is serious in his threats to kill Gabrielle," Kyle admitted. "But if Bobby really did kill both John Doe and Chloe, then it's very possible he will, especially if he thinks he's losing control of the situation. I also don't know if he has any way of knowing if police are involved or not, or if that's just a bluff. Maybe Gabrielle is right in thinking Bobby was well connected inside the police. But remember, it's my job to glean all the information I can and follow it until it leads me to the answers I need. Okay? You tell me the information you've got and I'll make the call. That's what we do."

Yeah, it was. And she had to trust they were both excellent at what they did.

"Okay." Slowly, she pulled her hand from his and then both of her hands through her hair. "Two months ago, Jared took me to see a plot of land that Gabrielle's parents were buying for them. He was making the down payment, and they were going to pay him back."

"Do you think you'd be able to find it?" Kyle asked.

"I'm pretty sure," she said. "I've got a good memory for details."

"Okay, we drive up there in your car," Kyle said. "I'm going to get in the back with Rocky and stay low, so if anybody's watching they will think you're driving up there alone. When we get there, Rocky and I will take a look around. If there's any signs of recent activity out there, we call for backup."

She pulled into the right-hand lane and slowed as he unbuckled his seat belt and climbed into the back seat beside his partner. They left the city and started toward the Rockies. She gritted her teeth.

"As much as I trust your memory," Kyle said. "I'm also going to call Isla and see if she can check property records to get an exact address for us. The property has to be in either Jared or Gabrielle's name."

He dialed and a moment later she heard Isla answer. But Ophelia tuned out his call and fixed her eyes on the road ahead, watching each intersection as they drove deeper and deeper into the untamed wilderness and counting on her memory to steer them right and lead them in the right direction.

She was sure she turned here. And there? No, wait. It had actually been two roads ahead over on her right.

Kyle ended the call and leaned forward between the seats. His brow creased with worry lines.

"The good news is that Isla thinks she's identified the jewelry store that sold the cuff links as one in Las Vegas," he said. "The bad news is she can't find any records for a Jared Clarke or Gabrielle Martinez owning a property anywhere near the Pecos Wilderness or even in the Santa Fe area."

The words hit her like a punch in the gut.

Had she remembered it wrong? Was she just driving deeper and deeper into the Rockies chasing a faulty memory?

"Maybe I was wrong, and it was registered under her parents or my great-aunt Evelyn?"

"I asked her to check by last name," he said. "Nothing under Evelyn Clarke, and while Martinez is a very common last name, there've been no new sales under that name the past six months."

She didn't even know what that meant.

But before she could worry about it, she saw a narrow road coming up ahead on her right. It was unmarked, but she could see the remnants of the ribbons where she'd once strung balloons hanging tattered from the trees and bleached from the sun.

"Well, I don't know who owns it," she said. "But we're here now."

"Okay." Kyle's voice came from the back seat. "Go slow. Keep an eye out and be prepared to get out of here in a moment's notice."

"Understood." She turned down the narrow dirt path.

"Lord," she prayed, "keep me safe and help me see what I need to see."

"Amen," Kyle echoed.

The cabin appeared in the woods through the trees ahead. It was wooden and faded, barely more than a shack. The dilapidated building had also been the only structure on it the last time she'd been there and now it looked even smaller than before. Then she saw the white van parked beyond it.

"Okay, we've got more than what we need," Kyle said. "Let's get out of here—"

But then a desperate and panicked cry rose on the air, freezing the words on Kyle's tongue and cutting a chill through Ophelia's heart like a knife.

"Help me!" Gabrielle screamed from somewhere within the shack. "Somebody help me! Please!"

"Ophelia, call 911!" Kyle shouted, leaping from the back seat and summoning Rocky to his side. "If something kicks off I want you to drive out of here and whatever happens don't get out of the car!"

He'd already slammed the door and started running toward the cabin with his gun drawn when he heard Ophelia call his name.

"Kyle! Stop! It might be a trap! You might be running into danger."

"I know." He stopped and looked back. "But that's the job I signed up for."

He was a law enforcement officer who'd sworn an oath to rescue and protect those in trouble. Even when his life was on the line or it meant running into danger. Somewhere inside that shack Gabrielle was calling for help. He had no choice but to do whatever it took to rescue her.

"But you could get killed," Ophelia pleaded.

Yeah, he knew that, too, and yet the depth

of worry in her eyes was so strong it took all the power he had to break her gaze.

"You're right," he said. "But I'm going to stand up, do what I know is right, and trust God to keep us safe and make it all right in the end."

She nodded and pulled her phone from her bag. Together, Kyle and Rocky turned and ran swiftly toward the cabin, staying close to the tree line and away from any sightlines that might put him in the line of fire.

Two voices rose on the wind.

One was male and his bellowing voice was punctuated with curses and shaking with rage. "Shut up! Just shut your face now! Not one more word out of you. I'm done putting up with your nonsense!"

The other was Gabrielle's, bargaining one moment, screaming and crying the next, as if desperately trying to figure out what to say to calm down the monster holding her captive. "It's not what you think. Jared and I are really in love—"

He snorted. "You're a liar!"

"What do you want from me?" Gabrielle shouted. "You want money? I'll get you money! I promise. Just let me go!"

"You think I'm letting you out of my sight? You so much as flinch and I'll kill you."

Kyle glanced through the filthy window at the scene unfolding in front of him. Gabrielle was down on her knees, tears rolling down her cheek. Her hands were unbound and yet an ugly bruise under her eye made it clear her kidnapper wouldn't hesitate to strike. The man he guessed was Bobby stood over her, limping from a left leg injury Kyle recognized all too well, as he paced back and forth waving a gun in her face. And for the first time, Kyle got a really good look at the masked man who'd shot at them in the barn, tried to kidnap Ophelia and probably killed Chloe. He was in his late twenties or even early thirties, with unremarkable brown hair and narrow eyes, and one pupil so pale that Kyle wondered if he was blind in one eye.

So this was Bobby? Kyle had never seen his face before.

Rocky growled softly, and even without looking down, Kyle could sense his partner's hackles rise. His partner could detect the smell of death. Kyle thought of Chloe's locket, which had been snapped in half. Maybe Bobby had kept some kind of gruesome trophies of his kills nearby.

"You're not thinking right," Gabrielle said. "Please just calm down and listen."

"I'm done listening to you!" He lunged toward her and aimed the gun between her eyes. "No more stories. No more lies. This time I'm in charge!"

Not if Kyle had anything to do about it. He raised his weapon, prayed that God would guide his hand and fired through the window, sending glass shattering across the floor. The bullet clipped the man in the shoulder before his finger could even brush the trigger.

He swore in pain. The gun fell from his hand and clattered to the ground. Then he pelted from the cabin and took off running down the mountain.

"Who's there?" Gabrielle called. "Jared?"

But Kyle didn't stop to answer her. He wasn't about to let her attacker escape.

He ran through the woods after the man who had to be Bobby.

"Agent Kyle West of the Mountain Country K-9 Unit!" his voice rose. His partner barked. "Stop! You're under arrest!"

The man was limping and bleeding, and yet

dodging around trees and tumbling over rocks as he practically threw his body down the steep mountainside in a desperate attempt to get away.

Not this time.

Kyle leaped, catching the man by this unwounded shoulder and pulling him down to the ground. For moment they rolled and tumbled down the rocky mountainside, while Rocky ran after them. But it was Kyle who found his footing first.

"Stay down!" he shouted, standing over the wounded man lying at his feet. "You put up an impressive fight. But Bobby Whatever-your-last-name-is, you're now under arrest for kidnapping and murder."

The sound of sirens filled the woods above him. Kyle read the man his rights. When he was done, the man swore. "I'm not Bobby, you idiot."

"Well, whoever you are, I'm arresting you." He hauled the man to his feet and cuffed his hands in front of him as gently as he could, so as to not aggravate his injury. Then he patted him down and found a wallet in his jacket pocket. He pulled out the driver's license. It was from Las Vegas. The photo matched. He read the name. "Dylan Brown. Is that your name?"

"Yeah!" Dylan shouted. "Told you I'm not Bobby! He was a stupid fool who didn't know when to quit!"

Whatever that meant.

"Is Bobby the man you killed in the barn?"

"I didn't kill anyone." Dylan scowled, his single, very pale iris gave his face an unsettlingly uneven look, and Kyle realized that must be why the mask he'd worn to commit his crimes had included a dark mesh that covered his eyes.

"Why did you kidnap Gabrielle?" Kyle demanded. "Why did you attack Ophelia?"

"Because I got tired of being used and treated like a fool. And that's all I'm going to say!"

Kyle looked down at Rocky. *I don't have a clue what to make of any of that. I'm just glad I finally got cuffs on this guy.* His partner growled softly. Did Dylan smell of a fresh death or had Kyle's hunch about trophies been right?

Voices rose from the trees. Backup had arrived. Kyle quickly snapped a photo of the man's face and driver's license and sent them off to Isla with the request she find out whatever she could about him. Then he turned and marched Dylan up the hill as he swore and complained.

Santa Fe PD officers and paramedics met him as he neared the top of the slope.

"This is Dylan Brown from Las Vegas," Kyle said. "He's under arrest for murder and kidnapping. He needs immediate medical attention, for a fresh bullet wound in the shoulder and another in the calf yesterday, which I'm guessing he didn't get medical treatment for. Don't underestimate him. He's tough."

"And I don't need a doctor," Dylan grumbled.

Kyle had no doubt that when they scratched the surface of this man's life they'd find a rough upbringing and very long criminal history.

Suddenly his mind flashed back to the RMK. The Rocky Mountain Killer had murdered three men ten years ago, then another three in the past few months. And like Dylan, Kyle thought there had to some be something tragic behind his cruelty.

Lord, what pain in the RMK's life led him to become the vindictive and taunting killer he is today? Help the MCK9 find him, and please heal the hearts of all those impacted by his crimes.

"Kyle!" Ophelia called. He looked up to see her running toward him. He jogged toward her. Instinctively his arms opened to embrace her. But instead, she stopped a few paces away from him and folded her arms across her chest, and he found himself doing the same.

"Gabrielle just left in an ambulance," she said. "Patricia Gonzales went with her. Gabrielle says that Bobby didn't hurt her beyond slapping and scaring her, and she was just in a hurry to get back to Jared. But she's promised to give Patricia a full and complete statement." She smiled. "I'm so happy and relieved you finally got him."

Kyle frowned.

"Me, too," he said and thanked God for the fact. "But he says his name is not Bobby and he's carrying a Las Vegas driver's license that says he's Dylan Brown."

Ophelia blinked.

"Do you think he lied to Gabrielle about his name being Bobby?" she asked. "Or lied to you about his name being Dylan? Is it possible his ID is fake?"

"No idea," Kyle said. "But he clearly has some kind of history with her and he hates her. Did you notice he had two different colored eyes?"

"Yeah, it's called heterochromia," Ophelia said. "It's very rare in human DNA, impacting less than one percent of the population. It's much more common in animals. It could be heredity or the result of something he was exposed to as a young child."

"My impression is that this criminal hasn't had an easy life," Kyle said, "not that it justifies anything he's done. Thankfully, at this point, putting the case together becomes the prosecutor's job. I'm just glad we caught this guy, he's off the streets, this part of the case is over and I don't have to worry about my little guy and mother having to go stay in a safe house."

But even as he said the words a doubt crossed his mind. What if Dylan hadn't been working alone? Did he have an accomplice? Was it Bobby?

"And I can finally get back to my lab," Ophelia said. "Although I expect that I'm still going to have a wedding to show up at tonight. I don't think anything's going to stop those two from getting married, even if it's a five-minute ceremony."

And if they did, Kyle wouldn't be there. The guy had been caught. He wasn't her pretend wedding date anymore. Rocky barked softly and sniffed the air. Whatever the K-9 was alerting to, it wasn't Dylan.

"Sorry, he's been alerting since we got here," Kyle said. "Even though he's trained to detect bodies, sometimes cadaver dogs will detect something that's touched a corpse, like what was used to transport it recently."

"Well, you should go see what he wants to show you," Ophelia said.

Yeah, he should. And even though he'd finally caught his man, he hoped that whatever Rocky was signaling to would be that final piece of the puzzle that wrapped up the case for good. He turned to Rocky. "Show me."

Rocky barked and started sniffing the ground. The dog took off toward the cabin, which was now swarming with investigators. Kyle followed closely behind. The K-9 led him past the cabin, to a soft mound of earth and rock. The footsteps that surrounded it looked fresh. Rocky woofed confidently and sat in front of it.

"Good job," Kyle said sadly.

He crouched down and pulled the rocks back. It was the body of a young man. This time, the victim's body wasn't wrapped in anything, but just lay there in the shallow grave, under a pile of rocks. He heard Ophelia gasp and looked up to see her standing behind him.

"I thought we were done," she said. "You

caught him. He's in custody where he won't be able to kill ever again."

"I know," Kyle said. Slowly he moved the rocks one by one. "But I guess he managed to kill one more time before we could stop him."

He sat back on his heels. Sadness filled his core as the face came into view.

It was Nolan.

Chapter Eleven

"We have three dead bodies." Kyle slapped the pictures of Chloe, John Doe and Nolan down on the interrogation table in front of Dylan. "Why these three? What do they have in common?"

It had been almost two hours since Rocky had led Kyle to Nolan's body. Nolan, like John Doe and Chloe before him, had taken a single gunshot wound to the chest. The time after that had passed in a blur as he coordinated with the police, crime scene techs and paramedics who'd retrieved the body and documented how it had been found. Once again, Ophelia had slipped off and headed back to town while he was busy doing his job and managing the scene. This time he'd caught her wave goodbye. But there'd been no time alone for a conversation, let alone a hug goodbye.

For all he knew, they'd never be alone like that again.

He'd returned to the same Santa Fe PD station where he'd interviewed Nolan just a few hours earlier. And since then, he'd been sitting in an interrogation room across from Dylan, locked in the same frustrating conversation as it went around in circles.

"I'm not telling you nothing!" Dylan said. Thankfully, both of his injuries had been minor and easy for paramedics to patch up.

Kyle looked down at Nolan's picture. The same man had sat in that very room a few hours earlier, after warning Kyle that someone had placed an explosive in his SUV. Not only had Dylan's fingerprints confirmed his identity, they'd also been found, along with explosive residue, on a bag found where Kyle's vehicle had been parked when the bomb had been planted, confirming Dylan was indeed the man Nolan had seen.

Nolan might've saved Kyle's life. But Kyle had been unable to save his.

"My colleague emailed me your rap sheet," Kyle said and opened the email from Isla on his phone. "You're right, you're Dylan Brown. No known aliases. And you've got a long record for theft, burglary and assault. But no murder, until these three. I'll ask you again, why them?"

Dylan crossed his arms leaned back in the chair. "I'm not a killer."

"Look, you're a muscle for hire," Kyle said. "You do jobs and favors for people. So, my theory is someone asked you to murder these three people, tamper with the gas tank of my vehicle and terrorize both Gabrielle Martinez and Ophelia Clarke. I think that if I hadn't stopped you, you would've killed both Gabrielle and Ophelia. Why? Who has a vendetta against all these people?"

Dylan cursed under his breath and didn't answer.

Lord, how can I be so close to getting an answer and still have nothing?

There was a knock on the door. Rocky's head rose. The K-9's tail started to thump on the floor, letting Kyle know that whoever was on the other side of the door was a friend.

Kyle stood. "I'll give you a moment to think."

Dylan only grunted in response. Kyle and Rocky stepped out into the hallway, where he found Meadow and her K-9 partner, Grace, waiting for him.

"I hear congratulations are in order," she said. "I was told you got your man."

Kyle glanced back through the small, reinforced window at where Dylan still sat at the table. "I know I should feel more relieved. I am certain he's the man behind every violent crime related to this case and yet I'd just feel better if I knew what his motive was."

"And you don't think it's related to the RMK?" Meadow asked.

"No." Kyle shook his head. He knew he should be relieved that the criminal he'd been chasing was finally off the street. But still it felt like something was missing. He quickly ran Meadow through all of the details of the case as he knew them so far, starting with the moment Ophelia heard gunshots.

"What if Dylan is in love with Gabrielle?" Meadow asked. "Wasn't that your original theory? So it turns out his name is Dylan and not Bobby, but it could be that simple. He came to the wedding looking to kill Jared but shot John Doe by mistake. He killed Chloe for trying to warn Ophelia that he was coming to stop the wedding and attacked you and Ophelia for trying to investigate the case. Finally, he killed

Nolan in revenge for telling you about the fact that he tampered with the SUV. It all fits."

"It's too simple." Ophelia's words from earlier brushed the back of my mind. *"And in my experience most things are more complicated than that."*

"Except who's Bobby?" Kyle said, "And why did an unidentified blond man who looked like the groom get lured to the barn where the reception was taking place on the day before the wedding?"

It was like a sweater that only looked neat and tidy until someone pulled on one the loose threads and then the whole thing unraveled.

"I don't know," Meadow admitted. "By the way, I ran into Ophelia in the waiting room. She was just dropping by on the way to the wedding, and she asked me to give you this."

She picked up something soft and white off a chair and handed it to him. It was his short-sleeved shirt that Ophelia had borrowed. Without even thinking, he held it close to his face and smelled in the scent of her.

The fact that she'd chosen to drop it off at the police station where he was working instead of his home told him everything he needed to know—their time working closely together was well and truly over. They wouldn't be going for long nighttime walks or sharing coffee together in the morning. There'd never again be a reason for them to suddenly throw their arms around each other, or for their lips to unexpectedly meet in a kiss. And that was how he wanted it, right? Because he'd decided he wasn't looking for a relationship and obviously neither was she.

Meadow looked at him curiously and he wondered if she'd caught him cradling the shirt.

"I found out why your mother has been going to the pharmacy so often," she said. "Turns out she has a crush on the pharmacist. I met him earlier today when we popped in to buy a few overnight things, when we were still thinking that we'd have to go to the safe house. He's a nice guy. He's a widower her age, and a man of faith. I think she wants to date him but is worried about how you'll react."

"That's ridiculous." Kyle crossed his arms.

"Is it?" Meadow said. "Sorry if this is too personal, but your mom also mentioned that your father was bad news. She told me about the whole dating site debacle, and my impression was that she thought that maybe if you started dating you'd be okay with her starting a new relationship, too."

Really? Was his mother holding herself back because of him?

"I don't have a problem with my mom starting a new life," Kyle said. "I'm not going to start dating, because I'm worried for Brody and need to focus on being his father. I can't risk starting a relationship that might fail or getting Brody attached to someone who might leave our lives. What if I fall in love and marry someone, and then it doesn't work out?"

And what about his own heart? All this time Kyle had kept telling himself he was choosing to be single for fear of hurting Brody or putting him through the turmoil that Kyle had grown up in. But the way his heart beat painfully even now at the memory of just how terrified he'd been when Ophelia was in danger made him realize that maybe Brody wasn't the only who he was trying to save from pain.

"I guess that's a choice you need to make," Meadow said. "I had to walk away from someone I loved once. I didn't have a choice and it broke my heart." She glanced down at the shirt Kyle was still holding in his hands. "Look, I only just met Ophelia today and already it's clear to me how much you two care about each other. And that's rare. So you're just going to have to decide if that's a risk you're willing to take."

The sun dipped low in the New Mexico sky, sending pink and gold streaks across the horizon. As Ophelia walked down the path to Cherish Ranch's outdoor wedding chapel, dark purple shadows spread out beneath her feet. Truth was, she wasn't sure what to think about the fact that Jared and Gabrielle were still getting married, although with a much smaller celebration than originally planned.

Then again, if she had the opportunity to marry a man whom she loved with her whole heart, would she let anything stand in her way?

The outdoor chapel itself was simple and beautiful, with rows of chairs overlooking the glorious vista and a simple archway of wooden branches stretching up to the sky.

She sat in the back row, in her favorite turquoise dress and sandals. Ophelia couldn't remember ever seeing a more romantic scene or feeling such a depth of sadness inside her own heart. She closed her eyes and tried to settle her thoughts, only to find Kyle's handsome face fill her mind.

Lord, I've never liked a man as much as I like

Kyle. He's not just handsome, funny, kind and brave. He likes the things about me that I like about my-self. I want a man like him by my side. And yet, I looked him in the eyes and told him I could never let it happen. Have I been so convinced that Your plan for me doesn't include that kind of happiness that I closed my heart?

"Oh, I'm so glad you're here, dear," Great-Aunt Evelyn's voice cut through her prayers. Ophelia opened her eyes as her aunt slid into the chair beside her, in a resplendent yellow dress that somehow reminded her of baby ducks without looking the slightest bit cutesy.

"I think you're meant to sit in the front row," Ophelia said.

"I know, I just wanted to sit with you." Ev-elyn's delicate hand patted Ophelia's affection-ately, and Ophelia realized for the first time just how frail her great-aunt had gotten. "This whole wedding thing doesn't feel right and it never really has. You know I don't like being negative and I promised my grandson I wouldn't question his decisions, but maybe I was wrong to support this wedding. What do you think?"

She fixed her eyes on Ophelia's face. They were the same shade of blue as hers. And Oph-elia realized this might actually be the first time her great-aunt had asked her opinion about something significant.

"I think Jared really loves Gabrielle and will stop at nothing to marry her," Ophelia said.

"I can understand loving someone so much you want to marry them immediately," Evelyn said, "even in the face of tragedy. I remember when I was a little girl hearing stories about people lining up at the church to get married days before their fella shipped off to the war. My mama said when you loved somebody you don't let the bad things in life stop you from the good ones."

Maybe like eating scrambled eggs in the morning, Ophelia thought, and playing trucks with Brody in the sandbox.

"I never had a wedding," Evelyn added, almost wistfully. "I always wanted one, but we didn't have the money. The business was struggling and it was either pay the rent or get married. So we just eloped one night and then my mom made us chicken dinner. I didn't even have a dress."

Ophelia's eyes widened. "But what about all those beautiful wedding pictures you have up on the wall?"

"Oh, we just took those in the park behind

the church three years later, because we'd never gotten pictures and we'd been given this beautiful set of frames. I was actually four months' pregnant with Jared's dad by then. I just hid the little bump behind my bouquet."

"You never told me any of that," Ophelia said.

Ophelia searched her seventy-four-year-old great-aunt's face and realized that she'd never heard a story about a time they hadn't been well off.

"That sounds really lovely," Ophelia said. "I thought if I ever got married you'd be disappointed if I didn't do a big wedding like Jared."

"Oh, you do what's right for you." Evelyn patted her hand. "It's not for me to tell you what to do. Or judge. I just give you my best advice and leave it up to you."

Ophelia hid a smile. She couldn't imagine her great-aunt was about to start keeping her opinions to herself, especially if Ophelia ever did end up having the unexpected blessing of finding a man to marry her. But it was kind of nice to know that was the kind of person Evelyn wanted to be.

"I mean, I did my best to keep my mouth shut about this whole wedding mess and keep writing checks every time Jared said he needed me to." Evelyn waved her hands in the air. "But now I'm beginning to think I should've pushed back instead of just going ahead and paying for all this."

"What do you mean you paid for all this?" Ophelia asked. "You paid for the wedding? I thought the bride's family pays for the wedding. Or the couple themselves."

And wasn't Gabrielle's family supposed to be unbelievably wealthy?

"Oh, there as some problem with the international payments," Evelyn said, "and they said they were going to go to my bank with me and sort it all out when they got here." But then Gabrielle's parents had never showed up. Ophelia thought back to how stressed her great-aunt had been about everything when she'd asked Ophelia to step in as a bridesmaid. "Jared just kept calling me up and saying that Gabrielle was upset, and they needed money for this and money for that. The wedding venue. Dresses. Catering. A private jet to whisk them off to Mexico for their honeymoon. I don't even know where it all went."

Ophelia's mouth went dry.

"Auntie." Ophelia gently reached for Evelyn's

and took it in both of hers. "How much money have you given Jared and Gabrielle?"

"Oh, I don't know." Evelyn didn't meet her eyes and shrugged. "Jared would just give me these different bank accounts to wire money to. Gabrielle always said her parents would pay me back."

But Gabrielle's parents were conveniently overseas and had never materialized. For all she knew, Gabrielle had been lying about her parents the whole time and they never intended to pay Evelyn back a single cent. The taste in Ophelia's mouth turned bitter. "It was a lot of money, wasn't it? More than you could afford to give."

Now she could actually see tears building in the corner of her great-aunt's eyes. Ophelia's heart ached. She enveloped her great-aunt in her arms and hugged her.

"You know I love you, right?" Ophelia asked. "I know we don't always agree on everything. And we don't always like the words each other says. But I love you, you matter to me, and I'm sorry that Jared and Gabrielle were taking advantage of you."

For a long moment her great-aunt hugged her back and didn't say anything. Then she pulled away and stood.

"I'm fine." Evelyn patted Ophelia on the shoulder. "You are sweet and I am so thankful to have a great-niece like you. Now I'm just going to go check in and see what's keeping Jared and Gabrielle so long. They left the hotel before I did and I can't believe they haven't arrived yet."

Evelyn started down the path toward the main lodge. The toes of Ophelia's sandals tapped against the ground as she fought the urge to rush to the lodge, look for Jared herself and ask him how he could possibly be so selfish as to take advantage of his grandmother like that. She had half a mind to take her great-aunt to the bank and see what she could do to help her get her money back. Not to mention asking the ranch for receipts to see just how much of her money really went to the wedding.

Without even pausing to think about why, she pulled out her phone and called Kyle.

The phone rang twice, then clicked.

"Hey, Kyle, it's Ophelia. I don't know if this has anything to do with anything but I just found out that Gabrielle and Jared have been taking advantage of my great-aunt and getting her to pay for everything—"

"Hello, you've reached Agent Kyle West of

the Mountain Country K-9 Task Force." His voice came down the line crisp, professional and slightly tinny. "Please leave your message at the tone."

She hung up. What had she been thinking? The masked man had been arrested. The case was over. She couldn't just call Kyle on a whim anymore to offload about what her family was doing and how she felt about it. Somehow in just twenty-four hours they'd gone from being colleagues who'd barely spoken, to a professional pair that worked together, to friends, and then what? To something else entirely that she didn't yet have the courage to try to put into words.

It was only then that she noticed a red dot on the corner of the screen telling her that she'd missed a call. She clicked on it hoping it was Kyle.

It was Isla.

Ophelia looked around. It didn't look like the wedding was about to start anytime soon. She stood up, walked down the path toward the parking lot and dialed Isla's number. She answered before it had even rung once. "Hey, Ophelia! Aren't you supposed to be at a wedding right now?"

"I am, but the bride and groom are running late," she said. "I missed a call from you?"

"You did!" She could hear Isla smiling down the phone. "I tracked down the cuff link to the jewelry store where it was bought and I think I found our John Doe."

"Really?" Now, that was good news. "Who is he?"

"Robert Wesley Norrs, professional gambler and online investor, last seen in Las Vegas a week ago," Isla said. "And yes, I was able to get a visual match to our John Doe from the jewelry store surveillance cameras."

"Robert as in Bobby," Ophelia said.

"I've got a picture," Isla said. "Want me to send it through?"

"Absolutely." A second later her phone dinged and Ophelia looked down to see a handsome blond man with arrogant eyes. "That's our John Doe. He's the man who was shot in the barn yesterday. Have you shown this to Kyle yet?"

"I left a message on his phone," Isla said, "but he didn't call me back. But get this, last year Robert came into the Las Vegas jewelry store with his fiancée, Lisette Austin. He bought her a huge diamond ring as well as the pair of cuff links for him. She said it was to celebrate their engagement. From what I could glean from his social media, Lisette dumped Robert and left town after a gambling loss."

"Who's Lisette Austin, though?" Ophelia said. "I've never heard of her."

"That's because she doesn't exist," Isla said. "At least not under that name. A woman matching her description is suspected of romancing and even marrying men under fake identities and robbing them blind in Connecticut, Texas, Florida and Vermont. Sometimes she's even suspected of killing them. But they've never managed to track down who she really is or pin down her identity. It's all conjecture. No proof."

Ophelia's phone pinged. Then a black-and-white picture appeared on the screen of a woman with long blond hair. Ophelia's mouth gaped. Despite the different hair color, the face was clear. "That's my cousin's fiancée, Gabrielle."

Isla gasped. "Are you sure?"

"Definitely." And now she was pretty certain wherever Jared and "Gabrielle" were now, they weren't about to show up here to get married. No wonder "Gabrielle" hadn't wanted police poking around and had been in such a hurry to marry Jared.

"According to the files I can read on her, she's a pretty talented manipulator," Isla said. "She zeroes in on wealthy and lonely men, convinces them that she's in love with them and then bleeds them dry. Sometimes she even cons their family members out of money."

Like Evelyn. Ophelia thought back to all their interactions with Gabrielle in the past twenty-four hours. The way Gabrielle would cling to Ophelia like they were best buddies, or smile one moment and cry theatrically. "It was like she was always trying to figure out what button to push to make me like her and could never quite find the right one. How many ex-husbands is she suspected of killing?"

"Four," Isla said. "Plus, quite a few she just robbed."

"Then either way my cousin is in trouble," Ophelia said.

"Again, I've got to stress that police have never successfully pegged anything on this woman," Isla said. "There's not even a single warrant out anywhere for her arrest. She's too slippery to be charged with anything, and all we have are theories."

And Ophelia didn't peddle in theories. Only facts. And the fact was there wasn't a single scrap of DNA, fingerprint evidence or anything else sitting back at the forensic laboratory that pointed to Gabrielle committing a crime, let alone killing anyone.

Lord, please help me find the facts I need to protect my cousin and stop her from hurting anyone else.

"My great-aunt said they were taking a private jet to Mexico for their honeymoon," she said. "If they disappear into Mexico, there's any number of ways she could kill my cousin and vanish."

She heard the sound of Isla typing quickly. Ophelia could feel all the evidence she'd gathered in the past twenty-four hours finally clicking together in her mind.

So Gabrielle was a con artist who romanced men for their money. She got engaged to Robert Willian Norrs, aka RWN, aka Bobby. Then she moved on to Jared. But then Bobby wasn't about to let her go so easily. He started stalking her and came to Santa Fe to stop the wedding. And then what? Bobby was murdered. How did she prove Gabrielle had anything to do with Bobby's, Chloe's and Nolan's deaths?

Bobby could've exposed Gabrielle as a con artist. Chloe had talked to Bobby and tried to share her concerns with Ophelia. Nolan had given Gabrielle an alibi for the time of Bobby's murder and then warned Kyle of the bomb Dylan had planted in his car.

So they were all liabilities. But it was still all circumstantial.

And how did Dylan fit into this? He definitely didn't fit the type Gabrielle would pursue romantically.

"Okay, I've found them," Isla said. "Gabrielle and Jared are at the Santa Fe Airport now, scheduled to fly to Tijuana. I'm going to alert officials not to let them on the plane. But they'll only be able to delay them. They won't be able to stop them from just walking out of the airport and vanishing."

"I'm heading there now," Ophelia said. She climbed into her car and plugged her phone into the vehicle's hands-free speaker. "Hopefully, they can delay Jared long enough for me to get there and try to talk to him. My cousin is so blindly in love he's not going to believe anything they tell him. But maybe if I can get him alone, I can talk some sense into him."

"Tell him he's not the first person she's fooled," Isla said.

"I don't think that's going to help," Ophelia said. The problem with being the kind of man who just arrogantly assumed everyone was going to do what he wanted was he wouldn't accept he'd been duped by a con woman. "I'm going to hang up and try Kyle again. In the meantime, send me everything you can on Gabrielle for now."

"Will do," Isla said. "Police still don't know her real identity, but there are a lot of photos of her with different hair and eye colors."

They ended the call and the technical analyst's final two words continued to ring in Ophelia's mind. *Eye color. Eye color.* What was her mind trying to tell her or remind her of?

Ophelia pulled out of the parking lot and drove down the twisting mountain road. The Santa Fe Airport was on the outskirts of town. If she stuck to back roads she could be there in fifteen minutes, give or take. She dialed Kyle's number. But again, it went through to voice mail. All right, so he must still be in interrogation.

Now what? Just how brave could she be? Just how certain was she that she was right? She gritted her teeth and dialed Detective Patricia Gonzales directly.

"Gonzales." The detective's voice was on the line in a moment.

"Hi, it's CSI Ophelia Clarke," she said. "I'm so sorry to do this, but I know Kyle West is in the police station right now and I have urgent information for the case and need to talk to him immediately."

"Understood," she said.

The phone went silent as Ophelia was put on hold. She drove and prayed. Then she heard a new call beginning to ring on her phone. It was Kyle.

Thank You, God.

She ended the call with Patricia and answered.

"Ophelia, hi!" Kyle sounded flustered. "Someone just knocked on the door of my interrogation room and said it was an emergency. I've been going around in circles with Dylan for hours. Whatever he's hiding, he's not about to crack."

"Isla has identified our John Doe as a gambler from Las Vegas called Robert Wesley Norrs," she said quickly. The sky was growing darker around her. "So that's our Bobby. He was engaged to marry Gabrielle, who at the time was going by the name Lisette. Gabrielle was there when he bought the cuff links to celebrate their engagement. Maybe he brought them to return to her—"

"Or maybe she demanded them back," Kyle said. She could practically hear the wheels in his head turning.

"Gabrielle is a con woman with a history of crossing the country, changing her name and look, romancing men and robbing them," Ophelia said. "She's even suspected of killing a few."

Kyle sucked a breath.

"Turns out she got Jared to milk my great-aunt for a whole lot of money," she went on. "She and Jared are supposed to hop a plane to Tijuana, and Isla's asked police to delay them."

She quickly outlined her theory from how Gabrielle had conned multiple men under various identities, set her sights on Jared in the hotel, convinced him to marry her and take advantage of Evelyn's generous nature to weasel her out of money. But then her last target, Bobby, hadn't wanted to give up on her easily and tracked her down. Maybe she'd even led him on romantically while being engaged to Jared, in order to con more money of out him. Bobby had said something to Chloe, which made Gabrielle's roommate a liability. Nolan was Gabrielle's alibi for the time of Bobby's murder.

Bobby, Chloe and Nolan had all been liabilities, who knew something about Gabrielle that could've thwarted her scheme.

She switched her headlights on as the last sliver of the sun vanished beyond the horizon.

"But I don't have evidence," she said, "and we need evidence. Otherwise, I won't be able to convince Jared not to trust her. He'll never believe me. Police have no reason to detain them indefinitely. And sooner or later he'll just take off with Gabrielle, she'll kill him and I'll never see him alive again."

She could hear Kyle praying quietly down the line. She joined in his prayers.

Lord, help me trust in the work I do and the skills I've honed that You've given me. I'm used to noticing the little things. Sometimes the smallest thing is the key to catching a serial killer.

"Gabrielle was only wearing one contact yesterday," Ophelia said suddenly. "What if she doesn't need them for her eyesight but only to disguise her eye color. And if she was only wearing one—"

"She might have the same DNA condition as Dylan," Kyle said.

"Heterochromia," Ophelia said. "Which means he might not only be her accomplice, but also her brother."

"Which might explain why he won't turn on her," Kyle said, "and also what I need to get him to crack." He whistled. "You're incredible, Ophelia? You know that?"

Then before she could reply she heard the sound of a door opening and closing again, a chair scraping and Kyle setting the phone down on the table, without ending the call.

"I'm still not talking," Dylan said.

"It doesn't matter if you talk or not," Kyle said. "Because we know that Gabrielle is your sister. She's been conning men into marrying her, robbing them and even killing a few. And I expect she's going to pin it all on you, cut a sweet little deal with prosecutors and tell them that you're the one who's been making her do it. Who do you think a jury's going to believe? Your sister or you?"

Silence crackled on the line. Ophelia held her breath and prayed that Kyle's bluff would work. She could see the airport in the distance now, the beautiful adobe orange rectangles and squares, looking like something built from children's blocks.

Lord, please help me get through to Jared. Protect my heart and mind.

"My sister's a liar!" Dylan's voice shouted

down the phone. "Her name isn't even Gabrielle. It's Dorothy Brown. I had nothing to do with all her nonsense and scams. She just called me because she needed help with this Bobby person. She wanted me to meet him in the barn, rough him up a bit and convince him to leave her alone. But apparently she got there first, they started fighting and he threw a pair of cuff links at her. Anyway, she lost it. So, when I got there turns out she's already killed him and begs me to make it look like she didn't do it. I've been cleaning up her mess ever since. Take care of this person, take care of that or that person, I've had enough of her. Now get me a lawyer! I want to cut a deal!"

Prayers of thanksgiving filled Ophelia's heart. Now police had enough to arrest Gabrielle, or Dorothy or whatever her name was, and protect her from hurting Jared or anyone else ever again. It would still be a matter of whom a jury believed and a testimony wasn't the same as DNA evidence, but it was a good start and she was confident they'd get what they needed to put her away for good.

She heard Kyle stepping out of the interrogation room and informing someone that Dylan had requested a lawyer and that a warrant needed to be issued for Dorothy Brown aka Gabrielle Martinez.

The airport grew closer. A construction vehicle with reflective triangular stickers was parked at the side of the road. A woman with long blond and curly hair, reflective sunglasses and bright orange vest stepped in front of Ophelia's vehicle and held up a stop sign.

Ophelia slowed to a stop and rolled the window down.

"You gotta turn back!" The woman strode over to Ophelia's car. "We've got a downed power line ahead."

Ophelia glanced at the road ahead. She didn't see any downed power lines.

Then she felt something sharp jab into her side. A quick and painful blast of electricity shot through her limbs. She cried out in pain.

"Ophelia!" Kyle's voice yelled down the phone line and filled the car.

Ophelia whimpered from the lingering pain and she glanced in disbelief at the woman who'd just jabbed a stun gun into her side.

It was Gabrielle.

"Can you hear me, Agent West?" Gabrielle leaned into the car. Her voice was cold, calculating and stripped of all the fake sweetness that had once dripped from it like honey. "Nice try getting someone to delay my flight and separate me and Jared. You think I didn't know how to slip out a window? But now I have Ophelia and you tell Evelyn that if she ever wants to see her again, she's got twenty-four hours to wire me three million dollars. I'm getting out of this state, one way or another, and if I so much as see a police car or helicopter, Ophelia dies."

Chapter Twelve

"Don't you hurt her!" Kyle shouted down the phone line, even as he heard Gabrielle ordering Ophelia to end the call and toss the phone. The phone clattered.

His stomach wrenched. Rocky whined as if sensing his fear.

"What's going on?" Meadow asked. He looked up to see the US marshal and Grace running down the hallway toward him. "Your voice reverberated all the way to the lobby."

"Ophelia's been kidnapped by a serial killer," he said. "It was the bride all along. She says if she even sees a cop car or helicopter, she'll kill her."

"Where are they?" Meadow asked.

"They just left the airport," he said. "I don't know where they're heading."

"Let's go," Meadow turned sharply and ran for the side door, her K-9 partner at her side.

"Thankfully I flew in and my Jeep's a rental without any police marking. You can fill me in as we go." She tossed him her keys. "You drive, I don't know Santa Fe."

Seconds later they were in the vehicle speeding down the highway. Meadow was in the passenger seat and on the phone with dispatch, putting law enforcement across the state on the lookout for Gabrielle and Ophelia, and filling in the Santa Fe State Police's emergency response unit on the details of the kidnapping and ransom demands, so a crisis response officer could be in touch with Evelyn. Rocky and Grace sat at attention beside each other in the back seat. Kyle's fingers tightened on the steering wheel. He glanced to where he'd plugged his cell phone into the hands-free. The call still hadn't ended. By the sound of things, the phone was now hidden somewhere in Ophelia's back seat, live but on mute, like she'd let him listen in to her conversation with Jared hours before.

Minutes ticked past. The airport loomed ahead in the distance, but there was no sign of Ophelia's car anywhere. But if Ophelia had hoped to be able to give Kyle directions on where she was and how to find her, it wasn't working. Instead, tense silence spread down the line, punctuated only by cryptic directions from Gabrielle to Ophelia like "turn here," "there" and "stop fidgeting."

Help me, Lord, please give me the information I need to find her.

He focused his mind and listened, knowing that she'd be trying to communicate with him. It was just up to him to decipher the clues. A comment Ophelia made about the sun visor told him they were going south. Another about the lack of stop signs told him they were heading into the desert. The sound of the engine slowing meant they were slowing to a stop.

"Park there," Gabrielle said.

"By the sandstone caves?" Ophelia said.

But there were hundreds of caves spread like labyrinths across Santa Fe. Which one was she taking her to? Then he heard a rhythmic tapping down the phone line as if Ophelia was drumming her fingers on the steering wheel. Long taps, short taps, deliberate and rhythmic.

It was Morse code. She was giving him the GPS coordinates of where she was.

Hope sprang in his chest.

Hang on, Ophelia, I'm coming for you.

Then he heard a car door open. "What's this?" Gabrielle's voice was suddenly loud down the line as he heard her pick up the phone off the floor. Then he heard the sound of the phone smash against something hard. The call went dead.

He glanced at Meadow.

Worry filled her green eyes. "It's going to be okay. We'll find her."

He hoped so. He plugged the GPS coordinates he thought he'd heard Ophelia tapping out into his phone. A blue dot appeared on the screen, eight miles away to the southwest. He drove toward it, explaining to Meadow as he went what he thought Ophelia had signaled to him.

Desert plains spread out cold and dark in front of his headlights, punctuated by buttes and sandstone outcroppings. A tapestry of bright stars appeared above in the dark sky. He just passed the dot on the screen when he saw Ophelia's car, abandoned and alone at the side of the road.

He pulled over and they leaped out. Meadow grabbed a flashlight from the trunk and started scanning the ground, looking for footprints. Rocky sniffed the air and growled. Pain surged through Kyle's heart. His partner smelled death.

Was he too late? Was Ophelia already gone?

Please Lord, Ophelia can't be dead. She's incredible, smart, caring, beautiful and kind. She's the only woman I've ever been able to imagine spending the rest of my life with and I've just found her. Please, I can't lose her now.

He ran his hand over the dog's side. "Show me," he said softly.

Kyle barked and sniffed the ground, walking this way and that. Then the dog woofed in frustration. Whatever Rocky smelled, it wasn't strong enough to track.

"Do you still have the shirt Ophelia wore?" Meadow said. "I can get Grace to track it."

He pulled it from his jacket pocket and handed it to her. "She only wore it a few hours. Do you think the scent is strong enough?"

In the glow of the flashlight he saw Meadow look down confidently at her K-9 partner. "For Grace? Absolutely."

Kyle stood back and watched as Meadow summoned Grace to her side, instructed her to sniff the shirt Ophelia had worn and track the scent. The vizsla howled and took off running, with Meadow at her side. Kyle and Rocky followed just a few steps behind, as the dog darted this way and that through the towering maze of stone and rock that rose out of the desert.

A cave loomed ahead, like a large mouth in the earth ready to swallow them whole. Rocky barked. Grace howled. The scents both dogs could detect ended in there. The dogs plunged through the opening and into the cave. Meadow and Kyle were on their heels. Her flashlight beams bounced off the walls.

Then he saw them. Ophelia and Gabrielle were down on the ground, battling over a gun. Gabrielle was striking out against Ophelia with all she had, hitting and punching her like a fury. But courage shone brightly in Ophelia's eyes, and he knew she wasn't about to give up easily.

"Down on the ground!" Kyle shouted. "Dorothy Brown, aka Gabrielle Martinez, you're under arrest for murder and kidnapping."

Gabrielle stumbled back. He watched as her calculating eyes glanced from Kyle to Meadow, and suddenly tears sprang to her eyes.

"You've got to help me!" Gabrielle whimpered and ran toward Meadow. "Ophelia kidnapped me and Kyle is a corrupt cop. They've set me up and they're going to kill me."

"Don't even try." Meadow snorted and raised her gun. "You can't pull that nonsense with me." She ordered Gabrielle to her knees and handcuffed her.

"They don't have any evidence," Gabrielle protested. "It's my word against theirs and Dylan's. No one's going to believe them."

Kyle ran past her and scooped Ophelia up into his arms, even as she collapsed into him as if the last of her fight had finally left her limbs.

"I knew you'd come." She laid her head against his chest. "And that all I had to do was stay alive until you rescued me."

He cupped her face in his hands. "I'm so glad I found you."

"I never had any doubt you would."

He leaned toward her and brushed a kiss across her forehead as she nestled into the crook of his neck. He wanted to tell her that it felt like he'd spent his whole life looking for her without even knowing it, and now that he'd found her, he didn't ever want to let her go.

But before he could even find the words to say, he heard Rocky bark. He turned. The dog was pawing at a duffel bag that lay up against a cave wall.

Ophelia pulled out of his arms. "What did he find?"

"I don't know." Kyle took his phone from his pocket and used it as a flashlight as he walked over to the bag and carefully undid the zipper. Trinkets fell out and clattered on the floor. There was RWN's matching cuff link, the missing piece of Chloe's broken locket, plus an assortment of other rings, necklaces and cuff links, as well as clothing, bundles of cash and multiple driver's licenses and passports.

"It looks like she kept souvenirs of her victims." He sat back on his heels and glanced at Ophelia. "Enough to keep your lab busy for a few days."

He may not have caught the Rocky Mountain Killer, but there was enough evidence in this bag to put a serial killer away for a long time. But as his eyes lingered on Ophelia's face, there was still one question ringing in his heart that he couldn't answer.

Now what?

"See 'oats!" Brody requested loudly and tugged on Ophelia's hand. "Pat now!"

She smiled and looked down at him as they crossed the Cherish Ranch parking lot, feeling a special kind of joy she'd never known before filling her heart. It had been two days since Gabrielle, aka Dorothy, and her brother, Dylan, were arrested and charged with multiple murders, and the manager of Cherish Ranch had agreed to make a meeting room available for investigators to brief ranch staff, Jared and Gabrielle's wedding guests, and select members of the press about the state of the investigation. Ophelia and Kyle had promised to take Brody to the petting zoo after the meeting, along with Alice and her new pharmacist friend. The toddler had no desire to wait.

"We will take Ophelia to see the goats, I promise, buddy," Kyle said. He reached down and ruffled the toddler's hair. "Ophelia and I just have to talk to some people first. If you go with Grandma to the kitchen, I hear the chef has made some special cookies."

Brody hesitated. Then nodded.

"Okay," he said.

He dropped Ophelia's hand, patted Rocky on the head, hugged Ophelia's leg tightly and ran toward Alice. He then asked her to pick him up, despite the fact that she was already holding Taffy in her arms.

Ophelia laughed. "I wish I had his energy."

"Don't we all?" Kyle said. Kyle, Ophelia and Rocky watched as the others disappeared though the door to the kitchen. Then he turned to her. "How are you feeling about the briefing?"

"Nervous," she said. "Jared is still refusing to

talk to me. He can't believe that the woman he thought he loved was conning him. Thankfully, when police pulled him and Gabrielle aside at the airport, she realized the jig was up, stole a construction vehicle and bailed, leaving Jared with nothing but an empty bank account and a bruised ego. Could've been a lot worse."

"Yeah, but it still has to be a pretty big blow to his ego," Kyle said, "especially for the kind of person who doesn't ever consider he could be wrong."

"Yeah." Ophelia nodded. Her eyes searched the blue sky above. The sound of music floated through the flowering hedges. Someone was having a party in the courtyard. "At least he's agreed to be here today and listen. That's all I can ask."

The briefing was in a small dining room just off the lobby. Sure enough, Jared was there sitting in the back row, beside Evelyn. She also spotted all the bridesmaids and groomsmen and almost every guest she'd seen at the reception dinner, along with multiple other faces she didn't recognize. Apparently people who'd known Gabrielle had traveled there from Albuquerque, Las Vegas and beyond.

Patricia spoke first, welcoming them all, and

then introduced Kyle and Ophelia as the key investigators who'd solved the case.

Kyle quickly went over the basic facts of the case, including Gabrielle's long history of conning people. Dylan had struck a deal with prosecutors and pleaded guilty to helping Gabrielle dispose of Chloe's and Nolan's bodies, tampering with Kyle's vehicle and shooting into the barn. But he said Gabrielle had faked her own kidnapping to con Jared out of more money and that it was Gabrielle who'd fired the fatal shots into Bobby's, Chloe's and Nolan's chests. He claimed he'd only tried to kidnap Ophelia to hold her somewhere until Gabrielle was able to slip out of the hotel unnoticed and kill her herself. Police had since recovered the gun used in all three murders, with her fingerprints on it. As for threatening his sister at gunpoint in the cabin, Dylan claimed he was just looking for the payout she'd promised him.

In a twist that perhaps shouldn't have surprised Ophelia, Gabrielle had confessed as well, no doubt counting on her ability to charm investigators as she'd duped others in the past. In Gabrielle's version of the story, she'd been forced to keep changing her name and moving around the country to escape a long string of bad relationships. She made Bobby out to be a villain who'd discovered her multiple IDs, tried to blackmail her into getting back together with him, and when she'd refused, Bobby had gone to Chloe and convinced her that Gabrielle was a criminal. In her telling, killing Bobby had been an act of self-defense and she'd had no choice but to ask Dylan to kill Chloe. As for Nolan, he'd threatened to tell police that he'd lied when he'd given her an alibi for the time of John Doe's murder.

Kyle was sure neither sibling had told the full truth about their crimes, motives or involvements. But thankfully, they were behind bars now and due to the ongoing, diligent work of law enforcement and the crime lab, they were going to stay there for the rest of their lives.

"I want everyone to know," Kyle said, "that this case would not have been solved without the help of CSI Ophelia Clarke." His voice rose as he looked over the group. Was it her imagination or did his eyes alight specifically on her great-aunt as he spoke? "There's an unfortunate habit some people have of overlooking the people in the background and only focusing on the people running around with the badge and gun. But CSI Clarke is by far the most dedicated and talented crime scene investigator that I have ever worked with. Countless lives have been saved because of her work and the work of people like her." He looked down at her and Ophelia felt a flush rise to her cheeks as he fixed his dark, handsome eyes on her face. "And I mean it when I say, there's nobody else on the planet I'd rather have been partnered with."

Then he turned back to the gathered group.

"I urge you all to focus on the bright side wherever you can find it," Kyle said. "I won't sugarcoat it. This was a grim case and a very sad story. I wish I could say it had a happy ending. But I think we can be thankful for all the hard work the Santa Fe PD, the Mountain Country K-9 Task Force and Crime Scene Unit put into solving it, and all of you who answered questions and helped in the investigation."

He handed the microphone back to Patricia, who started to brief them on what they could expect to happen next with the case. As Kyle stepped back beside Ophelia, she felt his hand brush her arm. "Let's go for a quick walk, before she opens the floor and people start trying to ask us questions."

"Good idea."

His hand slid down her arm and his fingers linked with hers. Together they slipped out of the back door, with Rocky by their side and back out into the sunshine. There they followed the path through the flowers, toward where the sounds of celebration still rose from the courtyard.

It was a wedding, she realized as they drew closer. Much more modest than what Gabrielle and Jared had planned, but boisterous and full of laughter, as young people and old, from babies to seniors, hugged and celebrated.

They stopped at a rustic bench, not far from the one where she'd sat with Gabrielle just days before. Kyle and Ophelia sat side by side, still holding hands, and with Rocky stretched out of their feet. For a while they just watched the happiness unfolding before them.

"That's what I'd want for my wedding," Kyle said after a long moment. "Nothing expensive or fancy. Just celebrating with people who love me and each other."

"Sounds perfect," Ophelia said. She looked down at their linked hands. His thumb ran gently over her skin. "Do you really believe this story doesn't have a happy ending?"

"This case?" Kyle said. "No. But maybe it can have a happy beginning. Look, I still don't know how you and I are going to make time to get to know each other better, in the middle of everything that's going on in our lives. But how did I put it when we thought I might be running into gunfire? I'm going to stand up, do what I know is right, and trust God to keep us safe and make it all right in the end."

She thought of what Evelyn had said about people lining up at the church to get married on the eve of being shipped off to war because they weren't about to let the hard things in life stop them from the good ones.

"Maybe this isn't the timing I'd have chosen," Kyle said. "But you are the only person I can ever imagine picking to spend my life with. I admired you before we'd even met and now that I know you, you're even more stunning on the inside than you are on the outside." He ran his free hand along her cheek. "I'm falling in love with you and I can't imagine ever letting you go."

A sudden cheer rose from the wedding party and Ophelia looked up to see something flying through the air toward her, over a sea of outstretched hands. Instinctively she pulled away from Kyle and stood. Her arms opened as a huge bouquet of roses and ribbons landed in her hands.

"I think I just caught a wedding bouquet."

Faces from the crowd turned toward her as people laughed, clapped and cheered.

"I think they're waiting for me to do this," Kyle said. He slid off the bench and crouched down on one knee. Rocky cocked his head and watched. Kyle took Ophelia's hand. "I know we've only really known each other a few days, but I have all the evidence I need to know you're the treasure I've secretly been searching for my whole life. I know juggling the busyness of our lives won't be easy. But I have faith that we'll work it out one day at a time together—morning by morning, meal by meal and case by case. And I'd much rather fight to build an amazing life together, than face another day without you by my side. So would you please have dinner with me tonight, go to the park with Brody and me tomorrow, and when we're both ready, will you be please marry me and become by wife?"

Happy tears filled her eyes. "I will."

"I love you, Ophelia."

"I love you, too."

Then his arms went around her waist, she slid her free arm around his neck and their lips met in a kiss that promised a lifetime of joy to come.

★ ★ ★ ★ ★

Don't miss the stories in this mini series!

MOUNTAIN COUNTRY K-9 UNIT

Crime Scene Secrets
MAGGIE K. BLACK
June 2024

Montana Abduction Rescue
JODIE BAILEY
July 2024

Trail Of Threats
JESSICA R. PATCH
August 2024

MILLS & BOON

Widerness Witness Survival

Connie Queen

MILLS & BOON

Connie Queen has spent her life in Texas, where she met and married her high school sweetheart. Together they've raised eight children and are enjoying their grandchildren. Today, as an empty nester, Connie lives with her husband and her Great Dane, Nash, and is working on her next suspense novel.

Visit the Author Profile page
at millsandboon.com.au

And whoso shall receive one such little child
in my name receiveth me.

—*Matthew* 18:5

DEDICATION

To my wonderful partner in crime, Sharee Stover,
who joins me every day to write. For all the
that's-not-how-that-works and the "unique" ways
of answering the what-ifs, I thank you.
You're a great friend and make the journey more fun.

Chapter One

From this day forward, Everly Caroline Hunt is your child to have. Congratulations! The memory of balloons, coworkers clapping, and Judge Torbett handing his gavel to eight-year-old Everly to slam on his desk in celebration of the adoption evaporated in the muggy Texas night air.

How could Josie Hunt's dreams of being a mom go so wrong in only four months of parenthood?

Fear ran through her veins as she took another step into the dark woods wearing hiking boots. Had her daughter really run away? At ten thirty at night, no less. She called again, "Everly!"

Only silence greeted her.

She couldn't have gone far. Josie had planned this weekend vacation to the secluded cabin, believing it would help her and Everly bond. A little fun with no worries. S'mores by a campfire and taking daily hikes while admiring nature type of thing.

Evidently not.

The first chance her daughter had gotten, she'd taken off. Maybe Josie should've sensed something was wrong. Everly had been even quieter than normal after they stopped to pick up pizza at a hole-in-the-wall place on the outskirts of the boonies. Josie had chalked it up to being tired after the drive, but now she wondered if her daughter had been making her plans to run.

But why? Was Josie really that bad of a mom?

The eight-year-old had been left an orphan when her dad, an acquaintance of Josie's, died in a tragic home accident a few months ago—a fall into the hot tub while trimming the grass with an electric trimmer and he was electrocuted. Everly's mom died of a rare heart disorder when the girl was a toddler. Josie had dreamed of having a family for a long time, but out of the guys she'd dated, one had let her down by getting into trouble with the law and the other had been mainly interested in a career. Family was important and there was no room to put a child on the back burner. How could she give a romantic relationship a chance if he wasn't a family man?

Josie had jumped at the chance to adopt the sweet girl, seeing there weren't family members willing to take Everly in. Even though normally there was a six-month waiting period to adopt in Texas, the judge waived the time because her parents were deceased, and he was familiar with Josie.

But being a competent investigator with the sheriff's department and for the Bring the Children Home Project—a volunteer organization of professionals who worked with law enforcement to help find missing children—had not prepared Josie for motherhood.

A footstep sounded behind her. Just as Josie started to turn, a powerful arm wrapped around her collarbone from behind. The sharp tip of a knife bit into the side of her neck. "Where is your daughter?"

She froze. *Oh, Lord. Please help me!* Who is this man? Her Sig rested out of reach in her ankle holster as the man pulled her against his chest. Being that she was five feet eight and her shoulders came to his chest meant he must be over six feet tall. "I don't know."

"If you want to live, you better start talking." The hoarse male voice held a drawl, which meant he was probably a local.

The last time she'd seen her daughter was when Everly went to bed with Dexter, her border collie. The next thing Josie knew, she was awakened by Dexter's sharp bark from somewhere outside. Everly's window was open, and her daughter and dog were gone. Josie had grabbed her weapon and cell phone and stepped into the night calling her name. A lump in Josie's throat grew, making it difficult to swallow, the blade digging deeper. "I don't know," she repeated. "She's gone."

The man hesitated.

Did he believe her? Or was he contemplating slashing her throat? One thing was certain, she had to get away from him to find her daughter.

"You're going to help me find her."

No, I'm not. Defense training kicked in, and she held up her hands as if in surrender. She said, "Okay. Okay." As soon as his hold relaxed, she shifted her hip, and in one swift move, grabbed his right wrist with both hands and yanked downward. His arm bent over her shoulder, hyperextending his elbow.

He dropped the knife and cursed.

She took off through the woods at a sprint,

dodging trees. As she leaped over a fallen branch, her knee almost buckled when she landed, but she kept going several more yards before stopping to retrieve her Sig from her holster.

"You're going to pay for that!" the man called. Snapping twigs told her he was coming for her.

Keeping her weapon in her grip, she took off again, but this time at a quieter, slower pace. She could've shot at him, but she couldn't take the chance since she didn't know Everly's location. Her mind scrambled with what the guy wanted as she weaved through the brush in search of Everly. If she and Dexter were close by, surely the dog would've barked.

The vacation cabin she'd rented sat on over twenty-five acres. Since Dexter's barking had awakened her, the two couldn't be that far ahead. Unless Everly had gone in the opposite direction.

Her daughter didn't own a cell phone, but as Josie moved deeper into the woods, she thought of calling Bliss, her boss at Bring the Children Home Project. Not slowing down, she reached into the pocket on her shorts, but the Velcro was no longer fastened. Her phone was gone. She must've dropped it while wrestling with the guy.

Was there more than one attacker? Had someone kidnapped Everly? Working with Bring the Children Home Project tended to make her believe every child was a potential kidnapping victim. Her stomach knotted at the thought.

Everly was a timid child. Surely, she wouldn't have run this far. Josie must've gone the wrong way. She was about to switch course when something shiny dangling in the brush grabbed her attention. It was Everly's pink butterfly necklace that her daddy had given her on her last birthday.

Jose untangled it from the limb and noticed the chain was broken. She shoved it into her pocket.

"Everly. Are you here?" She kept her voice down, but maybe the girl had stopped to hide. "Honey, it's me. Come out if you hear me."

When she received no answer, she picked her way through the woods again. Every few seconds, she looked over her shoulder to see if the tall man had closed in on her.

The longer she went, the more her heart raced with disbelief that the eight-year-old had run this far. She picked up the pace and trekked the uneven ground, watching for more signs Everly had gone this way. If she didn't locate her soon, she'd hurry back to where she thought she had lost her phone. Then she'd call the authorities and her team to help search for her and, hopefully, to arrest the man who'd pulled the knife on her.

"Everly," she called again. Frustration settled in.

Black shadows blended into the trees, making it almost impossible to see. The toe of her running shoe hung on a limb and caused her to fall hard. Dirt and gravel bit into her hands as pain radiated through her. She climbed back to her feet and dusted her hands on her legs before taking off again at a fast walk. A frog croaked somewhere, and crickets chirped.

Crash.

Josie jerked at the sound that came from behind her and to the left as she searched for the source. In the opposite direction, a dog barked. That had to be Dexter.

She came to a clearing and listened.

A branch snapped. This time the noise was closer, as if the source was on the move. "Everly. Is that you?" No response. "If you're out here, please answer me."

More popping and rustling came from the woods.

She switched her Sig to her other hand while

wiping the sweat away, before transferring the weapon again to her shooting hand. Hunching low, she wove her way through the brush.

A bulky shadow presented itself against an oak.

She froze. Her breath hitched as she concentrated on making out the silhouette, and she stayed low. Being that the man had been behind her when he'd pulled the knife, she hadn't gotten a clear look at him.

A child's scream sounded in the darkness. *Everly!*

Suddenly, the shadow vanished. She blinked, trying to clear her vision. There were only the trees.

With her gun ready, she hurried to the oak. Nothing.

She took off, determined to find her daughter before the man did. Snaking through the woods, she heard water running like that from a creek.

Another scream sent chills down Josie's neck.

Even though the darkness hung like a black, impassable curtain, she dashed through the trees. Something cracked to her right, but she kept going.

She'd been in dangerous situations before.

Exchanged gunfire. Helped rescue children. But Everly was *her* child.

Gripping her gun tighter, she mentally prepared for the unknown.

Dane Haggerty moved through the woods, crouched low as he maneuvered the tunnel-like trail in search of what sounded like a girl's scream. There was nothing for miles except for wilderness and wild animals. At first, he'd thought the scream might be that of a mountain lion, but he was certain it was that of a child.

His flashlight remained on his belt until he found out what had made the noise. If there was a child out here, he could only guess he or she was lost.

"Everly," a lady's voice called.

Dane stopped in his tracks and automatically pulled the baseball cap down further on his head. Did he dare take the chance of being found now? Maybe he should return to his hideout since an adult—probably the parent—was nearby.

But it wasn't in him not to help someone in trouble, even if there was a warrant for his arrest.

A dog yipped somewhere close.

A growl rose on the wind. As the heavy grunts grew louder, he tried to place the animal.

The growl didn't come from a dog or a wild pig.

A terrifying scream provoked him to move. He clicked on his flashlight and took off again. As he came out in a clearing on the edge of a creek bank, an ominous black shadow moved in the night.

The girl's cries were pure terror. He moved closer and aimed the flashlight. The outline of a burly bear with his nose on the inside of a fallen tree trunk was illuminated from the shadows.

The child's squeals came from inside the rotted wooden log.

Ignoring the dangerous predicament, he moved in and yelled, "Get back." He removed his Glock from his holster, although he doubted it was powerful enough to stop the animal from mauling him should it attack.

The black bear suddenly looked up, his nose pointing upward, and gave a horrifying growl.

"Go on. Get away from there." Dane stood tall and waved the light again. "Get."

The bear swung his head and snarled.

Dane had never been confronted by a bear, but as the child cried out again, he took another step forward, putting him within twenty feet of the beast. He looked around. If the animal charged, he'd have no place to hide except to take a chance of jumping into the creek and hoping he could move fast enough to escape.

The bear looked back at the hollow log and then ran off into the trees, disappearing.

Dane hurried forward and pointed his light inside the open end of the trunk. A young girl with braids huddled in the far end with her arms wrapped around a dog. "The bear is gone. You can come out now."

Large, tearful eyes stared back, and she shook her head vehemently.

"Where is your family?" She must have been scared to death. How did she get separated from her parents? Especially at this time of night. When she didn't answer, he said, "My name is Dane. I live right over there." He pointed to the north. "I will not hurt you. I have a cell phone where we can call your parents." As soon as the words were out, he regretted them. How could he help her and keep his identity hidden at the same time? Tears continued to flow down her cheeks. "I know you must be frightened, but I assure you the bear is gone."

A huff-like growl came from the trees, making the fluffy dog bark.

This was not a good time for the animal to return. "We need to go. I'm climbing in to get you."

"No." She held up her hand.

"Look, the bear is gone, but he's still moving around in the woods. We need to get you out of there." *Please, Lord, help her not panic and run.* He went down on all fours and crawled into the dark, musty log.

"No!" The girl held her hand out.

"I'm trying to help you. The bear is coming back. Come on." He pumped his hands closed, indicating she should move to him now.

The snarl came from somewhere close, and the girl didn't fight when Dane scooped her into his arms and backed out of the log. The collie crawled out after them. When Dane got to his feet, he spotted the bear moving through the trees. Quickly, he fired a shot into a nearby tree, hoping to scare the animal away. The beast hesitated.

Dane wasted no time stuffing his gun in the back of his waistband and heading in the opposite direction, with the girl in his grasp and the dog at his feet. He weaved in and out of the brush.

"Everly," a woman's voice called. "Where are you?"

"Mom!"

A lady wearing a pink T-shirt and shorts would've run into him if he hadn't come to a halt.

"Give me my daughter. Now." Shadows hid her features.

She held her hands out to the girl, but Dane pulled her back. "No time. There's a bear out here, and we need to move now. It'll be faster if I carry her."

"There are no bears in north Texas."

Yeah, right. Without arguing, he continued through the trees, away from the animal. He didn't know if bears would track a man, but he wasn't taking any chances.

"Stop," the woman demanded. Moonlight glistened from the end of a gun barrel. "I'm armed."

"I can see that." Panting for breath, he stopped long enough to eye the pistol in her hand. Unless the darkness gave him cover, his scruffy beard, faded black T-shirt, cap, and holey jeans gave her the wrong impression. He put the girl on her feet. "Let's keep moving."

"Are you okay, Everly?"

The concern in the woman's voice wasn't lost on him. He wanted to ask why the girl would go wandering off by herself, but it wasn't his business. Sometimes kids did dumb things.

"I'm fine, Mom."

"We'll talk later." The lady turned on him. "Throw down your knife."

"I don't have a knife." He glanced around to make certain the bear hadn't followed them.

She continued with her pistol trained on him. "I won't ask again."

"Listen, lady. I don't know who you think I am, but I don't have a knife." Since he shot to scare the bear away, and she'd probably heard, he added, "I do have a gun, but I'm not giving it up. We need to get out of here. Come with me if you want."

He took off, hoping she wouldn't shoot him. What was wrong with the woman? Who did she mistake him for?

The two followed close behind him. Once they'd gone several hundred yards without seeing any signs of the bear, curiosity got the best of him. He glanced over his shoulder. "What are you doing out here? There's nothing around for miles."

Even in the dark, he was certain that was a frown. He tried not to look her straight on to keep his identity hidden.

"You're not fooling anyone, mister. But we'll get to the bottom of this." She paused. "I could ask you the same thing."

The woman sounded familiar. Not so much the voice, but the attitude when she talked. Being two hours from his stomping grounds, it was doubtful he knew her. What had she asked? What he was doing out here. He held his hands in the air. "I heard the girl calling for help."

She clipped, "I'm sure she was."

"Where are you staying?" There weren't many homes or people in the area. Being that it was night, the woman probably hadn't made out his features, but he didn't need anyone recognizing him. And he sure wouldn't compromise his hideout.

"I'm not certain. Maybe a half a mile to the south." She looked at him and their eyes met, causing him to freeze momentarily.

Josie Hunt? What were the chances of him meeting up with her in the middle of nowhere when he just happened to be wanted for murder? Not likely.

"My name's Josie and this is Everly."

Oh no. He still didn't believe it. She was the last person he wanted to see. He had to keep her from recognizing him if she hadn't already. "Let's get you back." Purposefully, he kept his voice low. He needed to keep moving, so he started back on the trail again and was glad when they followed. He glanced to the right and pointed. "That way."

"You don't have a vehicle?" Suspicion laced her voice.

He did, but he couldn't give away his identity. If possible, he needed to keep to the shadows of the trees so she couldn't make out his features. He'd stayed off the grid for four months. But he also didn't want to leave the two alone with a bear wandering the area. "I do."

Everly faced her mom. "I don't want to go back with you. I'll just run away again."

Her words had him taking another glance at the girl. What had made her run from Josie?

"Don't say that. I know you miss your daddy, but *we're* a family now." Josie turned to him. "We can find our way on our own." Josie ran her hand down Everly's braids in a comforting gesture, but the girl jerked away.

"I don't want to go back to the cabin or home."

The fear in the girl's voice was clear, and Dane was torn as to what to do. Had Josie been abusive? The woman he knew could never hurt a child. Maybe she had a violent husband or boyfriend. *I know you miss your daddy.* Had Josie's husband left her?

"I can protect you." Josie eyed her daughter. "As soon as we make it back to the cabin, we'll get in our vehicle and go home."

"No!" Everly wrapped her arms around Dane's waist. "I want to go with him. I'm scared."

The girl's action rocked him, making him cringe. Even in the dark, the sharp prick of the daughter's words could be felt. He could relate to not wanting to go home as a child, but Josie was nothing like his family. She'd always been kind to him. Well, almost always. If you didn't count the time she turned him in to the police for theft—a crime that he didn't commit.

Clouds drifted away from the moon, causing the light to shine on their faces.

Josie's eyebrows scrunched as she looked at him. "You look familiar."

Purposefully, he took a step into the shadows and turned away. "I get that a lot."

Not only had he and Josie dated in high school—he didn't know if she even remembered him—but she'd been the one person in school to make him believe in himself and give him hope that he didn't have to follow in his father's footsteps. They'd only been teens, but her actions had meant everything to him—until she betrayed him. A pang in his heart still ached more than it should have. The last few months, his picture had been all over the news. The last thing he needed was Josie to blow his cover. If he had any intention of not going to prison for murder, he needed to escape these two now.

Framed for killing his business partner, Harlan Schmidt, Dane had been in hiding while trying to find evidence that exonerated him. Was he doomed to be incarcerated again? If authorities arrested him this time, he was certain he'd never see daylight again. He couldn't let that happen.

Not if he wanted to save Violet.

The court date for his thirteen-year-old sister to become a ward of the state was in less than three weeks. There was no one else in his family who could fight for her. He had worked tirelessly for a spotless reputation and to have a successful business. No one knew better than Dane how being raised not knowing where your next meal was coming from could cause you to make poor decisions.

Something rustled in the trees. All three of them turned toward the sound.

The girl wrapped her arms around his arm. "Don't let him take me."

"Stay close. I won't let the bear get you." Dane pulled her against him.

As he searched out the animal's location, movement caught his attention, and he realized the culprit's silhouette only had two legs and a rifle in his hands. Maybe he was a camper who'd heard Dane's shots.

Everly cried and moved behind Dane. "Don't let him hurt me."

Josie eyed her daughter.

The rifle must've frightened the girl, but Dane wanted the man to know they had shot to scare a dangerous animal. "We were warning off a bear. There's no need to be alarmed."

Suddenly, the man raised his rifle and aimed it at them.

A microsecond later, the attacker's intentions dawned on him, and Dane pulled Everly into his grasp as he dove for cover. They rolled underneath thick foliage.

As shots lit up the night, he looked for Josie. He and Josie warned in unison, "Get down."

But Josie was already on the ground, propped up on her elbows with her pistol in her grip. She didn't take her eyes off the shooter as she readied her aim and fired two rounds.

Dread filled him, as he didn't know what kind of trouble had followed his old high school sweetheart into the wilderness. Which also spelled trouble for him if it led authorities to his doorstep.

As the thoughts stabbed him like a thousand needles, he also realized he couldn't leave Josie and Everly's sides until he knew they were safe.

He slid his weapon from his waistband.

The guy shot once more before he turned and barreled into the foliage.

Everly buried her head under Dane's arm. "This is all my fault."

"No." Dane gave her a gentle squeeze. He didn't know how a kid could come to that conclusion, but she needed to understand. "This is not your fault."

Josie rushed forward. "Are you okay, honey? Were you hurt?"

"I'm not hurt." The girl's voice came out loud and frustrated. She climbed to her knees and clung to the collie as sobs racked her body.

"Let's go back to the cabin, pack up and go home." Josie motioned with her hand.

"You're not listening." Finally, she looked at her mom and shouted with tears in her eyes. "It won't matter. That man is going to kill me."

"Everly, no." Josie moved to her side. "I won't let anyone hurt you."

"The man will kill you like he did my daddy. We're all going to die because of me!"

The dog barked and danced at the girl's feet.

"Someone killed her dad?" Dane glanced from her to Josie as he returned his weapon to his waistband.

Josie shook her head and whispered, "Her father died in an accident."

"No." Everly balled her fists. "It was on purpose! I saw that man with the gun drown him in our hot tub. He held him under. The man's been following me ever since. He's watched me at school, and he was at the pizza place."

"Oh, baby. I will protect you." Josie wrapped her arms around the girl, and then she looked at Dane. "We're leaving and going straight to the sheriff's department."

Of course, Josie needed to go to the authorities. But what would she do when she recognized his identity? No doubt she'd turn him in. And he wouldn't blame her one bit.

His gaze went from Josie to the girl. "Come on. I'll see you safely back to your cabin." There was no way Dane would let Josie and Everly walk back alone when there was a killer after them.

Chapter Two

Josie held her daughter, her heart breaking, while tuning out the stranger's comment about walking them back to the cabin. Her mind tried to sort through everything at a hundred miles per hour. She pulled back from the embrace and ran her hand over Everly's face and repeated, "No one is going to kill you or me. Do you understand?"

Her daughter's forehead wrinkled into a frown before the tears flowed freely. "Yes, he will. If Daddy couldn't stop him, neither can you."

A knife stabbed Josie in the heart. "Oh, baby. I'll do everything to keep you safe. Do you know the man's name?"

Everly shook her head. "No, but I got a good look at him. He went into the pizza place. That's why I ran. Please don't be mad. I was trying to find a place to hide and lead him away from you."

A lump formed in Josie's throat. She hugged her daughter once again as she tried to remember the people who had been in the store. The place was small and almost deserted. She simply hadn't paid attention to anyone except to the woman behind the counter. "I could never be mad at you. I wish I would've known."

"I'm sorry."

"Don't be. I'm glad you told me."

"Josie." The stranger's voice interrupted their moment. "We need to get moving. Now that we know who he's targeting, we don't need to be caught out here on foot. With him or the bear."

She wanted to console her daughter, but the stranger was right. "Let's go."

Dark shadows had kept her from making out the gunman's identity, but maybe when they got back to Liberty, Everly could identify the man from mug shots.

"There's still no sign of that guy. Let's get you two to safety."

Suspicions arose. Josie turned back to the trees where the guy had stood to make certain he was gone. Satisfied, she holstered her Sig into the largest pocket of her shorts and Velcroed it shut. She looked at the stranger and noticed he glanced away. "What are *you* doing out here?"

"I've already answered that. I heard your child scream."

Something wasn't right. Was this man in cahoots with the gunman? Possibly. If he was, at least she'd know where one man was. Right now, all she wanted was to get somewhere safe. She grasped Everly's hand without a word and they wove their way through the trees at a fast pace toward the cabin. If the gunman tried to circle around and get in front of them, he'd have to run.

Ten minutes later, they came to a trail, and the woods thinned. She stopped and turned to the stranger. "Who are you?"

She observed him. His dark eyes disappeared under that bib of his cap in the moonlight, and his scraggly beard covered most of his face. Her attention returned to the eyes. They were almost familiar.

He glanced down and stared at his feet. "Ma'am, I'd be glad to see you two back to wherever you're staying."

"And your name?"

"It's not important."

She gave him another look. Irritation crawled over her. The relationship with her daughter was not going as planned, and now someone was targeting them. If Everly was correct and she witnessed Pierce's murder, then the killer would need to dispose of her.

Josie wanted to dismiss the stranger but trekking through the woods had not been in a straight line and the darkness had prevented her from noticing landmarks. Stubbornness was something she struggled with, but she had Everly to consider. It was time to swallow her pride. "Are you familiar with the Hidden Oaks cabin?"

"Yes, ma'am. I know the location if that's what you're asking. I can lead you there."

The stranger's manners confused her. He appeared rough and unkempt in contrast to his speech. "That won't be necessary." She pointed to the right, which felt like the south. "Is it that way?"

"Yes, ma'am. If you stay on this trail, it's about a half mile to a metal walkthrough gate to the backyard of your place."

She wished he'd quit calling her ma'am. "I lost my cell phone back there. Can you call in the shooter to the sheriff's department?"

"I will let them know."

She held out her hand. "If you let me borrow your phone, I can call them now."

"It won't do any good. There's no reception out here. I'll call them in a bit."

She squinted. There was something about him she didn't trust. She wasn't about to let him lead them back to the cabin. They would pack and leave as quickly as possible. She rested a hand on Everly's shoulder and pulled her close in a protective gesture. "We don't need help."

He said, "Be careful."

She slipped into the darkness with her daughter's hand in hers. After they went several yards, she glanced back. The stranger was nowhere in sight.

Thankfully, Everly stayed close to her. As they hiked down the rugged path, her mind kept returning to the stranger.

Where did he go? Was he camping in the woods? He claimed to hear Everly scream. Maybe. The most important question was what if he was working with the gunman.

They made tracks through the brush, hurrying toward their cabin with Dexter trotting happily at their side. After several minutes,

Everly tugged on her hand, and Josie released her grip.

By the time they got back to the rental cabin, Josie was exhausted, and her feet ached. Nothing would be better than curling up in bed and getting a good night's rest, but sleep wasn't in her future.

Maybe she could reschedule this getaway in the summer after authorities found Pierce's killer and Everly visited with Kennedy, the psychologist for Bring the Children Home Project.

The back door was left unlocked from when Josie rushed outside to find Everly. She retrieved her gun from her pocket. Uncertainty whether she should have Everly wait outside or follow her inside nagged at her, but she decided on the latter. "Follow me and stay close."

They walked through the log structure together, including Everly's room, with Dexter at their side. By all appearances, nothing had been touched. As they stopped between the kitchen and living room, the border collie immediately lay at Everly's feet with his tail in rapid motion, slapping the wooden floor.

A smile crossed Josie's lips. "I think we're all tired." She turned back to Everly. "Pack your bag, and I'll get my things together. We'll leave in two minutes."

Everly went into her room, taking Dexter with her. She left the door wide open.

Sadness fell on Josie that Everly had witnessed such atrocities at such a young age. Hopefully, the girl would learn to trust her and could begin healing after her father's murderer was caught.

As she rushed to throw her clothes and toiletries into her bag, she wondered whether the authorities would believe Everly's story. At only eight, Everly could have easily misinterpreted what had happened. But Josie believed her. Being that she'd seen the man several times and that he'd followed them on their vacation told Josie the girl had not misunderstood.

Moonlight seeped into the cabin, making use of lights optional. The rustic home was in the middle of nowhere, but if someone was outside, they could easily see through the large floor-to-ceiling glass panes in the living room. The eerie feeling that someone was watching her slid down her spine.

Slowly, she turned toward the windows. Short shrubs lined the lower two feet, and the branches of a cedar tree danced in the breeze as clouds drifted across the moon.

It took a moment for her eyes to adjust. She could see no one, but the feeling of being watched grew.

"Everly, hurry up. We need to leave now."

Her daughter stood in the doorway with Dexter. "I'm ready."

But when Josie went to the front entryway to leave, she saw the silhouette of a man through the small pane on the door. He moved to the back of her Bronco, where the security light did not reach. Her hand shot out, and she whispered, "Go out the back door."

Everly's eyes grew large, but she hurried through the dark house to the back, evidently feeling the urgency.

"Leave your bag here." They dropped their stuff on the floor at the same time and all three of them fled the cabin to the backyard.

As soon as they moved under the covering of a huge pecan tree, Everly whispered, "Is the man here again?"

"Yes, honey, and it's important he doesn't hear us. Try to keep Dexter quiet."

Everly nodded. "Okay."

After they'd gone to the edge of the yard, about twenty yards from the home, Josie stopped. "Let's stay here and see if the man leaves. Be ready to move quickly."

Again, she nodded.

Poor thing. Josie hated scaring her, but it would do no good to go traipsing about in the woods. They wouldn't know if the gunman left the cabin, had someone pick him up or if he was following them. If it weren't for having Everly with her, Josie would confront the man. There was no way she could put her daughter's life at risk.

Her mind went back to the stranger who'd helped them. Surely it wasn't a coincidence. He knew they were headed back to the cabin, and the gunman was waiting for them. Why didn't the man give his name?

Dexter's ear went up as he stared toward the cabin.

The man stood at the back door, which meant he'd been inside and must now realize they'd spotted him.

Josie pulled Everly closer as she bent down. "Shh. Let's move back."

"That's him."

She gave her shoulder a squeeze and stepped deeper into the shadows. A narrow trail cut across the yard to a gate that led to the woods, but Josie kept to the left of it, afraid if the man ran after them, he'd stick to the path.

She patted her leg to draw Dexter's attention. Too late. The dog gave three quick barks.

"No, Dex." Everly's face lit up in alarm.

"Let's go!" Josie whisper-yelled. They took off through the trees behind the shed and down the fence row.

A bullet whizzed past her ear, followed by the resounding pop. "Stay down." She returned fire, two shots with her Sig. As they weaved through the trees, Josie hoped to deter the gunman, but another shot blasted.

Wood splintered above them and a heavy limb from the pecan tree fell, hitting her on the top of the head. Pain radiated throughout her body as she hit the ground.

"Mom!"

"I'm okay." Josie struggled to stand, but not before Dexter licked her on the cheek. "We've got to keep moving."

"This way." Everly zigzagged through the trees.

But Josie's world spun out of control and lights danced before her, making it difficult to stay on her feet. She turned one last time and fired another shot toward the cabin. Hopefully, the gunman would keep his distance.

As the trees blended into the sky, the moon bounced up and down in a blur. Her head swirled, but she kept following Everly and Dexter. If they could just find a good hiding place.

"Come on. This way." Everly held back a bush branch so that Josie could get by. "You don't look good."

Josie would've laughed if it wasn't for her head throbbing. She didn't ask where they were going because it didn't matter as long as it bought her time to get her bearings. They came to a clearing, and she recognized this was where she'd found Everly earlier. Her head continued to swim. "Stop. I need to rest."

"I'll go get help."

"No. We stick together." Josie drew a deep breath. The spinning slowed, but she didn't think it'd take much activity to grow worse again.

A twig snapped from somewhere close by. Both of them looked to the south from where the sound came. Dexter raised his hackles.

"Mom, did you hear that? It's either the man or the bear."

"Don't worry. I'll protect you." But could

she keep her word? She had no choice but to get going. Her dizziness had only slightly lessened. "Let's move again."

A deep growl came from the west, sending chills down her spine. She hadn't believed there was a bear, but that certainly sounded like one. Seconds later, an engine rumbled from behind them to the south where the gunman would've been.

With danger coming for them from two directions, Josie picked up the pace to a run.

Everly said in a panicked voice, "Let me get help. I can do it faster without you."

Her words wreaked havoc on Josie's mind. "From who? Not that stranger. He may be working with the gunman. You can't run off. It's too dangerous."

"Dane helped us. He told me his place was that way. Since he heard me screaming, he can't be far away."

Had the man told Josie his name? No, she didn't think so. He'd refused. There was only one person she knew who went by the name Dane.

Dane Haggerty.

Josie asked, "How do you know his name?"

"He told me when he was trying to get me to come out of the log."

No. Surely not. She would've recognized him. But his face was covered by a bushy beard, and he'd worn a cap low on his head. She could kick herself. He had never looked at her directly after he'd met her in the woods. Which meant he'd recognized her. *That low-down, good-for-nothing Haggerty boy.* Her grandfather's words played through her mind like it was yesterday.

Her cheeks burned with heat as they hiked through the wilderness. She'd turned Dane in once to the police for stealing a car their senior year in high school. And she'd seen the news that he was a suspect in a murder case. If there was any other option for protection, she'd choose it.

However, she had little choice but to seek refuge from a fugitive.

Dane took long strides toward his hideout. Unknown to Josie, he'd followed the duo at a distance to the cabin to make certain they arrived safely. At first, he couldn't help but think the gunman may've been a bounty hunter hoping to bring him in.

But now he was ninety percent certain the

man had targeted Josie and her daughter if Everly had truly witnessed her father's murder. He kept a constant watch for a sign of the man. He had started to keep an eye on the cabin until Josie left, but then he got to thinking about his hideout. If it were a bounty hunter, he might be in search of his place right now.

He pulled his burner cell phone out of his pocket, but there was no signal. Hopefully, reception would improve when he got back to his place.

Maybe he should find a new hideout. Either way, Dane needed transportation, and his old truck was back at the barn he used for cover. He hurried through the trees toward his shelter while keeping a lookout for the bear.

Frustration bit at him. His life had been on a solid trajectory for several years, giving him confidence that staying on the straight and narrow had served him well. After working in the construction business for seven years, he finally took a leap of faith and started North Texas Custom Builders with his good friend, Harlan Schmidt. The business had its bumps in the road, but nothing that hard work and careful planning hadn't solved. Then, several months ago, Child Protective Services took his younger sister away from his mom and put Violet into foster care for neglect. It's not that he doubted his mom had not taken good care of his sister—his mom had always battled problems from drinking to putting food on the table. But he could only imagine how it felt to be forced to live with strangers—following new family rules and maybe going to a new school. Everything Violet had ever known ripped from underneath her. That in itself could create a whole list of new problems, even if the foster family were decent and kind people. Dane hoped to gain custody of his younger sister and filed with the court.

Yes, things had not been seamless, but his life derailed four months ago when he walked in to find Harlan lying on the floor in Dane's office with his granddaddy's antique hay hook embedded in his back. Uncertain if Harlan was breathing, he tried to remove the hook from his back so he could roll him over. But it was no use. Someone must've called the police because a cruiser pulled into the drive and Dane took off out the back.

He probably shouldn't have run, but the timing had been too perfect, and Dane had been on the losing side of the law before. Within hours, a warrant had been issued for his arrest, and he'd been running ever since. He planned to turn himself in once he found evidence to clear his name.

Even though he hadn't seen Josie in years, he'd heard she worked with the sheriff's department as an investigator for a while. Was she being near him just a coincidence? He doubted it. Maybe she was a bounty hunter.

He rubbed his hands through his hair. Not only was he not making good progress figuring out who murdered Harlan because it was too risky to return to his house or the office to search for evidence, but now he had to wonder if his hideout was compromised. He couldn't hide out forever, but he'd hoped to be closer to figuring out who framed him.

Harlan had believed money was missing from North Texas Custom Builders, and there had to be a paper trail. Making matters worse was the fact that money had shown up in his own account that Dane hadn't deposited himself.

It would make it easier if Dane had family or someone in law enforcement who was looking to clear his name, but his family was the last place he could turn. A glance to his Bible reminded him of the verse in Ecclesiastes he'd read earlier in the day. *Two are better than one; because they have a good reward for their labour.*

Harlan had been his closest friend and had introduced him to God. Maybe if Dane had been a better friend to others, he might have someone else to turn to.

He'd listened to scanners and read the news daily to catch updates about the murder case, but all information had dropped to virtually nothing after the first two weeks. The past four months had been the longest of his life.

Darkness shrouded the old wooden barn. Tree limbs blew in the breeze and crickets chirped. Stopping at the edge of the woods, he watched his hideout for several minutes. No strange sounds or movements could be detected. Slowly, he stepped through the weeds, sticking close to the protection of the trees. He walked around the perimeter and then moved in.

A minute later, he unlocked the chain on the barn's double doors and put his hand on the thick handle to open it when he heard a voice. He froze.

There it was again.

Dropping the chain, he stepped outside into the shadows.

A slight figure ran toward him, and a dog

barked. As the girl grew closer, her features became clear.

Panting for breath, Everly said, "The man came back. Mom… Mom needs help."

His chest tightened. "Show me." He headed in the direction, but someone came out of the darkness.

"It's me." Josie's voice sounded tired, and maybe a tad angry. "Don't shoot."

He never should've left them alone. He hurried her way, but when he got close, her hand shot in the air.

"Dane Haggerty, if you'll help us get away, I promise I won't turn you in to authorities until I get back to Liberty."

All air left his lungs as his shoulders slumped. All the trying to live right, to change his life for good, had brought him back full circle. His fate lay in Josie Hunt's hands. He was certain he didn't like that at all.

Chapter Three

Josie's head throbbed as she rubbed her forehead, but they didn't have time to stand around.

Dane stepped beside her. "Let me see that." He gently removed her hand. "Ouch."

She instinctively pulled away from his touch. "Our guy fired at us and caused a heavy limb to fall on me. I'm fine."

Everly stepped close. "My daddy's killer was at our cabin, and we came looking for you."

Dane glanced from Everly to Josie. "Did he see where you went?"

"No, but I know which way he went. We heard something crashing in the woods and then an engine. He has some kind of vehicle."

"We need to get you to a hospital and away from here. Come on."

When Josie tried to walk, her knees wobbled, causing her to stumble into him.

"There's no time for this." Dane scooped her

into his arms and headed in the direction they'd been traveling.

"Wait. This isn't necessary. The hit on the head made me a little loopy, but I'm feeling better."

His dark eyes stared down at her. "We have no time. I don't want to be caught in the open."

She was used to doing things herself, but even as the thought came to her, her head swam, dizziness causing her to close her eyes and lean against the strong shoulder. Her stomach didn't feel so good. Nausea was a sign of a concussion. Maybe he was right.

Even as she kept her eyes closed while trying to stop the swirling, she listened to the sound of his footsteps. A minute later, he paused, and she opened her eyes.

He swung a wooden door wide and carried her into a large building—a barn. The constant moving up and down made it difficult to concentrate on what she was seeing. He opened another door and then put her down on a leather couch.

"Where is Everly?"

"I'm right here." Her daughter moved beside her.

Josie squinted. "Is this a camper?"

"Yes."

She went to sit up but grabbed her head in pain. "I need to call my boss."

"Maybe later."

"No. We have people on my team and in the sheriff's department who can help. Law officers need to arrest the shooter before he hurts anyone else. And if he is the one who killed Pierce, he needs to be off the streets."

Dane frowned. "We're out of Jarvis County's jurisdiction."

"There's someone out there with a gun who's targeting us." Even though Everly knew they were in danger, Josie thought it best not to use the phrase "he's trying to kill us." The girl was scared enough already. "I know you're running from the law, but we must get out of here."

He frowned. "Did you get a better look at him this time? Did you recognize him?"

She shook her head and instantly regretted it. "I'm certain he was watching while we were packing in the cabin. I glanced out the door before opening it and saw him standing beside my Bronco with the rifle, like he was waiting for us. We left our things and hurried out the back door." Maybe if she'd been by herself, she could've challenged him since she was armed, but all she could think of was getting Everly away from this guy. "It was too dark to see his features, but he was tall and slim."

"I'm assuming the guy followed you."

"Probably. We heard something moving in the trees, and I think your bear friend was out there, too."

Quickly, he turned to a kitchen cabinet. "I have ibuprofen if you need it."

"I'd appreciate that. I'll take one. Do you have a vehicle?"

She sat against the cushions, pushing aside the headache. After she took the medicine, she glanced around at the granite countertops, nice stainless-steel refrigerator, and a genuine wood floor. Everything looked top of the line. It hadn't escaped her attention that he didn't argue about being a fugitive. "This is a nice camper. Yours?"

Dexter whimpered and came over to the couch, looking at Josie with his tail wagging.

"I'm all right, Dex." She patted his head, then turned her gaze back to Dane. "Is this RV in a barn, or did I imagine that?"

"It's a barn. Helps keep the energy costs down."

"Yeah." She laughed. "And keeps it hidden

from those nearby. Great hideout." The sarcasm wasn't necessary, but she tended to lean on it when she was nervous.

His gaze met hers, but he didn't say a word.

Her eyes squinted. "Do you have a phone I can borrow? Earlier, you said you'd call the sheriff's department. Did you do that?"

"I tried. Here you go." He pulled a cell phone from his pocket and held it out to her. "This place is hard to find, but if you found it, someone else can, too. I need to make certain the gunman didn't follow you." Before she had time to react, he turned and stepped out of the camper.

Oh no, you don't. She struggled to her feet and waited several seconds to get her bearings before moving toward the door. Everly and Dexter followed her.

The barn was tall and open, but the camper took up much of the space. She saw Dane walk between the home and a motorcycle that was propped against the wall to the back door. A rusty pickup truck that was parked inside looked to have seen better days. Probably didn't run.

Slowly, he pushed the door open and stepped outside.

They needed help, and fast. A glance at his

cell phone showed two bars, and she punched 9-1-1.

Where did he go? She stepped toward the door he'd exited.

The dispatcher answered, "9-1-1. What is your emergency?"

"My name is Josie Hunt, a man shot at me and my daughter..."

Something clanked from outside. The door swung open, and Dane hurried inside with a gun in his hand when a gunshot blasted.

The cell phone went flying out of her hand and landed on the floor in pieces. More bullets sprayed the doorframe, sending wood splinters into the air.

Everly squealed and moved behind Josie.

Dexter sprinted underneath the pickup and launched into a barking tirade.

"Our shooter is back. Get in my truck. Now." He hurried to the driver's side and put Everly in the middle as Josie ran to the passenger door. Dexter leaped onto the floorboard before climbing onto Josie's lap. "Put your heads down. Hang on."

More gunfire from outside.

When he turned the key, his old Ford roared to life, and he stomped on the gas.

One of the big double doors swung wide, and the gunman stepped into the opening, taking aim. This guy looked heavier than the one she'd seen at the cabin.

Dane's truck hesitated, spinning in loose hay. They gained traction, shot forward and blasted through the doors.

The gunman leaped out of the way barely in time.

One of the barn's doors ripped from its hinges and landed on the hood before sliding off.

The man shot several more times, once hitting Dane's side window.

"Is this guy trying to kill all of us?" Josie yelled over the roaring engine.

"I don't know. I can ask him later."

As he flew down the grassy drive, headlights came from in front of them.

"Dane! Watch out!"

He jerked the wheel to the left and into a barbwire fence to avoid hitting the other vehicle. T-posts bent under the impact and dented the front of his bumper. After half the fence was gone, he pulled the wheel back to the right, ran over brush and kept going.

Josie looked over the seat. Headlights from a

pickup bounced through the pasture, making a wide circle. "He's turning around."

"There's two of them."

She glanced again. Sure enough, another set of headlights, but narrower, flew out from behind his barn.

"One looks to be a four-wheeler or some kind of ATV." At the end of the grass drive, he turned left onto the rock road without slowing down.

A dust cloud appeared in the reflection from the brake lights. On the left, she saw the ATV tearing through the pasture parallel to them.

Everly covered her ears and bent forward with her head lowered. Dexter had already crawled back to the floorboard, evidently not liking the bumpy ride.

Josie called out, "Do you know where you're going?"

"I've been this way several times. Right now, I'm just trying to get away."

She checked the twenty-round magazine on her Sig and then slid it back into her pocket but didn't fasten it shut. Her two extra magazines were locked in a case in the back of the Bronco. Tension racked her body as they came to a sharp curve. Dane hit his brakes as he slid through the turn. Centripetal force tugged his tires into the ditch before they got back to the middle of the road. She held onto the door handle with one hand while the other squeezed the back of Everly's shirt, trying to keep her upright.

The road came to another *T.* When he hesitated, Josie asked, "Are you familiar with this area?"

"I don't recognize this road. Did you call the sheriff?"

She yelled. "I tried, but a bullet hit your phone, destroying it. Sorry."

"This is not good."

As they neared a wooden bridge, a large grove of trees appeared to the left. Just as he was in the middle of the dilapidated passage, the ATV shot out from the brush, headlights blaring through the driver's side window.

"Watch out." Josie looked back over her shoulder as the headlights shone in the back window. "Everly, I want you to stay down. Okay?"

"Okay." The girl frowned and sank lower into the seat.

"I'm going to get him to back off." Josie rolled down the passenger side window and climbed into the opening and sat on the door frame. She aimed her Sig and fired three shots.

Dane's truck hit a pothole, sending it jolting.

"Whoa." Her heart leaped, and her free hand grabbed the interior of the cab, regaining her balance.

The driver swerved and backed off.

She plopped back into her seat. "That should get him to keep his distance."

Dane glanced her way. "I thought you were an investigator, not a deputy. I'm assuming you worked in the field and did more than search documents on a computer from the office when you were employed at the sheriff's department."

Her gaze connected with his. "You could say that."

Headlights came from in front of him. She realized the driver must know these back roads as well as Dane. "Here we go again. Hang on."

A sour taste bubbled up in her throat as she braced for more danger, and she prayed they got out of this alive.

Dane had to get off the road before the two men sandwiched them in. If he was alone, maybe he could take the chance. But not with Josie and Everly with him.

A rocky driveway appeared up ahead. Johnsongrass grew around a large metal sign, making it impossible to read. He figured it'd be best to take his chances than to hit the other truck. He whipped into the driveway. Not knowing what kind of place this was, he slowed down a tad.

Headlights shone in his rearview mirror, and another set came from the trees. He had to lose these guys.

After a mile or so, they topped out on a large hill. A giant sand hole spread out in front of them. Dane swerved right to keep on the rim that was covered with small trees.

Josie leaned over to peer out his side of the window. "That looks like some kind of quarry."

"Yeah, one that hasn't been used in years." His truck bounced with the rugged terrain. Narrow gullies created by rainwater streaked across the rim.

Lights again shone on his back window. "They're gaining on us."

He pressed the gas pedal, but the engine roared, and the truck slowed. "This can't be happening."

"What's wrong?"

"I think my transmission is out." He shifted

the gear into neutral and then back to drive again, but the truck rolled to a stop.

"Dane, we need to move."

"I'm trying." He slammed it into Park before shifting into Drive, but it was no use. As the gunmen bore down on them, he rammed the gear into Reverse. The transmission popped, and the truck jumped. As shots sprayed the hood, he spun the truck around and took off, going backward.

"Whoa!" Everly yelled as she fell sideways. She climbed into the seat.

Josie joined in. "Oh… Dane!"

He dodged trees and worked to keep the tires on the rim of the giant man-made hole, avoiding cave-ins on the edge.

Josie leaned forward and dug her fingers into the dash.

The quarry took in about ten acres with deep, steep sides. If he were to go over the edge, the truck would roll. The other vehicle, a black Dodge, took off around the other side, its lights bouncing with the movement. With only his backup lights, he could barely see where he was going. Red reflected on the tree trunks, barely giving him time to react. Like a ball in a pinball game, he weaved in and out of the brush.

The pickup flew up on them, being able to go faster forward. Headlights blinded him, making him glance away.

He warned, "Hang on."

The Dodge slammed into his front bumper, sending them fishtailing toward the outside of the rim into the trees. Everly planted her feet against the dash, just as they were hit again. "Ow." She removed her feet and returned to the floorboard beside Dexter.

Branches scraped the side of his truck. Their bumpers stayed locked as the other truck pushed them faster.

"That's enough." Josie fired two quick shots out the window.

The truck kept coming but gave them distance.

She looked back in the other direction. "The ATV is headed this way."

"Great. I really don't want to hit the guy."

Her hand touched his arm. "Try not to do that." She glanced at Everly as she lay with her head in Josie's lap.

"I understand." As his truck continued to bounce and run along the overgrowth, he looked for a way out. In less than twenty seconds, the ATV would come up behind him.

While trying to keep his truck from going over the rim's edge, he searched for an escape.

Suddenly, his headlights flashed on a road that snaked down into the hole used by the haul trucks. In his mirror, the ATV swung wide, getting ready to force him into the pit. He had to take this opportunity. "Hang on."

Everly squealed as he jerked the wheel to the right, whipping the truck toward the rim in a tight circle until he was hightailing it back toward the ramp.

Brake lights flashed from the ATV before it slammed into a tree. The other truck continued coming his way.

Keeping the accelerator pressed, he descended the ramp, spiraling downward.

"I hope you know what you're doing!" Josie held on to Everly and the dashboard.

Parts of the ramp were washed away, and he gritted his teeth as they hit each crevice. He could only see the quarry in bits and pieces as he made his way down the incline, but it looked to have water in the bottom. There was no way to tell how deep it was. If he made it to the base, then what?

They'd be trapped.

He'd known that was a possibility when he'd

chosen this route, but his goal was to ensnare their pursuers here and then hightail it out, a risky tactic, but he'd been in dicey situations before.

On the other side of the pit, the truck raced down the road. With only Reverse, there was no way to outrun these guys. Once they got near the bottom, the gunmen could easily pick them off.

"What's the plan? Do we need to get out and run for it?"

"We don't know how much ammunition they have. I only have about twenty more cartridges besides what's in my gun."

"I'm a skilled marksman, but I'd hate to get shot down with no help for miles."

It'd been years since he'd participated in stunts of jumping his motorcycle and leaping ravines in his old Mustang. He'd even bungee jumped strapped to a couch from a railroad overpass. He wasn't that guy anymore and had spent years trying to redeem himself and prove he could be a businessman and an asset to the community.

Not that it had stopped him from being framed for murder.

But he'd never had an innocent woman and

child with him. He glanced at her. "Do you trust me?"

"Not really." She looked at him with scrutiny. "But do I have a choice?"

Ouch. He had to admit she had little alternative. "I'll get us out of here. Make certain your daughter's seatbelt is snug. It tends to loosen easily." He patted the seat. "Just try to keep your head low."

Josie nodded and then did as he asked.

He didn't know if he could get out of this pit, but he wasn't ready to give up. Still going in Reverse, he turned the truck off the road and straight up the pit. As no one had excavated the quarry in years, the sand was packed, and the thick vegetation should give him traction. It was crucial he back straight up and not sideways, or else they would roll.

His passengers were silent as the engine revved, plowing up the sandy terrain.

He glanced at Josie and noticed her eyes were closed. Whether scared or praying, he didn't know.

The back end slid to the right, where the ground broke off in a serious crevice. He fought to keep the momentum. His tires slid, but he kept the gas down and slowly his old truck slithered toward the top of the hill.

Below them, the gunman's truck slid sideways, the driver foolishly jerking the wheel to the right, which was the wrong move. The truck careened down the pit and crashed into a bottomless ravine. Seconds later, steam floated from under the hood.

"Let's go," Josie shouted.

Dane made it to the rim and took off toward the exit, trying not to jolt his passengers. But it was no use. The road was simply too rough. All was quiet in the cab as they made it back to the road, and then he maneuvered through the countryside going backwards. He hoped the transmission didn't totally go out.

A loud sigh came from his passenger once they had traveled several miles away from the quarry. "I have to admit. Your driving abilities are just as good as they were in high school."

He didn't look her way. "Thanks. I think."

When they got to safety, *if* they made it safety, did he escort her to the sheriff's department? Even as the thought crossed his mind, his stomach knotted. Could he give up Violet so easily?

Suddenly, the engine grew loud, and the truck rolled to a stop. He and Josie exchanged glances. He put it in and out of gear several times, but the vehicle didn't move. "Looks like this is as far as it goes."

Josie gazed out her window. "At least we're miles from the quarry and the gunmen."

"True."

As they got out on the passenger side in the tall grass, Everly lifted her shoe. "Oh."

"What's wrong?" Josie asked as she knelt beside her and felt her foot. When her hands touched the ankle, Everly grimaced.

Dane came around their side of the truck.

Dexter sniffed the girl's foot like he understood it bothered her. Josie stared at her daughter. "Can you walk on it?"

Everly took a few steps, but then limped.

"Come on. I've got you." Dane scooped her into his arms.

"I can carry my own daughter."

"I realize that. I'll give you a turn when I get tired. Deal?"

A slight smile tugged at her lips. "Thanks, Dane."

Her tiny gesture shed a sliver of light into a dark situation. "Let's stay close to the road until daylight. If the guys return, we should see their headlights in plenty of time to get out of sight."

Everly laid her head against his shoulder, and almost immediately, her eyes closed.

They walked for several minutes, and he noted Josie's frown only deepened. "Are you okay? Is your head still hurting?"

"I have a slight headache, but it's not as strong. The good news is I'm no longer dizzy."

"That's good." He hated seeing her this way. "I know my truck is broken down, and we're miles from your vehicle, but if it's any consolation, I plan to see you back to safety."

Her gaze cut to him like she was insinuating he didn't have a clue.

"What?"

"Don't you get it? These guys are serious about doing what is necessary to stop Everly from identifying her father's murderer. And now we've been added to the equation. That means killing all three of us."

Chapter Four

As the three of them hiked through the pasture under the light of the moon, Josie had time to ponder their situation. The main concern was to get to her Bronco so they could contact the sheriff of McCade County or find a phone to call for assistance.

"What can I do to help?" Dane asked.

"I don't know. Nothing." Irritation crept into her tone. She kept her gaze on where she was going instead of looking at him. She had been too busy with her daughter to think about him, but she couldn't help being annoyed that he had stolen that car, thus rupturing their friendship years ago. He'd shattered her trust—something she didn't give easily. Even though Dane had always been carefree and rambunctious, she never thought he'd break the law. After he was sent off to juvenile detention to finish out his senior year, she had mostly stayed to herself. Selena and Bridgett had been her friends, but once they began dating guys, it was like she was the third wheel.

Spending time with her granddad was a gift—no matter how eccentric, and even sometimes embarrassing, she found him when she young. His hobby of making music with spoons had been exciting and curious to some, but for a teenager who'd moved to a new school, it'd brought unwanted attention when he performed at local events. A few times a week, he'd meet his friends and practice, and occasionally they'd play at festivals or break out the spoons after a meal at a local diner. It was one thing she and Dane had in common—they were two of a few teens who didn't have a parent at home. She lived with a grandparent, and he lived in different places—sometimes with a neighbor and other times with his grandmother.

"I didn't do it."

"Do what?"

"You're thinking about me stealing Principal Scruggs's Mustang. I didn't knowingly steal it. Keaton Stebbins gave me the keys and told me to take *his* car for a spin. Looking back, it wasn't too bright of me, but I believed him and was excited to show off my driving skills."

She sighed and shook her head. They'd had this short and to-the-point discussion eleven years ago in high school. "I'm not going to argue because I saw you, Dane. I wished I hadn't, but I did. The red Mustang pulled out of Principal Scruggs's driveway, and you were the one to get out of the driver's seat at Talley Field. Everyone knew the Mustang belonged to Scruggs."

"Not me." He shook his head. "I was a dumb kid, trying to get attention. But I was no thief. Like I said, Keaton gave me the keys. I assumed that was *his* house and *his* car. I didn't ask questions. I was just glad to be included."

Josie refused to argue with him. She knew what she saw, even though it brought her no pleasure. Did he really expect her to believe he didn't know the muscle car belonged to the principal? Keaton Stebbins's dad was the county district attorney. From what Josie knew of Keaton, he was a good kid. Dane had disappointed her more than she let anyone know. She had needed him back then. Before her family had perished in the fire and Josie had been the sole survivor, she'd been confident and had plenty of friends. Then in one moment, everything changed.

"I'm not my dad."

Not in everything, no. "I never said you were."

He squinted his eyes at her, indicating he knew what she thought. "You want to tell me about Everly's dad?"

His change of subject was a relief. "I don't know what there is to tell. He was a great man—a caring dad and a competent investigator."

He nodded. "So, he was an investigator. That's how you met him."

"Yeah. I got into law enforcement with the encouragement of my granddad, a family tradition type of thing, but you knew my plans. We talked about our futures enough times." Not only had her granddad been a small-town police officer, but he also had a couple of retired friends from the department who had invited her to spend time with their families. To this day, Granddad spent time with two of his retired police buddies playing spoons and talking about the old days. "Even though Pierce didn't work for the sheriff's department, occasionally we'd talk on the phone or see each other in the same circles."

She glanced at Dane. Everly's head was snuggled into his neck, her long braids dangling down to his chest, and she was still fast asleep.

Poor thing. She was sure to be missing her dad, which probably made her instant attachment to Dane unavoidable.

"How long were you two married?"

She stopped in her tracks. "What? We weren't married."

"Oh. Sorry." He shrugged. "I just assumed..."

If the situation weren't so serious, she might've laughed. "He wasn't my boyfriend either."

Confusion etched across his brow.

"His wife died six years ago, and upon his death, Everly was left alone with no family who wanted to take in an eight-year-old. I adopted her."

"I didn't know."

Was that relief in his expression? She shook her head, and a smile crept up.

Dane threw his free hand in the air defensively. "Being shot at hasn't exactly given us time to talk. I guess you've never been married?"

"No. And you?"

He shook his head. "Too busy trying to build the business with Harlan. I've gone out on a few dates."

She almost laughed out loud. Even though

she hadn't seen Dane in years, in a graduating class of forty-one, everyone tended to keep up with one another. One of her friends, Tara, had told her she'd heard Dane had moved about thirty minutes west of Liberty and was working in construction. Then a couple of years ago, Susan told her Dane had gone into business for himself, and she saw him driving a black sports car with a pretty blonde in the passenger seat. Susan laughed and made a crack wondering if he'd stolen the car.

Being annoyed, Josie had quickly cut Susan's conversation short. She didn't know if it was the callous joke or that Dane was with a girl, but she had no desire to talk anymore.

Josie had dated a couple of guys, but nothing serious. She didn't want to discuss her personal life with Dane or anyone. Personal life. Ha. As if she had one. The last few years, her energy and time had been taken up with her private investigation company and volunteering with the Bring the Children Home Project. There were times she longed to have someone besides her grandfather to share good news with—such as when a missing child was reunited with their family. Or like last year when she was shot under the ribcage while helping Chandler Murphy, the K-9 handler for the team, work a case to find a missing boy. It would've been nice to have someone at her side during her hospital stay and recovery. But at what cost? How would she deal with it if she lost someone else? She didn't know if she could survive that kind of loss again.

One thing was certain, she didn't need to be distracted with Dane. Her daughter had to be her top priority. "I'll take Everly now."

Dane started to tell her he could handle carrying the girl, especially since Everly might be too heavy and awkward for Josie to carry. He could see that Josie had made up her mind, so he handed her daughter over.

Once Josie positioned her against her chest, and her arms were securely wrapped around the girl, they took off again.

He shouldn't have cared that Josie wasn't married, but he was glad. Even though their relationship had ended terribly, he had thought of her often and occasionally looked her up on social media. It had been a year or more since he'd searched. That was why he'd been so surprised to realize she had a daughter. He couldn't figure out how he had missed that when most people posted news of their kids all the time. Now it made sense.

Back in high school, she had been the one person who seemed to *get* him. He told himself she was too good for him. Since they'd lived on the same road, they had gotten to know each other. One day his car—his grandmother's vehicle that he drove—broke down some five miles from his house, and he started walking. Josie came along and gave him a ride the rest of the way home. Since neither had a vehicle of their own but used their grandparents', they began to share rides and soon talked for hours like best friends. The summer between his junior and senior year, they'd finally begun to date.

Going out with Josie had been the first sign of hope in his life, a sign that made him believe he didn't have to turn out like his family. He'd heard the whispers, and sometimes experienced downright animosity because of his family. It was no secret to the community his dad, Tyrus, had done time in prison for theft. The theft had been personal to many in the community. He loved not only to steal from neighbors when they went on vacation or were at work, but also to nab packages that were delivered to businesses and homes. Many times, Dane thought how much his dad would've loved the apps nowadays that show where the delivery trucks were making stops.

But it was when his dad turned to robbing banks that the authorities really took notice. If he had just robbed the one bank, he may've never been caught. But it was dad's third time that did him in. There was an off-duty police officer in the lobby who took him down.

His dad caught pneumonia while in prison and died after only serving two years.

His older brother, Randy, had been sent to an alternative school for threatening a teacher with a knife. Before Josie, Dane had tried to do anything for attention—most of the time it leaned toward the dangerous side. Like riding his motorcycle recklessly and trying stunts. It had worked, too. Kids took notice of him and so did the adults.

"Oh." Josie tripped over something, almost causing her to fall with Everly.

He stepped forward to prepare to catch her. "Are you all right?"

"I'm fine. I stepped in a hole."

The girl wiggled in Josie's arms and opened her eyes, before falling back asleep.

"If you need me to take another turn, I don't mind." But as he figured, she shook her head, not taking him up on his offer.

After a few minutes he asked, "What was in the police report from when Everly's dad died?"

"I don't think there was a police report, but only the autopsy. I didn't realize anything at the time was suspect. I received a copy of the official documents when I adopted her, but with Pierce's house being in probate, the estate needed to be cleaned out, so I never saw the need to dig further, and I haven't gone back over everything."

"Totally understandable. Sounds like the police didn't either."

"I should've gone through everything by now. It's my job to perform mundane activities like sifting through paperwork. My daughter had been living with this burden for months..."

"Josie, you can't beat yourself up over this. There was no way you could know." She didn't respond but kept trekking across the pasture. He understood wanting to blame oneself for not noticing something like that, but it could only prove a distraction to her ability to keep Everly safe now.

Dane mulled over the situation, and ways to

make it easier on them kept returning to his mind. "I'd like to run ahead and retrieve your Bronco to come back and pick you two up, so you don't have to walk. Or I could get my motorcycle and ride it to get your vehicle. Would you be comfortable with that if we find a place for you to hide?"

She shook her head. "That thought crossed my mind, too. But I think we'd be safer sticking together. Two guns are better than one should the two men find us. Even if you aren't trained."

Dane didn't particularly like being reminded he wasn't trained to use a gun. He'd hunted when he was younger and knew how to shoot. Evening the score should another shoot-out happen had occurred to him, too. "I can protect us if need be."

"It'd be helpful if we knew the men's identities."

Everly's head popped up. "Has my daddy's killer found us again?"

Josie exchanged glances with Dane as she patted Everly on the back. "No, baby. We were just talking."

They needed to be careful of what they discussed in front of the girl. No doubt she was scared enough. He couldn't imagine Violet being in this predicament.

"Honey, what happened to your dad?" Josie asked.

Brown eyes stared at Josie. "I don't want..."

"It's okay." Josie smiled. "No one's going to hurt me or you."

Dane's gut tightened at the heartbreaking concern that laced Josie's voice.

"My daddy and me were working in the backyard. He was using the weed trimmer, and I was putting away my toys. The man drove up, and Daddy started talking to him. I went inside to get us something to drink and use the bathroom. When I came out of the bathroom, I heard yelling and ran to the window. The man hit my dad in the face and then they started fighting. I yelled for them to stop. The man pulled a knife and tried to stab my dad. Daddy was too fast and dodged.

"I screamed. When Daddy looked at me, the man tackled him into the hot tub and held him under. When Daddy stopped kicking, the man saw me, and I ran out the front door and hid in my treehouse. Dexter had been barking and growling. I peeked through the window to see Dex bite the man's arm.

"And then a delivery truck pulled up. The man yelled at me that he would kill me like he did my dad if I told anyone. Then he ran into the woods."

"Oh, honey, I'm so sorry."

He wished Everly would've told Josie, but the killer had made certain she was too scared. Dane clenched his jaw. How could a man threaten the girl? "Do you know the man's name? Had you ever seen him before?"

Everly shook her head. "Never."

Josie glanced over her shoulder at Dane. "We need to let—" she cleared her throat "—let authorities know about this as soon as possible."

"No. No." Everly wiggled in her grasp. "He'll kill me."

Josie released a sigh as she clung to her daughter. "I'll protect you. Do you understand? As long as you're with me, nothing is going to happen to you."

A long hill appeared in front of them, and Dane held out his hands. "Can I have a turn?"

Creases lined Josie's forehead, but she handed over the girl.

As soon as Everly was in his arms, he asked, "How's that foot feeling?"

"It's hurts a little."

"Not too bad?"

"I can walk."

"How about you let me carry you for a while, at least as far as your mama did. You wouldn't want me to think your mama is stronger than me, would you?"

She giggled. "No."

Dexter trotted beside them, occasionally sniffing the ground and wandering in and out of the brush.

Josie whispered, "I'll be glad when I can call my boss and get some protection."

He would keep them safe. He'd be glad when Josie understood that. They had to be several miles from the cabin. He wasn't certain how far they would go, but they needed to keep heading south. He had stayed around the barn and had traveled into town a few times but hadn't gone in this direction much at all.

"I never thought I would say this, but I wish there were more houses out this way. A farm—anything."

"I know what you mean."

The night sounds were mild with only a gentle breeze blowing the grass and an occasional bawl of a cow. Not even the chirp of crickets or croaking of frogs could be heard, so when a light hum sounded in the distance, he looked at Josie and said, "Let's move closer to the tree line."

"You think that's them?"

"I'd say so. Not much traffic this time of night out here."

Everly's eyes grew large. "They found us again?"

"Everything is going to be okay. You can count on it." He tapped her under the chin to show his confidence in his words.

Headlights suddenly appeared behind them.

Keeping one step ahead of these guys might be more complicated than initially thought. "It's time to run."

Chapter Five

They hurried across the open pasture, and the trees had to be a hundred yards away.

A cow bawled and then another. The Angus herd came into view as they topped the hill—their stocky black bodies barely detectable in the moonlight.

Josie looked over her shoulder as headlights bounced along the path. The bashed-up truck flew up the road. The guys should be coming up on their disabled truck. Sure enough, the men stopped. "They must know our vehicle broke down."

A few seconds later, the men took off again.

Lights shone in the pasture on the opposite side of the road and then swung back in their direction.

Dane yelled, "Get down."

She dropped to her stomach in the tall grass,

Dane beside her. He put a protective arm around Everly. "Stay down, honey."

"Lie down, Dexter." The collie sprawled next to Everly. Her daughter didn't say a word, but the fear on her face said enough.

A door slammed, and something crossed in front of the lights. The men were walking around. "Are they searching for beaten-down grass to determine which way we went?"

"Looks like it."

Suddenly, the man hurried back into the truck and gassed it toward them through the pasture. The urge to get up and run for the trees called her name, but then they'd give away their hiding place. Indecision plagued her. "You think we should run for it?"

"Wait." He held up a finger. "I doubt our tracks are that visible."

"But they may have nothing else to do but drive around. I can't just lie here and wait for them to find us. Everly, come with me but stay low." She got to her feet and took off when the headlights swung away from them. "Go."

Her daughter ran, but it was slow and with a limp. Dane scooped her up. They'd gone only about twenty yards when he again yelled, "Down."

They all dropped again. Josie watched the lights bounce across the terraces in the pasture. *Dear God, help us know what to do. I don't want to get in a shoot-out.*

The cows continued to bawl and suddenly an idea crossed her mind. She'd probably watched too many Westerns, but people were always using a stampede in the movies. That probably wasn't a good idea unless the men were on foot. As soon as the truck turned in a parallel direction, she said, "Come on. And don't stop."

They ran across the open field, Josie moving fast. Even while carrying Everly, Dane remained close to her side. Dexter stayed beside them. Only fifty more yards until they would be under the protection of the trees, and the area illuminated around them.

The engine revved as it came across the open place, and the cattle watched. A few of the calves trotted to get beside their mothers.

A gunshot went off.

They weren't going to make it. Her boot stepped into a hole, and she almost went down. As she regained her footing another shot went off.

She drew her gun. "Go. Get to the trees."

But instead of doing as she said, Dane put

Everly on the ground. He removed his gun from his waistband. "I've got this. Hurry. Protect the girl."

Josie wanted to argue, but he was right. She picked Everly up and sprinted as fast as she could for the woods with Dexter.

"I can walk." Everly squirmed in her grasp.

"Not yet."

Dane fired his Glock, and then more shots were returned at them. One whizzed past Josie's head, and she ducked as if it would help.

There was more bawling from the cattle, and then they were running. The herd turned straight at them with several cows leading the pack, jumping over brush and dodging others. The stampede had started. There was nowhere to go. Not knowing what else to do, she waved her free arm at the cows and yelled, "Yaw! Get back!"

The herd split, and she was able to make for the trees. She put Everly down behind a large pecan tree. "Stay behind the trunk with Dexter. I don't want you getting hit by a stray bullet."

"Okay. Be careful."

She made eye contact and gave her daughter a reassuring smile. "I will."

When she turned around, the truck was still

heading toward them, but Dane was nowhere in sight. The sound of gunfire had dissipated among the running cattle. Her heart sped up as she looked around. The cows were still on the move, but she could barely see them on the far side of the pasture.

A few washes cut across the land and the truck bounced up and down as it made tracks toward them.

"Where's Dane?" Everly asked.

"I don't know, but he knows how to stay out of trouble." Ever since the day she'd met him, he'd been good at getting out of messes, even dangerous ones. She hoped he did this time as well. "We need to keep moving."

But as they headed deeper into the woods, she wondered what had happened to him. Had he taken off to escape and wasn't coming back? Or had he been trampled by the cattle?

There was no benefit to fretting about her ex-boyfriend. Her focus needed to be on getting Everly to safety and figuring out how she was going to get to her vehicle.

Before the men found them again.

Dane lay in the tall grass, the back of his leg throbbing with pain. A cow had rushed toward him. He'd tried to move but wasn't quick enough. He was knocked to the ground and then another cow tried to leap him, but her back leg came down on his hamstring.

He'd seen Josie and Everly make it into the thicket. He was glad they kept going and didn't wait for him. The men were almost to the trees. Their window was down, and their hollering at each other was easy to hear. "In there. She disappeared into the woods."

Oh no, you don't. He aimed his Glock and waited for them to draw closer. *Closer. Closer.* When they were thirty yards in front of him, he shot. Sparks from the bullet hit the side of the cab.

One of the men yelled something and returned fire, but his aim was off since they didn't know his location. He waited for the vehicle to pass. Josie couldn't be seen, but the truck made several passes. Finally, the driver stopped, and his passenger got out and headed into the woods. The truck proceeded along the tree line in the direction of the cabin.

Dane's chest tightened. He had hoped the men wouldn't separate. Once the truck had gone farther away, he climbed to his feet and made his way toward the trees. The back of his leg cramped but he was determined not to let it slow him down. Following at a distance, he stayed to the edge of the tree line while being on the lookout for Josie.

There was no noise, which concerned him. After all this time, he still couldn't believe he was helping Josie Hunt. He'd had a crush on her in high school, but like many others, it took a while for her to know he existed. Once they began to talk, they'd become friends almost instantly. He'd felt betrayed when she told the police he was the one responsible for the theft. And if he was totally honest, deeply hurt. She had acted like he'd let her down. Well, he wouldn't disappoint her this time.

The truck had all but disappeared—the sound of the engine fading in the night.

He kept a constant watch on the trees and the pasture while occasionally turning around to make certain the gunman hadn't come up behind him.

Several minutes passed and then more time. Worry began to set in. Where had she gone? Surely, she hadn't kept going deeper into the woods. Their plan had been to go to the cabin.

What if the man had found her? Surely, he would've heard the commotion. Josie would shoot to protect them—unless the man had snuck up on her catching her unaware.

Another glance at the woods produced no sightings of anyone.

A growl rose in the night.

Chills popped up on his arms. Heavy animal breathing accompanied the distinctive sounds. It was one thing to hear a bear on television, but quite a different story in the country at night. Was he on Josie and Everly's trail?

Dane took off through the tall grass at a run. With the gunman and the bear close by, he needed to find them quickly.

Limbs snapped and the sound of running through the trees came from his left. *Josie.* His chest grew tight with each step, and he turned toward the growing sounds.

Just as he got to the end of the pasture, a figure ran out of the forest. The gunman. The black bear was on all fours right behind him.

Dane stopped.

The gunman squealed and dropped his weapon.

He watched as the guy trekked across the pasture. After several yards, the bear stopped his pursuit to a walk, and the man kept going while looking over his shoulder.

The animal turned and put his nose into the air.

Dane stood still, holding his breath.

With a final grunt, the beast trotted back to the woods and disappeared.

It took a few seconds before he moved again. And when he did, the hamstring pain returned full force. Even though he hadn't checked the injury, he was certain it wasn't serious. More annoying than anything.

Hopefully, Josie knew to keep going, but he could only guess she had continued moving south toward the cabin. The thought that the gunman had killed Everly's dad didn't sit well in his gut. The man must've determined he had no choice but to get rid of her. Dane needed to catch up to the mother-daughter team before the killer did.

He skirted wide of the area where the bear had gone while keeping watch and picked up the rifle the man had dropped. The silhouette of the gunman could only be seen occasionally. The herd of cattle was out of view. A towering oak tree stood out from among the rest about thirty yards ahead. If he made it to that tree without seeing Josie, he would enter the woods.

As he approached the oak and didn't see her, he started to veer toward the woods.

"Where are you going?"

He flinched at the sudden female voice. Josie stepped out from behind a large bush.

"How long have you been waiting here?"

"Several minutes." She moved closer as Everly limped beside her. "When we hit the woods, we hoofed it through the trees. I heard the bear again and didn't stick around."

"I can see that. The gunman caught the bear's attention." A chuckle creeped into his voice. "Chased him for a bit."

"Really? I wished I could've witnessed that."

"The bear returned into the woods, so let's get moving."

"I heard something crash in the trees. It must've been him."

Everly walked between them with Dexter. Her limp wasn't as prominent.

"How's the ankle? Feeling better?"

"A little. It doesn't hurt as much after I walk on it."

"Would you like for me to carry you?"

The girl shook her head. Her shoulders sagged. "Nah. I'm good. Just tired."

Josie looked down at her, and he thought she

was going to say something but then changed her mind. Then she glanced at him.

He mouthed, "She's okay."

Josie whispered, "I know."

But the worry lines on her face said she'd prefer it if Everly accepted help.

As they traveled, Dane kept a lookout for the bear, the gunman, and their truck. Over the next hour, there were a couple of times he thought he heard an engine in the distance, but he never saw them. At one point, Everly allowed him to carry her for a while before asking to be put back down.

Eventually, the cabin came into sight, and he put out his hand. "Wait. I want to make sure the men aren't waiting for us."

Everly dropped to the ground, folded her legs crisscross and rested her chin on her hands. Dexter lay beside her and placed his head on her lap.

They watched the home for several minutes. He finally said, "There's no sign of the truck. I think we're clear."

"Yeah, and I thought that earlier, too. But he was here waiting for us."

Dane nodded. She was right. Their man could've parked up the road or in the pasture somewhere hidden from sight. "Let me check it out. You stay here with Everly."

She reached into her pocket and pulled out her keys to her. "Here."

He took them and kept an eye out as he made his way to the yard. He skirted around her Bronco. By all appearances the men had not messed with it. He climbed in and started it. When he looked up, Josie and Everly headed his way. He got out to let her climb in. "Let me grab our suitcases."

"I'm going in with you."

She glanced over her shoulder at him but didn't comment. All three of them stuck together walking into the cabin and Dane grabbed their luggage. He didn't know how they'd left the cabin, but nothing looked out of place to him. They hurried back down the porch. Seconds later, Josie was in the driver's seat.

"Hop in the back, Everly." The girl did as she was asked.

He wanted to go with her, but he also didn't want to put her in danger. "I think I should stay here."

Josie shook her head. "Those men will be back."

"I know. But I can't have authorities searching for me."

"They're searching for you anyways. And those men just found your hiding place. I don't care what you do, but you need to make up your mind."

Everything in him told him once he was back in town, it'd be difficult to stay hidden. Headlights shone in the distance. He looked over his shoulder.

"Well?" Her eyebrows shot up.

He'd just have to find a new place. "Hit it." He hopped in.

She peeled out of the driveway and headed down the rock road at a fast past. Her lifted vehicle sported leather seats and the engine ran smoothly. His mind whirled where she could drop him off that wouldn't compromise his safety. There was nowhere. His business partner and friend had been murdered. He'd made few friends. He'd disappointed Josie once and he didn't intend on a repeat.

If he got himself thrown in jail, she and her daughter would be on their own. He couldn't allow that to happen.

Chapter Six

Josie made it to the highway without incident. Her mind struggled to make sense of everything. She still couldn't believe Everly had seen Pierce murdered. The police had believed it was an accident immediately, and the coroner must've agreed.

If Pierce had drowned, then surely there would've been water in his lungs. If he'd died of electrocution, burns on the skin would've been present.

A few minutes later, she glanced over the backseat and saw that Everly was slumped in her seat fast asleep. Her heart constricted. She couldn't imagine the fear she must've been going through.

"She's a sweet girl."

She glanced at Dane and took in his beard and the black T-shirt with the small hole in it. No one would've guessed he had been a business owner. Even though she'd dated him, she'd heard the rumors and insults. He was branded a bad apple, a troublemaker—someone the teachers griped openly about. His dad had spent time in prison and his mom drank a lot. He had an older brother who had gotten kicked out of school for something. For what she couldn't remember. By the time Josie came on the scene, his brother wasn't in the picture.

Even though their relationship had ended on a sour note, she still owed him appreciation. "Thank you for helping us."

"You don't have to thank me."

Other than the hum of the engine, silence filled the cab. Her lights melted into the highway. No other vehicles were in sight. Awkwardness grew. She was probably careless to take him with her since he was a wanted man, but she couldn't leave him back there with those men hunting them. Still, she had a duty to do. "I'll have to tell my boss and the sheriff about you."

Alert blue eyes glistened back at her even with the darkness of the cab. "I would expect no less. I don't suppose it matters that I didn't kill my partner."

She turned her attention back to the road. Of course, he would claim he was innocent. But he'd claimed innocence over stealing the car, too. And she'd seen that with her own eyes. "That's not my place to judge. A jury will decide."

He nodded. "Because the system always gets it right?"

Almost, yes. The system was as good as they had. But she refused to reply to that question. She could feel his eyes on her. It was unnerving. He wasn't going to make her feel guilty. The police had tried to arrest him, and he'd run. Why would an innocent man do that? He wouldn't.

The highway dead-ended into the interstate, and she turned right toward Liberty. It was four forty-two in the morning—meaning she'd been up almost twenty-four hours. Her body was racked with exhaustion and a headache crawled from the front of her head to the back. The tree limb had almost knocked her unconscious. Dane hadn't hesitated to carry her back to his place.

Correction—his hideout.

He didn't have to help her. And he'd saved Everly from the bear. And his truck was worthless now. She tried to push the guilt aside, but it wouldn't budge. He couldn't expect her to hide a fugitive.

"Mind if I ask you something personal?"

She glanced at him and took in the seriousness of his expression. "Ask away. No guarantees, though."

"How long did it take for the adoption process for Everly?"

This was not what she expected. She scrutinized him, trying to figure out if he was attempting to divert her attention away from the talk of running from authorities.

His gaze went to the floorboard.

Because she had dreamed about having a family for years, when Everly's single dad died and there was the first mention of the state taking conservatorship, she'd moved quickly. She didn't want the girl to go into foster care if she could help it.

She'd met Everly a couple of times and had taken to her immediately. But still, Josie was protective over Everly and didn't like to talk about her adoption. Josie remembered after her family died and her grandfather took her in, people would ask her about her *real* parents. The constant reminder that her granddad wasn't "real" frustrated her. And it was like everything else that used to make her *her* had taken a backseat to the fire or what it was like to be raised by her grandfather. Almost like it changed her identity. In her previous school, she'd played tennis, was the first-string pitcher in softball, and her team had gone to state in volleyball. Because Liberty was smaller, only track, basketball, and drill team were offered for females. Her mom had also been teaching Josie and her sister to quilt. Josie had won a blue ribbon at the 4-H fair.

She had struggled to fit in and didn't want to see that happen to Everly, starting with not subjecting her to going on about the adoption. "Four months."

He frowned and mumbled, "That's not much time."

"What does that mean? Time for what?"

"Nothing." He shook his head. "I know you have other things on your mind, like getting Everly back to Liberty and going to the police."

He was right, of course. But still, he bugged her. Why would Dane Haggerty want to know about adoption? Surely, with him being a fugitive he wasn't thinking of adopting a child. "Spill it, Dane."

He turned to her, amusement dancing in his

eyes, and then he sobered. "Violet, my sister. She's being taken away by the courts. For now, she's in foster care. Don't laugh, but I want to raise her."

"I would never laugh at that." She could see by his expression, he was serious. Josie barely remembered his curly-haired little sister. When she'd dated Dane, he lived with his maternal grandmother and then moved in with a neighbor. He'd talked of Violet often. "How old is she now?"

He worked his jaw. "Thirteen."

"Wow. I can't believe it. She was practically a baby when we were in school." As the hum of the tires on the pavement filled the silence, Josie realized he was done with the subject. A pang in her heart made it difficult to swallow. That was the age she'd been when her family died. She couldn't imagine being in foster care at such a fragile age. He had been enamored with his younger sister, so she didn't know why it surprised her he wanted to adopt her. But could he really offer her a better life?

She glanced his way and caught him fidgeting with his jeans. Violet was a difficult subject for him, but she had the feeling he hadn't made the decision lightly.

"You can quit staring at me. I don't want to go to prison for a crime I didn't commit, but I also have things I want to live for. That shouldn't shock you."

It was like he'd read her mind. Even though he had a reckless nature, she'd always believed Dane Haggerty had a soft heart. "You…" She swallowed. "You'll make a great dad."

To her surprise, she meant it.

He turned to her. "I hope so. I pray about it every day."

The pink of morning showed in her rear-view mirror as she was about ten miles outside of Liberty. They stopped at an all-night gas station, and she filled up with gas and picked up a burner phone that she used to call her boss, Bliss.

"Hello."

"Bliss, it me, Josie."

"What's going on? I know it must be important for you to call this early. I thought you were on a camping trip."

She drew a deep breath, still debating whether to tell her about Dane. "I realize you're busy but thought you would want to know what's going on. Everly and I were attacked last night. Long story short, after being chased through the woods by a guy with a gun, Everly admitted she witnessed her father's murder, and this guy threatened her. He's been following her ever since and finally caught up to her on our trip."

"Oh my! What a horrible thing to witness! I'm so sorry. Poor girl. I had thought Pierce died of an accident."

"Me too."

"Have you talked with law enforcement yet?"

"I'm going to call them as soon as I hang up from you. I lost my phone and just now picked up a new one."

There was a second of silence. "You know I'm in San Antonio on Mitchell's case, or I'd drive up. If you need help, call Chandler or Kennedy. Annie and Riggs are working on a case right now."

"I will. Have you learned anything valuable?"

"It looks promising. But I want you to get protection for you and your daughter. This is not the time to be alone."

Josie cringed inwardly and took a deep breath. "I will not be alone. If you need help once this thing with Everly is cleared up, give me a holler."

After they disconnected, she glanced over to Dane and their eyes met.

"I didn't ask you not to tell your boss about me."

"I know. And I would've given her more details if she didn't have important things going on in her life."

"Important case?"

"The most important case of her life. I don't suppose you've heard of Bliss Walker. Well, now her name is Bliss Adcock. She got married last year to a Texas Ranger."

He shook his head. "I know you try to find missing children."

"Bliss is the founder of our group. Years ago, while working for the US Marshals, her husband was killed in a car accident, and her son went missing from the wreckage. After years of searching for and not finding her son, she took early retirement and created the Bring the Children Home Project. Last year, her son's remains were found. A couple of weeks ago, a similar case happened where an FBI agent's wife was killed in an obvious hit-and-run just as the agent was narrowing in on a suspect in a drug smuggling ring. The same suspect Bliss had been working. I don't know all the details, but it sounds like the two may be connected."

Josie prayed Bliss found closure and the persons responsible for their deaths were brought to justice.

"Oh, that's tough. I'll pray they find who was behind it."

Was Dane for real? He rarely mentioned God or prayed back when they dated except when he visited worship services with her. She mainly believed he went with her just to have more time with her. But there was no benefit to having an in-depth conversation with him. She wasn't looking to rekindle an old flame.

She hated to drop him off at the sheriff's department, but she firmly believed in the law and doing the right thing. As they neared town, she needed to make up her mind.

"You can drop me off anywhere out here."

"What?" She turned to him and could see he was serious. "The law is hunting you, and now a killer may also be after you."

He stared. "Thanks. I won't need anyone's help."

"There's no need in getting an attitude with me. You chose to run from the law. That wasn't my fault."

"You would've, too, if someone would've framed you."

"That's where you're wrong." She pointed a

finger at him. "I would trust the law officers to do their job."

"Oh, how the girl from high school who finished in the top of our class and whose granddad was in law enforcement thinks she knows everything about the rest of us."

"I worked hard in school."

"So did I. Kindly pull over at the next road and let me out."

She shook her head. "No. You need to set this straight."

"If you don't pull over, I'll jump out."

Her gaze went to his hand on the door handle and then back to his dark steely eyes as they locked onto her—daring her to doubt his resolve. He'd always been willing to take risks. "You haven't changed a bit, Dane Haggerty."

"Actually, I have. But I'm not about to go down for a crime I didn't commit. Not when a young girl is depending on me."

The Bronco came to a stop on the shoulder of the road. Everly sat up in the back seat. "What's going on?"

"Take care, Everly," he said as he exited the vehicle. His gaze went from Everly back to Josie. Before he slammed the door, he said, "I'm sorry it had to end this way."

"Why are we leaving him?" Everly leaned over the seat, resting her arm on top.

How did she answer her? Everly already had too much to worry about. "He wants me to leave him there, honey. Right now, I'm taking you home to talk with the police."

Everly stared out the back window. "But there's nothing back there. No car or house. What's he going to do?"

Her teeth ground together as she pulled away. "I'm not certain."

As Josie checked her rearview mirror, headlights came over the horizon. She kept her speed down and watched the vehicle draw closer. Suddenly, she recognized the black truck the men had driven. She stopped and put the Bronco in Reverse and floored it.

"Watch out!" Josie's warning came out as the truck whipped onto the road she'd left Dane on. He must've just noticed them, for he ran into the ditch and the truck followed.

Dane opened fire on the truck, but it kept coming. Right as it got to him, he dodged being hit by rolling back into the road and lying flat on his belly.

Josie turned onto the road just as a grain dump

truck came from the other direction straight at Dane.

Everly yelled, “No!”

Dane ducked his head as the grain truck appeared to run over him.

Josie’s heart stopped. The large vehicle halted in the middle of the road, its engine humming.

Meanwhile, the black truck continued into the ditch and then pulled back onto the road going in the other direction.

She stopped on the shoulder, got out and ran to Dane, who was on the other side of the grain truck.

His hands covered his head. Slowly, he looked up at her. “I’m still alive?”

“You won’t be for long if we don’t get you out of here.” She bent over and gave him a hand up.

“What are you doing?” The driver of the grain truck hurried his way. “I almost killed you.”

“I’m glad you didn’t.” Dane shot him a smile as Josie hurried him toward her vehicle.

As soon as he was back in, she pointed her finger at him. “Don’t ever threaten to pull such a dangerous stunt on me again, or I’ll...” Everly's eyes grew large from the backseat, and Josie warned, "Just don't."

"I would've waited for you to slow a little." He smiled.

"I don't care." She hoped her voice conveyed the seriousness she intended.

"Understood. Now let me go from here."

She shook her head, but then she knew he was right. He wouldn't allow her to take him to the sheriff's department, but it wouldn't be smart for her to know where he was going. "Okay."

He hurried into the adjoining pasture. He took off at a jog, and she watched him disappear into some trees. When she was satisfied he was out of sight and the men's truck hadn't returned, she got back on the road.

"I don't know why you let him go." Everly frowned.

"There are things you don't understand." But as Josie got her speed up on the highway, Dane's words replayed through her mind. *I don't suppose it matters that I didn't kill my partner.* If he didn't, then he had nothing to hide. Why run? Especially now that he knew the man who had targeted them at the cabin was also after him?

Her phone rang and Bliss's name showed on the screen. "This is Josie."

"I talked with Sheriff Van Carroll. He's out of town but he's sending a deputy to meet you at your house, and Chandler should be giving you a call."

"I plan to do more research on the victim to find potential suspects." Josie purposely didn't mention Pierce's name in front of Everly. Bliss had a great working relationship with the sheriff, so she appreciated her making the call. "The sooner we find this guy, the better."

"I agree."

"I know. Thanks." After she disconnected, she turned on the white rock road to her house. The older farmhouse sat in the middle of a large pasture, with only a scattering of trees. The home was fashioned as a Queen Anne Victorian, but much smaller than most with only a single-story and a wrap-around porch.

Everly's bike leaned against the white fence. The front porch light was on, but the rest of the house was dark—just the way she'd left it. Neither the deputy nor Chandler was here yet. She pulled across the cattle guard and kept an eye out for anything out of the ordinary. The doorless garage sat ten yards from the home, and she drove inside. "We're home."

"Will we be safe here?"

Josie gave her what she hoped was a reassuring smile. "Yes. But remember to let me know anything—" how to say it? "—anything that happens that I need to know about. Please don't be nervous confiding in me."

"Okay." Everly got out of the back seat. Dexter leaped down after her.

Josie grabbed their bags as Everly and the dog ran up the steps to the back porch. Her daughter retrieved the keys from under the ceramic frog. As she thought about Pierce's killer following Everly for months, it suddenly dawned on her that he would know where they lived. She dropped the bags. "Everly, wait!"

But she'd already opened the door and disappeared inside.

Josie was hurrying up the steps when Everly screamed. Her heart constricted at the sound as she removed her Sig from her pocket and stepped inside.

Crying reached her as she ran to the back of her house to Everly's room. Her daughter wrapped her arms around herself. Her teddy bear was lying on the bed with a piece of cloth wrapped around its mouth and a note pinned to it.

Dane made tracks through the woods and came out on the other side—where the backyard of a modest brick house blended into the morning sunrise. He shielded his eyes as he strode to the residence. A tabby cat jumped from a planter's box in the window and followed him around the front of the home. Before he could rap on the door, it opened.

"Dane Haggerty. It's good of you to drop by. Haven't seen you in forever."

He hated to involve this woman, but he had little choice. "I need help, Nellie."

The older lady waved him in. "Come on in."

Nellie Hickman had cleaned North Texas Custom Builder's offices twice a week since the day they opened. Harlan had known the woman for years before then. "I guess you haven't heard."

The woman wore an apron that read *Never Trust a Skinny Chef.* "I hear things all the time. That doesn't mean I believe them."

He looked up into kind eyes. "That means a lot to me."

"Have you eaten breakfast?"

He'd skipped supper last night but didn't want to stay longer than necessary. "I don't want to bring trouble to your door. I need a ride."

She folded her arms across her chest and stared at him for several seconds as if in thought. "Come with me."

Dane followed her out the back door to the garage. A large beige tarp lay on top of a couple of vehicles, and she peeled it off to reveal an old classic blue pickup. He let out a whistle. "That's nice, but I couldn't..."

"I wasn't offering it to you." She smiled. "My father-in-law bought this new in 1962 and my Roger restored it. I ain't gettin' no younger and figure it's about time I drive it." She jerked her head at the other vehicle. "That one is for you."

A four-door silver sedan that was probably fifteen years old, and the paint was beginning to fade was parked beside the truck. Nellie tossed Dane the keys. He admitted this vehicle would bring him less attention, which was what he needed.

"You don't have to do this."

"I know it. Bring it back to me when you're done with it."

"I will."

"It won't do you no good to leave here on an

empty stomach. Come in and I'll fix you some bacon and eggs. Won't take five minutes and I don't want no argument."

Dane followed the lady back instead.

"Fishing has been good this year. Have you been?"

"A couple of times. Caught me a large catfish." Even though he was on the run, it was important to blend in. He'd gone fishing on a stock tank on the land where he'd stayed.

The woman's bright eyes glistened. "It's been a while since I had fish fry. Alec hasn't had much time to go this year. You need to stop by later, and we'll have one." She started frying bacon while she talked, and then cracked some eggs in a bowl where she gave them a quick whisk. Soon, she had them in a separate pan.

"I'd like that. Let's plan on it." Alec was Nellie's son who'd worked for Harlan and him a while back before they had to let him go due to problems with alcohol. It was a shame, too, because Nellie was a gem. Back when Dane was young, Nellie often gave him odd jobs to do around the yard and always paid. That might seem small to some people, but for Dane, who had little spending money, it had meant the world.

True to her word, Nellie had the food ready in minutes. She handed him the meal on a paper plate with a plastic fork and knife, along with coffee in a foam cup. "Have a good day. I hope you can get the business back up and running soon."

"Me too. Thank you." Dane settled into the sedan and put his food in the console, then pulled out of the driveway. There were few people he could depend on, and appreciation for the older woman grew.

He turned left onto the highway—the opposite direction Josie had gone. He had to stay in hiding. Josie had worked with the sheriff's department and now with the Bring Home the Children Project, which employed many with backgrounds in law enforcement. She would be in good hands. Much better than Dane was.

Time was closing in on getting custody of Violet. It may already be too late because he'd have to prove his innocence and then that he could be a suitable parent. Being a fugitive made it almost impossible.

He needed to go to his office to see if any evidence had been missed. Driving Nellie's car, he had to be careful. He didn't want to get her in trouble in case he was pulled over or caught.

Although unlikely, he didn't want to take the chance of her being charged as an accomplice. He figured she'd play ignorant of his runaway status, though, if questioned, just as she had with him. Anyone seeing her car at the office would assume she was working.

The sun shone bright and summer flowers were in bloom. Everything seemed normal, completely unlike his world, which had been turned upside down.

His office building sat on a county highway. Not expensive real estate, but in an easy to get to location. It was nine thirty in the morning with the normal business traffic of work pickups, semitrucks and a variety of other vehicles. As he neared his office, the neighboring business, Kountry Kuts, had three cars parked out front, and the heavy equipment rental place had several pickups in the parking lot.

His foot eased off the gas as he passed North Texas Custom Builders. No vehicles were parked out front, and a closed sign stood in the window. He continued past and drove to the next road about a half mile down. After turning around, he kept a lookout for anyone suspicious who could be looking for him, but he saw no one. Maybe in the months he'd been in hiding, the authorities or bounty hunters had quit staking out the place. Instead of going slow, he blended in with the traffic and then pulled around to the back.

With a quick glance, he climbed out of Nellie's sedan and strode to the back door. He put his key in, half expecting it not to work, but it turned. From the terms of their partnership, Harlan's widow would inherit half of the business. He stepped in and when he tried the lights, they came on. That was good. He'd done research to find out what would happen to the business should he be arrested, and from what he found, the company would be in the hands of the court. All assets would be sold, and profits would pay off the debts. Harlan's widow could buy out Dane's half. The court date had not appeared online yet.

A quick walkthrough of the downstairs showed no change except the surfaces were now dusty. Hurriedly he went up the metal stairs to his office where he had found Harlan on the floor. The bloodstains had been cleaned and the murder weapon—his granddad's hay hook—was not there. Not that he expected it to be. It was surreal looking at the business he and Harlan had worked hard to build and knowing his partner was gone and he was on the run for his murder. Their business would be dissolved. Or maybe bought by someone else. The scripture in Luke came to him that talked about a man building bigger barns to lay up treasures, but in the end, the man died. God asked who shall receive those things you have provided. As much as it made his gut tighten, Dane didn't like the thought of someone else receiving everything he and Harlan had worked for.

No doubt the police had gone through the desk and file cabinets searching for evidence. But he glanced through the paperwork anyway. Maybe something had been overlooked that only Dane would recognize.

Why had someone gone to the trouble to frame him? If it had been a simple robbery, they could've killed Harlan and run. And why use his grandfather's hay hook? Maybe the killer hadn't come with the intent to murder his partner and didn't know it belonged to him. But he didn't think so.

As these thoughts came to him, he knew he must search fast. A stack of bills was piled on the corner of the desk, and he quickly sifted through them. Besides utility and mortgage information, the only other bills were for contractors they'd used. The large desk calendar in the center of the desktop was still on the date four months prior. A quick glance at the couple of weeks before showed three deadlines for bids on upcoming jobs and several dates for completion of jobs. As always, the completion of jobs could vary depending upon a number of factors, but Harlan used a color-coded system to indicate early, goal, and last possible dates. He'd been a stickler for being on time, something their customers often commented on.

Everything looked in order on the calendar with no unknown names or appointments to draw suspicions. Next, he went through the filing cabinets. Even though the computers were used for records, Harlan liked to have a hard copy of important documents. Dane scanned them quickly and disappointment hit him when nothing presented itself as unusual.

He put his hands on his hips and glanced around the room. Some people brought work home with them, but Harlan used to advise Dane to draw a line between work and family. His partner worked long hours, but when he left for the day, work stayed here.

But did Harlan ever take things home? Was there some clue at his home office? Possibly.

Especially since the money missing from their business later turned up in his account. Dane had met Layla, Harlan's widow, on numerous occasions, but most conversations had simply been quick small talk.

Had there been something Dane had missed the days before the murder? The trash cans were empty. The murder happened on a Tuesday. Nellie cleaned on Monday and Thursday nights so that would make sense. And since Dane had found Harlan a little past seven in the morning, there'd be nothing in the receptacles.

Again, the place on the floor where Harlan's body had been lying caught his attention. He couldn't believe his friend was really gone. More like he'd left on a vacation and would be back in a couple of days.

Harlan had been an inspirational man.

Dane felt bad for not visiting Layla. After Harlan's first wife died, he married Layla—a woman eighteen years his junior—but that was before Dane knew him. Over a year ago, the accountant, Jim Price, who helped do the books for North Texas Custom Builders moved to the Dallas metroplex, and even though Layla retired from being a personal secretary to a CEO of an oil company, she showed no interest in helping with their company. Harlan tried to keep up with ledgers, and only hired Jim before tax season.

Harlan's twin daughters from his first marriage were at Baylor College, one for a BA in communications and the other a BS in biochemistry. Harlan talked about his daughters often and went to many of the college's events. With the girls away, his wife was probably lonely. He didn't know how close Layla was to her stepdaughters, being that she was only a few years older than them.

He wondered again if it was possible Harlan started taking work home with him. If so, he hadn't mentioned it.

Dane needed to get moving. He quickly went through the closets in both offices and then the tiny kitchen that contained a mini refrigerator and a microwave.

He didn't know what he was hoping to find but he was certain there had to be evidence that would exonerate him. Or at least provide another suspect.

The sound of a door slamming came from somewhere outside. He hurried to the window and looked out. A silver pickup sat in the parking lot below and two men stepped out. Dane eased to the side to avoid being spotted. All he could see from this point was the top of their cowboy hats. The man who'd driven was bulky, and the one who got out on the passenger side was younger, lanky and dark, curly hair stuck out from under his hat. His heart thumped in this chest. Who would be coming by the business? One of them gave Nellie's car a look over, and then said something to the younger one.

He needed to get out of there but if he went downstairs, he might not have time to stay hidden before they came in. Deciding to wait, he watched them, trying to learn their identities. They moved toward the back door that he'd entered, and before they disappeared under the awning, the bigger guy glanced up.

Dane jerked back and out of the way, but he didn't know if the man had spotted him.

A door slammed shut and footsteps clicked on the tile below.

He hurried into the closet and silently shut the door.

Footsteps came up the stairs. Not in a big hurry. Once they made it to the top floor, one man moved toward Dane's office.

Anger burned his insides as he thought about someone invading his personal space. The construction company was his and Harlan's. It'd been bought with hard work and sacrifice. Eager to learn the man's identity, Dane eased the door open a crack and peeked out. The older man's back was to him. But there was something familiar about the way the fellow moved.

The other man disappeared into his office but was not quiet. A crash sounded and then papers flitted into the doorway. A deep voice mumbled, "Where did you hide it?"

More commotion as drawers slammed and then there was the playing of an oldie's tune. It was the guy's ringtone on his cell phone. "What?" After a pause, he said, "Not yet. I just got here. Give me two minutes to look and then I'll be there shortly."

Dane stayed hidden until the young man walked by. The only thing he could make out was dark curly hair, and then he disappeared into his office. There was more banging and chatter between the two men until finally the footsteps retreated downstairs.

Byron Ferguson had a stocky build like the older man. Once the door slammed, Dane came out and looked back out the window. As the truck drove off, he tried to read his license plate, but the sun reflected from the metal bumper, obscuring the view before it disappeared around the building—he only made out four numbers. He didn't recognize the vehicle, but it was new.

Byron Ferguson—his job foreman.

What was his old job foreman looking for? It had been difficult to investigate the murder while on the run. In the movies, a person always had someone on the inside willing to slip the fugitive information. But Dane had no one he could trust. Not his family, and he didn't trust his coworkers.

He moved to the door and stepped out onto the balcony. Just months before he'd jumped from this railing to the ground below and had injured his ribs.

Trust.

Harlan used to quote the proverb, *Trust in the Lord with all thine heart; and lean not unto thine own understanding.*

Trust the Lord, yes. But his ex-coworkers?

He wanted to ask Josie to run a check on their old foreman to see what he'd been doing since he left the company and where he got the money for a new vehicle. But could he trust her?

He had to take a leap of faith sometime.

Chapter Seven

Josie hurried across the floor and picked up the bear.

Keep your mouth shut or people will die.

What kind of sick person would leave a threatening note for a child? She wrapped her arms around her daughter and pulled her close. "I'm so sorry. No one is going to die. We're going to find this guy and he will be arrested."

"No." Everly shrugged out of her grasp. "He's going to find and kill me. Just like he did my daddy. My dad was strong, and if the bad guy could take him down, there's no way you'll be able to stop him."

Josie's heart ached at her words, and she kneeled on one knee in front of her. "I won't let that happen. Your dad must've been taken by surprise. He didn't expect an attack. But now the authorities and I are watching for this man. We'll protect you." Even as she said the words, she prayed they were true. She'd never been responsible for anyone besides herself. Well, considering she worked with teams of others who'd sworn to protect, that wasn't exactly true. But she'd never had a family of her own since she was thirteen.

Everly frowned. "I hope you're right."

A child shouldn't have to worry about such things. She should be playing hopscotch or other games with friends.

She'd learned a long time ago that doing chores and staying busy helped keep the mind occupied. "How about you put your clothes away and feed Dexter."

"Okay."

Taking the bear with her, Josie walked into the kitchen and made a call to Sheriff Van Carroll's office. "Hattie, is the sheriff available?"

"Hey, Josie. It's been a while since I heard from you."

"Yeah, it's been a few months and we should get together. But this is important. Is he available?"

The deputy's jovial tone turned serious. "No, he isn't. He got called out of town for some family thing. Speaking of, I can't wait to meet your new daughter."

Bliss had mentioned him being out of town. "I have a situation and was hoping for his assistance." She knew Bliss had reached out to his office, but she needed to make sure help was on the way.

"Is there anything I can do?"

She gave her the abbreviated version of what had happened in the past day, ending with the note attached to the bear.

"You know not to touch the note. I doubt it, but maybe the guy left his fingerprints on it."

"We touched the bear, but not the note. I would love to have a protection detail for me and Everly."

"Oh, you know what? According to this message on my desk, Bliss already called. Deputy Green must have taken the call while I was on break. We're stretched tight, but I'll get the word to one of the deputies or will help you myself. You know, a wellness check on your place may be the best we can do."

"Thanks, Hattie. I'm going to dive into Pierce's case and see what I can find. Makes me wonder if he was investigating something that got him killed."

A creak sounded behind her.

She cringed when she turned to see Everly

staring at her and holding the dog food scoop. "I'll be in touch." She disconnected the phone and said, "Do you need help feeding Dexter?"

"His bowl is in the Bronco. I thought maybe you wanted to get it for me. Do you think Daddy's killer was somebody who worked with him?"

"It's possible." Josie hadn't gotten used to someone being in her house every minute and how easy it was for her daughter to overhear her conversations. "Did your dad mention anyone by name?"

Everly shook her head. "Not that I remember."

"Did he talk about the cases he was working?"

"Sometimes." She shrugged. "It mainly depends. One time he was paid to track down a lady's missing cat named Percy that ran away during a thunderstorm. He found her two weeks later in a shed in the backyard. Percy had five kittens."

Josie smiled. "Let me get Dexter's bowl for you."

She placed the stuffed animal in a gallon plastic bag, being careful not to touch the note. As Everly followed her out the back door to the porch, she grabbed his feeding container from her SUV and brought it to her. It didn't hit her until now that Everly must have been afraid to go outside by herself with her dad's killer threatening her. Her gaze went to Everly's bicycle leaning against the fence. Josie had bought it for her since the girl's aunt had disposed of her other bike. She had assumed Everly never rode it because she was depressed. Now it made sense.

"Daddy talked on the phone a lot and I wasn't supposed to listen, but sometimes I heard him anyway."

Josie stopped and looked at her. Her head hung down, but she stared up with her brown eyes like what she had to say was important.

"Did you hear anything lately?"

"Maybe. He talked with a woman named Nellie. There were others, but I can't remember anything specific. I wish I could remember more."

Nellie wasn't a common name around Liberty. The only Nellie that Josie knew was a woman who worked in billing for a rural trash service. "That's okay. But if you recall anything else, can you let me know?"

A vehicle sounded out front. Josie looked around the corner to see a Jarvis County Sheriff's SUV pull into the drive and stop in front of them. Deputy Green got out.

"Are you okay, Josie? Bliss called earlier and said someone shot at you?"

"Yeah. I called Hattie a few minutes ago. I have something for you. Hold on." She hurried inside and retrieved the bear. After she handed him the stuffed animal, she explained about it being left in Everly's room.

He asked several more questions and typed her answers into an electronic device. A voice came over his radio. He stepped away and answered it. A minute later, he was back. "I have another call I need to take. We're a little shorthanded, but we'll continue to check on you."

"Thanks."

After Dexter was fed and watered, Josie asked Everly to stay inside. She didn't want her outdoors, even though they lived in the country in a safe area. She set the suitcase on her bed in her room but hurried to get on her laptop. She could put her clothes away later.

The first thing she did was call and request the coroner's report on Pierce's death. Then she scrolled back through her texts to the last time she'd talked with Everly's dad. Every so often they'd share information or discuss a case, but her last contact was over seven months ago—three months before his death. He had texted her stating his old pair of night vision goggles were scratched and out of date and asked which night vision optics she recommended. And the text prior to that one was when he'd invited her to his Independence Day party almost a year ago.

That was as far back as the texts went. She'd gotten a new number when she resigned from the sheriff's department and started her own private investigator company while volunteering with the Bring Home the Children Project. If only they had talked more recently, maybe she could've had a clue as to who his clients were. Getting access to his files now would be more complicated. After the adoption was finalized, Everly had come to live with her and had brought several boxes of items with her. The rest of Pierce Browning's belongings had been either sold or donated by Pierce's sister who lived in Florida. Much of the family's savings had been wiped out due to his wife's illness several years prior, and Pierce had taken out a second mortgage on their home. Basically, it went back to the bank at his death. Pierce and his wife had set up a prepaid tuition plan for college that Everly could use when she became eighteen.

The rest of Pierce's living extended family were either elderly or not interested in raising a young girl.

Where would his work files have been stored? What had happened to his laptop? Josie still hadn't gone through the boxes, but maybe Everly knew what had been packed.

"Everly, come here please."

Seconds later, she came into the room. "Yeah?"

"Do you know what happened to your dad's things? Like his laptop or business files?"

She shrugged, and her gaze went to the floor. "I dunno. After his death, I stayed with my aunt until you adopted me. My aunt and uncle went to our house, but they made me stay in the car while they loaded up his things they said I would want."

The girl wouldn't look at her. "Honey, is there something you want to tell me? Have you looked through the boxes?"

"I don't want to lie." Her frown deepened. "I went through them once."

"You're not in trouble." Josie sighed. She wished Everly would've told her. Josie had no idea what her aunt thought the girl needed to keep. Irritation crawled all over her. She wasn't an expert on the law, but Everly should've inherited all of her parents' things. Poor child. And Josie had considered looking through boxes but had put it off because she hadn't found the time. Life had been a whirlwind of activity since Everly moved in.

"Aunt Ruby told me not to go through his things, that it was best to move on with my new life."

"Oh, honey. His things belong to you. I wouldn't have minded." Josie desperately wanted to wrap her in a hug, but that tended to make Everly shy away. She settled for a hand on her shoulder. "Grief takes a while. I lost my family when I was a child and I still miss them every day."

Everly cocked her head at her. "What happened?"

A lump formed in Josie's throat. Rarely did she talk about that night even to this day. If only she hadn't been pouting because her parents told her she couldn't have a friend over, she would've been on the first floor and could've saved them. "Our house caught on fire. They weren't able to get out." She could still see their faces today. But as time went on, their faces began to blur and that scared her.

"Did you have brothers and sisters?"

"I had a younger sister. Audrey."

"I'm sorry. I always wanted a sister. Were you the only who got out of the fire?"

"Yes." Josie forced a smile past the emotion that bubbled inside of her. She didn't want to talk about the fire. Or her family. "Do you mind if we look through the boxes?"

"I would love to."

"Okay. I don't know if we can make it through all of them, but we can get started."

Everly moved quickly out the door, but then turned back. "I'm sorry about your family." Then she hurried toward the detached garage.

A lump formed in Josie's throat. Somehow Everly's condolences meant more than she believed possible. She drew a deep breath before performing a quick survey around the place to make certain there were no signs of the men who'd attacked them. Her gun rested safely in her pocket. Satisfied no one was lurking, they entered the door to the storage room at the back of the garage. A variety of unmarked boxes and tubs were stacked in the corner. For the moment, Josie was only interested in finding

Pierce's laptop and work files, but she stood back while Everly opened the first container.

The girl's face wrinkled into a frown.

Josie moved closer and glanced inside. A pile of shirts and ties were stuffed inside. When Everly pulled out one of the ties, several shirts fell out onto the concrete floor. She quickly picked up a sweatshirt and held it against her face. Then she paused and looked up at Josie. "This was one of his favorites." She held up the faded and soft shirt showing the logo of Browning Investigations printed on it. "He said my mom bought it for him a long time ago. One time when we were camping, he let me wear it when I got cold."

"That was kind of him. I know you miss your dad." From what Josie witnessed, Pierce was a loving father. "Would you like to take that one in the house with us?"

"Yeah." Everly glanced down. "But I lost my butterfly necklace that Daddy gave me on my last birthday. I'm sorry."

"Oh no, honey. I should've told you. I found it in the woods last night dangling from a tree. The chain is broken, but I'll get it repaired as soon as possible."

Her mouth dropped open. "Thank you!

When Daddy gave it to me he told me to take good care of it."

Josie patted her on the back. Then she looked up at the dozen or so containers and knew it would take a while to sift through them. She needed to find his records now.

"Would it be all right if I bring this in?" Everly held up a man's baseball cap.

"Certainly. You don't have to ask. These items are yours." The only thing she would prefer was for Everly not to find something personal or too stressful for a girl of her age to see. Josie grabbed the next container, which held a stack of photograph albums and pictures. She shoved it over to Everly. While her daughter went through those, she quickly opened four more before finding one that contained mail, electronics and things that looked to be from his office. "Do you mind if I take this one inside so I can go through it?"

Everly nodded. "Sure. And I'd like to take the pictures to my room."

They hurried into the house, each carrying a box. Everly disappeared into her room while Josie unpacked her box on the dining room table. Bingo. At the bottom was his laptop. A few minutes later, she had it plugged in and charging. When the screen lit up, it asked for a password. She tried several common variations containing family names and birthdates. When that didn't work, she hollered at Everly.

"Yeah?"

"Do you know your dad's password for his computer?"

She shrugged. "I'm not sure."

"What did he call your mom?"

"Her name was Melody, but he called her Mel."

"Okay. Thanks." Josie tried multiple combinations and finally, "Melsguy" worked. The computer powered opened. Several of the programs were the same as Josie used and she was thankful. She opened an Excel sheet titled Browning Investigation Clients. That made it easy.

She scrolled to the bottom of the list. Her heart picked up the pace. The last name was Harlan Schmidt, Dane's business partner.

Pierce had been investigating Dane's construction business. Was it just a coincidence Dane was in the woods where they had rented the cabin? She'd been deceived by him before. Did she dare take a chance on him again?

Suddenly an engine rumbled up her driveway. A glance out the window showed Dane riding his motorcycle. Time to make a decision had just run out.

Chapter Eight

As Dane cut the engine on his motorcycle, he saw Josie coming out the back door and onto the porch. He put the kickstand down and hurried her way.

"What is it?"

"I got a hunch." At her raised eyebrows in question, he continued. "I went by my office today at the construction business..."

"Yeah..." Impatience radiated from her tone. "And where did you get the motorcycle?"

"It's mine. It was in the barn with my old pickup. I borrowed a car from the woman who cleaned our offices and drove back out to the barn and exchanged it for this. She's one of the few people I trust. Anyway, I got a hunch. I definitely believe Harlan's murder and Everly's dad's murder may be connected. While I was at the office, I'm ninety percent certain Byron Ferguson, our job foreman, came by. I could only read four of the numbers on his license plate. Can you run it for me?" He removed a piece of paper from his shirt pocket and handed it to her.

She glanced at it. "I'll see what I can do. What did he want?"

Dane shrugged. "I didn't find out because I hid. And there was a younger man with him I didn't recognize. I figure it's better not to trust anyone until I learn who killed Harlan. I know this is shaky ground with you working for the Bring the Children Home Project and often with law enforcement, but can you check out some people for me? I'd never ask this if it weren't important." He hated requesting this of her. She'd trusted him once and believed he'd let her down. "If the same person who killed Harlan also killed Pierce, then we could be helping each other."

"I think you're right."

His defensiveness fell. "You do?"

She nodded. "I found some of Pierce's notes. Harlan's name was listed as one of his clients—his last client."

For the first time in months, Dane's heart lifted. Almost afraid to hope, he asked, "What did it say he was investigating? Did it give names or conclusions on what he found?"

She put up her hand. "Not so fast. I haven't had time to go over everything. All I know is Harlan's name was the last on the list. It stands to reason there's a connection. But I need to let the authorities know. Turn yourself in and that way we can look into the cases without worrying about you being arrested."

He sighed. "I'm going to repeat myself. I did not steal that car in high school, but it did not stop me from going into juvenile detention. I don't trust law enforcement. It's easy for you. You were not judged because of your family."

She frowned, frustration showing on her face, and then she turned and walked toward the house. "If you weren't guilty of stealing, then why were you in Principal Scruggs's car? The police said someone kicked in his back door and stole the Mustang's keys before taking the car. For an innocent guy, you sure did a terrific job making yourself look guilty."

He followed her as she kept talking.

"You were hot rodding and ran his car on two wheels. Not exactly the actions of someone trying to avoid trouble." She took a deep breath. "But you're not a kid anymore and you ran a thriving business. They'll believe you. And the evidence should be lacking."

"I did not kick in Scruggs's door, but it was part of the lie that was repeated. Seems like no one questioned the other kids or considered one of them may have broken into the principal's house. It did no good to say it, though. Even *you* believed the lie. And if they don't believe me this time?"

"Trust in the system."

Nope. He wasn't going to do it. He reached out for her hand to get her to stop walking. "I have Violet to think about. I'm her last hope."

"Instead of letting the authorities investigate, you'd rather live as a fugitive?" She pulled away. "Being on the run raises your chances of something going wrong. You'll have no protection if this guy comes after you. You could easily lose your life."

Again, he reached for her, but his hand just managed to snag her shirt, which tugged up a little on the side. A terrible pink scar showed. "What is that?"

"Nothing." She yanked her shirt down.

"Is that what I think it is?" Disbelief hit him. He could tell by her flaring eyes it was true. "You took a bullet? Was it serious?"

"Aren't they all?"

"You know what I mean."

She looked thoughtful for a moment. "Yeah. It was. I suppose that's the closest I've ever come to death."

He couldn't believe she hadn't mentioned being shot before. "Who did this? When did this happen?"

"Last year when I was helping Chandler Murphy bring home a missing child. I was shot."

A door slammed, and he turned to see Everly standing on the steps with Dexter at her side. The frown she wore told him she'd overheard the last comment.

"Everly." Josie hurried her way.

Her eyebrows furrowed into a frown. "I don't want you to be hurt, Mom. I don't want to lose you."

"Oh, honey." Josie knelt in front of her and placed her hands on her shoulders. "I didn't mean for you to overhear that."

Dane stood where he was, giving them room. He never should've come by here. "I'll be going now."

He waited for Josie to argue and tell him to stay, but she just stared at him. "I'll contact you if I learn anything."

As he climbed on his motorcycle, Dexter ran over barking at him and Everly followed. Dane flicked his hand at the dog. He didn't know if he was more upset about finding out Josie had taken a bullet last year or that Everly had overheard. All he knew was he needed to find out who was targeting them and put an end to this madness. He looked at the collie. "Stay back, boy."

"I don't want you to go. Stay here." The girl's brown eyes stared up at him, which reminded him so much of Violet.

Dane shot her a smile. If only Josie wanted him to stay, then they could work together to find out who framed him. "I'll be fine."

Josie called with a frustrated expression, "Come on in, and we'll get something to eat."

Even though he was still hungry after the breakfast Nellie had made for him, he didn't want to stay if she didn't want him there. "I don't want to intrude. I understand I've put you in a bad position."

Josie shook her head. "I wouldn't offer if it wasn't okay." She turned and walked to the house.

Everly came up beside him. "I like your motorcycle. I wish I had one."

"You have to be very careful, but maybe your mom will allow me to give you a ride sometime."

She shrugged. "Maybe."

When he came into the kitchen a few moments later, Josie was hurriedly setting out the fixings for sandwiches. He opened the cabinet door closest to the sink and found the glasses then put them on the counter. "Everly, what would you like to drink?"

"Milk. But I can get it." She grabbed the jug, and he filled his glass with water from the refrigerator dispenser.

"I'll take milk, too," Josie said to Everly, then turned her attention to him. "Thanks."

He took in the red face and quick movements, telling him she was frustrated. "Welcome."

They all sat at the table and then Josie said, "Everly, would you like to say the blessing?"

"Sure." The girl's gaze met his before she bowed her head and said grace.

It was odd because growing up, his family never prayed. It wasn't until he met Harlan that Dane had seriously considered God and prayer. He had to admit he was glad Josie and Everly had faith.

Everyone helped themselves to make their own sandwiches and grab chips. They remained quiet while they were eating; evidently everyone was hungry or too distracted to talk.

Dane knew he'd eaten too fast, but he was certain the food would catch up soon and he'd regret it if he ate more. He pushed back from the table. "That was good. I didn't realize how hungry I was."

Josie smiled as she finished the last bite of her sandwich. "Me either."

Everly glanced at them and seemingly understood they needed to be alone. "I'm going to my room."

"Leave the door cracked, please."

Everly stared at her mom. "I will."

Ever since her family perished in the fire, she couldn't relax if the bedroom doors were closed. Technically, it was safer to cut back on oxygen to control a fire by keeping doors closed, but Josie feared not knowing if one broke out. She'd told Everly the rule, but not the reason. It was probably time she explained.

After Everly had left the kitchen, Josie started clearing the table. "I need to be more careful when talking around her because she overhears a lot. I think she may be trying to figure out what is going on and purposely listening in."

"Wouldn't it be better if you had her shut her bedroom door then?"

Josie shook her head. "No, I like to be able to see where she's at."

"Any particular reason?"

Her head jerked. "I just do."

There was more to her statement. Much more. He remembered Josie had been extra careful about fires back when they dated. Things like unplugging cords from wall outlets and refusing to use space heaters ever. It wouldn't be such a big deal, but when he lived with a neighbor during his junior year, a single space heater was all they had to heat with. A glance at the living room wall showed a smoke alarm, and there was one in the hallway he could see. "I thought it was safer to leave doors shut."

Her gaze connected with his. "I realize this."

He was glad she didn't pretend not to know what he was referring to.

She cleared her throat. "The sheriff won't be back for a couple of days. I know many of the deputies, but the ones on duty haven't been with the department for long. And with the annual July Fourth jamboree taking place at the fairgrounds with the rodeo, they're short-handed. We haven't been hit since we've been home, but I don't want to be a sitting duck."

"I agree. I'll help watch over you two."

She smiled. "I appreciate that. Being that Harlan appears to be Pierce's last client, I'd like to check out his office. Do you think that's possible?"

"Sure."

"What is it?" She looked at him curiously.

"I don't know what you're talking about."

"That smile. What's going on?"

He shook his head. "You're asking to look for evidence in the case. I know you're investigating because of Pierce, but I've been on my own for the past few months while trying to stay hidden. I would've done anything to have someone examine the facts with me. It's a resounding yes that you check out the office."

She nodded. "You're not afraid of what I might find?"

"Not hardly." Even if she didn't fully believe him, maybe she would come around once she saw for herself that he was innocent.

"What about Everly? Is there anyone she can stay with?"

Josie's face etched in concern. "I could let my granddad watch her, if necessary, but I don't want to alarm him. I'd rather her stay by my side."

"I hate to ask, but...do you think she could look at mug shots? If we could learn who killed her dad, authorities could arrest him. And it'd make it easier to clear my name."

"Let me pray on it. I realize the best thing for her would be to know this man can't reach any of us."

"Okay. You're her mom."

She gave him a double take. Was it his imagination or was she extra sensitive concerning her daughter?

"I'm ready to go when you are," he said.

She looked thoughtful. "I'm trying to make up my mind whether we should wait until dark or not."

"Good question. I don't want to be spotted, so my vote is to wait." At her annoyed look, he wished he'd kept his mouth shut. He knew she didn't like helping him hide. Not that he blamed her, but from here on out he wouldn't mention it.

"Come on back." She jerked her head toward the table in the living room. "Remind me of the name of your foreman again?"

"Byron Ferguson."

"Hold on." She typed fast onto her cell phone. "I sent Chandler his name. I talked to him earlier, and he said he'd be glad to look at some suspects."

He stood at her side as she sat in the chair and typed on the laptop. A list of names came up on an Excel sheet. "Is Chandler an investigator?"

Without looking up, she shook her head. "He works with the K-9 unit for the sheriff's department and for our team. But we all help each other out when possible."

What must it be like to be a part of a team with people like Josie? She seemed to be comfortable with her career choice. He didn't like the idea of her being in dangerous situations where she could be shot, but he believed the mission of her team was important.

He knew when he'd met her as a teen that she would do something important with her life.

She scrolled down the Excel sheet. Harlan's name was at the bottom. Even though Josie had already told Dane about it, it was still unreal to see it. She clicked on his name, but there was no more information. It was blank.

"Is there another place Pierce kept his notes? He must've written down his findings."

"I was thinking the same thing. If you'll look at the date of entry, it was over six months ago—about two months before his death. And Harlan's death was only a week before Pierce's."

"Pierce had probably found his conclusions or was close by then. And since a company's bank statement was found under Harlan's body, we can conclude it had to do with missing money at our company."

"Do you know how much was missing?"

"Not the exact amount, but it was a thousand here and there for a period of several months. And then thirty thousand dollars went missing all at once, and I think that's when Harlan believed the missing money was not some clerical error. Harlan handled the money and business end, while I talked with contractors and dealt with sales."

Josie looked up at him. "That's a *lot* of money. How come it took so long to notice?"

Dane shrugged. "I don't think it did. At first, it was a hundred here or there that the books were off. And then the amounts increased. Harlan didn't discuss the specifics with me, but normally with our accountant or the job foreman."

"He trusted you?"

Instantly, his heart picked up the pace. He wasn't a thief. "Harlan and I were close. He had no reason to doubt me."

At his sharp tone, she waved her hand downward, telling him to calm down. "I'm not accusing. Were the accountant and job foreman questioned?"

He nodded. "I think so, at least by Harlan. My partner had several closed-door meetings with both men. I can only assume they were ruled out. When Harlan was murdered and the was money found in my account, the authorities zoomed in on me."

"Okay. Byron is the foreman. And the accountant..."

"Jim Price. Price and Monroe Accounting in Dallas."

"Thanks." She jotted down the name and glanced back to the laptop. "I'm going to continue to go through more of his files. Hopefully, I'll find the name of who he was looking into. If it was the accountant or job foreman there might be something in his notes.

"Thanks." Dane walked out of the room

and when he passed by Everly's door, he noticed she wasn't in sight. He stopped and looked in, not wanting to alarm Josie. He whispered, "Everly?"

Dexter wasn't in the room either. Surely, the girl wouldn't have disappeared either. He was tempted to go look for her before he alerted Josie, but that wouldn't be right. If he was her dad, he'd want to know. He stuck his head in the room. "Everly's not in her room."

Josie jumped to her feet and hurried past him. He followed on her heels out the back door. Josie hollered Everly's name.

While she checked the house, he went straight to the shed. When he opened the door, he stopped in his tracks. Everly was sitting on a plastic tub with her face in her hands and Dexter at her feet. Was she crying?

"Everly?"

She glanced up at him and quickly turned her back to him. "Go away."

He turned and yelled toward the house to Josie. "I found her." He stepped closer to the girl. "Are you okay? I was worried about you."

Slowly her chin lifted as she made eye contact. "I heard you talking about my daddy with Mom. I wish I could remember more about the man who killed him. I try to remember, but it's just the same thing over and over. Him holding my daddy underwater while he fought."

"You don't have to go back over the story again. We'll find him."

"The man looked at me. But I can't even tell you what color hair he had."

"That's not uncommon for people not to be able to recall details. Even for adults. Didn't you say you were inside the house?"

She nodded.

"That makes it even more difficult. You've been a big help."

That seemed to calm her, and she shot him a half smile.

Besides Violet, Dane had never spent much time with children. And since he'd moved out of his parents' house at an early age, he'd not even spent much time with her. Yes, he'd practically raised her with his mom drinking and his dad's absence, but after he moved out and got a place of his own, his mom asked him not to come around. Said that it upset Violet.

He had a hard time believing that. His sister had adored him. Had something changed her mind? Or had his parents made the story up? But to what end?

Either way, he intended to gain custody of her. He brought his attention back to Everly. "Hey, you've had a lot of changes in the last months. You're doing great, kiddo."

"I don't want to be the cause of anyone getting hurt."

He cocked his head at her. "You don't really believe that, do you? The only person responsible for hurting anyone is the person doing it. You're only ever, ever responsible for your own actions. Do you understand?"

She nodded. "I get it. I am eight."

"And smart as a whip." If the situation wasn't so serious, he could've laughed. To take so much burden on at such a young age was cruel.

"Everyone all right out here?" Josie stepped into the shed.

"Come on in. We were just talking."

Josie glanced from Everly to him—a strange expression on her face. "It'll be dark soon. Are you ready to go?"

"Sure." He dusted off his jeans and gave Everly a hand up from the box she was sitting on. He wished he knew what Josie was thinking. One thing was clear, she wasn't happy. Almost like she'd looked years ago when he'd disappointed her.

No matter how hard he tried, it seemed he kept letting her down?

Chapter Nine

Silence followed her as Josie settled into her chair in her living room after they returned from going to Dane's and Harlan's construction offices. To her disappointment, they had found no more evidence. On first visit to a crime scene, often an investigator could see things more clearly than a person who was familiar with the premises.

She couldn't help but feel like she'd let Dane and Everly down.

After seeing the building though, her appreciation grew for Dane and the effort he'd put into their construction business. The offices were tidy and looked professional. When they were through searching the office, they returned Nellie's car back to her home. She remembered Everly's mention of the name Nellie whom she'd overheard her dad reference.

Since Chandler was researching the foreman,

she'd called Kennedy and Silas to get their expertise. They both agreed Everly needed to look at mug shots. Technically, Silas was a Texas Ranger and not on the team, but he was a good guy to have around on cases anyway. The sun set low in the sky in her living room window.

Irritation nipped at her, but she wasn't sure why. Was she jealous Dane seemed to have a way with her daughter? Hopefully not. Josie had never been petty. Everly had a close relationship with her dad, and that was probably why she seemed to draw close to Dane. The girl was only three when her mom died so she wouldn't have memories of her.

Patience was the key, but she'd never guessed how insecure or hurtful it would be that Everly hadn't trusted her enough to share the story of her father's death right off the bat. She knew better, but still she struggled to keep the feelings from surfacing.

The next morning, Josie called investigator Patty Lynch at the Liberty police station to set up an appointment. She didn't want to put pressure on Everly, but it'd be a big help if she could identify her dad's killer, and Josie had just received the call saying she could bring her in.

She stepped into her room. "Honey, can I talk to you?"

"Sure." Everly scooted over on the bed.

She sat beside her daughter. "How do you feel about going down to the police station and looking at mug shots? Would that be okay? Or would it make you nervous?"

"What are mug shots?"

"When a person is arrested, the police take a photo of them."

"Oh, you mean when they turn sideways or look at the camera?" At Josie's nod, she continued. "I've seen those. Will the people in jail be able to see me?"

"No. You can sit in an office at a desk. I don't want you to confuse this with a lineup where you're in a room looking at suspects."

"Oh. Okay. I don't mind."

Poor thing. Josie could understand how she got the two confused. Many shows or movies showed the lineup. She patted her leg. "Let me know if you have any more questions."

Everly nodded. "Can Dexter go, too?"

"Hmm." The collie was a barker. That might be distracting. "You want to see if Dane wants to ride with us and he can sit in the Bronco with Dexter?"

"Okay." Her shoulders shrugged.

Several minutes later, they all rode in silence. Josie was learning that Everly's quietness did not necessarily mean something was wrong, so she let her enjoy the peaceful time.

When they grew close, Jose turned into a city park and pulled to the back of parking lot, closet to the trees. Everly hugged Dexter bye.

Dane climbed out with Dexter's leash in his hand and looked at Josie. "I'll stay here unless you need me."

"Thanks. We'll be fine." As she drove out of the park, she noted there were only a handful of people there—two were walking their dogs and another appeared to be a mom with her two young children. The police station sat only thirty yards on the other side of the woods.

Josie and Everly walked up the steps and through the glass door. Tile floors and an open reception area greeted them. Josie had been here several times and recognized Mark behind the desk. "Good morning."

"Hi, Josie. Investigator Lynch is waiting for you in her office." He looked at Everly and then back to Josie. "Can she have a snack or something to drink? We have donuts in the break room, and I can get her a soda?"

She glanced down. "Would you like that?"

"Sure." Everly smiled.

A minute later, he came back with a soda and a chocolate donut with sprinkles. "Here you go, princess."

Everly took them and thanked him.

Josie shot him a smile and was glad they did everything possible to make children less nervous. Events like this had a way of staying with a child for the rest of their life—whether good or bad.

"Hello," Patty said when they walked into her office.

"Patty, this is Everly." Josie rested her hand on her daughter's shoulder.

Everly shook Patty's outstretched hand.

Patty kept a smile on her lips. "Your mom told me you saw a man at your house when your daddy died. Is that right?"

Everly nodded.

Josie stood off to the side to allow Patty room, but she also wanted Everly to know she was there for her. Her chest tightened at what her daughter must be feeling right now. Remembering her own childhood during and after the fire had been life changing. Although Everly witnessing her father's murder couldn't be undone, Josie hoped to offer Everly comfort and a safe place to talk.

"This seat is for you." Patty pushed a chair on wheels next to Everly. "Here's a place for your donut and soda. First, I want you to know what a brave girl you are to come in and do this for us. After I'm through explaining how this works, if you have any questions, please ask. There are no silly questions. If I ask you something and you don't know the answer, just say you don't know. Okay?"

"Okay." Everly nodded.

"When your mom called, she gave me a description of the man you saw. But I'd like to hear what happened from you. Can you tell me what you saw that day?"

"Sure." Everly's eyebrows scrunched together. "My dad and I were working outside. He mowed our lawn and then was using the weed trimmer. Daddy made me pick up my toys and Dexter's chew toys in the yard. I went inside to go to the bathroom and to get us some lemonade because it was hot outside."

Josie realized she was holding her breath and tried to relax. It was no use. Her heart hurt for the girl.

The investigator nodded. "That was helpful of you."

Everly half smiled. "I poured us some glasses, but then heard somebody yelling. I looked out the window and there was a man arguing with my daddy. I was afraid to go outside so I hid behind the door and peeked out the window."

"What did you see?" Patty coaxed her.

"The man hit my daddy and then they started fighting. My daddy got in several punches when the man tried to stab him with a knife.

"I screamed. Daddy looked at me and the man shoved my daddy into the hot tub and held him under water. Daddy fought and kicked the man in the face, but the bad man kept holding him under. Once Daddy quit moving, the man threw the weed trimmer into the water and sparks flew. I screamed again, and the man looked at me. Then the electricity went off in the house.

"I ran out the front to my treehouse. That's when Dexter, my dog, bit the man, and he kicked my dog. Then the FedEx truck pulled up and I saw the man run behind the house. He yelled at me that if I told anyone, he would kill me. A car started up, and I didn't see him anymore."

Moisture lined Patty's eyes as she gave Everly a hug. She glanced at Josie with an *I'm sorry* look.

A tear rolled down Josie's cheek.

"You did fantastic, Everly. Now let's go back to the man and what he looked like. Can you recall how tall he was, or if he was fat or skinny?"

"I don't know how tall, but he wasn't fat or skinny."

"Good. Do you know if he was taller than your dad?"

She shrugged. "Not really."

Josie's heart went out to her as she tried to recall such an incident.

"Did he have a moustache or a beard?"

She shook her head. "I don't think so."

Josie noticed Patty used easy words such as beard instead of asking if he had facial hair. She appreciated the simple gesture. Patty had been with the police department for several years, but Josie didn't know if she had kids or a family.

"Where did Dexter bite the man?" Patty asked.

"On his arm."

"You're doing great, Everly. Now think, do you know which arm?"

Everly's eyebrows knitted. "Uh, this one." She patted her arm. "Right."

"Excellent. Okay, we're going to look through some photographs and if you see the man who was at your daddy's house, just let me know. Even if you aren't certain, let me know if any of the people look like the man. Can you do that?"

"Yeah." Everly moved closer to the desk as Patty typed a couple of things into the computer and then turned the screen for Everly to view.

Josie watched intently as Patty scrolled through several slides.

"Maybe that one." Everly pointed to a dark-haired man. Robert Latham. Forty-one years old.

Josie didn't recognize him.

"Or maybe him." This man had lighter hair and was thirty-two years old.

Patty said, "Okay..."

Josie tried not to be disappointed, but she knew it was difficult even for adults to be able to recall details in the middle of a dangerous event. Several more minutes passed, and Everly pointed out another man.

Her daughter rubbed her eyes and sighed.

Patty patted her on the shoulder. "You're doing wonderful, Everly. Why don't we take a small break? You can finish your donut while I speak with your mom."

She stepped to the corner with Josie. "I don't want you to be disheartened. Everly is really doing great. Even if none of these are the man, we're building a base for the sketch artist. If it's all right with you, I'll set up an appointment with him later in the week."

They'd been attacked several times, and she didn't want to put off finding this jerk any longer than necessary. "Is there any way Everly can meet with him today?"

"You know we're a small department, but I'll give him a call in a minute and see what I can do. No promises, though."

"I appreciate that."

While Patty left to check on schedules, Josie went over to Everly and visited quietly. Soon Patty returned.

"He rearranged his schedule and can get to you on Thursday."

At least that was better than Friday. "Thanks."

"Do you think she can look for a few more minutes?"

"I'm sure that's fine but let me ask." Everly

agreed. Thirty minutes later, they walked out of the investigator's office with a few leads. Everly had picked a total of five men she believed could be the man. One man by the name of Ronnie Hugg Josie recognized. When she looked at his file, she remembered why. He had a prior arrest for possession of cocaine with intent to sell when she'd worked for the sheriff's department. Ronnie had sold primarily to kids in junior and high schools. Josie had been the one to stake out a popular hangout close to the lake that he worked.

She tried to recall what the man with the knife had sounded like. She didn't know if he was the same or not because she'd barely talked to Ronnie. According to his file, he was six feet tall. Even though he was tall, she would've thought the knife man was taller. It wouldn't hurt to check him out.

They drove to the park and found Dane leaning against a picnic table with Dexter.

"Did he get tired of waiting?"

"You could say that." Dane shook his head in playful disgust. "Dexter was running around smelling of everything. But when he started barking at the kids on the climbing tower, I decided we were better off hiking through the trees as to not draw attention to ourselves."

Everly patted him on the head. "Oh, Dexter. You're supposed to be quiet." The collie cocked his head to the side.

Dane glanced at Josie. She was certain he was wondering if Everly identified her daddy's killer. Instead of discussing it in front of her, she held her finger up, telling him they would talk in a bit.

After they climbed in her vehicle, she asked, "Besides Dexter taking advantage of you, did anything else happen?"

"No. I kept my eye on the traffic in front of the station but nothing suspicious."

She read between the lines that he didn't spot the silver GMC or the black Dodge. That was good that the guy hadn't followed them to the police station. "Let's go back to my place where I can do some research."

His gaze crossed to her. "Okay."

She could tell by his look that he knew she had at least one lead. It'd been years since she'd seen Dane, but it was funny that they still seemed to be able to communicate without saying words. She'd forgotten about that connection with him and missed it. In school, she'd always been a good student who stayed out of trouble and who most teachers liked. But there was that day in Mrs. Dillard's class that she and Dane had gotten in trouble for laughing during a movie and not being able to stop. The thing was they were sitting across the room from each other and still were able to converse just by reading each other's facial expressions. She looked at him, and he looked back. There was something about his eyes that made her stomach do a little flip. He'd always been a good-looking guy, even if he never realized it. She needed to be careful. They'd been high school sweethearts. Nothing more. The feelings were probably more sentimental than real since he was her first love. But with him once again running from the law, he'd not make a good family man.

She needed to keep that in mind. It was going to be hard considering how much he was risking his life to help her and Everly.

Dane sensed Josie had learned something while at the station, but he knew better than to ask in front of Everly.

Twenty minutes later, they pulled up to Josie's home. He agreed to sit with Everly while she checked out the house. There was no sign of anything out of order and they went in.

Everly had no sooner half-shut her bedroom door, before he asked, "What did you learn?"

"Not much." She pulled out her laptop and opened it up. "Everly identified five men that looked like her daddy's killer, but she wasn't certain on any of them. Do you know Ronnie Hugg?"

"The name sounds familiar. Did he play college football?"

She frowned. "No, I don't think that's the same guy. Do you mean Ron Huston?"

"Yeah, that was him. I didn't know Huston very well either, just heard his name."

As she started to type on her keyboard, she pushed a piece of paper across the table. "What about the rest of these guys?"

He glanced down at the list of names and photos and pointed. "Only this one."

"Robert Latham? Where do you know him from?"

"I didn't know his name, but he used to work at the convenience store close to our company."

"Did you or Harlan have issues with him?" Josie asked. "A disagreement? Anything that would make him want to come after Harlan?"

"No. About two years ago, he worked the early shift, and I'd stop in and buy coffee in the mornings. Then one day there was a lady behind the counter, and I never saw him again. But it's not unusual to have a high turnover rate at those kinds of places."

"Okay. Let me see what we can find on him. First, his arrest record." A minute later, she had it pulled. "DWI and vehicular manslaughter. There are a few older things on here from when he was younger. Driving under the influence and driving without a license."

Dane shook his head. "Those charges should have nothing to do with me or Harlan."

"It doesn't sound like it, but let me see who died in the accident, and I'll also check out Ronnie Hugg's family to make certain there are no connections." Her fingers paused on the keyboard as she glanced at the list again. "I'm going to look at all five of these men and see if we can find a tie-in."

At the mention of family, Dane wondered about his dad's incarceration. He'd been concentrating his efforts on the people he and Harlan both knew; he hadn't thought about anyone else. "My dad was in the Beto Unit near Tennessee Colony in Anderson County.

Can you make sure none of the men served at the same time?"

"Certainly."

He glanced back to make sure Everly wasn't standing at the door. "How did Everly do? Is she okay?"

Brown eyes stared back at him before her shoulders slumped. "It's difficult for her. The investigator had Everly tell everything again she remembered about the day her daddy died."

At her pause, Dane's chest constricted. Pain radiated in her face, and her lip trembled so slightly that he wondered if he imagined it. He scooted over a chair and sat beside her. "I'm sorry, Josie." He wanted to take her into his arms to offer comfort but remembering how slow she'd been to warm up to people, he simply rested his hand on hers. "That must've been excruciating for you to endure, too. You're good with her."

A sharp laugh came from her. "I don't think so."

"What? Are you serious? You're patient with her and getting an eight-year-old child to confide in you at all is a big accomplishment."

She stared down and shrugged. "I feel like I'm failing her at every turn. If she would've trusted me, she wouldn't have run away but told me what happened."

"You sound pathetic."

Her head jerked up. "I'm not pathetic. I don't feel sorry for myself."

"Ah, there's the old Josie." He chuckled. He'd known the crack would make her come up fighting. The truth was Josie rarely bemoaned her troubles, even when deserved. She was a tough lady that preferred to hit a problem head on. "It takes time to build trust. Don't rush it. You of all people should know that. It took me forever to get you to accept a ride in my grandma's Oldsmobile with the dented fender."

A smile tugged at her lips. "It's been forever since I've thought of that car. I know you're right." As if she just noticed his hand was still on hers, she pulled away. "I need to get back to work."

"I'd like to sit here if you don't mind."

"Make yourself comfortable."

He stayed there looking over her shoulder as she researched each person thoroughly. When Everly came out of her room, Dane prepared them all something to eat, and then he and Josie ate by her desk. After four hours of digging, nothing significant popped up.

She pushed back from her desk and stretched.

"Do you think we're missing a connection?"

"Could be." She shrugged. "As the pieces come together into one place and a whole picture is developed, normally it rules people out or warrants more questions to be answered."

"Any person nagging at you? Because right now, none of the people stand out. Robert Latham is the only person I had a brief acquaintance with. The other four are strangers to me."

"But the person may not have any connection to you but may have with Harlan."

"What about Byron Ferguson, my job foreman?"

"Chandler didn't find anything concerning him. He's forty-two years old, divorced as of five years ago and he has a twenty-one-year-old son. And I checked on the partial license plate, but nothing came up belonging to your foreman. I don't mind digging deeper. Besides him being at your office, what bugs you?"

"I guess it's just that he and his friend were there and seemed to be looking for something. But what? And why now? The younger guy was talking on his cell phone to someone like he was being guided."

"Like he was on a quest for someone else?"

"Yeah, maybe." Dane ran his fingers through his hair. "He asked where he hid it. Makes me think they were searching for something that could be incriminating."

"If that's true, then it's possible something was left by another employee or by the killer when he struck Harlan."

"Yeah." He drew a deep breath. "But I looked through the office and didn't find anything—unless Byron took something with him."

"Are you certain it was a friend with Byron?"

"Why are you asking?"

"Hold on. I saw something earlier." She looked back to her laptop. "Right here on Samantha Ferguson's social media account." She scrolled down. "Is that your guy?"

A man about twenty stood with his arm wrapped around a girl of about the same age, at what looked like a pro football game. "That looks like him. Hard to tell with him in a baseball cap, but he has the same build and age. Who is he?"

"Kyle Ferguson. The foreman's son. I couldn't find a social media account for Byron, but I looked up his ex-wife. Let me see if I can find a better picture."

Dane watched from over her shoulder. Another photo came up without the cap, showing his dark, curly hair. "Stop. That's him."

"Okay. I'll try to learn what Kyle and Byron were doing there."

"Good." They needed to make progress. "I think I need to go visit my mom and brother. Maybe the crime has to do with them."

She nodded. "The gunman and the murder of Harlan may not have anything to do with you. But you were simply at the wrong place at the wrong time."

He got to his feet. "You don't know how many times I've told myself that. But if so, how did the money get into my account? Someone wanted the blame put on me."

"Good point. How would someone find your account number to do that?"

He shrugged. "Did I mention it showed the money was deposited *after* Harlan's death?"

"After? Wouldn't that suggest Harlan wasn't investigating the missing money then?"

"It went missing weeks before his murder. I still get monthly bank statements in the mail. Someone could steal that from my mailbox."

"Have you missed any statements?"

"Not that I know of, unless it was the last one. Of course, the envelope could've been opened and then resealed. Maybe far-fetched, but possible. Now that I think about it, I don't think they put the account number on the statement. Wait." He snapped his fingers. "Direct deposit. When I was going through the employee files, I came across the paperwork with my bank information for direct deposit. It had my account number."

"That would make sense. Most companies shred sensitive documents after the information is entered online. But maybe not smaller companies."

Dane shoved his hands into his pockets. "I need to walk around and burn off a little energy because I tend to think better when on the move."

"I understand." She gave a big yawn and stood. "Sitting in a chair tends to exhaust me, almost like driving."

"Will you be okay while I go visit with my mom tomorrow or do I need to stay here?"

"We'll be fine." She shooed her hands at him.

"What about tonight?"

"Deputies are driving by occasionally."

"And yet no one has stopped since I've been here." Did they not notice his motorcycle in the backyard? He needed to move it out of sight. "I can sleep outside..."

Her hands went into the air. "No need to say anything more. I don't think I need protection, but I also didn't think I would need any on the camping trip. Would you like to stay here, at least until tomorrow and one of my team members is available?"

He nodded. "Yeah, I would. If I didn't, I'd never be able to sleep anyways unless I knew you and Everly were safe."

Like she said, this was temporary. As the thought came to him, he couldn't imagine leaving her safety to anyone else. For Josie to agree to let him stay meant she understood the dangers were high.

Chapter Ten

Josie checked the house once more, making certain all the doors were locked and nothing appeared out of the ordinary. On the way to the living room, she stopped at Everly's open door. The poor child must be exhausted. She was fast asleep with Dexter lying at her side. Josie wasn't certain she wanted the dog in the bed, but for now, she wasn't about to stop the practice. For several seconds she watched her daughter breathe. Emotion clogged her throat. She would protect her no matter the costs.

Hopefully, the list of suspects they'd assembled tonight would help catch the man who'd attacked them. She padded back to the couch and prepared it with a sheet and pillow for her to sleep. After she brushed her teeth, she noted the light on under her door. Dane must still be up and working. It was nice to have him working the case with her, but she wished he'd get some sleep.

She could've given him the couch, but she wanted to be closer to Everly. Silly as it was, the living room was only a few feet closer to her daughter's room than her own bedroom, but it was enough to make a difference.

The door swung open, making her jump.

"Good night." His voice sounded way too jolly for this time of night. "I want to thank you for your help. For the first time since I found my partner murdered, I feel…some hope."

She cleared her throat. "Try to get some rest. I'm sure we'll have a busy day tomorrow." Inwardly, she shook her head. She sounded like Fretful Frieda, a character in a children's book she'd had as a child. Certainly, Dane was old enough to know when to go to bed.

"I will." A smile crossed his lips. "And I didn't mean to scare you. I heard your footsteps outside my door. Thought maybe you'd heard from one of your team members."

"Not yet. I may try to contact them again. I'm going to get some sleep."

"Let me know if you learn anything. I'm going to stay awake for a while so if you hear me walking around, just know I'm keeping an eye on things."

"Okay." She headed back to the living room and heard his door shut. She hoped tomorrow would be a good day for both of them. If Dane had been framed, and she believed he was, then he needed to prove his innocence.

She clicked on the lamp next to the couch and turned off the overhead light. Once she was settled under the sheet, she stared up at the ceiling and the swirling fan. Her legs hurt and her head slightly ached probably due to the lack of sleep and getting hit in the head by that limb. Suddenly, her mind went to the laptop she'd left plugged in on the coffee table. There was no reason it would start a fire, was there? Quietly, she climbed out from the sheet and walked to the table and shut down her computer. Logically, she knew most people left things plugged in all the time and nothing happened, but she couldn't relax until everything was safe.

Seconds later, she lay back down and turned off the lamp. With Dane in the house to help watch for intruders, she hoped to get some much-needed rest. With a fluff of her pillow, she rolled to her side and closed her eyes. Today's events went through her mind as she tried to relax. Once Pierce's murderer was behind bars, she planned to get Everly into counseling with Kennedy. There was no shame in getting help, and her team member's specialty was working with families of missing children. Surely if Kennedy could help with the trauma of missing children, she could help Everly with the death of her father. Not only for Everly, but Josie hoped Kennedy could help her with the loss of her family.

She'd never told anyone the details about the fire—nothing besides the fact that the family couldn't get out in time. How did you explain that it was your fault the fire started that killed your family? That she'd been angry her parents wouldn't let her have her best friend, Stacy, over for a sleepover. Josie had already set up the play tent in her room so she and Stacy could sleep inside while listening to some new music Stacy had downloaded. When her parents told her it wasn't a good night for company, she was mad and decided to sleep in the basement to get far away from everyone and be alone. If she hadn't been in the basement, she would've died with the rest of the family.

Or, as she preferred to believe, she could've saved them.

It was later determined the fire had started in her bedroom with an electrical cord that ran under the tent.

Looking back, she realized that had not been the healthiest decision not to seek counseling.

A door creaked and soft footsteps came out of her bedroom.

"It's just me," Dane's voice whispered to her.

"Okay," she whispered back. She was glad he was there. Ever since she'd adopted Everly, she'd constantly worried about keeping her safe and struggled to rest. Her eyes drifted shut.

Dane tried to be quiet as he stepped through the house, taking his time staring out of each window. Clouds drifted over the moon and a few stars sparkled. A gentle breeze made the limbs dance in the oak outside. The only light was near the old shed, which shone on the ground below. A frog hopped across the grass and out of sight.

His gun was in a holster shoved into the back of his waistband just in case there was trouble. Josie was competent at protecting her daughter, he had no doubt. But even the best law officer, or in her case former law officer, could be overtaken if the conditions were just right.

With the list of suspects, he prayed he could turn himself in once the sheriff had returned.

Trust had never come easy, and he hoped he wasn't wrong in putting his faith in Josie. Her watching as he was arrested was scorched into his memory—the shiny eyes, the corner of her lips drawn downward. Not only did she appear sad, but also resigned. Like she was doing what she must. If she'd just come to his defense, maybe the police would've believed him—or at least asked more questions about Keaton. With Keaton being the DA's son, it had been easy to accept his word, and pin the theft on Dane.

They had gone out for months, and he remembered being blown away that she accepted his date when other kids pulled away from him or ignored him. But Josie had been different. Beautiful and athletic. She had been one of the few who talked with him. If it hadn't been for her living a half mile from him, he never would've had the chance. He had been a goofy kid, but she'd given him confidence.

Her grandpa didn't seem to have much money, but that didn't stop her from being popular by his standards.

Protectiveness consumed him at the thought of the same man who killed Harlan, targeting her and her daughter. Besides Violet, there wasn't anyone in his life he cared so much about.

Clank.

The noise came somewhere from outside. He stiffened as he peered through the window. A leaf blew across the drive, but there were no other activities nor shadows. It sounded like it came from the right of his vantage point, so he hurried back to his bedroom. He intended to look out the window, but when he came through the door, movement came from the closet.

He reached back for his gun, and something hard came down on his head. Fireflies danced in the air.

And then he was stumbling, trying to keep his footing. Josie and Everly were vulnerable sleeping.

He tried to put his hands out to break the fall, but his arms collapsed as he hit the floor. Everything went black.

Josie's brain wrestled in a fog of memories. Her childhood home filled with breath-stealing smoke. Family members' shouts reverberated from the top floor.

Her dad's voice echoed through the dark home, "Fire! Get out!"

"Audrey!" her mom called. "Where are you?"

Footsteps pounded across the floor above her. Josie fumbled out of the bed in the basement and hurried up the stairs. The smoke grew thicker the higher she climbed. Dizziness descended on her as she reached the top. When she swung the door open, flames whooshed in front of her. She yelled, "Mom!"

The dark haze blinded her, but flickers from the flames illuminated her dad's silhouette. "Josie. Go back downstairs and climb out the window."

"What about Audrey?"

"I'll get your sister. Go now! Get out of the house and don't come back in." His shout spurred her into action as she sprinted down the dark stairs. She hacked, her lungs begging for air.

The cough racked her body and her chest burned.

"Mom!" The child's voice called from far away.

The word demanded her attention, and Josie shot straight up on the couch. Barking came from the other room.

Everly!

"Get down on the floor. I'm coming for you." Smoke burned her eyes, making it difficult to see. She'd scarcely made it to her feet when the blazing ceiling fell on her, and she was barely able to block it to keep from taking the brunt of it. Burning debris dropped like rain all around her.

More barking came from Everly's room. The fire would spread slower if there was no oxygen.

"Shut the door, Everly."

But it was too late.

"Help me." Her daughter's voice came from the hallway.

"Get down on the floor. I'm coming to you." Heat blocked her path, but she had to save her daughter. She turned and ran toward the kitchen and away from Everly. The fire had not engulfed this part of the house yet. Before running out the back door, she hollered one last time. "Go back in your room and shut the door. Trust me."

Moving faster than she believed possible, she sprinted barefoot down the porch and around the side of the house to Everly's room. In her mind, she prepared to break out the window since she knew it was locked, but the girl had the pane open. Dexter barked.

Josie held out her hands. "Come here."

Everly leaped into her arms, Dexter right behind her. The girl coughed and gagged, and Josie carried her away from the flames. With all of her might, she tried not to break down, flooded with relief, but it was no use. Her limbs shook uncontrollably. "Are you hurt? Did you get burned?"

"I'm okay."

Despite her words, tears ran down her daughter's face; no doubt, scared to death. Dexter continued to bark and circle them with excitement as the flames reached high into the sky. Small explosions mixed with whooshing, and pops filled the void.

"Mom, where's Dane?"

She inhaled a sharp intake of breath. She'd been so concerned with saving Everly, she'd forgotten about him. As she ran around the backside of the house, an explosion rocked the ground. As if danger was everywhere and closing in, it suddenly hit her, someone must have started the fire.

That person might still be close by.

"Everly." She turned. "Get inside my Bronco and lock the doors. Take Dexter with you."

While her daughter ran barefoot in her gown

toward the garage, déjà vu swept over her. She couldn't lose another person in a fire. The last she'd seen of Dane he was walking through the house trying to protect her and Everly.

She prayed he wasn't in the home, but his motorcycle was still in the driveway. She ran toward the flames. *Please, Lord, help him be okay.*

Chapter Eleven

A massive ache pounded through Dane's head and stampeded back and forth like a jackhammer. His lungs burned, making it impossible to breathe, and the heat was unbearable. It took a millisecond for the cobwebs to clear and for him to realize something was wrong.

Deadly wrong.

Deafening pops and a constant sizzling encompassed him. Even the wooden floor felt warm to his cheek. He rolled over to see the ceiling above him ablaze while pieces of sheetrock crashed to the floor.

Josie and Everly. He had to get to them.

He climbed to his feet, making the heat increase, and dizziness swirled through him. He stumbled toward the door. Orange flames kicked up all around, singeing the side of his jeans. When he opened the door, a raging inferno whooshed through the opening.

He couldn't exit this way and shoved the door closed. He'd have to go around the side of the house to get them out. As he turned and staggered back toward the window, his world spun. No matter how much he attempted to take a breath, his lungs wouldn't fill. It felt like he was breathing through a coffee straw.

Over the crackling of the flames, a faint voice called his name.

Josie? "In here." As soon as the words were out, a burning board fell from above and hit him in the shoulder, knocking him down. He still couldn't breathe.

Fear like he'd never felt before assaulted him. He wasn't going to survive. Not this time.

What would happen to Violet? And Josie and Everly? Had the killer already found them?

He had to get out of there. Shoving his pain aside, he attempted to get to his feet. But it was no use. The lack of oxygen zapped his energy.

"Dane." Josie's voice called again.

He opened his mouth to answer but gagged and coughed instead. *Stay out. Don't try to save me.* He didn't know if he said the words out loud, but he didn't want her to die.

Please, God, if You get me out of here alive, I

will try to do better. I'll try my hardest to help Josie, Everly, and Violet. Just let me live.

Somewhere in the distance, sirens wailed. There was no way Dane could survive by the time they reached her house. After running back to the shed, Josie found a box of bed sheets and grabbed a stack. A blanket would be better, but there was no time to search. She hurried to the water spigot and held the fabric underneath, then sprinted back to the house. A quick glance showed Everly's face plastered against the driver's side window of her Bronco watching her.

Please, let Dane be okay. She yelled, "Watch out. I'm going to break the window."

She prayed he was still in her bedroom. Using a bulky decorative rock from her landscaping, she threw it with all of her might. The stone went straight through, and left a decent hole in the pane, but not large enough for her to crawl through. Wrapping the sheet around her elbow and arm for protection, she finished knocking out the pane and climbed through.

Instantly a wall of heat suffocated her, and she pulled the wet sheet over her core. "Dane. Where are you?"

She dropped to the floor that was littered

with tiny fires. Heat burned her eyes, forcing her to temporarily close them. Not being able to see, she felt around with her hand. Was the door to the bedroom open? She couldn't remember. At this point, it didn't matter. Her bed was to her right and the bathroom on her left. She hadn't crawled a couple of feet when her hand touched something firm—his shoulder. "Dane. Are you okay?"

He groaned, and his hand reached out and touched her cheek. "Josie."

"Here. Cover up with this. Help is on the way, but we need to get you out of here. Can you crawl to the window?"

His voice was gravelly. "Save yourself. Get out."

"Not without you."

He got on his knees and elbows, while she helped keep the damp sheet around him. As she assisted him, her sheet got tangled under her knees and fell to the floor. It didn't take long to make it to the window, and Dane grabbed the frame and pulled himself up, his muscles trembling from the effort.

As smoke was sucked from the window, blackness descended on them. Something exploded—engulfing them in a heat cloud.

"Come on. Let's get you out of here." But Dane slumped back to the floor.

The flames grew larger. "Out the window. I can't pick you up."

He climbed to his knees and then to his feet, leaning against the window. With her help, he was able to fall and roll out of the window frame and onto the ground. More hissing and popping sounded. The house was old and used propane for heat. The tank sat on the other side of the building, and she wondered how much longer it would be until it exploded.

Sitting on the window frame, she jumped feet first and landed beside Dane. They stumbled across the yard as the sirens grew louder.

Boom! The ground shook as a huge fireball ballooned across the land.

Seconds later and neither of them would've made it.

Josie watched as the fire ravaged her house. "This was too close. We must catch whoever is targeting us."

Dane leaned up on his elbows, his face and clothes a dark mask of soot. He fought to get to his feet. "I've got to get out of here."

"Dane, no..."

Regret lined his face. His gaze searched hers

before he leaned forward and gave her a peck on her cheek. "Thanks for helping me out. I owe you." And then he took off between the outbuildings and disappeared into the darkness.

Josie made her way over to her Bronco, as the last of the fire trucks stopped in her drive. Multiple emergency vehicles arrived, including Deputy Hattie Perkins's from the sheriff's department.

As Everly eagerly climbed out of the SUV, Josie wrapped her arms around her, her knees still shaking. She didn't trust her voice and held her daughter for several moments.

"Is there anyone still inside?" a tall fireman asked.

"No. Everyone made it out." Had she really gotten them all out? The feeling like someone could still be in there caused her chest to constrict, but she knew it was just the three of them.

"Are you certain?"

"Yes, sir. Even our collie is out safely."

"Okay. Stay back."

Deputy Perkins walked up but waited for the fireman to leave before she drew close. Concerned eyes examined her. "Are you okay, Josie?"

"Scared, but I wasn't injured."

"Let's check your oxygen level just in case." A paramedic put a reader on her finger. "Eighty-nine. Let's get you on oxygen and check the rest of your vitals."

As Josie sat in the back of the ambulance, she watched as the same paramedic checked out Everly. Thankfully, her daughter had suffered no harm. Deputy Perkins decided to wait to ask more questions. She was glad, considering she was wearing the oxygen mask.

Josie glanced to the area behind the shed where Dane had disappeared. As quick as the kiss had been, her cheek still tingled from the brush of his lips and the prick of his beard—not a bad thing.

The peck had been a simple gesture of appreciation. Right? Because she wasn't looking for anything more. She had her hands full with Everly and didn't need to even consider a relationship, especially while he was running from the law.

Where was he? Had he kept running or was he close by watching the scene? Her gut told her he was close.

But did she really know him that well anymore to have a sixth sense? Surely not. He couldn't keep running. It only made him look guiltier. If only he would trust the system.

Her attention returned to the home as the firemen got the blaze under control. The house would be a total loss. Thankfully, she had renter's insurance. Fifteen minutes later, she was off the oxygen and felt much better. As she walked around the perimeter of what used to be her home, Deputy Perkins caught back up with her.

"Tell me what happened, Josie."

She sighed. "I'm not certain where to begin. I told you about Everly and me being attacked at our vacation cabin."

The deputy nodded.

"I was going through some of Everly's dad's things—his laptop that was stored in boxes in my garage. I didn't even realize I had it with me until yesterday. I woke to the house being filled with smoke."

For several seconds, the woman stared at Josie. "Tel me about your involvement with Dane Haggerty."

Her heart dropped. She couldn't and wouldn't lie. But what if he was right and someone had framed him and the law didn't believe it? She had to trust in the justice system. *That's easy for you to say.* His words echoed in her mind. "How did you know about Dane?"

Perkins shrugged with a slight smile. "I didn't know for sure. But that looks like his motorcycle over there." She jerked her head.

Oh no. And Josie had fallen for the leading question. "Dane believes the man who is after Everly and me is also the man who set him up. Pierce Browning, Everly's dad, had been hired to investigate Harlan and Dane's construction company. For the record, I came to that conclusion on my own, too."

This time Perkins kept her expression unreadable. "You realize that could mean Dane could've had reason to kill Browning, too."

"I do." Josie nodded. "But if that's so, why hasn't he left the area? Why remain close?"

"You know as well as I do that criminals don't always make the smartest moves. Having family or friends in the area is enough for them to stay with what's familiar."

Violet. His sister immediately came to Josie's mind. "Hattie, you know I would never break the law or hide a fugitive."

"Unless…"

She rubbed a hand across the back of her neck. If Dane was innocent, he needed her this time. She'd turned him in before, and now she realized she *could've* been wrong. It was at least a possibility. "Unless there was a really good reason. I don't take the law lightly."

"I won't lie to the sheriff. He needs to know." The deputy's stern expression told her there was no room for discussion.

"And I wouldn't ask you to."

Hattie pursed her lips and nodded. "Good."

After the deputy walked away, Josie considered what she'd just done. It was one thing to believe in somebody, but another to put her faith in them. Her gaze went to Everly. Not only was her own reputation at stake, but if she was wrong, it could affect her daughter's future, too.

An hour later, all emergency responders were gone except for the deputy—Hattie had agreed to see her to a hotel in town. Since her Bronco had been left unscathed, Josie climbed into the driver's seat and looked over to where Everly sat in the passenger seat fast asleep. Her daughter's eyes fluttered open as soon as Josie shut the door.

"Sorry. I didn't mean to wake you."

"I wasn't sleeping well anyway. Where will we live now?"

Josie tried to display confidence. “Home is wherever family is. It’s not a building. As long as we’re together, we’ll be fine.”

Everly didn’t reply, and she hoped that was because her answer satisfied her. The truth was, Josie had never invested much in a house, or put down deep roots, because she understood too well how fast a home could vanish. And family.

“I totally agree,” a male voice said from the back seat.

Josie let out a yelp. “Dane Haggerty. You scared me half to death.”

“There were too many people milling around. I knew you couldn’t stay here for the night, and I thought we should get on the same page.”

She glanced at him in her rearview mirror as she came to a stop at the end of her driveway.

He asked, “Where are you going?”

“To a hotel. I’m figuring Liberty Inn and Suites. Hattie is planning to be with us. That’s her vehicle.” Josie pointed to the deputy’s SUV that just pulled out. I think she’s waiting on me.”

“It’s good you’re staying with her. That makes me feel better.” He leaned forward and grimaced. “I’ll call you in the morning.”

Before she had time to ask anything, he exited the vehicle and moved along the fence row until he disappeared into the shadows. She noticed he hunched forward in pain, making her wonder about the extent of his injuries from the fire.

As she pulled onto the rock road, Josie looked for Dane and disappointment crashed into her when she didn't see him, leaving her with the dawning realization he was becoming important to her again.

No matter what she'd done to protect her heart, Dane had a way of breaking through the strongest of armor.

Chapter Twelve

From the cover of a lilac bush, Dane watched Josie's Bronco pull out of the drive until it topped the hill, disappearing from sight. Pierce Browning's laptop was in the house and no longer useful in proving Pierce had been hired by Harlan.

Should he give up and turn himself in? Maybe Josie was right, and he should trust law enforcement to do their job. But the looks on the faces of the DA, the judge, and the few other people in the courtroom were still ingrained in his memory. They all believed him guilty. And then his classmates and neighbors treated him differently after he'd gotten out of juvenile detention. He'd graduated high school from there.

As he climbed to his feet, his back burned, his shirt sticking to the wound. With each move, the cloth stuck, and instant pain felt like a knife stabbing an open wound. No doubt, he needed medical care. But if he sought help, it'd be the same as turning himself in.

Josie and Everly needed his help more. The quicker he found the guy who was targeting them, the better. The fire must've been started by him. Where did he go? Had he stayed around to watch his handiwork? Was he sending a message again, or had he really wanted to kill them? Or did he just want to destroy the laptop and anything else in those files?

So many questions and not enough answers.

As he surveyed his surroundings, his gaze stopped on the garage. Drawing his gun, he moved down the driveway, careful to stay in the shadows as much as possible. He stepped into the open garage and then the storage room at the back. A quick look produced nothing.

The man must have started the fire and left. But why not stay and act like a good neighbor or passerby? Because Everly could still identify him.

His motorcycle was still there. Thankfully, the machine had not been consumed by the fire. As he threw his leg over the seat, his back cramped in rebellion. He waited for the pain to subside before starting the motor. Cobwebs filled his mind from being only semiconscious due to the smoke—a terrible headache his reward.

Even as the idling engine rumbled, his head felt like it would explode. After he left Josie's place, he rode by the Liberty Inn and Suites. Josie and Everly were climbing the stairs to the second floor, the deputy behind them.

Now that he knew she was okay, he headed out of town to get ready for his next stop. The stakes were getting more dangerous, and he intended to do everything in his power to find out who was behind the attacks. He had the feeling the person may be closer to him than he'd first believed.

Dane knocked on the door as early morning light came over the horizon. The overgrown yard looked like it hadn't been mowed all year. Sadness hit hard. *Honor thy father and mother.* It was such a challenging commandment for him, even though he knew it was the right thing to do.

The door swung open.

Shock was the best word to describe his reaction. His mother was hunched over, and her hair had thinned and grayed. He almost didn't recognize her. "Mom."

She squinted. "Dane. Is that you?" Her voice came out weak and shaky.

"Yes, Mama. It's me." He hoped she hadn't been drinking being it was early in the morning. "Can I come in?"

"Of course. Of course." She stepped back.

The smell of cigarette smoke and something burning assaulted him as he entered the living room. Trash and junk were piled up on almost every surface in the living space. Even her old recliner was full of yarn and crochet needles. "Is something burning?"

She waved her hand. "My peas and carrots ran out of water and scorched the pan last night. I don't have no money."

"I didn't come for money." He held his breath for her to say she'd heard about the warrant for his arrest, but she didn't continue.

"Have a seat." She indicated the couch.

"No, thanks. While I'm here, I figured I might lend you a hand." He smiled and stepped into the kitchen. Dishes were stacked in the sink, and he went about transferring them to the counter. After he rinsed the sink, he ran water and squeezed in a good amount of dish-washing liquid.

His mom cleared a place at her table and sat. "What do I owe this visit to?"

He glanced at her. "I wanted to check on Violet."

"Violet?" Her voice dropped. "The court took your sister away."

"I'm sure there was an investigation. When did it start?"

"Over a year ago. They threatened to take Violet away if I didn't take parenting classes and get a job. I had been working at the diner for over thirteen years, and then they let me go."

The Greasy Spoon had fired her over two years ago for showing up intoxicated. They'd even given her time off at a rehabilitation center to help—something small businesses couldn't always afford. But his mom had not stayed sober. After he washed several glasses and plates, he went for the bowls and larger spoons. His mom appeared frailer than he'd believed possible.

He turned to her. "I'm sorry, Mom. Is there anything I can do?"

"For Violet? No. She's gone." She rubbed her forehead. "And maybe it's for the best. Teachers and other people tended to get involved. I just couldn't be a good mom anymore. Not after you and Randy."

Dane held his tongue. His dad had been in and out of trouble, including jail, for most of Dane's life. And his dad used Randy to help steal things in stores. The first time Dane had witnessed it, he couldn't have been more than five, and Randy was about seven. His dad had gone into a jewelry store and told the clerk he wanted to buy a bracelet for his wife for her birthday. Dane remembered being surprised because he didn't realize it was her birthday. But he was also excited, believing she'd be getting a nice present. As soon as the lady had a group of bracelets displayed on the counter, Randy ran inside the store and grabbed a carousel of earrings at the end of an aisle. The whole thing crashed to the floor. The clerk told his dad to hold on, and when she hurried across the store to stop Randy, his dad stuffed several bracelets into his pockets.

They hurried to the car and then pawned the pieces on the way home.

Randy didn't have a chance to stay out of trouble as a kid. Dane didn't have much to do with his brother, but the last he'd heard, Randy was doing time in county jail.

After a load of dishes was drying, he continued to put items away and clean the kitchen.

"Why are you here? You haven't been by in a couple of years."

Did she not remember asking him not to come by? That seeing him made Violet act out. Like he was to blame. "I've got a few questions for you if you have time."

"Honey, I don't hardly get out or talk to anyone besides Alma and Stanley Hastings. They pick up food for me at the store or take me to my doctor appointments if needed. I don't have no money if that's your game."

"No game, Mom." Guilt descended on him with her words. Even though she'd asked him to not come by anymore, he should've argued or made more of an effort. "I don't know how to ask this."

"Just be honest like we've taught you."

He wasn't going to take the bait on that opening. "Did Dad have any enemies? Any that would come after our family?"

Her eyebrows furrowed. "Most people liked your father, although I'm sure there may be a few who felt otherwise. That's normal."

"Mom, he went to jail for stealing. That's bound to upset the ones he stole from."

"I'll not have you speaking ill of the dead."

He sighed and ran his hand through his hair. "I'm not trying to. I promise. I just need to know if there is anyone who may have been mad enough to target our family."

"Is someone bothering you, Dane?"

"Yeah." He grabbed the cereal boxes from the table and put them in the cabinet.

"I'd rather you leave those on the table. It makes it easier for me."

"Sorry." He put them back where he found them.

"There were a few people who didn't get along with your father. Joe Tonelli and Demarcus Howard are the worst."

"I remember them. Joe claimed Dad owed him money for work done on his old Chevy pickup, and Demarcus got into it with him over some tools that went missing when Dad did some work for him."

She nodded. "That's right. Joe rebuilt an alternator, but your dad said it didn't fix the problem, and he wasn't going to pay for it. And then he helped Demarcus combine during wheat harvest, and then the man said Tyrus stole his post-hole digger and air compressor from his shop. Your daddy had no use for those things and wouldn't have taken them."

He also had no use for diamond bracelets, but that hadn't stopped him from pawning them. "Is there anyone else that might have it in for him or our family? Maybe someone from jail?"

"Not that I can remember. He never talked much about people from those times. You know, Dane, he had his problems, but Tyrus was a good man. What's this all about?" The back door opened as she was speaking. "Are you in some kind of trouble?"

Randy walked into the room. His face lit up into a greasy smile. "Yeah, he's in trouble," his brother busted out. "Ain't that right, little brother? Running from the law. Didn't think you had it in you."

Dane had thought Randy was still serving time, but evidently he'd been released early. "Been a while, Randy."

"Mama, you know your darling Dane has a warrant for his arrest for murder?"

Her mouth dropped open and concerned etched her forehead. "For what?"

"Come on, Randy." His older brother had called him "darling Dane" for as long as he could remember, and it still grated on his nerves.

He turned his attention back to their mom. "There's nothing to worry about."

His brother grabbed a beer from the refrigerator and took a big swig. Oily hair swung to his shoulders and his T-shirt was wrinkled and had a crude picture of a woman complete with a nasty saying printed across the front. "I knew you wasn't the goody-two-shoe like you thought."

Dane didn't bother with a response, although he could feel the heat rise to his cheeks. Maybe it was no one that had known their dad causing him trouble, but Randy. Did he dare ask the question? Could it be his own brother who framed him?

His stomach turned. That would be too much for even Randy.

Dane had always been a little afraid of his older brother. Maybe it was that way with a lot of siblings, but Randy took trouble to a new level. "Was this your doing?"

Randy's lips slowly turned upward. "What? That I killed somebody?" He let out a boisterous laugh. "Not hardly. Although, I could if I wanted to, and I can guarantee I wouldn't get caught. If you want me to testify for you, lil' bro, just give me the word. I have no doubt you've never hurt anyone in your life. You ain't that tough."

Dane was about to get into it with Randy. He sure wasn't going to argue that killing someone made you tough.

Worry lines formed across his mom's forehead, and he turned his attention back to her. "Mom don't be concerned. I didn't do anything wrong. I'll check on you later."

Randy dropped to the sofa, his beer sloshing to the carpet, and he watched Dane.

He gave his mom a kiss on the cheek and left without acknowledging Randy. As he strode out the door, he wanted to tell his brother to lay off and quit upsetting their mom. But it'd do no good. Randy would welcome a confrontation.

As he took off on his motorcycle, the wind blew through his hair. Could his brother have set him up? But why? What would be the purpose? They had never been close, but they weren't enemies, not enough to lead to killing two people.

When he was several miles away from his mom's place, he pulled over at a roadside park and killed the engine. He called Josie.

"Hello."

"I have another person I'd like you to investigate if you can."

"Okay, Grandpa. Let me step out." Her voice was barely more than a whisper.

"Is the deputy close by?"

"Yeah."

It felt like a knife went into his chest. "I don't want you to lie for me, Josie. I'll make this quick. Randy Haggerty. I thought he was in prison, but he's not."

Several seconds of silence crawled by. "I can do that. I hope you're wrong, Dane."

"Me too. Can we meet so we can talk freely? How about at the old Tatum drive-in on Preston Bend."

Several seconds of silence went by. The drive-in was already closed when he and Josie started dating, but they would sometimes meet to talk there. After a few meetings, it became their place.

"I'll be there at nine o'clock tonight. Everly is still asleep. Technically, Hattie is off duty right now and said she could watch Everly if I needed to get a couple of things done. She'll be back on duty this afternoon."

"Okay. I'll see you there."

"Oh, one more thing. Do you know anyone who drives a black Ford Raptor?"

He thought for a moment. "No. Why?"

"One has driven by the hotel several times, but I wasn't able to see the license plate."

That didn't sound good. And if she left to meet him, whoever was in the Raptor might target her. "Josie, be careful."

After they disconnected, he stared at the phone. He was starting to care for her again. A lot. Just as things were becoming more dangerous.

Josie arrived at the drive-in fifteen minutes early, and Dane's motorcycle was already parked between a grove of trees and what was left of the concession stand. She pulled her Bronco next to him and killed the engine.

He opened her door for her. "You're early."

"So are you." She stepped out onto the green, overgrown grass. Even though it had been a hot day, a welcome breeze blew across the open area, reminding her of the summer nights when they used to come here.

Without thought she moved to the old metal picnic table where they used to talk for hours. She sat in her normal place on top of the table and rested her feet on the bench seat.

He stood in front of her and glanced down. "Did you learn anything more?"

"Several things. Chandler paid a visit to Byron to find out why he and his son were at the office."

"Yeah." Hope sounded in his voice. "Tell me you learned something helpful."

"It looks like nothing but dead ends. A few days after the murder, Byron stopped by to grab his personal belongings, and Kyle and his girlfriend came with him. While Byron was loading up his things, Kyle and his girlfriend were looking at the murder scene and the offices. His girlfriend accidentally left her purse or wallet there that contained her identity. Being that her parents didn't want her dating Kyle and her dad is police officer in Pine Hollow, she was afraid her parents would find out if investigators searched the premises. Kyle agreed to grab the wallet and give it back."

He held his hands out to his side. "It took them months to figure that out?"

"The two were no longer talking, and it took her that long to remember where she'd left it. Chandler believed them."

Dane rubbed the back of his neck. "I always

liked Byron, so I suppose I should be relieved. Anything else?"

"Chandler also checked out Jim Price, the accountant. He seems clean with no red flags. I researched your brother. Randy was paroled over two months ago. I didn't find any connections to Pierce or anyone who worked with you, including Harlan."

Stormy eyes stared back at her. She couldn't tell what he was thinking, but emotions swirled. What must it be like not to trust your own family?

"What about my dad?"

She shook her head. "I'm sorry. There's nothing there either. There were no connections to prisoners in Tennessee Colony." She shrugged. "We can keep looking, but my gut says Harlan's and Pierce's murders had nothing to do with either Randy or your dad."

"I guess that's good." He looked up at the sky. "It's beautiful tonight."

The sudden change of subject surprised her. She leaned back and put her hands on the table and gazed at the sky. "The moon and stars are so bright."

Dane was silent for a few seconds, and then he sat beside her. "Reminds me of when we used to come here. I missed those days—the long talks...and stuff."

The stuff was what she didn't want to think about right now. They'd been young and in love; besides talking, they'd come here to hold hands and kiss. Once, Dane had brought a blanket so they could watch airplanes and occasionally see a shooting star. Their budding romance hadn't happened over night, but rather they'd been friends at first. He'd lived with his grandma when Josie met him, but he confided he'd lived with neighbors before then.

Even though Josie had lost her family to the fire, she'd been proud to be part of the Hunt clan. Her dad had been a supervisor at a factory, and her mom had stayed home with her and Audrey until they started school. Then she went to work for the rural water company. Nothing grand, but her parents were well thought of in the community and provided a stable homelife.

"Dane, you've done good."

Even though she wasn't looking at him, she could feel him studying her. "What's that supposed to mean?"

She turned to him then. "In business. In life."

He chuckled. "You're kidding me, right? I've

been accused of murdering my business partner and best friend."

"I know it sounds silly. But I'm proud of you. Harlan believed in you. Your parents…had a difficult time."

"That's putting it lightly. Dad was a thief and Mom was an alcoholic."

Her chest constricted. "But yet you managed to help start and run a successful business."

He glanced away and gazed back at the stars. "It's more than that. Harlan introduced me to God. I realized no matter the struggles my family had, I had choices. I could choose a different path. When I started going to worship services, I also realized everyone has problems. Even the people that seem to have their life together." He turned back to her. "I was younger when I went to church with you. I didn't quite get it. I mainly went to be around you, so when you turned me in, I was ready to give up."

"I'm sorry about that." Rarely did Josie apologize. Normally the sentiment tasted bitter, but not this time. "I should've believed in you."

"What changed your mind?"

She shrugged. "Just you. You kept telling me Keaton gave you the keys and you didn't know the car belonged to the principal. In my mind, that was unbelievable."

His eyes searched her face before he wrapped his arms around her.

She started to pull away because she didn't want to give him the wrong idea. Didn't want him to think she was interested in anything more than helping put away whoever was targeting them and clear his name. But as he held her tight, she couldn't make herself let go.

"Thank you, Josie. You don't know what it means to have your support." He released her and climbed back to his feet. "We need to find the real killer."

Instantly she missed his warmth. She cleared her throat. "You're right. Who would have something to gain?"

He shoved his hands into his pockets. "I don't know. I've gone over this a hundred times. It has to be the money. I think we should visit Layla."

"Harlan's wife?"

"Yeah.

Headlights shone along the road and then a vehicle pulled into the abandoned drive-in. Josie slid her gun from the holster and then placed it against her leg. Dane moved closer to her and pulled the bill of his ballcap further down as a squad car pulled up.

The car stopped in front of them and then an unfamiliar officer stepped out.

Josie's heart thumped in her chest. If the lady recognized Dane, he would be arrested.

"Can I ask what you two are doing out here? This is private property."

Dane eased into the shadows of the concession stand.

"Hello, officer." Josie let out a friendly laugh. "This is a little embarrassing. My high school sweetheart and I used to come here years ago. We reunited a few days ago and decided it'd be a good place to talk."

The officer shined a flashlight on Josie's face. Josie was careful to keep her gun out of view. It'd be hard to explain why she had it on her. Her mouth went dry, and her stomach rolled as the officer shined the light on Dane.

"Okay." She clicked the light off. "The owner has listed this place for sale, and he calls in to complain when someone trespasses—there's been vandals recently. You two need to move along."

"Yes, ma'am," Dane said.

The officer glanced from Dane back to Josie.

"Just to give you two a piece of advice, find somewhere else to *talk.*"

Awkwardness hung in the air as they watched her pull out until her taillights disappeared over the hill.

Josie released a high sigh of relief. "That was a little too close."

"You're not kidding." He looked back the way the officer had disappeared. "I'm going the other way. I don't want to take a chance of crossing paths again."

"I'll see you in the morning. I'm praying things go well when we visit Layla." The seriousness of the situation weighed heavy on her. The only thing she knew for certain was they were running out of leads and were no closer to learning who was trying to kill them. How many more times could they be attacked and come out alive? She prayed they didn't find out.

Chapter Thirteen

Josie took a deep breath and knocked on Layla's door.

The gorgeous stone home was trimmed in cedar and had bulky porch posts. A wide, winding stone walk accented the colorful landscaping. She glanced over her shoulder at Dane, but he was no longer in sight. He must be down in the seat.

A banging sounded from inside the house and then she watched through the glass panes of the door a pretty lady walk into the foyer. The slender woman with fiery red hair wore soft makeup that gave her a flawless look. The dark complexion shouted either she was outside a lot or suntanned at a facility. Josie figured the latter.

"May I help you?"

She smiled and held out her hand. "Yes, ma'am. I'm Josie Hunt and I'd like to ask you some questions about your husband."

The woman gave her hand a quick shake. "I've already talked with the police. I have nothing more to say."

"Oh, no, ma'am, I'm not with the police. I'm an investigator with Bring the Children Home Project." She smiled. One mention of the organization that helped find missing kids brought down most people's defenses. Who could be rude to a person who helped reunite children with their families? Josie wasn't above using this tactic to get her foot in the door.

The woman's smile waned a bit. "Come on in. Although I'm not certain how I can help. Is there a missing child?"

"No." Josie followed her inside the entryway and cool air hit her. Tall ceilings made the home feel even larger. A huge stairway led to the second story. Plants and flowers sat along the wall, giving the place a welcoming feel. She followed the woman into a cozy room with all white furniture and bright floral pillows.

Somehow Dane's description of Harlan as down to earth didn't quite match the grand house or his exquisite wife.

"Can I get you something to drink? Lemonade? Bottled water?"

"No, thank you. First, let me offer my condolences. I can only imagine what you are going through." The woman's bright-colored shirt and teal leggings were a far cry from mourning clothes, but some people didn't tend to hold to such traditions anymore. "I'd like to know if there is anything you can tell me about Harlan before his death. Like if he was distracted."

The woman's green eyes stared straight at her. "Harlan was always distracted with work. He lived and breathed the construction business. Work is what made him the happiest, which is why it breaks my heart his partner took advantage by stealing from him. A tragic case of betrayal."

The words annoyed Josie, but they also sounded rehearsed. *A tragic case of betrayal.* Had she read that line in a book somewhere? "Yes, of course, that would be tragic. But I'm not certain Dane Haggerty is the man who killed your husband. Did Harlan keep records or documents here? I've looked at the office, but it seems some paperwork may be missing."

Layla stiffened, her face paling. "Well, you're wrong. It's obvious he killed my Harlan. Dane Haggerty is a greedy low-life varmint that couldn't wait to get his hands on my husband's business. Harlan was considering selling his half to Dane, but Haggerty was too impatient and killed Harlan with his granddaddy's hay hook."

Josie inwardly took a deep breath and gave the woman some latitude because she'd lost her husband. Dane had complained how people easily wrote him off. "But if he killed Harlan with the hay hook, why didn't he take it with him? Surely, no killer would be that ignorant."

Layla got to her feet. "He most certainly was that dumb. Harlan complained about his incompetence all the time. Why that man ever took pity on that scum I'll never understand."

A door shut somewhere in the back of the house, and Josie turned toward the sound. When she looked back to the widow, their gazes met.

"Just the AC coming on. Sometimes it causes a door to close." The woman waved her hand, dismissing the noise.

"I'm sorry for your loss, Mrs. Schmidt. I didn't mean to upset you." She asked again, "Did Harlan bring paperwork home?"

"No, he didn't." Layla's gaze wouldn't meet Josie's. "Is there something in particular you were searching for?"

"Honestly, anything that could give me insight as to why someone killed Harlan. The authorities have the bank statement that was discovered at the scene, but the previous statements appear to be missing." Financial information could easily be subpoenaed at the bank, but Josie wanted to get the widow's reaction.

Layla tugged at her collar irritably. "I understood Haggerty had the stolen money in his account. If you truly care about justice, tell the man to return the money and turn himself in. I won't be able to sleep well until my husband's killer is behind bars."

Josie smiled. "I understand. There seems to be a question of why he deposited the money in his account *after* Harlan's death. Do you know why your husband hired a PI?"

"I have no idea what you're talking about."

"Harlan hired Pierce Browning and then the investigator was killed."

Layla shook her head, but her eyes displayed doubt.

"Seems too coincidental that he was killed right after Harlan was murdered." Josie paused to see if she would reply, but Layla simply stared. "If you think of anything else, would you please give me a call?" She withdrew a business card from her purse and held it out.

The woman snatched it away from her. "I

won't. And it sounds like Dane must've killed two people."

"I'll see myself out." But as Josie walked toward the front door, Layla stayed on her heels.

"If Dane wasn't guilty, why did he run? Innocent people don't run."

"Maybe. Unless they're framed." Josie shot her a smile. But as she turned to leave, a shadow presented itself on the hallway floor. Someone was listening around the corner. Who? She lowered her voice. "Layla, if I'm right and Dane wasn't the one to murder your husband, surely you realize that could put you in danger. If you ever need to talk..."

The woman glared at her, and Josie could feel Layla's eyes on her as she walked down the pathway. She resisted the urge to turn around until she got to her Bronco. Layla stood on her porch.

When Josie opened her door, she quickly warned under her breath, "Don't get up yet. She's watching."

Dane whispered, "Okay."

As she pulled away, she gave Layla a quick wave before disappearing up the drive and out of the gate. "You can get up now."

He was slow to look out the window back at the house. "How did it go? Did you learn anything?"

"I'm certain someone else was in the house."

Dane sat up straight. "Who?"

She shook her head. "I don't know. I heard a door shut and there was a shadow around the corner."

His gaze took her in. "I didn't see any vehicles, but I probably wouldn't since she has a three-car garage. Did she say who else might be involved?"

"No. She blamed Harlan's death on you. How did you get along with Layla before he died?"

He shrugged. "She was friendly. We got together several times a year, like at the Christmas employee party and then a few times for burgers or barbeque. Mainly, though, I saw Layla when she went to worship services."

"How was that? I mean, did she seem sincere?" Josie couldn't shake the feeling that Layla was a fake. But maybe not. Everyone handled grief differently.

Dane looked thoughtful for a moment. "I have no idea. I've never thought about it, but she was nice enough. She never seemed to mind that Harlan would invite me over or that he included me with their family."

Like a fifth wheel. Josie could fill in the blanks and realized how much Dane had felt like an outcast. At times, she had felt the same way. But it was more than that. She detected the strain in his voice. A glance to him showed him staring out his window. She'd never considered how much he might be grieving for his partner. "You miss him, don't you?"

"Yeah, I do." He nodded. "We used to work together at Red River Construction, and he was my supervisor. After high school, I'd worked several odd jobs and then applied at Red River from an online advertisement. Harlan hired me. Back then, I walked around with a chip on my shoulder and got into arguments with other employees. Harlan called me into his office and had a talk with me. I was expecting to be reprimanded, but he talked to me about needing me to be a part of his team. He complimented me on driving a forklift and that it was beneficial I wasn't afraid of heights."

Josie caught the smile on Dane's lips.

"I was always a kind of daredevil as a kid, and this was the first time someone had said to me it gave me an advantage."

"Yeah, I guess you're right." Something in

his demeanor told her Harlan had been much more than a boss.

"He made me feel like I could be a part of a team." Almost as if he read her thoughts, he added, "Harlan invited me to worship services. He never preached to me, but rather, included me. It didn't take long for me to see how much I'd been missing. Gave me purpose besides being angry all the time."

As Josie listened to him, she realized Layla was wrong. Harlan hadn't pitied Dane but had been a sort of mentor to him. There's no way Dane had misinterpreted their relationship. "What made you two go into business together?"

"I'd taken a couple of business classes online and began to want to go out on my own. I know, it was kind of a silly dream."

She looked at him. "Not at all."

He shot her a smile. "I didn't have the money. At first when I mentioned it, Harlan didn't seem interested, but then a local construction company went out of business and was put up for sale. The owner had been young and made poor decisions. Being that Harlan was twenty years older than me, he had no desire to start a business by himself but loved the idea of starting one together. He told me retirement would come soon enough, but he liked the idea of running a company. In his words, he had the capital and connections, I had the energy."

Josie said, "He sounds like a good man."

"You would've liked him. I'm sure of it." He pointed toward his rearview mirror. "That silver GMC has been following you for a while."

"I noticed that, too. It's possible the driver is simply headed to Liberty like us. Our guy back at the cabin drove a black Dodge."

Dane continued to watch.

She switched on her signal and turned off onto a county highway, headed north.

"Where are you going?"

"Just seeing if he is following." She looked in her rearview mirror and the truck whizzed past, continuing on the main road.

He straightened. "I guess you were right. Where to now?"

"Bliss said I could use their place while she's gone. I want to do some digging into Layla's background."

"Really? Something bothering you?"

"Not so much. But I always like to dig into people to see whether they're on the up-and-up or not." When they came to an intersection, she turned right on a road that would take them the back way into Liberty.

"Who do you think was in the house?"

"I don't know. I keep thinking about that. Do you think Layla may have already met someone?"

He shrugged. "It's possible. Harlan seemed happy, but he also wasn't the kind to talk about his personal life."

"So, if Pierce was investigating something, what do you think it was?"

"Again, I don't know. It wouldn't have been the missing thirty thousand dollars because Pierce was hired before the money went missing."

"Yeah, you're right. Maybe it had nothing to do with the money, but something more personal."

Suddenly something appeared in the road, and she didn't have time to swerve. With a loud bang, her passenger-side tire blew, and the SUV pulled to the right. She hit the brakes and fought to keep it on the road.

Dane pulled his gun out. "Do you see anyone?"

She glanced around. Only pastures and trees. "Not yet. Wait—" she pointed "—over there."

A man jumped up from the grass only ten yards away and aimed his gun. At the same time, Dane raised his.

Flat tire or not, she floored the gas.

The Bronco jumped, causing Dane's aim to be off. His shot went high as bullets kicked up dirt behind the SUV. Josie kept the accelerator down even as the wheel went *thwack, thwack, thwack, thwack* on the pavement. "I don't know where the guy's vehicle is, but I think we're out of reach of his gun."

The back window shattered, causing him to cringe. Josie let out a squeal.

"Are you hit?"

She shook her head. "No, but ever since I took that bullet last year, I have no desire to have a repeat."

He kept watch behind them to see if they were being pursued, but there was no sign of a vehicle.

Dane didn't like the sound of that. He knew a relationship with Josie was unlikely—there would never be trust if she didn't believe his word—but still his stomach tightened at the thought of her being injured—or worse. Maybe it was because she had been his first love, or that he felt partially to blame, but either way, he couldn't let anything happen to her. "I shouldn't have asked."

She laughed. "It's not your fault."

"I know." Again, he checked his mirror, but no one appeared to be following them. A driveway to a ranch house appeared in front of them, and he pointed. "How's your spare?"

"It's a new tire, and it's full size. Not the donut kind."

"Pull in there, and I'll change it for you."

"I can change it myself, but since you offered..." She turned into the drive and moved several yards from the entrance.

She was smart getting off the road. The three doors on the garage were closed and there were no vehicles in the drive. "Doesn't look like there's anyone around, but I'll hurry."

Most people were still friendly in the country and wouldn't mind them being parked there for a few minutes, but one never knew. He got out and noticed the wheel was bent. He hurried to the back and removed the spare from the back door along with the jack and four-way lug nut wrench.

Josie got out and came around to his side of

the vehicle. "I hope that didn't damage more than the wheel."

"Doesn't look like it." After he pulled off the wheel, he looked at the tire. "There are spikes in the tread. This was definitely a trap."

She rubbed her wrist across her forehead to wipe off the sweat and looked to the south, the direction they'd just come. "But there was no way for anyone to know we were going to take that road, especially the silver GMC. The driver must have called his partner."

"That makes sense." He hurriedly put on the new tire and had started to tighten down the lug nuts when a vehicle showed in the distance.

"Dane. Looks like we have company."

"I see them." He spun the tool fast and tightened it as much as he could. As he slid on the last nut, the approaching vehicle's engine roared.

"Come on. We've got to go. You can finish that later." Josie slammed the driver's side door shut.

Dane threw the ruined tire and the tool into the back seat as he jumped in.

"I'll have to turn around in a minute." She took off down the driveway toward the rancher's house. The front door opened, and a lady came out with a baby on her hip, a look of curiosity on her face.

"Oh, no."

"Turn around. Turn around." Dane hung on as Josie whipped into the adjoining pasture. "I didn't mean to go into the pasture."

"I'm trying to get far away from the house."

The silver GMC barreled down the driveway and then whipped into the same open gate Josie had used.

"Here he comes. You need to get back on the road."

She gritted her teeth. "I'm trying. I didn't want to meet them head-on in the lady's driveway."

"I wasn't criticizing." He held on as she flew across the rough terrain. The Bronco approached a narrow but deep washout. "Watch out."

The front tires hit hard and then half bounced, half flew across the opening and landed with a jolt. Glancing his way, she said, "I've driven my fair share of backroads in my time. You're not the only one who can jump a ditch."

"It's scarier in the passenger seat. I'd rather you not show me what it feels like to drive on two wheels, though."

A grove of trees appeared in front of them.

Her teeth gritted as she sped between two trees. When they came out on the other side, the pickup was farther back. She floored it again and raced along a barbwire fence. She plowed through it and got back on the road. "I'll find out who the owner is and pay him later."

"I don't care as long as we leave these guys behind."

"My thoughts exactly."

After they had gone another mile, she turned to him. "Why do you think these guys just keep coming after us? I mean, I know they want us dead, but so far, the attacks have been away from others."

"I noticed that, too. Could be that when they find us, we just happen to be in remote areas."

She nodded. "Yeah. Or others would recognize him, and he doesn't want to take the chance of being recognized."

"Could be, but I don't want to bet my life on it."

"Me either."

Dane continued to keep a look out for the silver truck, but there were no more sightings.

As they came to the edge of town, Josie said, "I'm going to drop by the tire shop to get a new one."

Dane waited in the Bronco while the technician retrieved the wheel out of the back, and he said he'd be an hour before he had a new tire mounted.

Josie turned to him. "Would you like to get something to eat while we wait?"

"I'm starving, so yeah."

"Okay. There's a burger place over there within walking distance. I'll pick up something for Hattie and Everly. Hattie must work the afternoon shift, so I'll need to do something."

He climbed out of the SUV and walked over to her.

"I don't mind having a deputy watch Everly, but I would rather have someone closer to me keep an eye on her until this case is wrapped up."

"You mean like your grandpa?"

"Yeah."

As they walked beside each other, Dane kept a watch out for the silver truck. There was no way around this. Leaving the girl at a retirement home would not be his first option. But they had little choice with danger hitting them at every turn. Until this man was caught, none of them would be safe again.

Chapter Fourteen

The glass door opened as Phillip, the doorman, stepped aside. "Good afternoon, Miss Hunt."

"Hello, Phillip." She shot him a smile. It made her feel better to know security was at least present at the retirement home.

The door closed silently behind her. The padded carpet felt good under her feet, and the cool air was fresh and welcoming. But when the lady at the reception desk did a double take as she walked past with Everly, Josie figured she should've cleaned up before she came by. There simply wasn't time. She plastered on a smile. "Good afternoon."

"Afternoon." The woman's smile feigned cheer. "Your grandfather is in the rec room."

Josie glanced down at her dirty wrist. Had she gotten grime on her face? Her hair hung in her face, and it tended to curl when damp. A glance down to her work boots made her almost laugh. When she was younger, she remembered her grandfather's mannerisms would embarrass her sometimes. Now, here she was in his retirement home doing the same thing.

A group of men was sitting at a table playing dominoes when she entered. A tall, white-haired man in the middle glanced up. As she approached, his eyes lit up.

"Josie Sue." He looked from her boots to the top of her head. "Been out mudding?"

"Ha, ha, Grandpa. Not really."

He nodded a greeting toward Everly. "Hello, young lady."

"Hi." Everly glanced shyly at the group.

"Can I talk with you?" As the rest of the guys looked on, Josie added, "Alone."

Bill, a man in his nineties, scrutinized her. Some of her grandpa's friends had been in law enforcement or worked in law offices. She didn't know who worked where, but they all enjoyed telling stories about the good old days and tended to complain about recent times. Judges. Lawyers. The laws. The DA. Schools. Politics. Nothing was off limits in the complaint department.

Her grandpa climbed to his feet. "Certainly. Come here and give your grandpa a hug."

Josie stepped his way, and he wrapped his arm around her and squeezed. The smell of his shirt brought back good memories. The action made her want to cry and tell him all of her problems just like she had when she was a girl, but she held back.

"Come on back to my room."

She walked beside him, holding Everly's hand. Even though her grandpa still kept up a decent pace, he'd slowed a bit since the last time she'd visited him. He opened the door to his room, and they filed in. She turned to Everly, leaning over and placing her hands on her shoulders.

"Wait here by the door. I'll be right back."

Everly nodded, her eyes wide, and Josie knew she had to make this quick.

She went in her grandfather's living room, to where she could still see Everly.

He turned to her. "What's going on?"

"I need help," she whispered.

"Does this have to do with that sweet girl you adopted?"

He struggled to remember Everly's name. "It does. I just learned her daddy, Pierce Browning, was murdered and Everly witnessed it."

"Are you sure?" His eyebrows knitted in concern as he glanced back at her.

She nodded. "Positive. I took her to the police station, and she went through mug shots. There were several men she identified as looking like the man, but none were conclusive."

He gave a slow whistle and shook his head. "What is wrong with people? Why would someone do that? I will never understand what causes someone to hurt or kill another. You'd think I was used to it by now, but a person should never grow accustomed to evil."

Her grandpa could complain about this for several minutes, so she interrupted. "I need help."

His face softened. "Are you in danger?"

"No. Yes. I need you to watch Everly for me. Whoever killed Pierce realizes she can identify him. I don't know who the killer is, but we believe he also killed Dane's business partner."

He frowned, making his wrinkles bunch up. "Dane Haggerty? Please tell me you're not talking to that boy again."

"Grandpa, he's twenty-eight years old. He's hardly a boy." She didn't want to talk about Dane, but it was only fair if he was going to keep an eye on Everly that he understood what was at stake. "I don't know if you heard, but Dane was accused of—"

"Killed his partner." He cut her off while his face turned red. "There's a warrant for his arrest. He's not the kind of man I want you hanging around. Especially with my great-granddaughter."

She planted her hand on her hip and cocked her head to the side. "Would you please trust that you raised a smart lady?"

"I know that," he said irritably.

"I don't have much time. But I need you to keep her inside."

"Where is Sheriff Van Carroll? Surely, he can give you protection."

"He's out of town. Kennedy and Silas from my team are here."

"I want you to stay with me. Let the authorities do their job."

She smiled. "I would love to, but I can't sit back and wait. I'm the best person to find this guy. The sooner he's off of the streets, the safer me and Everly will be."

"I still say you're better off with me. And it's more than that. Several of the old gang are here."

"I know." She patted him on the chest. "I love you, Grandpa. Please keep an eye on her."

"I love you, too."

She looked over her shoulder and waved at Everly to enter. "Come on."

Everly gave a hesitant smile as she hurried over to him.

A door shut from somewhere close, and then Dane glanced around the corner before stepping into the room. "We appreciate this. Please know that I'll do everything I can to keep your granddaughter safe."

Totally ignoring him, Grandpa looked back at her. "Are you sure this is how you want it?"

"Yes. He's innocent."

The older man shook his head, before looking back at Dane. He pointed. "Don't let her get hurt. I'm warning you."

Her chest tightened. Her grandfather had been a strong man when younger, but he didn't realize he was getting older.

Thankfully, Dane had the sense to nod. "Yes, sir."

Doubts whether she should leave Everly there plagued her. But she'd gone over this in her mind multiple times. There was no easy solution. The retirement home allowed residents to have overnight guests. She leaned down and got close. "Your great grandpa is going to take good care of you. If you need anything, ask him. Do you understand?"

"I'll be fine."

"Okay. Listen to him. You have my phone number?"

"I do. It's in my pocket." She gave Josie a little push. "Go."

As she caught up to Dane and they walked toward the back exit, she turned back for one more look and gave her a little wave.

Please, Lord, watch over Everly and Grandpa.

They walked out and got in the Bronco. After she shut the door and started the engine, warmth touched her hand. She glanced down at Dane's hand on hers.

"Everly will be fine."

She looked into his serious brown eyes. "I realize you're trying to help, but you can't know that."

"But I prayed to God. No matter what happens, everything will turn out for the best."

She let out a loud sigh and pulled her hand back then put it on the steering wheel. "I've always believed in God, as did my parents, and Grandpa. But I'm scared. It may be wrong, but I can't help but worry about her safety."

"You wouldn't be human if you didn't. Let's go find this guy."

Dane's words did help a little. The quicker the killer was arrested, the sooner she could get on with her life. As she traveled across town to the edge of Liberty, she passed a parking lot and noticed a silver GMC traveling fast toward the exit. A white coupe braked in front of her, causing her almost to rear-end the car. "Did you see that?"

"Silver truck? Yeah." Dane turned sideways in his seat as he looked through the back window. "He's headed the other direction."

"Oh no, you don't." She whipped into the next available parking lot and turned around. When there was a break in the traffic, she gassed it and headed in the same direction as the truck. "Do you see him?"

"Not yet." Dane leaned forward. "He didn't turn down that street. Wait. There. He disappeared behind that building." He pointed at a large empty building that used to be a grocery store.

Josie followed his directions and sped across the bare pavement. This wasn't the best part of town, but she didn't want to lose this guy. "Do you think he was following us? Like he saw where I dropped Everly off?"

"I don't know. That question crossed my mind, too."

As she approached the corner of the building, she slowed and eased into the back alley. There was no sign of the vehicle. "Where did he go?"

Dane twisted, looking around. "I don't see him. Ease forward. We know he went to the left."

She did as he said, her heart racing in her chest. Something wasn't right. Had the guy seen her? She reached down to her ankle holster to retrieve her gun as her driver's side window exploded.

"Get down!"

She ducked and then yanked on the wheel, slamming the Bronco into a trash dumpster. She fumbled to put the vehicle into Reverse as tires squealed on pavement.

"Stay down." Dane peeked over the seat and fired two shots through the broken window.

It was a trap, and she'd fallen right into it.

Fierce protectiveness came over Dane as he searched for the gunman. The man had fired from somewhere between the narrow space among two buildings but had disappeared. If Josie hadn't leaned down, she probably would've taken at least one bullet.

His blood pumped through his veins at an alarming rate. "Let me drive." At the scowl he received, he added, "I know it's your vehicle, but you're a better shooter than me, and I'm capable of driving. There's no time for discussion."

Her face paled, but she nodded and quickly climbed over the console as he scooted to the driver's seat. He didn't move as smoothly with his long legs, but it was better than being in the open.

He put the Bronco in gear and eased forward, until he was even with the narrow alley between the structures. It was empty except for trash littering the ground. Continuing forward, he looked for the silver pickup. It had to be close. The next building had a shop door. He stopped. "I'm going to check this out. If we were lured here, I want to know who's setting the bait."

She nodded. "I'll cover you."

They got out at the same time, and he waited for her to get into position at the front of her SUV. He nodded before reaching down and yanking the shop door handle up. The door squeaked as it rolled open.

The GMC sat inside with the bed facing him. There was no one inside that he could see. He mouthed, "I'm going to check it out" once more.

She moved closer with her gun ready.

The bay was narrow, not leaving much of a path. After peering under the vehicle to make certain no feet could be seen underneath the carriage, he approached the driver's side door while keeping his eyes on the front seat. With his gun aimed, he glanced inside. Empty.

He looked back at Josie and shook his head, telling her no one was inside. Suddenly, a jacked-up Ford Raptor pulled up in the alley behind them. Josie turned her back to Dane and her arm fell to her side, with her palm facing him as she waved him backward.

Was she trying to tell him to stay back? Dane hunched down and moved toward the front of the pickup.

A stocky man wearing a baseball cap, jeans and running shoes stepped out of the vehicle. Muscles bulged from beneath his T-shirt. He slammed the door and strutted over to her. "Josie, you are a hard person to track down."

Even though the man was slightly turned, and his facial details not clear, Dane knew his identity.

"How can I help you, Tyler?" Josie cocked her head to the side—a telling move when she was annoyed.

Big Tyler Jorgenson. Dane had only viewed pictures and heard stories of the rough, not-by-the-book bounty hunter.

"I need help finding someone who has a warrant for his arrest. Dane Haggerty. Have you seen him?"

"What makes you think I've seen him?" Josie stalled.

Dane slowly stepped back deeper into the shop until he made it to the front of the vehicle. With Harlan's killer targeting them, the last thing he needed to worry about was a bounty hunter trying to bring him in. A door stood on the other side of the shelves, and Dane moved closer.

"The sheriff's department over in McCade County had a report of an exchange of gunfire. Your name was mentioned along with Haggerty's."

"I wish I could help you."

The large bounty hunter frowned at her.

"You wouldn't be protecting him, would you, Hunt? I heard your daughter was in danger. I would think the safest thing for everyone would be if I brought him in. After I receive my payment, he can trust his fate to the law."

Anger tugged at Dane as he restrained himself from pummeling Tyler for bringing Everly into this fight—not that he would fare well in a physical confrontation with the brawny man. He didn't want Josie to be tempted to lie for him. Gently, he turned the knob and eased the door open, sunlight pouring in. He stepped out of the room and to the front of the building. The parking lot was empty. He had no idea where the driver of the silver GMC had gone, but his gut told him he was still nearby.

Unless he'd taken another vehicle after stashing the truck. But there hadn't been enough time. Or maybe he and Josie had been so intent on seeing where the truck had gone, they'd missed a man on foot.

He wasn't certain of anything except that they needed to be ready for the unexpected.

Dane hurried along the storefronts while keeping aware of the parking lot and the buildings as he passed by each one. At the last store—

an empty tile and floor-covering business—he stopped and peeked around the corner.

Nothing.

In front of him lay a few trees and a narrow rock road leading to a building. He glanced around the corner again to make sure it was clear and then dashed toward three scraggly trees. Instead of stopping to look back, he wove through the brush and came out near the driveway. The metal building was an old car wash with two bays. The hoses were gone, and graffiti covered the walls.

He skirted to the far side of the trees and hurried across the driveway to the protection of the car wash. From that vantage point, he could see the backside of the building he'd just vacated. Josie remained beside her vehicle. The bounty hunter was gone, but his truck was still there.

Josie appeared relaxed but then she looked over her shoulder toward him. Had she seen where he'd gone?

A few seconds later, a tall man came out of the front of the last building and proceeded around the corner. When he got to the back edge of the building, he peered about. He wore dark clothes and held something in his hand. Josie had her back turned toward the man.

"Look behind you, Josie," Dane whispered under his breath.

The suspect raised his gun, and Dane did the same. He'd never shot anyone before, but he would not sit there and watch a killer shoot Josie.

The man stepped out from around the corner just as the bounty hunter came from the far side of the building.

"Look out, Josie!"

Her head snapped up, and Dane pulled the trigger. A bullet hit above the suspect's head and into the brick building. The guy rolled for cover on the ground.

Josie dashed for the passenger side of her vehicle.

Tyler Jorgenson's attention went to the gunman and then to Dane's direction.

Dane ran through the wash bay and into the steep gully on the other side. He half slid and half fell to the bottom, his boots landing with a splash. The stream was only about a foot deep, but he took off through the ditch as fast as he could move.

Tires squealed.

That was probably Big Tyler coming for him, but he wished it were Josie. His thoughts went to her as he trucked through marshy ground. He hoped the gunman didn't come after her, and after being shot at, the man would be more likely cautious with his moves. Josie knew her stuff, and he had to trust her to get away from this guy.

Up ahead was a large metal culvert, about three feet in diameter. He started to go in and hide, but if Tyler crossed this way, it would be the first place he searched. Dane crawled back up the bank on the far side to take a look.

Tyler's Ford Raptor raced down the road. The land was grassy here. Taking a chance, he climbed out of the gully and ran as fast as he could while staying low. The highway crossed in front of him, and a bridge lay to his right.

He sprinted for it.

He glanced over his left shoulder to see Tyler stop and check the tinhorn. No doubt the truck would catch him quickly, but not if he weren't spotted. His breath came in pants, but adrenaline kept him going. As his side began to ache, he stood straight to ease the discomfort.

Tyler's truck was headed his way, the engine revving as rocks spewed.

Sirens sounded in the distance.

Dane didn't turn to look but ran. The rumble

of the approaching vehicle and the sirens grew louder. Only a few more yards to the bridge. With all his might, he ran to the middle of the bridge. The river flowed at a lazy rate beneath him.

"Dane Haggerty, I'm taking you in for the murder of Harlan Schmidt. Stop. Put your hands above your head."

The bounty hunter's command rang through his mind, but Dane had no intention of being arrested today. He prayed the man would not shoot him, and his instincts told him he had to get away if he wanted to survive.

Chapter Fifteen

Josie's chest tightened as she watched the bounty hunter take off after Dane. With her gun still in her hand, she ran around her Bronco and climbed into the driver's seat. She fired it up and took off. As she approached the corner of the building, movement caught her eye from the left. She jerked the wheel just as a bullet whizzed past her head and into the dash.

She fired out of her window at the man huddled on the sidewalk. She didn't know if she hit him, but a glance in her rearview mirror said he didn't follow her. She wanted to help Dane, but the gunman needed to be brought down. If Dane was arrested, she'd have to do everything in her power to find the true killer so he would be exonerated. Working with law enforcement had taught her that.

She turned her Bronco around and readied her gun as she approached the building. The man wasn't in sight, but he had to be close. She looked around, not wanting him to sneak up on her.

Using the speaker on her phone, she called 9-1-1. Deputies were already close, but they needed to know Pierce's killer suspect was there. All she had to do was subdue him until they arrived. When the dispatcher answered, Josie quickly relayed her location and the information about the shooter. She didn't stay on the line.

After she disconnected, she drove around to the back of the building where she'd been only minutes before. The man must be going back for his truck. She stopped and slid out of the Bronco. Making her way to the back, she skirted around the bumper and to the passenger side. Poised to shoot, she approached the garage opening.

She peeked around the edge.

Sure enough, a man sat behind the wheel and started the truck. Tinted windows kept her from identifying the man, but he appeared tall like the man in the woods the first night.

In her peripheral vision she saw a deputy's truck was headed this way.

She wasn't an officer, but she couldn't let the

man simply drive away. Nor could she just shoot him. In a flash, she hurried back to her Bronco and pulled forward, blocking the man's escape.

Her prized Bronco had been her dad's many years ago, and she hated the thought of wrecking it. She would do what she had to.

The man threw his truck into gear. Instead of ramming her vehicle, he shot backward, slammed into the shelves knocking them over before crashing through the back wall.

"No. No. No." Her foot hit the accelerator, and her SUV jumped forward. She tore around the building, down the alley, and to the front. The man's silver GMC flew onto the highway, and other motorists' tires squealed as they hit their brakes and one car went into the ditch to avoid a crash.

By the time Josie got to the highway, he passed three cars on the shoulder before returning to the road. When a break in the traffic appeared, she pulled out. But the man was so determined to get away, he passed a car while a semitruck was headed his way in oncoming traffic. The big rig driver jerked the wheel to the shoulder and halfway in the grass to avoid hitting him.

"He's going to kill an innocent person." At

the next driveway, she pulled in and turned around, heading back to the building. A deputy's pickup crossed the pavement and stopped by her Bronco. The man exited his vehicle and strode over.

She rolled down her window. "The suspect got away. He traveled that way in a newer model silver GMC truck driving erratic. I decided to let the authorities find him."

"Are you Miss Hunt?" At her nod, he continued. "That was smart thinking. We'll find him. Stick around. I'm certain one of the other deputies will need to talk with you."

When he got back into his vehicle, she saw him talking on his handheld radio. He turned on his lights and took off in pursuit.

As she headed in the direction Dane had gone, she couldn't help but believe the deputy wouldn't be able to catch the suspect. There had been no need to stop and speak to her since she'd relayed the information to the dispatcher. Frustration tugged at her. Was this guy ever going to be caught?

She sped down the narrow road past the car wash until she came out on the highway. Tyler's big truck, along with two deputies' vehicles, sat on a bridge about a half mile away. Two men appeared to be looking over the edge.

Oh no. What happened? Please tell her Dane didn't jump.

Blood thumped through her ears as she prepared for the worst. She parked behind a deputy's truck and hurried to the edge of the bridge.

She asked the deputies, "What happened?"

"Looks like our man jumped off the bridge."

Josie managed to keep her intake of breath quiet. Her gaze sought out movement in the shallow creek. The bridge was at least thirty feet high, but the water wasn't that deep.

One of the male deputies she didn't recognize stared at her. "I have to wonder, Miss Hunt. Did you know Dane was with you all along?"

Ignoring him, she looked at the female deputy. "Deputy Perkins, do you know what happened?"

"Maybe I should ask you the same thing." Hattie's tone carried reproach.

Not wanting to say anything that could be used against her, Josie shrugged.

Tyler climbed up the side of the riverbank. "No sign of him. I'll find him."

Josie stood back and let the man pass on his way to his truck. He slammed the door and took off, his tires squealing. On the other side of the river, the Raptor turned and raced along a dirt trail by the bank. She held her breath as a huge cloud of dust filled the air and then dissipated.

The male deputy talked on his cell phone a few feet away and then hurried to his truck. Before he climbed in, he said to Deputy Perkins, "I'm taking the highway and am going further downstream."

"Okay." After he pulled away, Perkins turned to her. "If you're hiding Haggerty, you know you can be arrested for harboring a fugitive."

"Yes, ma'am." The deputy's words hung in the air as Josie climbed into her Bronco. The day kept getting worse. First, she'd lost Pierce's killer, and now Dane tried to escape. There was no way to make that jump in the shallow without getting hurt. With Tyler on one side of the river and the deputy on the other, he'd be lucky if he wasn't arrested in the next few minutes.

As much as she didn't want to involve herself in his case, she whipped the Bronco onto the path Tyler had taken to turn around. When she started to back up, she glanced in the rearview mirror, and a face was staring back at her.

She squealed and put her hand to her chest. "Dane Haggerty. You scared me half to death."

"Get me out of here."

"You've got some explaining to do." She glanced around to make certain no deputies were still in the area. "I'd like to know how you got into my vehicle when you were nowhere to be found when I pulled up."

Dane remained hunched down in case someone was still nearby. "I thought I was caught. I started to jump into the river, but decided I'd probably break my neck because it was too shallow."

"You think?"

"I jumped to the bank and crawled to the other side under the bridge. Then I hid in the bed of Perkins's pickup."

Josie's jaw dropped. "You've got to be kidding me. That was taking a big chance."

"Not so much. She was the last vehicle here until you arrived. Chances were no one would be walking by the bed of her truck. Then you pulled up. While you were watching Tyler, I climbed in here."

She shook her head. "You haven't changed much since high school. You've always taken risks."

"Not really," he answered quickly. He didn't like her believing he was still the same immature teen he was in school. "I prefer to believe I've done well in business, especially with Harlan's help. But the old survival instincts kick in when I feel the walls closing in."

Again, she stared at him in the mirror. For two long seconds, they stared at one another until she looked back to the road. "Where to?"

"I'd like to look for that silver GMC, but since the deputy is in pursuit, we probably need to let them do their job. Did you get a good look at the guy?"

"A side view, but I didn't recognize him or get a good enough look to give a description."

"Yeah. It's like he knows if we see him, we'll recognize him. That could be a good lead."

She nodded and came to a stop at a red light at a main intersection on the edge of town. "It only makes sense since he knew Pierce and Harlan. Do you think it's someone we both know?"

The way she said it insinuated more. "You mean like someone we went to school with?"

She shrugged. "Could be. Since we haven't worked together since we graduated, that would be the most common denominator."

The DA's son kept returning to his mind. But why target Harlan and Pierce? He leaned forward. "I want to check out the DA's son." At her funny look, he replied, "What?"

"Nothing."

"No. Say what you're thinking."

She sighed. "You better have a great reason for mentioning him to others or it's going to look like revenge for the car incident."

"Josie, that was years ago. Yes, I was mad back then, real mad, for being accused and charged with theft. Keaton Stebbins set me up on purpose. When I tried to tell the judge that, he didn't listen. Nobody did. But I've moved on now. The only thing that bothers me is when people still assume I'm guilty of crimes without proof. It tends to get old."

The light turned green, and she took off. "What makes you think he's involved?"

"I don't, necessarily. First, not many people know I was charged with theft because I was a minor. The record was sealed. Someone stays one step ahead of me."

"Like they have inside knowledge? Come on. That seems like a stretch. Pierce was investigating something for Harlan, and he's in construction. What does that have to do with law enforcement?"

"I don't know yet. Stebbins is on the city

building committee." Even as Dane said the words, he wasn't certain of a connection. What could it be? Kickbacks? "You're an investigator. Can you find out what he was working on?"

"I will. But I'll need to be discreet. A person can get a bad rep for stepping on the toes of those in the upper crust, especially those in law enforcement."

"I hear you." Dane smiled.

"Do you? I mean, really hear me." Her gaze cut to him. "I could get into trouble, Dane. I have a daughter to think about. You plan to adopt Violet. Everything you do needs to be on the up-and-up."

He knew this was coming. She wanted him to turn himself in. What if it backfired? What if he spent the rest of his life in prison for a crime he didn't commit?

Josie's eyebrows rose in question. "Do you trust me?"

Dane stared at her. "That has nothing to do—"

"I was once told it was simple question." She looked at him with a quirked eyebrow, and repeated, "Do you trust me?"

He nodded. "Yeah, I trust you."

A smile crept across Josie's face. "Good. Then

please agree to see Sheriff Van Carroll. I'll go with you."

"He's out of town."

She shook her head. "He got back this morning."

Dane sighed. "I'll do it."

"Good. I've already called him and he's expecting you to contact him."

Dane clenched his teeth realizing that she knew he'd agree. His mind warred with itself. Part of him would be glad to quit running and hopefully have help. The other part was scared to death he'd regret his decision. He always remembered Harlan would tell him to have faith. Maybe this was what it felt like. A little scary, but hope danced in front of him.

Josie's cell phone rang as she pulled into Bliss's drive and parked beside Dane's motorcycle. She glanced at the screen. "It's Layla."

Dane's gaze connected with hers before he moved close so he could hear.

She hit Accept and put it on speaker while holding the phone between them. He didn't back away even though there was no need to be this close. The warmth of his breath felt good.

"Hello. This is Josie."

"I need to talk to you." Layla's voice sounded strained. "I have evidence."

The prospect of having good news had her holding her breath to see if Layla's news would finally wrap this case up.

Josie asked, "What did you find?"

"I'd rather not talk to you over the phone. I need to see you in person."

She and Dane exchanged looks. "Are you certain? If I knew what you—"

"I can't talk on the phone. Come right now to my house."

"Okay. I'll see you in a bit." She disconnected and then faced Dane. "What do you think this is about?"

"I don't know, but we need answers now. I'm going with you."

She shook her head. "Go turn yourself in. Violet is depending on you. When the killer is caught, I want you to be free. The longer you run, the harder it will be to clear your name."

His jaw tensed. "I don't like this. It could be a trap. It's too risky."

"I'm armed and trained. I'll call you as soon as I learn something."

"Not good enough, Josie. I can turn myself in after you meet with Layla, I promise."

She shook her head. "No. You have a bounty hunter on your tail who doesn't care if he takes you alive. You'll be safer under the sheriff's protection."

She whispered, "Trust me."

For several seconds their eyes connected. Dane leaned down and his lips touched hers in a light kiss.

After he pulled back, she could still feel his touch on her. "Be careful."

He shoved his baseball cap on his head. "I will. I'm ready to get there."

She followed him out the door and watched as he got on his bike and rode to the end of the driveway. He turned and gave her one more look before pulling out onto the road.

Please, Lord, be with Dane. Help him to learn to trust.

Chapter Sixteen

Dane dreaded talking with Sheriff Van Carroll. Even though Josie assured him he was not going to remain in jail, he couldn't help but think this might be a mistake. Would the sheriff lie to Josie? Maybe.

Josie kept talking about trust. Could he ever have faith in anyone again? He wanted to believe her. And to gain her trust, he was willing to take a chance on the authorities.

The wind blowing on his face felt cool and unfettered. He prayed this was not the last time he was free. He couldn't fail this time.

A car in front of him slowed, and he eased around it. The lady inside was talking on her cell phone. After he pulled back into his lane, the highway opened to not much traffic. As he tried to prepare his mind for his talk with the sheriff, he went over the details of the case and anticipated possible questions.

A shadow stretched from behind him. He checked his mirror and saw the grille of a pickup grow large before it rammed into him. His back tire swerved before he got it back under control. He gassed it, but something was wrong with his bike. The machine shook and veered to the left. The impact must've bent his wheel. He could've recovered, but then he was hit again.

He held on, but the back tire swung around to his left and slid on the pavement. The front tire dug in and then he flew forward, slapping his face against his mirrors before landing hard on the shoulder of the highway. Painful shock waves reverberated through his body. His shoulder hit first, followed by his helmet slamming the ground. His right eye stung, forcing him to squint against the agony. He ripped off his helmet.

The squeal of brakes added to the ringing in his head.

He scrambled to his feet, fell, and then got back up. He only took a couple of steps before someone seized him from behind. He grabbed for his gun in the back of his waistband, but before he reached it, strong hands manhandled him by the shirt and hauled him to the silver truck. Then he was shoved into the passenger seat.

Dane swung his fist at the man. It was a glancing blow. He tried to get his breath and swallow down the pain that continued to pulse through his body. He punched at him again, but his fist was knocked aside.

"You've been asking for this." Something hard jabbed him in the side. "You make a fast move, and I'll blow you away. Just so you don't try anything stupid, Josie and the girl are depending on you."

The gruff, familiar voice had him straining to look into the angry blue eyes of his captor. Alec Hickman. No doubt he'd love to pull the trigger of the pistol sticking him in the gut. The man hurried around to the driver's side of the truck.

A glance to the back seat showed no one. Thankful Josie or Everly weren't taken by Alec gave Dane time to clear his head and think. What did he mean Josie and Everly were depending on him?

Had Alec captured them? If so, where was he holding them?

Dane still had his gun, but he needed to use

it at the right time now that he knew the killer's identity.

A couple of cars stopped on the highway to check out the wreck, but Alec spun his truck around, almost hitting a teen dressed in a baseball uniform. The kid held his cell phone up, evidently snapping photos of them. Even if authorities were notified, there was a good chance it'd be too late to help Dane.

"Why did you kill Harlan?"

Hickman scowled as he looked at him. "The cold-hearted man shouldn't have fired me. He could've given me a second chance. Because of you two, my wife left me."

Alec blamed Dane also? Both he and Harlan had been doing their jobs. Alec had a drinking problem that made him a liability to keep with the company. This meant Alec had no intention of letting him live. He needed to get a message to Josie or the sheriff's department. He dropped his right hand to the seat beside him and slowly eased it toward his gun. His fingers touched the butt, but he couldn't withdraw it without being noticeable. He leaned forward to block the view from Hickman. To keep his attention diverted, Dane spoke while he withdrew the weapon. "You were drinking on the job."

The man slammed on his brakes and pointed at him. “It was one time. I didn’t deserve it.”

Fury shown in the man’s eyes as he took back off on the highway, and Dane knew he’d struck a nerve. Actually, he’d come to work intoxicated numerous times. The last time was the nail in the coffin. Dane’s cell phone buzzed in his back pocket.

Alec’s head jerked toward him. “Hand over the phone.”

In one move, he put his weapon on the seat and raised his left hand in the air as if in surrender while his right removed his phone. He placed it on the dash.

The man’s eyes narrowed and then a funny look crossed his face. He yanked the wheel to the shoulder of the road and stopped. A pistol appeared in his hand. “Give me the gun.”

Dane had never been much of a hunter, but there had been a time when he practiced shooting at targets attached to a tree and even gotten skilled at shooting disks. He’d never been good at backing away from a fight either. His hand came up with the Glock and aimed. “No.”

Both men pointed their guns at each other while less than two feet away. At this distance, both would die should they fire.

Sweat beaded across Alec's lip, and his eyes grew with rage.

Dane's heart stampeded in his chest. He'd had enough. And Josie still didn't know who the killer was. He couldn't take the chance of Alec getting to her and Everly. The man had big plans to take all of them down; no doubt he hadn't considered he might not come out of this alive. "Well, what's it going to be?"

Right then and there, they both had a decision to make. And Dane prayed with all his might that he'd made the right move because others were depending on him.

Josie was ready to learn something of value. She climbed into her Bronco and took off. Layla's place was about a twenty-minute drive. Time crawled as her mind tried to figure out what evidence Layla had found. Concern for Everly continued to nag at her. Hopefully, her grandpa would keep her safe and they could all go home after Pierce's killer was found and arrested.

Home. It had burned down. Where would they start over? What must it be like for Everly to lose her only remaining parent and then when she does get adopted by an almost stranger, your house is lost in a fire and you must start over again. Kids were resilient, but she knew this was pushing the sentiment too far. Josie had heard the saying many times after her family perished. She prayed nightly Everly would have an easier recovery than what she had experienced.

When she pulled into Layla's drive, the first thing she noticed was her car was parked outside instead of inside the garage like before. No other vehicles were around. She pulled behind Layla's luxury vehicle and walked swiftly to the front door. A quick hit to the doorbell, and she waited.

No answer.

After a few more seconds, she tried again. Still with no response, she tried the door and it opened. "Layla. It's me. I'm coming in."

She stepped inside and called her name again. Even though Layla had asked her to come over, she hated walking into someone's house. The dining area was empty, and she turned toward the living room.

A gasp escaped her. Layla lay on the floor, a golf-size bump on her head. Blood stained the carpet. "Layla."

Josie felt for a pulse. A faint thump was her

return. Immediately, she hit three numbers on her cell phone.

"9-1-1. What's your emergency?"

"I have an unconscious victim with a bump on her head." The dispatcher asked a couple of questions and Josie gave her the address. Against the dispatcher's instructions, Josie informed her she couldn't stay on the line and hung up. Then she called Dane, but it immediately went to voicemail.

A bad feeling came over her. It wasn't like him not to answer, but maybe he was talking with Sheriff Van Carroll and didn't want to interrupt the visit. Josie had worked for the sheriff for years, and after she explained the situation, he agreed if Dane came in, he could have him on bail in a couple of hours, and then Dane could work with authorities instead of running.

She called the sheriff's department.

"Jarvis County sheriff's department."

Josie quickly explained about needing to talk with Dane to the person manning the desk.

"I'm sorry, ma'am, but he hasn't arrived yet."

Her chest tightened. Maybe he had talked with the sheriff and the dispatcher simply didn't know. "May I speak with Sheriff Van Carroll?"

"I'll put you through."

He answered on the first ring. "Van Carroll."

"This is Josie. Have you spoken with Dane Haggerty yet?"

"I'm waiting for him to get here. What's going on? You sound worried."

"He left over thirty minutes ago. He should've already arrived." She told him about Layla's call and finding her on the floor. "The paramedics are on their way."

The sheriff said, "If Haggerty arrives, I'll have him call you."

"Thank you." As soon as she disconnected, she checked on Layla again. Her breathing was still shallow, and her face was pasty white. For fear there might be other injuries, she didn't move the woman's body. While waiting for the paramedics, she decided to look around for a weapon, but none was found in the living room. A person had been here yesterday, so she walked through the house to see if there was anything to tell her the identity of Layla's visitor.

When she stepped into what appeared to be the main bedroom, she noted the bed was made. There were no pictures of Harlan. Maybe the woman wasn't the type to hang photos. She opened the nightstand, and a wallet-sized photo of Layla with a man rested in the bottom of the drawer. Josie had seen pictures of Harlan, but this wasn't him. When Josie checked the bathroom, men's deodorant and an electric shaver were on the counter.

Was Layla already seeing someone? It had only been four months. Some people moved on quickly after losing a spouse, but it made Josie wonder if she had been seeing someone before her husband's death. As she walked back through the home, she passed an office with glass doors. The desk was clear of clutter or stacks of paper, but a soft-sided briefcase sat in the leather chair. It could be Harlan's. Sirens sounded from outside, and she hurried to the front door to meet them.

After two female and one male paramedic came inside, Josie stepped back into the kitchen and texted Dane to call her.

Her phone rang, and she couldn't help but be disappointed to see Silas Boone's name instead of Dane's. "Please tell me you learned something."

"We found a match on the man Everly saw. Alec Hickman, an old employee of Harlan and Dane's. I'm sending you his photo."

A text came through on her cell phone. This

was the same man who was pictured with Layla. "Alec was their employee? I didn't know that."

"Do you know him?"

"Not really. I just saw a picture of him at Layla's house." She went on to explain how she found Layla after the woman had called claiming she had some kind of evidence and then about Dane not answering his phone.

"That's not good. Where's your daughter?"

Josie closed her eyes and took a deep breath. She'd been thinking about her, praying for her and Grandpa's safety. "She's staying with my grandpa at the retirement home. I felt that was safer than being with me."

"If you send me the address, I'll send Kennedy to stay with them until we see this case to an end."

Relief fell on her. "I'll do that. Thank you."

"Sure. I found an address for Hickman and I'm on my way to check it out."

"Let me know what you learn." After she disconnected, she sent the retirement home's information to Kennedy and then returned to the living room to find it empty. A look out the front door showed Layla being loaded into the awaiting ambulance. She hurried to her Bronco and was able to leave before the ambulance was ready to go.

Would Hickman be at his home? Possible, but it seemed unlikely to Josie. Even though the sheriff said he'd have Dane call, she tried the department one more time to make certain he hadn't shown up. The dispatcher put her straight through.

"Have you heard from him?"

Josie shook her head as she talked on the phone. "No, and I'm worried."

"Haggerty better not have run again."

"That's not it," she was quick to reply, amazed at how fast she felt protective over the fugitive. "Texas Ranger Silas Boone just called and said he found a match for the man Everly described. Alec Hickman."

"Hickman. Name sounds familiar."

"He worked with Harlan and Dane several years ago. Silas is on his way to his house as we speak. I'm going to check out the North Texas Custom Builder's office."

"Be careful, Hunt. And if you hear back from your boyfriend, let me know."

"He's not my—" she started to say boyfriend, but the sheriff had already disconnected. Annoyance hit her as she sped down the highway toward the construction office. Dane wouldn't run. He had before, but he wouldn't lie to her. She was almost certain of it.

A few minutes later, she pulled up to the building. There were no other cars in the parking lot. Using a key Dane had loaned her, she quickly let herself in. She hurried upstairs and went straight to the file cabinets. Dane had said Harlan kept hard copies of many documents. She tugged open the top drawer, but everything seemed to be customer information. The employee files were in the third drawer, and she quickly found Alec's. She laid it on the desk and flipped it open.

A scan of the application revealed basic employment history and his home address. Emergency contact information was Nellie Hickman. Her cell phone buzzed. Silas's name flashed on the screen.

"Did you find Alec?"

"No. There's no one home and the yard is overgrown and his mail looks like it hasn't been picked up in weeks. His curtains are drawn, so I can't see in. If I didn't know he was in town, I'd think the owner had moved out."

"I've been thinking about Layla. What did someone have to gain by hurting her?"

There was a slight pause. "You think they were in a relationship?"

"Yeah, I do. There was someone there the other day when I visited with her. What if they were having a romantic relationship?"

"It's possible."

"I'm worried about Dane. The sheriff suggested he ran again, but I don't believe that. I'm at the construction office. It doesn't look like anyone's been here. Where do you think Alec would take Dane if he has him?"

"I don't know. I'll call the hospital and see if Layla is able to have visitors."

"Okay. I'll let you know if I learn anything." She slid her phone into her back pocket. A glance at Alec's file showed it contained his termination notice. Josie scanned it down to the paragraph that talked about Dane finding Alec drinking in the company's boneyard in a portable office building.

Where was this boneyard? She found Byron Ferguson's, the job foreman, number and called him. He gave her the address to the boneyard.

Would he take Dane there? It'd make sense. On the way out the door, she called Silas, but it went to voicemail, and she left a message. Her next call was to Sheriff Van Carroll.

As she was en route, Bliss called her. Josie gave an update to her boss and let her know where she was headed. She sped down the road. What if he wasn't there? Dane had surprisingly become very important to her.

She didn't know what she would do if something were to happen to him. She simply hadn't planned on him becoming a part of her life again. But he had.

Chapter Seventeen

Dane's gaze intensified with Alec's. He didn't want to kill the man, but he was left with no choice. He had to act. As Dane lifted his hand to hit the man's head with the butt of his gun, Alec pulled his trigger.

The bullet whizzed past his shoulder, and as Dane lunged for him, his grip on the gun slipped. His Glock fell to the floorboard.

Alec still held his weapon, so Dane grabbed his wrist and kept his arm wide in case he pulled the trigger again. Like in a game of mercy, both of them held the other while jockeying for position using their bodies as leverage in the pickup.

His opponent's foot wrapped around his thigh, and then they were moving as Alec's foot slipped off the brake. The truck headed into the ditch and picked up speed. "I can't wait to kill you, Haggerty. Even more than Harlan."

No doubt the killer meant his threats. With

his left hand, Dane released Alec's arm and went for his throat. His thumb dug into the soft spot to the side of his Adam's apple.

Alec's face turned red, and he cursed.

The truck slammed into something hard, causing them to come to an abrupt stop. They lost their grip on each other, and Alec fired again.

But Dane was too close, and the shot went wild.

His former coworker gritted his teeth and slammed the gun down on the top of Dane's head. Lights danced in his vision, and a loud ringing shouted in his ears.

"Get back to your side of the vehicle." He swiped Dane's Glock from the floorboard and tossed it into the backseat.

Pain radiated throughout his very being as he scooted across the seat.

Alec put the end of his gun barrel up to Dane's temple. "Don't try anything again."

It took incredible effort to open his eyes. The truck was slammed up against the metal railing that kept them from going into a creek. A couple of cars stopped to help, but Alec sped away as one man approached.

A loud racket on the passenger side rang

out, making Dane's head hurt even more. The crash must've bent the bumper, causing it to rub against the tire. Against his will, he leaned against the side of the door and closed his eyes. He didn't open them until they made a right turn onto Miller Lane. The bumpy road was littered with potholes, causing the truck to jolt with each hit.

A mile later, Alec turned into a drive on the left.

The company's boneyard. The place contained old equipment that needed to be repaired and a surplus of building supplies. What was Alec's plan? Thankfully, Josie didn't know about his place so she wouldn't look here for him. He wanted her far away from this madman.

As he forced his eyes to stay open against the pain, he sought a way to escape. The large pile of metal and other materials were a blur as they whizzed past. He'd been meaning to organize the boneyard months prior to Harlan's death but had never found the time. He tried to remember what else was stored there.

The truck stopped in front of a portable office—the same metal building where Dane had caught Alec drinking and that had cost him his job.

"Get out." Alec waved his gun at him. "Don't try anything if you want to see Josie again."

As much as Dane wanted to rebel, he withheld the urge. Moisture ran across his head, telling him the hit from the gun had caused him to bleed. The ringing had lessened, but he still didn't feel at the top of his game. If Alec had wanted to kill him, surely he could've done so on the road and left his body in a ditch.

His boots hit the dirt.

"Do you have any other weapons on you?" Alec came up behind him and quickly patted him down. He poked him in the back with the gun. "Move inside."

Dane held his hands out in full view and did as he was asked. When he entered the small structure, it took a moment for his eyes to adjust.

"Sit." Alec waved his pistol in the direction of a ripped office chair. A small chain looped in and out through the chair's frame and was bolted to the leg of the desk.

He had no sooner sat down than Alec withdrew two long zip ties from his back pocket. Grabbing him roughly, he attached his wrist to the arm. Dane didn't put up a fight. He tried to keep his arm away from the metal arm to give him wiggle room, but Alec clamped it tight, the tie biting into his flesh.

"You can't get away with this."

"I have so far. No one connects me to you." Alec grinned big. He moved in front of him and leaned down so that Dane had no choice but to look at him. "The sheriff's department is looking for you and only you. I was so exhilarated when you ran, making you look even more guilty. As soon as Josie and Everly get here, you'll be blamed for their deaths, too. You know, it really doesn't matter if I kill you now or later, I can position your body however I want to make it look like you killed them, but Josie got off one shot. It's not that difficult. Some of the fun would be diminished, because I'd like for you to suffer."

Dane's blood thumped through his ears, angry that anyone could be so heartless. But most of all, fear of losing Josie drove him the most. Just when he'd started believing in the system and people and that he could have a chance at a good life again. One he intended to show Violet, and maybe his mom, if she'd let him. So many good things at his fingertips and this man could ruin everything.

Not if Dane could help it. At least if Alec was here, that meant Josie was safe for the moment.

Tires on the drive sounded outside. He recognized the sound of Josie's Bronco.

He didn't know if Alec heard it or not, but Dane had to do something.

Alec's cell phone dinged. The man moved to the door and turned to look at Dane with a smile. "I have a little surprise for you."

Josie noted the silver GMC which she concluded must belong to Alec was parked in front of a metal building. She pulled to the corner of the property behind a small dozer type of equipment called a skid steer.

She was confident that Sheriff Van Carroll and Texas Ranger Boone both should be on their way. She checked her gun and then quietly exited her vehicle. She eased around the piles of building materials, from metal beams to ceramic tile, and moved to the side of the portable building. Indecision as to whether she should enter to see how Dane was making out or wait for backup warred within her.

She decided on the safest route. Even though Dane had never been in law enforcement, he had a canny survival mode. Before she could settle in somewhere that hid her while giving her a good view of the building, the door swung open, and Alec strode out.

Although she'd never met the man, she realized Everly had done a great job describing his features. For an eight-year-old, she'd recalled Alec's characteristics better than Josie could've.

She watched the murderer and noted the grin tugging on his mouth. Disgust bit into her as she wondered if he'd hurt Dane. Remaining calm was essential. She couldn't panic like she had the day her family had perished.

Suddenly, dust lifted in the distance as a vehicle came toward them. She hoped it was the Texas Ranger. As the vehicle grew closer, she realized the beat-up black truck looked familiar. It was the same one that chased them through the quarry.

Alec's head turned directly to where she was hiding, causing her to back up. Had he seen her? She chanced a glance around the corner to see a smug expression on his face.

He knew she was there. But why hadn't Dane come out of the building?

Alec stepped toward the car and a man got out of the driver's door. She saw that it was

Phillip from the retirement home. Then Alec opened the back door and pulled Everly out of the vehicle. Then he looked across the yard to her.

Josie's heart stopped. "Let her go!"

Everly's head came up and their eyes locked. "Mom!"

Her heart hitched at the fear in her daughter's face. Everly's hair was tussled, making Josie wonder if the girl had put up a fight.

Alec tugged Everly's hand and dragged her toward the building even though her feet dug into the gravel, and she sank back almost until her bottom was on the ground. Alec called, "You can join us inside now, Miss Hunt."

With her gun still in her hand, she ran across the property, weaving in and out of the piles of junk and got to the door at the same time as they did. "Let her go."

Alec clucked his tongue and shook his head. "You know I can't do that." His eyebrows shot up and he waved the weapon in his hand. "Drop your weapon unless you want the girl to die right here."

Josie did as she was asked.

The man shoved the door open and stepped

inside with her daughter. Josie turned to Phillip. "I can't believe you helped Alec with this."

"Sorry, Josie. It was nothing personal." He shrugged. "My cousin needed help and I didn't want to turn him down. Sometimes a person needs money, and at my age, there's not many opportunities." Phillip was Alec's cousin? She'd had no idea. The man actually looked ashamed, but she had no sympathy. A person made choices. "Your grandpa was not hurt, if it's any consolation. I can't say the same for that psychologist lady."

Kennedy. Josie said a quick prayer her friend was not hurt. If what he said was true, she'd check on her grandfather and Kennedy as soon as she could. When she stepped inside the small building, she caught sight of Dane lying on the floor as if he'd tried to break free and fell, his wrists tied to a chair that was chained to the desk. His jaw twitched as defeat showed in his eyes.

"You can leave now, Phillip. Shut the door behind you."

The orderly hesitated, his gaze shifting to Josie. Then he walked out.

Josie hurried over to Dane and helped get his chair back to an upright position. Their eyes collided and in that moment, she thought Dane would kill Alec if given the opportunity.

"Let my daughter go, Alec."

He shook his head and pulled Everly against him. "Can't do that. She's seen too much. Now, get over there." He indicated the corner with his gun.

"No." She and Dane exchanged glances again and this time she detected something in his eyes. He had a plan. She didn't understand what it was, but at this point, she'd try anything. She looked up at Alec. "Whatever you intend to do, you need to rethink the situation."

Dane's gaze went to the window, telling her someone was out there. She hoped it was the sheriff. When he looked back to her, he nodded big. She ducked.

Dane swept out with his boot, kicking Alec in the leg.

The door burst open. Silas stood in the doorway with his gun drawn.

"Silas Boone, Texas Ranger. Drop your weapon."

Alec lay on the floor, and his face turned red. Instead of doing as he was told, he gave a loud yell, and his hand came up with his gun.

Silas pulled the trigger, shooting Alec once in the shoulder. The killer's gun fell to the floor. After the Ranger retrieved it, Bliss hurried through the door to Josie. "Are you okay?"

"Yeah, I think so." She turned to Everly and held her arms out. Her daughter flung herself against her, crying. Josie inhaled an emotional breath as she clung to her for several moments.

Silas cut Dane's restraints with a pocketknife, freeing him.

Finally, Josie let go of Everly and pulled back to look her in the face. "Are you all right? Did the man hurt you?"

Her face wrinkled into a frown. "I'm okay." She pointed at Alec. "He killed my daddy."

"I know, baby. I know." If she could, Josie would undo time and go back to help save Pierce from this man. "He'll be going to prison for a long time."

Deputy Hattie Perkins came through the door and slapped handcuffs on Hickman. She talked into her radio and asked for paramedics.

They all backed up to give the deputy room as she escorted Alec out of the room and into the back of her SUV. Needing air, Josie took Everly outside the stuffy building.

Dane strode over to her, his eyes full of concern. "Are you certain you two are okay?"

"I think so. And you?"

"I'm good now. Alec rammed into the back of my motorcycle when I was on the way to visit the sheriff." He nodded. "I'm glad this is over."

"Haggerty." Sheriff Van Carroll's voice traveled across the parking lot.

"Maybe I spoke too soon." He turned to the lawman. "Sheriff."

Josie moved forward. "Sheriff, Dane was on his way to turn himself in when Alec Hickman, the real killer, kidnapped him."

"I've got this," Dane whispered before continuing the conversation with Van Carroll. "I shouldn't have run, but I was afraid I'd be arrested and not get a fair trial."

The sheriff folded his arms across his chest as Dane gave the short version of what had happened months ago through today when Alec brought him to the boneyard.

"I'll need you to come by the department and fill out a statement. You will still be investigated, but if you're clean, all charges will be dropped."

"I'm clean." Dane walked back to Josie and

pulled her hands into hers. "I never could've done this without you."

"I told you to trust in the system."

A smile tugged at his mouth. "Easier said than done." His gaze stayed with hers like there was something he wanted to say but was hesitant. Everly stood close to him, and his arm went to her shoulder.

Josie stared at him. "What is it?"

"I'd like to stay in touch."

Somehow that's not the words she'd hoped to hear. "In touch? Like friends on social media? Or maybe the occasional visit over coffee?"

He took a step back before running his hands through his hair. "You know I'm not good at expressing myself, but I want more." He waved his hand between her and him. "Of this. Us."

Everly looked up at him. "Does that include me?"

Josie smiled, and he laughed.

"Of course, it does." Dane grew serious as he turned to Josie. "Since the day I met you, you've been important to me. I'd like you back in my life. You make me a better man. I love you."

Her spirits lifted. "It's going to take some time to sort through this, but I love you, too."

"Mom, I like him."

Josie smiled. "I know you do. Me, too. He's a good man."

Epilogue

"Mom. Help me!"

Josie glanced up to see Everly running around a tree with Violet in hot pursuit. Dexter barked excitedly as he danced around them.

As Violet touched her, she yelled, "You're it."

"Oh, come on," Everly complained. "You had a head start."

"Nuh-uh. I just took a shortcut. Besides, I had Wyatt with me."

Josie brought the tray of marshmallows, chocolate bars, and graham crackers out the back door. Dane sat beside the campfire straightening several wire coat hangers. "Here you go."

They were gathered at Dane's home in the country. Already, plans were in the works to add another bedroom to give each of the girls a room of their own.

All of the families of Bring Home the Children Project team were gathered around the campfire.

Josie couldn't have been happier. Dane had been exonerated of all charges. Of course, she knew he would. They married last month, just two months after Alec Hickman had been arrested.

Alec received life in prison without the possibility for parole for killing Pierce and Harlan, a plea deal that kept him from a trial where he might have received the death penalty. Layla turned in evidence against Alec to avoid jail time. She admitted after being pursued for months, she finally had an affair with Alec and began taking money from the business behind her husband's back. But Alec pressured her to leave Harlan. Ultimately, she agreed, and they planned to take a long vacation in Mexico, and they would live off the divorce settlement. But when she hesitated to steal thirty thousand dollars, Alec went behind her back and withdrew the money from the account. Alec often snooped while his mom cleaned the offices, and he found a receipt that showed Pierce had been hired to investigate him. Believing it had to do with the missing money, he approached Harlan to proclaim his innocence, but the owner informed him he knew of the affair. Alec went into a rage and killed Harlan and set up Dane to take the fall. Realizing the investigator could tie Alec to Harlan, he was forced to kill him, too.

Once Layla realized how much Alec despised Harlan and Dane for firing him, it was too late. She was afraid to go against him, but in the end, he attacked her anyway.

Except for the occasional argument, Violet and Everly had become best friends instantly. Even before the wedding, Kennedy had counseled their family, which mostly was intended to help the girls. Josie was surprised how much talking about her past and the fire had helped her to see things more clearly. It was common for victims of tragedy to feel guilt for being a survivor. Her main regret was not seeking counseling earlier. Even Dane claimed he'd learned a lot about himself and was glad to have participated.

The kids gathered around while the men assisted in loading the wires with marshmallows to hang over the flames. The women finished carrying out the snacks.

Bliss smiled. "This get-together was a great idea. Wyatt loves the great outdoors. He and Spencer have really gotten to be close friends."

Kennedy brought out a pitcher of lemonade. Thankfully she was not injured when Phillip abducted Everly from the retirement home. He'd pulled a gun on her and then locked her in the medication storage closet.

Silas got up and took the lemonade from her. "I've got this."

A yellow Jeep pulled up and Annie and Riggs Brenner climbed out with a baby, two women and a man. Josie hurried over to Annie. "I'm so glad you all could make it. I know it's a long drive from Palo Duro Canyon."

Annie smiled. "It is. Especially with a teething six-month-old baby."

"Oh, can I hold her?"

"Certainly. Josie, meet Kelsey." The adorable girl had lots of dark hair and a stream of drool running down her chin. "And you remember Tami."

Josie had helped Annie and Riggs with a case in West Texas. Not only had they found and brought two children to their parents, but Annie had been reunited with Tami, who'd been abducted many years earlier. Annie promised she'd help Tami find her missing sister. The woman had changed a lot since Josie had last seen her. She'd gained weight and appeared healthier.

"This is my sister, Casey, and her husband, Jake."

"Glad to meet you." With the precious baby in her arms, Josie followed them to the campfire where Annie introduced them to everyone. Recently Annie learned Casey had been adopted in New Mexico by an older couple. Annie found Casey by using a family genealogy website. The funny thing was, Casey had been searching for Tami for years, but since her DNA wasn't in the system, she hadn't been able to find her.

An arm went around Josie's waist, and she looked up into Dane's glistening eyes. "This was a great idea, honey."

She searched his face. "It's not too much? I realize you don't know many of my team members very well, and meeting new people—"

He placed his finger on her lips and shook his head. "I like them. I can't help but think that Harlan would've enjoyed their company, too."

"From everything you've told me about him, I can see that. Are you ready to roast the marshmallows?"

"First—" Dane leaned in, his warm breath on her cheek "—I need one more of these." He planted a kiss on her lips.

She playfully slapped his shoulder. "You have a lifetime of those."

"It won't be nearly enough."

Keep reading for an excerpt of a new title
from the Special Edition series,
ONE SUITE DEAL by Michele Dunaway

Prologue

"I doubt you could succeed even if you tried."

Only two people could speak to Edmund Clayton III like this, and thirty-six-year-old Reginald Justus—a man one year Edmund's senior—didn't qualify, because he wasn't Edmund's mother or sister. Edmund leveled his most haughty glare at his nemesis. Justus, whose tux made him more penguin than cover model, had the gall to add a belated laugh to his taunt.

Edmund tried not to respond with a sneer—the two men were at a New Year's Eve charity gala, after all. Edmund made his tone as smooth as the two fingers of bourbon he held in his left hand. A gold cuff link winked from beneath a tailored sleeve. "I always succeed. When have I not?"

"Perhaps in business. Your love life, however, is quite another story." Justus chuckled boldly, something he wouldn't dare be doing had he and Edmund been alone. But with people around he took the risk, reveling in the fact they glanced over. "Plenty of stories, actually. What's that word? Viral. But not in a good way, of course."

Edmund's broken engagement making headlines was a sore spot, but he certainly wasn't going to concede that point to Justus. Edmund relaxed clenched fingers. "What's that old saying? That there's no such thing as bad publicity?" Edmund sipped his whiskey, letting the smoky heat with hints of oak and vanilla slide down his parched throat.

"You were everywhere. Still are," Justus persisted. "Not in the best light either."

Edmund set the empty whiskey glass on a round, bar-height table covered with white linen. A tea light burned in the center. "I'm well aware of my broken engagement."

And the fact that a mere two weeks later his social media influencer ex, Veronica, had started dating someone else. She'd made Edmund out to be the villain to her one million followers, and six months later, the fallout from the viral breakup still followed Edmund around. The whole thing had been mortifying for a man of his stature.

"So that means you lost at something. Love." Justus, who'd never beaten Edmund at anything, laughed even longer, as if he'd told a great joke.

Edmund refused to let Justus under his skin. He kept his tone even, bored and dismissive. "Well, it's like Oscar Wilde said, 'There is only one thing in the world worse than being talked about, and that is not being talked about.' So let them talk."

"Aww, I hit a sore spot."

If Edmund didn't despise the man, he might just have admired Justus's courage for daring to keep prodding the snake. When Edmund struck, no one saw it coming. But Justus couldn't help that he was so full of himself, which meant he kept going. "Here's another one for you. I'm making the acquisition of Van Horn Hotels my business. They'll be mine by the end of January."

Ah, there it was. The gauntlet. Justus was so damn predictable that Edmund had been waiting for it ever since Justus sought him out from across the ballroom.

"I don't know why you're so smug. Those hotels won't

ever be yours. As you just admitted yourself, I always win in business."

"I did not say that," Justus protested. Then realizing he had, he puffed out his chest. "There's always a first time. You're going down."

Edmund zeroed in on his longtime rival, tuning out the low hum of guests' chatter and the more distant musical notes of a string quartet. He was at yet another high-priced, black-tie charity gala for some do-gooder cause demanding the appearance of Portland's A-list—his third event this holiday season. It was a tiring but necessary burden—the price of doing business in Oregon. "No, I'm not, but feel free to think that."

With a liquor-loosened tongue, Edmund's bitterest rival scoffed. "Been almost a year and you haven't closed the deal for Van Horn. I'd say my chances are better than good. You've lost your touch, golden boy. Can't get to the altar. Can't get a signature on the bottom line. The sharks are circling, and you're chum in the water. I can't wait to take a bite."

Competitors had sensed an opportunity when Edmund's cousin Jack had permanently relocated to Beaumont, Missouri, after he'd fallen in love with former naval lieutenant Sierra James during the acquisition of her family's winery. A happily married man with a baby on the way, Jack had decided investing locally in his own pet projects was far more important than running Clayton Holdings, the firm founded by both Jack's and Edmund's fathers, or as the business world called them, the Conquering Claytons. Starting with almost nothing, the two brothers had built a hospitality business that was worth billions. Now that Jack had abdicated, the responsibility for keeping the company profitable and at the forefront of success fell fully on Edmund's shoulders. He was more than up for the task.

"You know I'm not the only one ready to take a bite out of your market share," Justus added, his glee obvious. "You're slipping, Edmund. You don't have what it takes. Not for the long haul. You're already a has-been."

Edmund gritted his teeth, biting back a reply not fit for polite company. He'd never had an extended period without success, minus Van Horn, whose acquisition had been Edmund's first order of business after being named VP of Clayton Holdings, a promotion that had leapfrogged him to the highest level in terms of company succession. The Van Horn deal should have been signed, sealed and delivered already, but lately it was like he'd walked under a ladder—not that he was superstitious. Both Edmund's dad and his uncle Jonathan, Jack's dad, were rumbling that they wanted to retire, and if Edmund could close this deal, he'd be a shoo-in for the company presidency. And after that, CEO.

Edmund refused to be a has-been. He most certainly would not let Justus see how close the barb came to hitting Edmund's greatest fear. Edmund had big shoes to fill. He wasn't as likable or gregarious as Jack. Or as adventurous and carefree as his two brothers, or as fun and witty as his sister, Eva. No, Edmund was too studious. Too serious. Too formidable. Too focused on the prize. Well, he'd always won the prize, hadn't he?

As for Edmund's inability to close the deal on love, he'd decided that—at least for him—love wasn't worth it, especially after his very public breakup. The bachelor life suited him just fine. Business first. Look at what had happened to Jack. He'd given up his birthright. Edmund refused to do the same.

Edmund watched Margot Van Horn approach, a glass of

bubbly in her ruby-studded right hand. She'd been his late maternal grandmother's best friend. At seventy-five, Margot was one of Portland's most beloved and generous matriarchs, also known for her various eccentricities. Today she wore a glittering black gown with a flared skirt. "Gentlemen, good to see both of you. Fighting over me already?"

"Of course," Edmund inserted smoothly. He saluted her with a champagne flute he artfully plucked from a passing waiter. "You *are* the most beautiful woman here, after all."

Margot's cheeks pinked. Because her white hair was in a chignon, that flush was visible as it traveled down a neck that somehow defied aging. "Ah, Edmund, your mother raised a delightful cad. I shall scold her when I next see her. I wish she'd been able to attend tonight."

"I'm here in her stead, and your wish is my command." He kissed the back of the white-gloved hand she offered.

Margot trilled her pleasure. "Oh, if I were younger…" Then she waved a finger at them. "Gentlemen, I must tell you that flattery won't get you anywhere. A donation, however, will at least keep you both in my good graces."

"Then I will make a hefty one," Edmund said, beating Justus, who added a hearty, "Me too."

"Good." Margot gestured toward the glittering collection of who's who. "This is my favorite event, as it helps raise funds to reduce our homeless animal population."

Edmund had heard the rumors that Margot's four-thousand-square-foot mansion housed at least fourteen rescued cats and two rabbits. "A worthy cause."

"Speaking of worthy, you remember my grandson Lachlan, don't you? The one who went to NYU? He's in California working as a producer for a TV show."

"That's nice." Justus played along, but Edmund's gaze

narrowed. Margot might appear dotty, but she remained sharp and quick. She planned to drop Thor's hammer.

Margot beamed, and Edmund braced himself. "It's his big break. One of those shows where bosses go undercover. He's recruiting talent."

Edmund's internal radar flashed danger even before Margot said, "I fully support him in his new endeavor, so I've decided each of you should do his show."

"What?" Justus appeared stunned, and Edmund wished he held something stronger than France's best bubbly.

"You'll each do one week undercover, and whoever has the highest Nielsen ratings and subsequent social media exposure wins the right to purchase Van Horn Hotels, with mutually agreeable terms to be discussed at the appropriate time, of course," she added with a breathy rush. "But you have my word that, should we reach fair terms, I will sell. Besides, doing this show will be great publicity for your respective brands. It's a win-win."

More like a week of misery, Edmund thought. But he'd do whatever it took, including keeping his mouth shut, unlike his rival, whose mouth dropped open as Justus stared, agape.

"A friendly wager, gentlemen, and an end to all this speculation and bickering. What do you say? You're in, right? Of course you are. You both want my hotels and will do whatever it takes."

Margot's laugh tinkled as she lifted her champagne. Automatically the men did the same, and their glasses clinked together. Margot smiled, satisfied she'd won this round and all future ones. Both men would do whatever it took to please her. "This is going to be such fun. May the best undercover appearance win!"